Autumn Leaves

Autumn Leaves

Victor McGlothin

St. Martin's Press ✿ New York

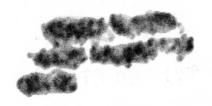

www.stmartins.com

ISBN 0-312-28676-7

First Edition: September 2002

10   9   8   7   6   5   4   3   2   1

To my lovely wife, Terre,

who has climbed this mountain

with me and sacrificed much in doing so

Abundant Thanks

FATHER—I could never say thank you enough but I'll certainly try

The First Family—Vera and Kim

"Aunt Glenda" Clement—please FedEx me some more peach cobbler

Elaine Koster—my agent, a.k.a. the "Miracle Worker"

Jennifer Enderlin—"The" editor, who made my crooked lines straight

Erica Bynote—who compelled me to do more than just talk about becoming a writer

Kimberla Lawson Roby and Lolita Files—for your kind words and insight

Erykah Badu—for blessing this novel

The Brothas—Vincent Alexandria, Rod "Bird" Johnson, and Andre Ford

Kappa Alpha Psi Fraternity, Inc.—(YITB)

LaShawn Scott and Beverly Nason—the first to see a diamond in the rough

Linda Walker and Harry Robinson, Ph.D.—my mentors

Emma Rogers of Black Images Books, Milton and Til Pettis of Jokae's Books, Sonja Babers of the Black Bookworm, Janet Mosley of Tenaj Books, Felicia Wintons of Books for Thought, Frances Utsey of the Cultural Connection Bookstore, Jackie Perkins of Montsho Books, and Anika of Shrine of the Black Madonna Bookstore

Walt Disney World's Terri Mitchell and Paul Bugge—I loved it!

Pam Walker-Williams, Mary Jones, Juanita Cole Howard, and the Good Book Club—my very first. Oh yeah, and PageTurner.net

Tom Joyner—the Original Fly Jock

K104's "Skip Murphy and the Morning Team"

K107.5's "Joe Soto and the Gang"

KISS 106's "Kidd Kraddick in the Morning"

Lavida @ DallasBlack.com

Sederrick Raphiel at The Design Factory

Jimmy Porch at Eclipse Magazine

Daphne Houston, Ph.D. @ Seesolutions.com

Betty Davis @ BlackBookNetwork.com

Writer'sReview.com

And lastly, a very special "thanks for believing" to all of the book clubs that offered me your ongoing kindness and support. I'll never forget you. Much Love, 67 times. See y'all soon.

Autumn Leaves

One

Stone Cold

Simpson adjusted his rearview mirror just enough to get a better look at his face. His mahogany-hued skin, ultrawhite capped teeth, and coal-black wavy hair made for quite a handsome but synthetic wrapper. The package was top rate but the product was another story. He was a shrewd businessman, a thirty-two-year-old who saw no limits, especially where love was concerned. Simpson's concrete heart was black, rock solid, and stone cold.

The orange sun set as he stepped out of his European sports car and casually put on an olive-colored jacket to complement his Italian linen trousers. Looking good was almost as satisfying to him as enjoying others admiring his expensive taste.

"Watch the doors, kid!" he ordered when the young valet attendant jingled his car keys with a little too much exuberance. "Last time I got it back with a scratch on it, and you don't park enough cars in a year to cover the cost. So don't let it happen again!"

Kennedy stood tensely embarrassed on the steps of the Mansion restaurant on Turtle Creek with her thin, pale arms folded across her chest. She despised the sun, like many black women, shuddering at the thought of getting a shade darker. Kennedy James was young and attractive. Although she was no more than five feet eight inches tall, her thin figure made her appear taller. Her naturally friendly persona was so likable, she easily could have been the national icon for *Girlfriend Next Door* magazine, except when she was with him, her boyfriend, Simpson Stone.

This wasn't the first occurrence in which her longtime boyfriend displayed his anal-retentive nature or passion for his expensive car and exotic things, but it was the first time it irked her to the point that she was repulsed by it. Still, she said nothing. She always said nothing when Simpson decided to just be himself, a real prick.

As they reached the top of the stairs leading into the restaurant, Simpson yanked on Kennedy, pulling her toward him by her elbow. Her dark-brown, shoulder-length hair whipped around as she angrily turned to face him. The large glass doors were pushed open from the inside. "You might want to brighten up, dear," he suggested firmly, making an attempt to look casual while doing it.

"We are at the Mansion, for God's sake. And each time I treat my girl to the top-rated eatery in the entire world, I expect her to enjoy herself. Now, then, straighten your gown and have fun."

She looked deeply into his tight, sullen, gray eyes with a scornful scowl. Her bottom lip quivered slightly. She was not in the mood to have fun and being told to straighten out her clothing didn't exactly ring joy throughout her inner being, either. Nonetheless, she manufactured a half smile before entering the lavish dining hall. Being in the public eye meant putting on a party face. And Kennedy knew her role well as the woman belonging to the wealthy and well-known bachelor businessman. She knew it involved playing the part of the fortunate lady of his choice, even during the times when she didn't feel so fortunate. Before she had the chance to remember when her Prince Charming began his metamorphosis into the nasty toad he'd become, Simpson tugged at her arm again to hurry her along.

Fleeting thoughts of how wonderfully he treated her in the beginning of their courtship faded quickly when they stepped inside and an older, distinguished maître d', who was bent over a podium with a small lamplight attached to the top of it, glanced up from his large black reservation book to greet them. "Good evening, sir. Ma'am. Just a moment, please." He drew a dark line through someone's name, then poised himself while adjusting his tightly fitted dark suit coat. "Ah, now, who do we have dining with us this evening?"

"That's two for Stone. Simpson Stone," Kennedy's date announced with authority.

A short line of guests began to form behind them while the maître d' plowed the reservation book for a seating time allocated to a Stone party of two. The man ran his stubby index finger up and down the page several times before asking Simpson to repeat his name. "Sir. Are you certain you have reservations for this restaurant? This particular evening?"

This was getting good. Kennedy strained to keep the big smile inside her lips contained. Clearing her throat helped, but it was a difficult task because the gentleman did not recognize Mr. Stone's face nor his name.

Simpson turned away briefly to shirk his displeasure. He was embarrassed and Kennedy knew it, even though he pretended not to be. It's strange how we sometimes get such a kick out of the little things in life. Thank God for the little things. That one forced Kennedy to take a deep breath, or else she'd risk losing it and burst with unbridled laughter in the greeting area. It was almost sad, but it wasn't. Had it been almost anyone else, it would have been. But it was *the* Simpson Stone being treated like a commoner for once. Even if it was only short lived, it served him right.

"Edward, do we have a problem?" a taller man asked, wearing an expensive tailored suit.

Edward, the maître d', was at a loss. "Well, Mr. Towns, I can't seem to locate, uh, Mr. Stone's reservation."

Mr. Towns, whose hair was overly moussed, was apparently a manager in charge of the front of the house. He recognized Simpson immediately. "Mr. Stone, I apologize for the delay. Edward here seems to have overlooked our VIP list for tonight." He quickly saved face by introducing Edward to Simpson and making a big to-do about it. "Edward, Mr. Stone here is a very special guest of ours. If he should wish to dine here in the future with or without a reservation, please do your best to accommodate him. He is responsible for the new additions to our wonderful wine selection."

"Please accept my humble apologies, sir," Edward pleaded, with sweat beading upon his balding head. "I really should have checked the owner's list of special guests. I assure you it will not happen again."

It was good while it lasted, Kennedy thought, as Simpson regained his arrogant posture. "I certainly hope that it doesn't, Edward," Mr. Towns threatened, obviously meaning it to sound as condescending as it did.

The elegant restaurant offered four-star ambience as well as an outstanding gourmet menu. After one gentleman escorted them to their table, another man pulled out the chair for Kennedy and commented on how beautiful she looked. He said it in a way that made it obvious he meant it; this was not the kind of place that lent itself to being overly complimentary. A young Hispanic man who wore a black tuxedo-style jacket and matching slacks lit the candle on their table.

"Someone will be along shortly to assist you," he said agreeably, then whisked away to another table to perform the same task. No matter how much they paid him for that service, it was too much. The whole joint was just that, too much.

Kennedy and Simpson sat at the charming dinner table barely looking at each other, as if one of them had something unfavorable to say and the other knew it was coming.

"It took long enough, but we've finally been seated," Simpson snarled, after they had gotten settled in. The bitterness was still apparent but should have been forgotten. "I can't stand incompetence. Edward had better be damned thankful I'm not in the mood to—"

"Good evening," the waiter interrupted, rather abruptly. He resembled a life-size Ken doll and obviously worked out. "Sorry to interrupt, but I thought I could introduce you to our wine list and answer any questions you might have."

Kennedy smiled cordially while thinking about how attractive the waiter was. When she extended her arm to receive the brochure that listed the selection of wines, Simpson intercepted her, then shot her a nasty stare before making an attempt to control the situation.

"Hmmm, I wonder." Simpson began to flip the tablets over to read both sides, as if they were different from each other. "Tell me. What might you suggest for this evening?" Kennedy looked down at her lap to avoid making eye contact with the waiter, who was about to be quizzed.

The waiter began the exam unknowingly. "Mr. Stone, if I may. Allow me to suggest something from your list of fine wines. Since you have undoubtedly sampled them all, perhaps the lady would like to try a chardonnay from the Clos du Bois winery. It's a light-bodied wine that's dry but full of fruit, or perhaps something from the Antonin Rodet, maybe? It's a French burgundy with a nice medium body, though it doesn't sacrifice a full flavor. It's also very nice."

Fortunately, the waiter knew his business and impressed even Simpson. Before congratulations could have been doled out on a job well done, Kennedy flashed a perky smile and insisted that they be brought a bottle of each. "You have done such an excellent job describing them that I can't possibly decide. You'll just have to bring them both."

The waiter smiled back, nodded, then disappeared. He returned shortly to pour a sample of each for her approval. Having dated Simpson for more than three years, Kennedy knew a thing or two about wines herself. "They will both do nicely. Thank you." She proceeded to order her meal while guzzling her first glass. It was the first step on her journey to Slosh-Town, that happy yet tormenting place where she sometimes found herself trying to hide from herself. After a few drinks on an empty stomach, she really didn't mind Simpson's company much. And after a few more, she might not mind him at all.

Looking around the exquisitely decorated room, Kennedy noticed that some couples were sitting closer than when they initially sat down, large parties were celebrating some special event or another, and other couples on dates sat and endured a less than memorable dinner, like she would and had before on too many similar occasions.

While drinking a lot more than eating, she began to wonder why those other women looked sad and lifeless. Were their men like Simpson? Driven to be successful, even to a fault, and willing to do anything to be on top? Did they work ten- and twelve-hour days too often only to negate the real reason they did so in the first place, to be able to have the finer things in life and share them with the ones they loved?

. Drudging through nearly fifteen minutes without a single word spoken between them, she decided to say the first thing that came to mind. "Did you know that husbands who kiss their wives before leaving home in the morning live five years longer than men who don't? Ah-hmm. It's a true fact. I read it in *Glamour* magazine a couple of years ago. They had this whole section on kissing." She leaned in closely, purposely placing her elbows on the table to piss him off. "If we get married, do you think you'll be the kind of husband who kisses his wife on his way out in the morning or the other kind? Those who die quicker?"

Simpson didn't find the comment the least bit amusing, nor did he appreciate her bringing up marriage or their relationship in public. "And which would you rather I be?" he questioned sarcastically, while swirling a glass of burgundy to note its consistency.

"I guess it doesn't really matter when you get right down to it. Think about it, Stoney, old pal." When she'd have too much to drink, she would resort to calling him that to keep from calling him

Simpleton or something even worse. "No matter what kind of husband a girl ends up with, she'll get what she's got. Get it, got it? Good. Now you're catching on, Stoney."

Contempt blanketed Simpson's face. "I thought you said you cut down on your consumption."

She poured another glass before she realized he was speaking to her. "What . . . did you say something? I could have sworn you said something."

He folded the white cloth napkin and pressed it firmly against his lips. "I said, haven't you had enough?"

Kennedy leaned forward again, almost touching the table with her chest. "You must have heard me wrong. I said I would cut down on my drinking around you, or something to that effect. I forget how I phrased it." She answered his first question unwittingly. The alcohol was running its course.

Simpson rudely summoned the waiter to the table with a series of hand gestures as other customers began to look on. He demanded loudly that the remaining wine be removed from the table immediately.

Promptly, someone from the service staff came by to collect all the glasses and bottles. Then, it seemed as soon as they disappeared, another man brought a dessert menu and two cups of coffee.

"Is everything all right here, Mr. Stone?" the waiter asked, looking Kennedy over.

"Everything is just jake. The lady just had a bad reaction. She forgot that her medication doesn't mix well with alcohol," Simpson explained. He frowned at Kennedy. "We'll be leaving soon. Would you prepare the bill, please? Thank you."

Simpson was put out. He was far beyond pissed off. She had openly defied him and he was forced to be polite for fear of drawing any more attention to his table while at a disadvantage and in public with an inebriated female on his hands. That evening was destined to bomb. It had all the makings of drama-to-go, like most of their dates had had lately. He would act like an arrogant jerk. She would start to drink; this was followed by more drinking, followed by

Simpson taking her home early and scolding her for ruining another evening. Each time, he'd threaten to leave her just before making a dash to exit her front door. It was a vicious cycle, and why should that evening have been any different. It wasn't.

Long gone were the wonderfully planned dinners for two that seemed to extend throughout the night. Their relationship hadn't always been so tumultuous. Somewhere, somehow, things just went wrong between them. As a result, Kennedy saw fit to return her man's meanness with trifling behavior of her own, after several months of being treated less than first-rate.

"Wait a minute, waaait!" Kennedy screamed, as Simpson pushed her in to the passenger seat of his canary-yellow convertible Porsche 911. "Don't push me, I don't feel so good," she complained, cradling her stomach with both hands. The wind had picked up quite a bit while they were in the restaurant. "It's cold! Please put the top up."

He ignored her pleas for leniency. Instead, he drove faster than normal, whipping around sharp turns and making quick stops and starts. He looked over at her occasionally to ensure that she was being tortured properly. Kennedy's fair complexion was turning a peculiar shade of green. "Let me out," she ranted. "Stop the damned car and let me out!"

Simpson refused initially, then pulled the car over on a quiet avenue and stared straight ahead. Kennedy climbed out and stumbled onto the shoulder of the road. A good meal and great wine had gone to waste. Unfortunately, it did not come up as easily as it went down.

The car peeled off down the winding street after she had wiped her mouth with the hem of her brown evening gown and fell back into the passenger seat. Simpson was disgusted. He rattled off a laundry list of reasons why he should have stopped seeing her a long time ago and why he had not considered proposing marriage. "You know I can't stand it when you disobey me. You promised to control your drinking and behave yourself. Tonight was utterly ridiculous. The mere thought of it is reason enough for me to leave you, but

I'll see you through this thing. That's the kind of man I am." He was near her apartment building and had not once looked in her direction since she'd climbed back into the car, nor did he display any signs of concern for her sickly condition. "I've tried to show you the finer side of life, the good life, but you, year after year, just get worse. You're pathetic. You don't even have the will to quit smoking."

Eventually, he cut his eyes at her. She was white as a sheet and huddled up in a tight ball. She was shivering, but he showed neither concern nor compassion. "You just don't get it, do you? You know the friends I have in this town. I'm well connected. Every woman would love to be involved with a man like me," he boasted, thinking she had fallen asleep. But she heard every word. "I guess it's true what they say at the club, you can take the girl out of the hood but the hood will be forever coming out of the girl. That's why I'll never marry you. Sometimes, you're so damned ghetto."

She opened her eyes as she thought of defending herself, but she couldn't find the strength to fight back. Sure, they'd had problems before, but this was life-altering. The cold night air coupled with his ranting intensified the pain, creating a terrible fate. She felt she was barely better off than she'd be dead. Just about. But she was so deep in love that she couldn't see her way out. Hope sustained her in the tumultuous love affair that had evolved into something much less desirable than what she dreamed of when they first met. Hope that it would all work out just fine kept her there. Hope that her love would prevail over Simpson's growing obsession with *other things* that didn't involve her was worth a little trouble, she concluded. Like with too many women in the same situation, Kennedy's hopes of changing him held her bondage in a relationship gone bad.

"I'll call the doorman, he'll help me get you upstairs," Simpson growled as they approached her building. Bradshaw, the night doorman of twenty years at the same apartment building, emerged from the front door with a thick red company-issued jacket. Seeing that Kennedy was freezing and in bad shape, the older black man removed his jacket and wrapped her in it. Simpson reluctantly stepped out of the car and helped him get Kennedy to the elevator. When they were completely inside it, Simpson turned and walked away slowly with his head down.

Kennedy stumbled from the elevator with a pair of medium-height, black sling-back pumps dangling from her hands. "Thanks, Bradshaw. I can take it from here."

"Are you sure, Ms. James?" he questioned. "Excuse me, but you don't look so good."

"Oh, that's nice to hear. Then I look like I feel. *Like crap!* Come on, Kennedy, you old barfly, you," she mumbled under her breath. "A few more steps and you can still make it without totally embarrassing yourself."

She stumbled down the long hallway, which had five doors on each side. Her apartment was the second one from the elevator, but grossly impaired motor skills accounted for her anxiety and lack of dexterity. It seemed like her refuge was miles away, over a shaky bridge. And after several unsuccessful attempts to put the key in the door lock, she finally managed to get it open. The helpful doorman was still standing in the doorway of the open elevator, looking on with concern.

"Thank you, Bradshaw," she yelled over her right shoulder. Kennedy didn't look to see if he was still there. She knew he would be until she was safely inside. That's the kind of man he was.

Soon after she disappeared behind the door, it slammed loudly. Bradshaw counted down. "Three, two, one . . ." Then he heard a loud thud. He chuckled and hunched his shoulders while shaking his head in disapproval. "These uppity Negroes gonna kill themselves."

Exiting the elevator, Bradshaw approached her front door and leaned in closely to listen for movement from inside. He poised himself to knock on it. Inside, Kennedy's legs had flopped from underneath her, as she lay sprawled out with her back pressed against the door. She felt him standing on the other side.

"I'm fine, Bradshaw," she admitted shamefully. It added insult to injury to have to get help to her apartment, then confirm that she had taken a nasty spill on the hardwood floor.

"Good night, Ms. James." He returned to the elevator.

Kennedy smiled softly. "Good night yourself, Bradshaw," she replied, as softly as she smiled.

She lay motionless for a moment before slowly raising her left leg nine or ten inches from the floor. "That's just great! I knew it! You see that, Lady Eleanor?" she whined, as her fluffy white Persian cat looked on. She was named Eleanor Rigby because she was an unwanted stray nobody cared about and Kennedy loved the Beatles hit by the same name. "I've got a runner in my panty hose." She continued to sit there, lying against the door and looking as ridiculous as she felt. "There's nothing like an elegant evening to put a run in your hose." Her befuddled facial expression faded to a blank stare as she lit up a cigarette and puffed away, still sprawled out on the floor and leaning against the door.

Half an hour later, Kennedy stood robed in her steamy bathroom with her hand against the large mirror and began rubbing in small clockwise circles. As she wiped the steam away, she began to see herself clearer until her flushed face was the only visible image in the mirror. At age twenty-seven, she was terribly paranoid about looking older than she was. Looking herself over, she pulled at her cheeks and checked for age lines at the corners of her eyes. Noticing the dark circles underneath her eyes caused by her all too familiar boy-mistreats-girl situation, she sighed heavily. "What in the hell are you doing to yourself?" she asked rhetorically, then turned off the light and slowly walked away.

By the time Simpson had arrived at his car, still parked on the street, he had concluded a business deal on his cell phone and lined up something, and someone, else to do that evening. After a short drive,

Simpson pulled up to the curb in front of an old refurbished apartment building in Deep Ellum, a liberal extension of the downtown arts district. A tall, thin white woman, wearing a shiny, navy-colored jumpsuit under a short jacket, exited from the front doors. She stepped down off the curb and waited for Simpson to open the car door for her and put the top up—two things he refused to do for Kennedy. This woman demanded chivalry and received it. She was obviously no run-of-the-mill date. She adjusted her outfit, then leaned in for a kiss from Simpson. He planted one on her red lips, then pulled away from the curb.

I'll Miss Yesterday by Tomorrow

Sweat from underneath Marshall's football helmet ran into his eyes as he peered straight ahead from the thirty-seven yard line and waited intently for the third-down play to begin. Then he looked down the line to his left to watch the ball being snapped. Rorey Garland boldly stepped up to the center and surveyed the defense before calling the signals. It didn't matter which play his quarterback called, Marshall decided there was only one he was interested in. The one that would send him deep enough to get him into the end zone.

Third down and seven yards to go with only thirteen seconds left in the game. "Red nineteen. Red nineteen . . .", Rorey shouted loudly, in order to be heard over the riotous crowd of well-wishers and adoring fans.

"Hut! Hut!" He took the snap and stepped off three or four

yards in a fast backpedal. The defensive linemen came crushing in hard. Both pass receivers to his left were well covered. Rorey looked left, then right, hoping his favorite receiver would make his way clear for a pass.

Marshall's white socks clung to his dark ebony skin; they resembled bouncing balls bobbing up and down as he streaked up the field twenty yards, only to pick up double coverage from the defense, just as he had for most of the game. He went into his break and turned to look back for the ball, but one of the opposing team members grabbed his jersey. He held it just long enough to slow Marshall down, leaving Rorey abandoned with no one to throw the ball to. The game was almost over and it appeared that the University of South Texas Coyotes would be the only team to shut them down, twice in one season.

The ball shot out of Rorey's left hand like a rocket and landed far out of bounds behind his teammates, who were looking on solemnly from the sideline. It bounced up into the marching band section of the bleachers. A loud, sharp squeal sounded when it hit an unaware clarinet player in the second row.

Disappointment loomed over the Stadium as stale, saddened glares shrouded the faces of nearly fifty thousand fans who had endured a thirty-six-degree chill at John Wesley Stadium to see the University of Texas Consolidated (UTC) Wranglers win their first conference football championship. Only a few years earlier, they had no hopes of contending at all. The previous year, they lost by seventeen points. Then they hired a new head coach who believed in putting points on the board and playing for all the marbles. The coaching change netted them nine wins during a ten-game season and brought them back to play the one team that handed them their loss.

The score clock stopped when the football traveled out of bounds. It held a tight grip on the seven seconds that remained. Head coach Myrick Dean called the last time-out and discussed what to do before ordering the kicking team on the field. Rorey jogged out onto the field slowly and made eye contact with Marshall as he kneeled down five yards behind Rex Longer, the center who was responsible for snapping the ball for field goal attempts. Rorey prepared to place the ball for Stevenson's field goal kick. The Wrangler offensive line drew in together close and tight. Standing shoulder to shoulder, all eleven Coyotes were packed against the line to block it, preserving the game and a third consecutive championship.

The massive crowd shushed for the final play of regulation. Marshall took his regular blocking stance and waited for the ball to be snapped. Rorey wiped his moist hands on a nearly soiled towel, which hung from the front of his pants, then called the signals, "Seeeh't . . . Hut!" The ball snapped toward him in a perfect spiral.

He sat the ball on its end for a forty-seven-yard field goal attempt. Stevenson was five of six for the year at field goals over forty-five yards. It was a perfect snap and ball placement on the ground. As the opposing team smashed against the middle of the line, Rorey's long index finger began to tremble atop the football's apex. All he had to do was hold it still while he counted his kicker's steps like he had always done. When the kicker approached the ball with quick, short strides, the Wranglers' front line collapsed.

Rorey quickly gripped the ball and pulled it away from the kicker's path, then popped up and ran as fast as he could to the left side of the backfield. It was much like he had imagined it as a kid tossing the ball around the school yard, the last play of the game with the clock running out and one last chance to win the championship. But he was not a child anymore and it was more serious than just school-yard pretending. This was it, the biggest play of his life.

Marshall blocked his defensive assignment until he noticed Rorey running with the ball and at least half of the other team chasing him down. It didn't look good. Not good at all. Marshall streaked down the middle of the field waving his right hand in the air with one of the men who had stopped him from catching the ball all afternoon closely behind. "Roarrr, throw it!" he yelled insistently, as if he could be heard. "Throwww it!"

The bleachers filled with pandemonium and both team's benches were emptied while everyone in attendance joined in hysterically to cheer and encourage their team. Screams of "Get 'emmmm!" became louder as Rorey ran closer to the Coyotes' sideline.

Being chased out of bounds with less than two ticks left on the game clock, he suddenly felt that his decision to take the game into his own hands was not such a good idea. Someone wrapped his arms around Rorey's waist from behind as he lofted the ball up the field as far as he could in Marshall's general direction. When he let it fly, everyone looked downfield to see who he was throwing it to. Anticipation and anxiety filled the stadium. Spatterings of Coyote burnt orange and navy blue melted into the landscape of Wrangler silver and green paraphernalia. The stadium was boiling over with excitement as all eyes followed the ball that seemed to have been overthrown.

As the football descended, Marshall's speed picked up. The defender stretched out his arms to grab Marshall's shirt again as he had done numerous times before, but Marshall had fallen out of reach. He was finally beaten. Rorey climbed to his knees with several blades of grass trapped between his face mask and helmet. He stuck out his arms and tilted his head in an awkward position, the way people do when they try to guide an object's course by using mental telepathy.

Marshall bit down hard on his mouthpiece. He dove from his feet and extended his body as far as he could with his hands outstretched to receive the ball. A split second before his long six-foot frame hit the ground, that beautiful, perfectly oblong brown leather football landed in the palm of his hands. The football must have been addressed "In Care of: Marshall Coates" because no one else could have caught it. After sliding along the dark green grass of the end zone, he rolled over and held the football high above his head, signaling it was a fair catch. The official hesitated briefly, then placed the whistle that was around his neck in his mouth and blew heartily. He gathered his arms against his sides, then thrust them over his shoulders, confirming Marshall's claim. It was a fair catch and a game-winning touchdown. Thirteen-ten Wranglers. Game over.

Marshall ran toward the network television cameras, pulled his helmet off, and struck his famous pose with his head tilted back. "Like Snapple, baby. Ahhhhhhhh . . . that's good," he said, celebrating with a triumphant smile.

"That million-dollar smile will easily bring more than a million dollars in endorsements for that young man," one sportscaster remarked. "When he enters the NFL next year, it should really be something to watch."

"I'll say. He's really something to watch now. He and Rorey Garland have cooked up something special this past season," added the other one. "Their Salt and Pepper dynamic duo earned them the championship as well as a clear path to the NFL. It's almost a shame in a way, but they'll more than likely play on opposing teams next year, folks. You've just witnessed a great one. For ABC Sports, this is Arnie Schram and Lou Miller saying so long. We have enjoyed you this year and hope you've enjoyed us, too. Good-bye."

The stands cleared instantly. Thousands of fanatical students mounted the goalposts and rocked them until they came crashing down in victorious splendor. It was glorious mayhem and impossible for the media to get interviews amid the scores of celebrations happening all over the football field. Marshall and Rorey found themselves embraced in jubilation at the bottom of an extremely enormous pile-on near the spot where the winning touchdown was caught.

Coach Dean shivered and wiped his eyes briskly after another barrel of Gatorade splashed over the top of his head near the Wrangler locker room. Film crews from the local news station, as well as those from nearby Dallas, aimed hot bright lights toward the lockers of the game's co-MVPs as they anticipated the press conference.

Like many of the other team members, Marshall milled around outside the player's entrance and soaked up all the adoration and praise he could milk from the moment. Rorey instead took the path of solitude and hid in the equipment room. He sat huddled against the wall with a blank stare and appearing to still be in utter disbelief. They'd won the game on a wing and a prayer. His wing. His prayer.

"There he is!" a tall cameraman yelled. "Let's get some footage," news reporters demanded. "Rorey Garland, Rorey . . . Rorey . . . over here," they urged. "Can we get a minute? How'd you pull it off?"

Rorey bent over abruptly. With one hard shake, he shed his jersey and shoulder pads like a thick wool sweater, then he ran his fingers through his short, sweat-soaked blond hair and shook his head briskly to help get some air to his scalp. He looked like the all-American boy, sporting a wet Woodstock hairdo from the Charlie Brown comic strip.

One of the network reporters guided the interview. "We have senior Rorey Garland here, a hero of the hour. Rorey, tell us how you did it. Seven seconds on the clock and you managed to pull it off. Was the fake kick designed that way?"

"Honestly, I just lost it," he admitted, followed by brief laughter from the media personnel. "Somewhere between the snap of the ball and that lame Hail Mary duck I threw up, I simply lost it. Lost my mind. Coach Dean called a field goal to tie the game because he thought we had a good chance making it and winning the game in overtime. I don't know, guys, I'll tell you. I just lost it, but lucky for us it all worked out."

Rorey began to push his way through the sea of cameras. "Thanks, guys, but I'm a shower away from being offensive. Whoaaa!" He ducked under flying bath towels and ice chips thrown by celebrating teammates. "How 'bout them Wranglers!"

Marshall emerged in the center of the media camp without his jersey, shoulder pads, or helmet. He'd sold them to wealthy fanatic alumni outside the dressing room for a couple thousand dollars. His street skills prevailed once again. This wasn't the first time he had sold something that did not rightfully belong to him. Growing up on the wrong side of the tracks did present its challenges and opportunities. Marshall was well suited for handling both of them.

Sweat trickled down his bare muscular chest like raindrops streaming down a glass windowpane. "Wait a minute. Wait a minute," he said unnecessarily. No one had gotten out of line or seemed to be overanxious, but he enjoyed orchestrating the media attention, especially when he was at the center of it. "I'm not going anyplace. Let's do this like we've been here before, folks."

"In case anyone in our viewing audience missed the catch of the decade, here it is again, and we have senior wide receiver Marshall Coates here to narrate it for us," a newsman with thick makeup directed. "Marshall, tell us what happened in your mind during the last and game-winning play."

As the TV viewing screen displayed the team's kicking alignment and the quick snap to Rorey, Marshall began to laugh and shake his head slowly. "Well, you see, we were prepared to attempt a field goal and tie the game. You know, maybe win it in overtime, but Rorey had other ideas. When he came up to the line before the play, he looked possessed. He stared right at me but I don't think he saw me. He was determined to win the game right then and there, so I kept an eye on him. And when the ball wasn't kicked, I knew he was in trouble. We've had an invisible umbilical cord keeping us in sync for the past three years. That's what the Salt and Pepper Show has been all about. You know what I'm saying? The Show. The rest is simple. He threw it; I saved his butt and made a spectacular catch. That's what friends are for. End of story."

Other questions were posed, but Marshall began to strip naked right there before making his way to the showers. The seasoned reporters knew Marshall's gift for no-nonsense, self-gratifying gab and had learned not to push the issue. Besides, he could never be accused of not giving the press enough to talk about.

Marshall and Rorey met at the walkway that led to the men's shower room. Rorey had a large white towel wrapped modestly around his waist while the other half of the Salt and Pepper tandem stood naked with one tossed over his shoulder. They flashed matching smiles and executed their personal soul handshake Marshall had taught Rorey when they both made the varsity team as sophomores.

"We did it, didn't we?" Rorey screamed.

Marshall nodded. "Together." Then he took a step back and

allowed Rorey to enter the shower room ahead of him. "Shall we? Mr. Garland."

"Let's," Rorey agreed, as they pretended to be pretentious, well-to-do Ivy Leaguers. "We shan't keep the boys waiting any longer."

The loud, rapturous atmosphere occupying the shower room screeched to a motionless halt once all the other varsity team members realized their superstar duo had arrived. "What took ya'll so damn long?" one of the largest men on the team charged.

"Don't ya'll know we get tired of waiting around for ya'll's slow, talking-to-the-press, asses," quipped Flea Johnson, the teams' smallest player.

Marshall sang, "Why can't we be friends?" in a soft melodic tone. A few of the other players softly joined in and repeated the phrase of the song, "Why can't we be friends?" Immediately the other two players, who seemed to have the biggest problems with the late arrivals, joined in. "Why can't we be friends?" Until all the young men sang the phrase in unison, "Why can't we be friennnds?"

"I'm first, I'm first," Rorey announced, while clearing his throat. "They came again looking for vic-tor-y but UTC out foxed the Coy-o-te." The chorus joined in hearty unison: "Why can't we be friends? Why can't we be friends? Why can't we be friennnds?"

Busta Griggs, a talented tailback, started in, "Later tonight I'm bound to get me some from a female coyote 'cause we finally won." The shower room erupted with laughter, then the players attempted to get the song back on beat.

They started up again in unison: "Why can't we be friends? Why can't we be friends? Why can't we be friends? Why can't we be friennnds?" "I got one, I got one," Marshall interjected. "We showed our guts and held our nuts like true champions should, there's just one thing left to say . . ." All the others knew what came next and joined in simultaneously with their heads tilted back, emulating his showy style. "Ahhhhhh! That's gooood."

They erupted even louder than before after their last participation and all began beating their chest and chanting, "Who you with? U-T-C. Who you with? U-T-C."

*   *   *

The following Monday, Professor Crayton entered the noisy lyceum-styled lecture hall, which seated 150 students. Section 4.02 of senior-level American Studies was a favorite course for many of the graduating class at UTC. It allowed them an opportunity to voice their opinions and critiques of the way the country had been run over the last one hundred years.

The student body came to attention when the distinguished black professor with a receding hairline began writing on a transparency laying on the top of a projector mounted on the far left side of the stage.

"I wonder what he is going to bore us—uh, I mean enlighten us—with today," whispered Marshall, as he searched his book bag for a pen to take notes with. Jasmine looked over at her boyfriend from the next desk. "If you'd keep up with your course syllabus, you'd know what should have been read for today's class."

Jasmine Reynolds was a cute brown maple-syrup-colored twenty-one-year-old from Dallas with nice hips and short, shiny black hair. Her parents were upper middle class and proud their daughter was on the dean's list every semester.

Marshall continued to ramble through his bag. "Why should I waste my time reading? That's why I've got you," he joked. "Hyyy gotcha."

"Well, Mr. Funny Man, let's see how well you take notes with your finger, then. Smarty."

Someone tossed a pencil from the next row. It hit him in the back of the head. "Ouch!" Marshall bellowed, rubbing his head as if to check for a hole in it. He looked behind him to see who threw it.

Rorey sat behind him grinning like the cat that ate the canary. "Shhhh! Now maybe you lovebirds can quiet down so we can hear."

"A pencil? This ain't math class," Marshall objected. "I need a pen!" Suddenly several ink pens came flying, each one hitting him in the back. "Very funny, very funny. That's all right, that's why I'm keeping 'em all." Light snickering proceeded from other students seated in the immediate area.

"That's what you get, Marshall," Jasmine teased. "Some people do take this class seriously. Not all of us are fortunate enough to be playing professional football next year. We still have to work on our futures."

He twisted his lips and mimicked her. "Noteverybodygonnabe blah, blah, blah. Jazz, you're always so serious. Too serious."

"Shhhhhhhhhhhh!" sprayed from several directions, just as the ink pens had earlier.

"All right, all right. I got it," Marshall conceded. He didn't like to study. He didn't enjoy class much, either, but he wanted to make his mother happy and be the first in his family to finish college. Besides, Jasmine would not have spent her college years dating a dumb jock. Her parents expected better of her and she could not see herself letting them down.

Professor Crayton paused suddenly, then interrupted his own lecture. After hitting the off switch on the overhead projector, when it seemed that a significant thought came to mind, a broad smile accentuated his round head. "Before we get any deeper into today's discussion, I would like to ask if there is anyone who doesn't know that the UTC Wranglers won the divisional conference championship on Saturday?"

Marshall sprang up from his chair with his hands motioning for applause, enjoying the broad ego strokes from his contemporaries. Clapping began and continued until Mr. Crayton raised his hands to quiet the room so that he could continue. "Might I add, there are several players in this section responsible for the win. Today's *Dallas Morning News* bears a front-page picture of one, Mr. Marshall Coates, and our very own Mr. Rorey Garland."

"The Catch," as the headline read, was the talk of the town. ESPN continued to show it over and over throughout the weekend in its sportscast.

After the class was over and most of the students had brushed by to congratulate Marshall and Rorey, Jasmine invited both of them to lunch, on her, but only if they promised to leave football out of their conversation. They promised.

*   *   *

As soon as they got to the Chili's restaurant off the interstate, all they could think about was the single important thing that joined them together, college football.

Marshall looked around the restaurant to find something hanging on the walls that might spark a conversation about something other than football, anything else. Rorey found himself doing the same while Jasmine studied the lunch menu.

"I bought a new hairbrush yesterday," Marshall blurted out. "It was on sale at Dollar World. I got it for ninety-nine cents. It's got this new revolutionary bristle construction or something like that."

As Jasmine glanced up from the dessert section, Rorey did his best to keep the drab conversation going. "I bet it's a fine brush. A fine brush indeed." Marshall nodded assuredly but had nothing else to offer.

"You guys are pathetic," Jasmine complained, noticing they both sat there trying to suppress their eager expressions. She began to feel the uneasiness, too. She had to give in. "Well, if you two are gonna be silly about this, do us all a favor and forget that promise y'all made before you two implode." Both of them let out deep sighs of relief as if they were in training for a breath-holding contest.

"Thanks, baby." Marshall pecked her on the cheek. "Rore, this whole 'The Catch' thing is getting to be more than even I can take. I've been staying over at Jazz's because my phone has been ringing off the hook with newspaper reporters and pro agents talking about representation. I can't lie, I was diggin' it at first, but damn, enough is enough."

Jasmine clenched her teeth and pinched her man on the side. "I thought you were spending quality time with me because football season was finally over?"

"Ouch, baby! Damn . . . oh yeah, baby, that too." Marshall grimaced and attempted to land on his feet. "Yeah, yeah. I've been waiting all season for this time to come. You know I can't get enough of yo' good stuff."

"Uh-huh," Jasmine murmured flatly. "You're drowning. And don't you try to save his butt, Rorey."

Rorey leaned back in his chair and put both hands up. "I . . . I . . . wasn't going to say nothing. Three years of watching you guys, I've learned to stay out of married people's business."

His comment made both of them laugh because he was right. Their relationship had been more like a marriage than a dating situation. Everyone on campus knew they were loyal to each other, inseparable, and bound to get married soon after graduation in the spring.

"Seriously, though, I've been just unplugging my phone," Rorey said nervously. "You could get in big trouble with the NCAA and the school could be fined if they even think you've been talking to an agent. Just ask those boys from UT." A few years ago, the NCAA interscholastic league tried to suspend three of the players from the University of Texas without substantiated proof that an infraction had taken place. It was rumored three players had lunch with a professional agent, who allegedly bought them sandwiches. It turned out to be much ado about nothing, but it did raise a stink in the college ranks.

"Yeah, I remember hearing something about that," Marshall acknowledged. "But that ain't my concern. I'm spending my energies in another arena, my baby's. Which reminds me, there's a victory dance at the Lambda frat house this Friday. Me and Jazz are gonna be there and so is everyone else. Now, Mr. You Ain't Had No Pudding Since Pudding Had You. Football season is over. So, who's gonna be getting your quality time for the rest of the year?"

"Would you stay out of that grown man's business," Jasmine insisted. "Like he's staying out of yours."

Marshall took note but continued to voice his opinion. "I'm just saying, my man, you owe it to yourself. Work hard. Play hard. That's the rule for successful people. Blow off a little steam."

Rorey's head sunk a couple inches. He cracked a quarter smile that was not too convincing. "You don't have to worry about me, Marshall, I gets mine." He remembered hearing some of the black players on the team say it with their chests stuck out.

"Then it's settled," Marshall resolved with a beaming smile. "We'll see you and your honey at the victory throw-down, then. And maybe we could all four hang out afterwards."

Jasmine looked uncomfortable about the entire conversation they shared with Rorey but restrained her sentiment until a more appropriate time. She didn't like sticking her nose into other people's affairs and couldn't stand for them to get into hers.

Later that day, she placed a bookmark in the folds of her marketing textbook and gathered her thoughts before addressing what happened earlier with Marshall. "Honey, there's something I wanted to talk to you about. Could you turn down the TV for a second?"

Marshall pressed the mute button on the remote control with his thumb.

"Yeah, baby. What is it?"

Jasmine knew her man's friendship with Rorey was almost as deep as theirs, maybe even deeper, so she treaded lightly. "I hope you don't take this the wrong way, but I don't think that it was fair for you to stay on Rorey's case today. If he wants to keep his private business private, you should respect that." Marshall rolled his eyes at her and attempted to blow it off, but she continued. "I know he's your best friend and y'all are tighter than panty hose two sizes too small, but it might be a better idea to leave his undercovers to him. You know what I mean?"

"Nah," he answered defensively. "I don't know what you mean, but I think I know what you're trying to in-sin-u-ate. The same thing that other people are running around here saying, but it ain't true."

Jasmine frowned when the conversation headed south. "See, that's why I hesitated to bring it to you. There you go getting defensive."

He became even more defensive and he raised his voice, one thing he had never done to her before. "How am I supposed to take it, Jazz? He's not just my best friend. He's my boy. My ace. We've been through too much together for him to be a damn faggot. Faggots can't do what he's done. It's all campus BS and it just ain't true. Ain't nobody ever seen him with a man or nothing, but just 'cause he ain't creepin' on the yard, people think there must be something wrong with him." He turned his face away from hers. "I don't want to talk about this anymore."

He was hurt that she would even consider that his best friend might be homosexual. He increased the volume on the TV to a level noticeably higher than it was before their discussion had begun. Jasmine got the message loud and clear. She knew he wanted to be alone and used the TV to help him retreat to his cave. She didn't have an opinion one way or another about Rorey's rumored sexuality. She just wanted Marshall to respect it, whatever the case turned out to be.

Three

Sometimes You Feel Like a Junior Miss

Morris *scurried around the small office* supply room gathering essentials to replenish the stash he kept at his desk. Paper clips, highlighters, ink pens, pencils, staples and Post-its. The phones were ringing off the hook and it wasn't close to opening time at the Johansen Art Gallery. He heard the phone lines sounding off their mad dramatic chorus, but he tried not to be pressured by them.

He placed the supplies on the reception desk, then quickly dashed away to the employee break room. "Filter, coffee. Darn, there's only domestic. Well, it will just have to do this once. Brew, baby, brew. Mother needs her java." Morris briskly walked down the long corridor with his legs brushing against each other. It seemed like he was trying to keep a thin sheet of paper from falling to the floor between each short stride. It was an extremely peculiar style of walking for a grown man.

In the rest room, he checked to assure all the toiletries were accessible and abundant. They were. One quick peek in the mirror as he passed. He could never pass one without making sure he looked his absolute best. "Charming but dusty," he said aloud when he noticed dust from the supply room was on his jacket. "How did I get . . . oh, darn, and I don't have the time to . . ." He tried to remove the thick dust from his clothes, but it was not coming out fast enough for him. Dust on his expensive outfit was not acceptable.

Morris was a perfectionist. He pulled two paper towels from the large dispenser mounted on the wall and ran cold water from the faucet over them. Then he began to lightly brush them against the dusty spots on his new designer business suit. "That'll do nicely for now. I guess."

After washing his hands, he wiped the water spots from the countertop to clean up the mess, then picked at his bleach-blond Julius Caesar hairdo for a moment. There were a few hairs out of place, even though he usually applied enough holding gel to freeze it solid. "Work with me," he said, as his thin feminine gold watch sounded several double beeps. "Now then, it's almost showtime." Everything was a production to him.

He ran his open palms gently down the lapels, then down the back of his pants where his butt met the top of his legs. He looked at his watch, which alarmed him it was nine-thirty. That meant other employees would be arriving soon and expecting the place to be ready for business. It wasn't Morris's duty to prepare the office, but it was his nature to take care of business, sometimes even if it was someone else's.

He had put away just about all the supplies when the front door opened. A distinguished and well-groomed white gentleman about fifty years old with a neatly trimmed graying beard entered the gallery and locked the door behind him. "Good morning, Mr. Johansen, the coffee's already brewing. It should warm you up."

"Morris," the owner said pretty matter-of-factly as he passed the reception desk. It hardly qualified as a salutation, Morris thought to himself. Actually, it was almost rude, but that's how Mr. Johansen was unless he really had something to say. His staff members secretly hoped he didn't have much to say at all. That usually meant he was pleased with the way things were going.

After Mr. Johansen took a few more steps past the desk, he stopped abruptly and walked back toward it. Morris winced and pretended he didn't notice his boss marching back to his work area. He should have known it was coming. "Morris, I thought we discussed your business attire last week." His stare was curt and disapproving.

"But it's a Donna Karan original," Morris replied, in his own defense, while admiring his newly acquired tailored woman's pantsuit.

Mr. Johansen must have realized that his talks with Morris were in vain, but he tried again.

"Morris, you and I both know that you're great at what you do. The customers as well as the other employees appreciate all that you do here, but your selection of professional wardrobe could use some stiffing up. I do believe that Brooks Brothers can accommodate something a bit more . . . conforming, shall we say." With that, he left Morris brooding.

Morris huffed. "You can't get any more *conforming* than this. It's a little something from this year's fall line." He mumbled under his breath as the owner disappeared into his spacious and extravagantly decorated corner office. "Humph, sometimes you feel like a junior miss."

More of the other employees had come in and gotten settled. It was almost ten o'clock when he unlocked the front door for business. As he turned to walk away, the door flew open against him. It was not enough force to injure him, but it startled the hell out of him.

"Uhhhhh!!!!" he screamed, throwing his hands up like someone caught on the bad end of a holdup. After realizing it was only Kennedy, he tried to compose himself by placing one hand over his mouth and the other over his heart. It was a bit overdone, but that was Morris's style.

"I'm sorry, Morris. I didn't know you were opening up. Is Mr. Johansen in yet?"

"Yes he is, honey, and we had words today. Beware, girl, he's on a rampage. He scoffed at Donna Karan herself. He's mad, I tell you. Maaad."

Most people probably would not have considered that brief encounter as having words, but Morris was widely known for his knack for exaggeration and embellishment.

"You look a little worn around the edges, let me put some herbal tea on for you. It'll perk you up," Morris said with excitement. He had another opportunity to help someone. He simply loved doing it. And away he went. Swish, swish, swish.

Kennedy pulled off her thick winter coat and was proceeding to her office when Mr. Johansen called for her to stop by his. "Ms. James, please come in and visit with me when you have a moment." She had been working at Johansen's for the past two years—long enough to know that when he called people by their last name, a reprimand was sure to follow. Running all ten fingers through her hair was more for relaxation than to make herself presentable for her boss.

She took a deep breath, then leaned her head into Johansen's office. "You wanted to see me?" she asked apprehensively.

"Yes, good morning, Ms. James. Have a seat." He put away his *Wall Street Journal*. That was the second "Ms. James." She must really be in for it, she thought.

Her body grew tense. "Yes, Mr. Johansen?"

Morris was listening in on the other side of the door with his ear pressed snugly against it. His attempt at eavesdropping was halted when someone began to run off what seemed to be a marathon of copies in the adjacent storeroom, making it impossible for him to hear another single word. He was foiled and would have to wait to hear the outcome secondhand.

When the boss's door opened, Morris hid in the storeroom and listened in on Mr. Johansen's last bit of discernment as he ushered Kennedy out. "You do good work around here and I would hate to lose you over something like this. But it must discontinue."

Kennedy was glad it was over, and it wasn't that bad after all. On the pilgrimage back to her office, she thought about Johansen taking the time to pull her into his office. It wasn't painful, but it easily could have been. Her boss was a kind man but took his business seriously, very seriously.

Morris brought her a steaming cup of herbal tea. He sat around anxiously but tried not to let on that he was. He sat squirming in the chair on the other side of Kennedy's desk, waiting for her to offer the information he was willing to kill for. He desperately wanted to know what they had to talk about at 10:05 A.M., just like he wanted to know everything that went on at the art gallery. Information was power.

He began rocking back and forth. As his anticipation began to boil over, he smiled suspiciously each time she took a sip of the delicious tea and looked up at him. Kennedy wondered why he was still there in her office but figured he would eventually get around to what he wanted. And he sat across the desk wondering when she would ask what he wanted. After several glances were tossed back and forth across her desk, the standoff had gotten ridiculous.

She finally broke the silence. "Morris, is there something else?" He grinned heartily with his lips pressed together.

"No, just wondering how you like the tea? It's echinacea, you know. Cures stuffy head, sinuses, even helps with some women's problems, I hear. I just love it."

She squinted at him, then tilted her head, thinking that if she focused on his face hard enough, maybe she could read what was on his mind. "The tea is great," she said out of nowhere. "Thanks a lot. You sure there's nothing else . . . you wanted?" Kennedy had a kind way of making people break when they had something on their minds but didn't want to say what it was.

"No, just thought I'd sit here and uh . . ." He primped his hair and looked away.

She liked Morris. She often thought of him as the gay brother, the overprotective sister she never had, the nosy bothersome neighbor, or the friend who always offered his advice, whether it was solicited or not. But he was too nosy. So she decided to push him to his nosy limit. "Just thought you'd sit there and . . . what, Morris?" she asked cunningly.

He looked at her with a panicked expression. She offered him a knowing stare in return. The time had come for him to ask her or leave her office. There they sat, peering awkwardly across the desk at each other. It had become a chess game of sorts. Each one watching the other's every move. Panicked expression . . . knowing stare . . . panicked . . . knowing . . . panicked . . . knowing . . . until Morris snapped.

He sprang up and pounced on top of her desk in desperation. "Okay, okay, you win and it hurts," he whined loudly. "You win, I lose, and I accept that. So please tell me before I have a stroke and die! Tell me, tell me . . . honey. How did it go in there? Was he brutal? Did he show his teeth or wag his tail? Come on, girl, share with me. Spill it! Spill it!"

Morris had lost his professionalism in the depths of his own need to snoop. He was on his knees on the desk with his hands around her throat. "Spill it! Spill it!" She managed to pull his hands away from her neck and gasped for air.

"Ahhhh-heeeh . . . ahhhh-heeh . . ." Kennedy panted. "Have you lost your mind? Morris, you could have killed me. If it's that important to you, I'll tell you everything. Just stay off my desk and keep away from my neck."

He agreed to calm himself down. He climbed off the desk and adjusted his jacket like an exasperated woman would do after being involved in an ugly altercation. "Please forgive me," he said slowly. "I slipped away but I'm back now." He took another minute to further compose himself. "Whewww . . . okay, that's better. That's the Morris I know and love," he said. "Well . . . let's have it. What happened in there?" Morris licked his lips like a large starving hound about to enjoy a ten-ounce New York steak. The only difference was that Morris's salivary glands were more active than any dog's. It was going to be good and he could taste it. "Was he vicious? Did he show his teeth or wag his tail?" he reiterated. "He was probably a savage, a real brute. Men can be so forceful."

Kennedy was amazed that a human could rattle off words so prophetically and so quickly. He was amazing to watch when he thought he was about to hear some dirt.

"Sorry to disappoint you, Morris, but it won't make the headlines. He gave me a pleasant but stern warning to stop coming in late or there would be a plastic chair down at the unemployment office with my name on it."

Morris was outraged. "That's it? That's all he said to you? Mr. J. called you in at ten-oh-five until ten-ten to scold you for being tardy? I thought surely it was something bigger, more scandalous."

"You timed me? You jerk!"

"I was looking out for your best interest, like always. Someone has to. Besides, what if it got heated and you needed a witness." He continued while she stared at him with a disapproving sneer. "You never know, it could have gotten out of hand, *Ms. James,*" he added, using the identical tone that Mr. Johansen had only moments before when reprimanding her.

"You're twisted, Morris. Mr. Johansen's not the raving maniac you've made him out to be in that little demented mind of yours."

"I'm going to disregard that insult, but you should consider yourself lucky. That drab gray dress may have gotten you some sympathy points. He couldn't have very well fired you in that rag. If he did, you might have gone right out and thrown yourself off a bridge, or worse . . . like run out and buy another dress like that one." Morris had had enough. He immediately threw his head back, left her office, and stormed out of sight in a huff. "Toodles." Swish, swish, swish.

Kennedy sat solemnly and still at her desk, looking at Simpson's photograph. She was losing him and she could feel it. They had begun fighting more than ever and had sex less than ever. She found herself wondering again where their relationship went wrong. Well, it didn't matter much, the damage had been done. She had to make up her mind. Stay in it, try to make it work, and be the superwoman Simpson expected her to be or give up and walk away. She did realize, however, that staying meant enduring more of what she had too much of already. Simpson's trifling ways.

Four

Twisted

Marshall *walked rapidly along the sidewalk* leading to the Business Administration building. His nylon green and silver Nike sweat suit made a whipping sound when his muscular thighs brushed against each other. His backpack was tightly harnessed on his shoulder. He made his way across campus, reciting notes and premises for the accounting quiz while frequently looking at his watch. "Okay. Discretionary costs. That's, uh . . . costs that arise from periodic, usually yearly, appropriation decisions regarding the maximum amounts incurred . . . blah, blah, blah. All right, all right. Homogeneous cost pool . . . that's, uh . . . uh, when the cost pool in which each activity whose costs are included therein has the same or a similar cause-and-effect relationship to a cost objective. Yes! I am ready."

It only took him a few quick bounds up the stairs to reach the second floor. The halls were almost empty. Many classes had already begun. His watch displayed 11:01. "Please be running fassst," he pleaded, as he approached classroom B-213. He stopped briefly at the door to catch his breath. "Okay, okay, please open." Marshall grabbed the door handle and pulled on it apprehensively. The door did not budge. He gave it a hard jerk to assure himself it was, in fact, locked. It was. He was one minute late. "One minute past and the door will be locked." Just as Dr. Grimes decreed earlier in the semester. Marshall had seen it happen to many other students who neglected to take Dr. Louise Grimes at her word. The sister was serious. She didn't play.

"Be on time or don't bother," she would always say. But this time, it was him who got caught in the tardy trap.

He contemplated knocking on the door and begging for leniency but remembered how she'd ridiculed other students who were stupid enough or daring enough to interrupt her class after it had begun and the door had been locked. Rationalizing the horror of the potential shame awaiting him on the other side of the door, and having been brought up by a single parent, he knew that no one could put a person in his place better than a sister could. And an educated one, a Ph.D. at that, forget about it. All things considered, receiving an "F" on the quiz didn't seem all that bad a deal.

He looked at his watch again. Two minutes after eleven. He had spent Thursday night at Jasmine's, his virtual other place to lay his head, and didn't allow himself enough time to get across the small but heavily populated college town on time. Marshall didn't like missing class. Jasmine convinced him years ago that every class period represented another ray of hope to those not fortunate enough to attend a university. She had a knack for inspiring him to reach deeper within himself than he thought possible. She was good for him. He was smart enough to realize it.

With no place in particular to be for the next hour, Marshall decided to take advantage of the situation and did as the other students did when they had no place in particular to be: hang out at the student center.

Walking much slower than before, he strolled casually toward the center of the UTC campus. Not much was going on, because those who had classes scheduled for the eleven o'clock hour were in them already, especially if their class happened to be in room B-213.

He stood at the corner of Avenue G and College Street waiting for the traffic light to change. Other people marched across the sluggish intersection without hesitation while he buried his face in the latest *College Football* magazine. Besides, he was in no hurry. He had missed his only class of the day.

Before the light changed, a green late-model Corvette pulled along the curb where he stood. The driver revved the powerful engine to get his attention. It was Shauni Woodbridge. The car was a gift from daddy. Shauni was the quintessential debutante, a white rich daddy's girl. Her family belonged to all the right clubs and had given her unlimited access to an American Express Gold card that she never left home without.

She was the first from a long line of Woodbridges to attend a public state school. Her interests in UTC's reputation as "party consolidated" was more than any upper-crust institution had to offer. Shauni was pretty, twenty-one, always in heat, and persistent. She was a rich miss who was accustomed to getting her way, a pedigree that reeked of danger.

At a glance, Marshall recognized the car and knew who it belonged to. Everyone knew. Shauni was the resident "big score" on campus even though she slept around, a lot. Marshall wondered what her daddy would say if he knew about his little princess, The *freakazoid*.

The window on the passenger side came down. "Marshall! Heyyy. You coming to the victory party tonight?" Shauni yelled in order to be heard over the street noise.

He bent down just low enough to get a good look inside and make eye contact. "Hey, what's up, Woodbridge? Yeah, I'll be there.

Round eleven. The whole crew'll be there. It's supposed to be all that and a Cadillac."

"Then I'll see you there. Save a dance for me." She winked and flashed a big old Texas-size smile as she pulled away.

Marshall didn't even entertain the thought of dancing with her or any other female. His woman was not having it. No hoochies, neither white ones nor black ones. Jasmine and Marshall had their share of disagreements in the past regarding trifling women hanging around outside the locker room and practice field. "Jock sniffers," as she liked to call them, were a sore spot for a good portion of their first year together. They came to an understanding, though. If he kept his zipper closed, he could keep her in his life. They were still together and the understanding was still enforced.

When it appeared clear to walk, Marshall stepped off the curb, looking to his right, watching the Corvette profile down College Street.

Scuuuuuuuurrrrrrr! A loud screeching of tires pressing against the cold concrete behind him made Marshall jump out of the way, dropping his backpack and magazine. An old rusted-out Ford F-150 truck came within inches of running him over but managed to stop just in time. Startled beyond comprehension, he stood panting and wide-eyed in the truck's path. He was too nervous to notice the truck was familiar to him. He was just happy to be alive and in one piece.

The truck door flew open. Rorey jumped from the driver's side and burst out with a hearty laugh when he realized it was his best friend he had almost run over. "Pepper . . . ," he said, still laughing hysterically. He rested his hands on his knees as he doubled over. Rorey often called him Pepper, or Pep for short, referring to half the tandem's nickname that one sports announcer coined after watching their dashing combination. Salt and Pepper, two spices that go so well together. The name stuck to them, much like they did to each other.

Rorey was still doubled over with laughter. "Maybe you need to get a little old lady to help you cross the street next time."

"Ha. Ha. Ha. That ain't even funny. It ain't!" Marshall was more scared than upset. "Stop laughing, man. Hey! That's not funny. You almost killed me."

"You're right, dude, it's not funny," Rorey agreed. "It's hilarious. I can't stop, I'm sorry but I can't." Rorey continued to tease.

Marshall gathered his things that had landed on the street as his best friend laughed on. "Whooooa . . . you should have seen your eyes pop out of your head when you thought you were going to be road pizza. You were like a deer staring into the headlights." Rorey tried to compose himself. "Okay, I'll stop tripping. Get in the truck so we can get something to eat."

After they were seated at Country Burger a few miles away, they both enjoyed a good laugh about the whole thing. "I bet it was a trip when I froze in the middle of the crosswalk," Marshall admitted.

"Yeah, just wait till I tell the guys tonight at the party, they'll get a kick out of it."

Marshall attempted to appeal to Rorey's sense of fairness. "Listen, Rorey, why don't you let a brotha slide and keep this on the down low." Marshall took the time to explain what the down low was, but Rorey still stuck to his guns.

"I gotta tell somebody, this is too good to keep to myself. You know you're my ace of spade and all, but this'n is a jewel. Maybe you should check your drawers?" Rorey laughed until he began to choke. The waitress brought over two waters when she heard the coughing. Rorey sang, "Why can't we be friends . . ." between coughs.

They placed a food order and sat talking about various articles in the football magazine Marshall had been reading. "Looks like those University of Texas boys got their stuff together these days," he said, while scanning the section naming the Associated Press top twenty teams. "All that scandal and still ranked in the top ten. They must be doing something right."

Rorey sat across from him with a stoic expression, barely listening. "Did you hear me, Rore?" Marshall repeated it after he realized Rorey wasn't involved in the conversation. "Ror-rey, did you hear me? I said, UTC ain't even ranked and we won the conference title. There ain't no justice. These polls are probably rigged, anyway, but I guess it don't matter much. We both goin' pro, big boy! All the way to the hall of fame, I bet. Me and you baby, all the way."

Rorey flashed a defeated smile and nodded his head slowly. "Yeah, right . . . me and you. The Salt and Pepper Show all the way."

Marshall looked up from the magazine. His bewildered frown went unnoticed. "Say, man . . . you all right? You've really been buggin' lately."

Rorey made a valiant effort at pretending all was well, but it wasn't convincing enough to fool Marshall. They had been through a lot of growing pains together. Rorey would have to put on a much better act if he was going to put one over on his best friend.

Rorey leaned back in his chair with his arms folded. "We do go back, don't we, Pep?"

"You know you're my boy. I love white chocolate," Marshall answered, now looking worried. He didn't recognize the desperate expression embedded deeply on Rorey's face. It was haunting and burned right through him.

Attempting to say what had him bothered, Rorey started in slowly. "There's something I've been wanting to tell you for a while now, but it never seemed like the right time, you know."

Marshall knew it had to be something deep, because Rorey found it difficult to look him in the eyes. "Whatever's on your mind, man, just spit it out. I ain't no miracle worker or nothing, but maybe I can help you with it. Anyway, it looks like you need to get it off your chest."

With a fluid exhale and a quick tug at the bill of his Texas Ranger baseball cap, Rorey looked more at ease but still not at peace with himself. "We're boys, right? You and me. Like always, right?"

"Hell yeah, like always," Marshall affirmed, while interlocking his fingers on the white Formica tabletop and posturing in the role of counselor.

"Yeah, well, you're probably right. I should just spit it out."

Fear replaced the worried look covering Marshall's face. "Well . . . out with it."

"I am buggin'," Rorey agreed, although nervously. "I just didn't know what you'd think of me or how you'd take it."

"Take what?"

"Well, check it out. You remember when I was a freshman and the upperclassmen rode me about not getting with that fine cheerleader Karen?"

"Yeah, I kinda remember," Marshall thought back. "So . . ."

"So, I didn't take it too hard because I had a girlfriend who lived in the Maple Hall dorm . . . she was everything to me. Pep, I thought I was in love and she really did a number on me."

Marshall hunched his shoulders. "What? You saying she cheated on you?"

Rorey looked down to hide his face. "We were together all the time. By spring semester, she was three months pregnant."

Eyes widening, Marshall leaned closer to the table, then looked around as if someone might overhear him. "So that's it? You're a daddy. You got a kid? That's great."

"N-n-n-no, that's not it," Rorey stuttered. "That's not nearly it. She was pregnant by someone else and lost the baby. She almost died and we had to tell her folks. Man, they pulled her out of here so fast. Didn't even give her a chance to pack up her things."

Marshall sat still. He contemplated the circumstances and was glad it wasn't him. "Damn, man. That's serious. So what's got you all twisted like this? She trying to get back in your life or something?"

"Naw, nothing like that, but she's still in my head."

"Just forget about her, man," Marshall suggested. "You're on your way to the big time. It's like my crazy uncle P. J. used to say.

The easiest way to get over a woman is to get another one under you." Marshall laughed at himself, but Rorey didn't seem to find it at all amusing.

"You're not making this any easier for me," he said, cracking his knuckles.

"What easier? I thought I solved it. Just get you another woman and it won't matter. She'll be sick that she messed up when she has to watch you on the tube every Sunday."

"She's dead, Marshall!" Rorey clamored loud enough to be heard several booths away.

"She's dead?" Marshall repeated in disbelief.

They were both so engrossed in the conversation that neither of them noticed their food orders had arrived and were getting cold. Marshall was at a loss for words, probably for the first time in his life. He put his hand over his face and tilted his head back to somehow help him absorb the news.

"I'm . . . I'm sorry, Rore. I had no idea. I'm . . ." He swallowed hard. "I'm really sorry. When . . . did it happen?"

Rorey's eyes watered. "She passed away on her twenty-first birthday last year. She never got the chance to live a decent life."

"Wow . . ." Marshall could barely speak above a whisper. "That is enough to blow your mind. And you've been carrying this around with you all this time?"

Rorey rubbed his eyes, then wiped the tears from them. "That's not the worst of it."

Marshall raised his brow. He was afraid to ask, but he did anyway. "What could be worse than dying?"

Rorey adjusted his cap again, then looked around to survey the area just as Marshall did earlier. "I'll tell you what's worse than death, and that's living with what she died from." There was a tense moment of silence before he could muster up enough nerve to say it. "AIDS."

Marshall heard it but it took a second to sink in. "AIDS! She died from HIV??" He could say it but he couldn't believe it. The only people he had heard of dying from the terrible disease were homosexual males and intravenous drug users. "Did she start shooting up or something?" Bewildered, he searched for an answer that would help him make sense of it. "I mean how else could she have gotten it?"

Rorey knew right away that Marshall, like most people, was drastically miseducated about AIDS. "Naw, she wasn't no drug user. She contracted it sometime while she was still in high school and brought it here with her to good old UTC."

"We gotta get you tested, come on," Marshall urged blindly as he felt his heart racing. "I know Coach can hook us up with a doctor. Let's go!"

Sitting still, Rorey didn't even blink. "Coach already knows about it and so do the team doctors."

The busy burger joint seemed to fade to silence. Marshall was sure he could hear his heart beating. Thump-thump . . . thump-thump. His eyes displayed the terror that ran through him. His lips had become dry and ashy, so he moistened them with the tip of his tongue. He became exasperated. "What do you mean, Coach and the doctors already know?" he asked, through somewhat clenched teeth. "Already know what, Rore?"

Rorey's hands trembled. He stared down at his cold French fries before answering. "That I've been HIV positive for over two years and now it's full-blown AIDS. That's why they always freaked out when I got hurt."

Marshall panicked. He instinctively bit his bottom lip to stop it from quivering. "Awww. No . . . Rorey, tell me you're joking, right? Please tell me you're joking with me." Tears ran from his eyes. Suddenly, his stomach started doing flip-flops. He felt violently ill. The kind that accompanies overwhelming suffering and grief. Rorey wanted to explain it to him but Marshall grew hysterical. "That's not fair! It's just not."

Before Rorey could get a word in, Marshall sprang up from the booth and bolted out of the restaurant with one hand over his mouth and the other holding his stomach. The news was too devastating. His plans of playing professional football included Rorey.

All of his plans included Rorey. They always did. But his world had just experienced a major catastrophe. It blew up in his face.

Rorey leaned back in his chair again. A single tear formed in the well of his eye and trickled down to the corner of his mouth. The more he thought about not having Marshall behind him, the more freely his tears flowed. He took some money out of his wallet, then threw it on the table and disappeared outside. The crisp twenty-dollar bill was more than enough to pay for the food, which neither of them bothered to eat.

Five

Low-Fat Popcorn

The past week had been a long one. Kennedy focused on getting to work on time, which wasn't a problem, since Simpson refused to see her at all. Actually, he neglected to return her calls, too. She was home alone with her cat, Lady Eleanor, lounging on her cordovan sofa. They watched *Seinfeld* reruns for hours. She had hundreds of episodes recorded on videotapes. She loved that show. And each time she embarked on a *Seinfeld* marathon, it meant she and Simpson had been fighting, and that meant she subsequently would be alone for days. It never occurred to her once that her man always managed to find some way to start an argument closer to the weekend than in the middle part of the week. He wanted his weekends to be freed up and he got them that way.

After two bags of low-fat popcorn and a liter of Diet Coke, she couldn't eat anymore, drink anymore, think anymore. She was home alone on another Friday night, another one with the cat and a chain of lit cigarettes to keep her company. She couldn't make sense of it anymore. As if she could before. Twenty-seven years old and home alone, again.

It was well after 2:00 A.M. when she turned off the television and all the lights in the house. Scented candles illuminated the den area and added tender relief while she endured the jagged loneliness.

While sitting curled up in her window seat puffing on a Marlboro cigarette and nursing a cup of coffee with hazelnut cream, she gazed out over the tranquil Dallas skyline and drifted into a deep trance. Her old Beatles LPs played until she fell asleep. Lady Eleanor looked on and enjoyed the quiet evening.

Simpson, on the other hand, wasn't heartbroken at all. His evening had been spent with a tall thin model type, one of those he picked up each time he and Kennedy couldn't keep it together for an entire evening. They were welcoming standbys and he treated them like diamonds, with spontaneously exciting late-night booty calls, expensive shows, and impromptu trips to exotic tropical places. Most of which he wouldn't think of taking Kennedy to.

Club Matrix was a ritzy hot spot in Deep Ellum. It was an artsy club in the entertainment district of Dallas, where mostly anything goes. Two of the rest rooms were unisex; one was exclusively for women, for those who couldn't grasp the adventure of a see-all water closet. And the one near the rear of the club had "Most Men" written on the door.

A busy tattoo parlor, Skin Graft, was next door to the Matrix. Sometimes, club goers who got too drunk ended up there and were quickly stamped with a permanent reminder why we should all drink responsibly. There were already far too many pairs of Mick Jagger's lips, cherries hanging from their stems, and interlocked hearts on hundreds of private parts in the inner city.

Simpson stopped near the club's entrance. He calmly stepped out of his car in the middle of the busy thoroughfare, blocking traffic.

Teenage kids behind him honked their horns relentlessly and shouted obscenities. They didn't like their cruising flow being obstructed, and Simpson's vanity license plate, NV THIS, didn't help the situation any.

Fancy blue suede Italian designer loafers stepped out onto the cold street top. A tailored azure-colored, double-breasted suit over a cream mock-neck sweater draped his thin body.

The valet darted out into the street, "Good evening, Mr. Stone. I remember, park it up front. No problem. Enjoy yourself."

Simpson walked up and shook the large doorman's hand briskly and slipped a twenty in his palm. He, big Franky the doorman, knew him well. Simpson frequented the club often and tipped a lot. "Go on in, Mr. Stone. Have a nice time," Franky said routinely.

Simpson had received the go-ahead to shoot by all the people standing in line to get in. He received the VIP treatment in practically every nightclub he paid visits to, at least where he was recognized. That was important to him.

He looked around to take in the sights, a spectacular laser light show, and the latest sounds. Scandalously clad women and some men, too, in the dead of winter, landscaped the first floor. The bartenders mixed drinks as ice cubes flew about behind them. When he climbed the back staircase to the manager's office, a man larger than Franky stood blocking the entrance to the doorway. He motioned for Simpson to spread his arms and prepare to be searched for weapons before entering.

Simpson objected harshly. "You gonna search me?" he barked.

"Sorry, Mr. Stone. I didn't recognize you at first," he quickly apologized. "Go on in. Mr. Glass is waiting for ya." Simpson knew the oversized help was not too bright, but exercising his IQ wasn't what he was being paid for.

The club's owner-operator, Richard Glass, was Italian. His real surname was Glassivido, but his parents changed it in the 1950s to give Richard, or Richey as his close friends called him, a better chance in life. He was a forty-something olive-skinned greasy black-haired hustler originally from Brooklyn, New York. He was ordered to take care of operations in the South after two NYPD officers turned up dead in a deserted warehouse belonging to Richey's connected uncle. Richey's hot head was to blame. It got him banished to faraway Dallas, Texas. As a rule, the mobster's family frowned on killing cops, dirty cops or otherwise.

His wardrobe consisted mainly of dark-colored designer suits, expensive shoes, jewelry, and silk shirts. It would be hard to imagine him in anything else. Richey also wore fine linens and virgin wools like a male fashion model. The scar on his right cheek was indicative of the kinds of things he had been involved in. It was an emblem of the kind of man he was, serious about getting what he wanted, even if he had to pay a severe price for it.

When Simpson entered the plush office, Richey stood up and walked around his desk, which was covered with stacks of crisp dead presidents. "Simpson, it's good to see you. You don't come up here to see me like you's use ta. I see you downstairs, though. You come in, score a nice little something for yourself, then vanish without a trace."

Simpson smiled heartily. He enjoyed picking up strange women and enjoyed it even more when someone knew he was very good at it. He liked the fact that someone might be envious of him. "Richey, you can't keep up with me, I'm too slick." They both laughed loudly. "How's things? You got what you need?"

"You know I don't. That's why I sent the message to your office. What did you think, huh?" Richey had sent a strip-o-gram to Simpson's office earlier in the day. It was a way to summon Simpson to visit the upstairs office and bring a package. Richey prided himself on doing things with pizzazz.

"How much do you need?" Simpson asked.

"Twice the normal ought to do it this time."

"Twice, huh? This for pleasure or business?"

The comment disrupted Richey's casual demeanor. Simpson immediately realized he had stepped over the line and quickly attempted to recover. "Just kidding, your party's your party." He unfastened his jacket and reached behind his back, then pulled a plastic bag out of his waistband. The five-by-seven bag contained several smaller zip-locked bags with a popular white powdery controlled substance in them.

Simpson's legit business was profitable, but he loved his side gig a lot more. It was one that gave him the clout he felt he needed. He wasn't a rough-cut, hard-core gangster like Richey Glass, but he relished feeling connected to powerful people.

"This should cover it." He threw the bag to Richey, who caught it with one hand. His pleasant disposition returned instantly.

"I knew you'd come through. Somehow, you always do."

"Enjoy, Richey. You know how to reach me."

Simpson reached for the doorknob, then turned around to get another look at the money stacked on the desk. When he did, Richey smiled and tossed him a stack of twenties totaling five thousand dollars. "Next time bill me," he said, then flashed him an undertaker's grin.

Simpson didn't have to worry about receiving payment from people like Richey. They had money to burn and were always in need of a little something to help get them by, get the party started.

Simpson shoved the strap of bills into his pocket, then exited to the downstairs bar. He ordered a bottle of Moët champagne and had it sent to a nearby table where four extremely beautiful women, all model types, sat. Just his type. Instead of picking out the one he wanted, he let his ego run wild. He thought it would be more interesting to see which one of the beauties would choose him. The waiter delivered the expensive champagne and four crystal glasses with a card bearing Simpson's name and phone number. The message read, "Thanx for the Beauty." Perhaps he should have written, "Thanx for the Booty," because that's what he wanted. Expensive champagne was his standard response to a can't-miss opportunity. It never failed. Not once.

The waiter pointed Simpson out as the one who sprung for the bubbly. Each of the ladies looked over and smiled. He returned their smiles with one of his own and nodded, acknowledging their appreciation. He sent for his car to be brought around and stood near the door, inside, impatiently waiting for it. Between the time he sent for the car and when it arrived, one of the women from the table had her coat on and her arms entangled with his, ready to be whisked away. It worked every time. Funny what charm champagne has on some women, or perhaps it's the charm of the money it takes to buy champagne that woos them so well. Whichever case it happened to be, Simpson could pick 'em.

That night, Kennedy was far from being in his arms and further from being on his mind.

Tequila Shots

*M*arshall *was slumped down* on the love seat in Jasmine's apartment. His only companion for the past six hours had been his thoughts surrounded by utter darkness. He didn't want to be alone, but he couldn't find the energy it would have taken to be around others. A forty-ounce bottle of beer didn't provide the tonic that he had hoped would dull his senses.

Rorey had stopped by earlier and banged on the door, pleading with him to open it, but Marshall had kept quiet and pretended no one was home, although Rorey knew that he was. Marshall hid in his confusion and pain but failed to elude the misery of it all. It would have taken much more than one forty of beer to pull that off.

His best friend shared both saddening and life-threatening news with him, and he couldn't handle it. Marshall sank into the abyss of his own sorrow and immersed himself in the horrible predicament that befell Rorey. He felt helpless and inadequate to say or do anything that could have made the situation better. His tough regimen of street wisdom and a nearly completed formal education both proved useless. During his youth, he witnessed people getting shot and stabbed to death in his very own neighborhood, a homeless woman at a bus stop giving birth in the rain, and countless other monstrosities too heinous to mention, but none of those had prepared him for Rorey's news.

He continued to sit motionless when Jasmine eventually came home from working her part-time job at the mall. She stumbled over Marshall's backpack, which Rorey had left against her door. When she flipped the light switch on, her eyes found Marshall sulking there. It was painfully obvious he had been crying.

"Marshall . . . Marshall . . . are you okay, baby?" He didn't answer. She cautiously walked over to where he sat. "Marshall . . . what's wrong?" she asked continually.

He gazed into her dark-brown eyes, then held her around the waist. "He's gonna be all right," he muttered. "I just know it, Jazz. Rorey's gonna be just fine. He's got to be."

She slowly lowered to her knees and leaned in between his legs, then wrapped her arms around him as tightly as she could. "You're right. Whatever it is, honey. It's gonna be just fine." She didn't know what happened to Rorey but knew it had to be catastrophic to affect Marshall this way. It was difficult to see her man broken up like he was. She had always seen the hard, insensitive, stereotypical male side of him, unless he softened up to comfort her pains.

Hours later, he still couldn't share his intimate pain with the woman he loved. He was lost in it and needed to find his own way out. Jasmine suggested he take a walk to clear his head, thinking he might feel better when he returned. Initially, he lacked the energy to move. Instead, he continued to stare at the television, which wasn't turned on. As he massaged his temples with his fingertips, she watched him intensely.

Suddenly, Marshall popped up off the love seat. He kissed Jasmine on the cheek, then disappeared outside without saying where he was going or when he was coming back. He'd had enough. The pity party was over. He wasn't sure of exactly what he'd do himself. He did know he couldn't help matters any by being a weak by-stander, doing nothing.

The night was cold. It got to be that way by late November but not too cold to go for a much needed stroll. Marshall had on loose-fitting blue jeans and a thick letterman's jacket over his favorite navy-colored Champion sweatshirt. Rorey had one just like it, identical.

Jasmine's apartment was less than a half mile off campus. Marshall started walking aimlessly until he ended up walking in circles, thinking. It only took two passes by Greek Row Boulevard before he mustered up the guts to head down the street where the sorority and fraternity houses were. All the homes on "the Row" were picturesque two-story dwellings with ten to fifteen rooms. Each one had its own sordid stories to tell, from invitation-only gay coming-out parties to late-night prostitution rings and everything else imaginable. The Row was also known widely for its ability to make things happen within its confines, unthinkable ideas that normally wouldn't have gone further than someone's thoughts that usually made it to confession by morning.

Marshall hit the Row wanting to talk to Rorey and apologize, to further discuss it, and maybe say something positive. Rorey was in a time of need and couldn't count on him. Marshall felt ashamed and alone, too, in his own way. He'd never turned his back on a friend before and promised himself he would never let it happen again. More than anything, he wanted to be there for Rorey, who was the closest thing to a brother he ever knew.

By the time he reached the Kappa house, with cream-colored trim and a crimson front door, he could hear the party going on five houses down at the Lambdas. He stopped and surveyed the long line of parked automobiles for Rorey's Ford truck. There it was, resting against the curb, up the street a ways.

Marshall wanted to ease into the party like nothing was wrong, find Rorey, and leave. Just like that, without any drama, but he began to feel nauseous while looking on from the sidewalk and see-ing carloads of people still arriving. He knew that he had to avoid them and take time to get his head together. Meanwhile, the cold weather began to rattle his bones. He could see his own breath in the cold night air when it came to him that the Wrangler diner stayed open late on the weekends. He hoped it was still open.

The victory party was off the hook. It was loud and hot, like college students liked it. Everybody who was somebody was there, except for Marshall and Jasmine. The lights were purposely dimmed. The music was hyped up and added funk to the atmosphere. Legacy Childs had his drawing stand set up near the DJ booth. He created booty sketch masterpieces for ten dollars a pop. Legacy was also known as Freelance around campus because he could always come up with another way to use his artistic talents to make money for himself. He was a product of an interracial relationship. Which races? No one knew. He had been orphaned at birth. At twenty-six years old, he was finishing his last year of undergraduate studies. His GI Bill was expiring, allowing him just time enough for grad-uation in the spring. He was an art major, well liked and possessed an uncanny ability to quick sketch anything he saw. Although he was a senior at UTC, he commuted twice a week for classes. His warehouse apartment was located north of downtown Dallas. He also worked part-time as a tollbooth change attendant. It allowed him the time to study and practice his skills while making a little change on the side, very little.

A medley of colognes and perfumes, intermingled with scented potpourri, almost disguised the distinct smell of a certain natural foliage so that it was at a bearable level, but it didn't. It was quite common for college students to get high from natural herbs, tradi-tionally passed from the left-hand side.

Rorey didn't seem to mind the odor as he danced the forbidden dance, the electric slide, and the good old ghetto bump and grind. He was sociable, as usual, and celebrated at the victory party like the rest of his teammates, irresponsibly. For the first time in three years, he was just one of the boys. He entered every drinking contest held. That is, before a three-hundred-pound lineman named Mike Lovelle, also known as Big Love, persuaded him to slow it down. Throughout his college lifetime, Big Love had seen more than his share of wasted athletes. He was usually the one who ended up making sure they got home safely. Watching Big Love was like watching an oversized doting mother grizzly bear looking after her cubs.

Rorey wasn't known to be an accomplished drinker, and for good reason. He went to the victory to get drunk, hard and fast. And he did. He was pissy drunk after ten long-neck beers and three tequila shot chasers.

"Where'd I put my drink?" Rorey yelled out, to no one in particular. "Somebody help me find my drink. It's a party and I'm an animal. Howwwl . . . party!" One more drink would have put him on his butt, or his knees, or his face for that matter. Which one depended on the way he fell when he passed out.

Shauni Woodbridge had been staring at him all night and waiting for the right time to strike. Finally, after one tequila chaser too many, the time had come, and she wasn't going to let some other adventurous hoochie bag her prey.

"Hey, Rorey, you having a nice time?" she asked, sizing up her potential victim.

"Good. I'm good." He was good, all right. Good and drunk is how he was.

"How're you enjoying this little swahhh-ray of ours, Shauni?" His words came out slow and slurred.

"Oh, you know my name?" she replied coyly, not expecting a response. "I didn't think you did. You never speak to me and I see you on campus all the time."

Rorey didn't think twice about her being there. More than three years had passed since he was sexually active with anyone. He missed the intimacy initially, then became too frustrated by it to continue going to the point of no return, only having to return unsatisfied.

After he and Shauni danced closely for a couple of slow-grooving songs, Rorey realized he needed someone to get him drinks past Big Love, so he kept his arm around her until the overgrown guardian eventually disappeared into one of the rest rooms on the second floor.

"Hey, Shauni, do me a favor and see if there're any more beers left. I'll check on the rest room situation so you won't have to wait when you're ready to go." She believed he was being thoughtful. He was. It took a lot of thought to come up with a plan to use her to smuggle drinks for him while he found a hiding place to slam beers at the same time.

Shortly, Shauni returned with two fresh, cold beers. Big Love appeared directly behind her to witness the handoff. "Rorey, here you go. How's the rest—"

"Thank you, little lady," Big Love announced, foiling the hand-off. "But he's had enough for tonight. His cup done runneth over an hour ago. I'll take that. My cup still has plenty of room left in it." He took the bottle from Rorey, then watched him from across the room periodically.

Shauni wasn't finished, not by a long shot. Rorey still wasn't in the mind-set she'd always hoped to catch him in. Confusion. She spent some time thinking about it, and then it hit her. She had a breakthrough. "Rorey, that big guy isn't going to let you near another drink here, but I know where you can get as much as you want."

He was getting bored and his buzz was starting to wear thin. "Where, the beer store?"

"No, silly. It's after midnight. They can't sell beer this late. I've got another place in mind and it's never closed." He didn't recognize her seductive strategy, but he couldn't pass up the free beer offering. The place could have been on the moon and he'd have gone along with her.

He licked his lips. They were drier than he expected them to be. "Hmm, I'm still thirsty," he admitted. There was also a lot of partying to be done and he was sobering up. He had planned on getting wasted, and wasted he was hell bent on getting. Considering that Big Love loomed near, he'd have to find another venue to get bombed in.

"Hold on, let me get my jacket," he said, with renewed hopes of getting more beer.

Before he could enjoy his short snooze on the way to her place, Shauni's Corvette was pulling into her condo parking lot. It didn't take long for them to get out of the cold and inside to something more comfortable. She poured him a stiff shot of bourbon and soda, then handed him a beer to chase it with while she sipped wine. Rorey wasn't thinking about being intimate. He was focused on the task at hand, getting zooted. "Drunker'n a skunk," as his father used to say.

He slammed the beer down his throat as fast as he could, then gulped the mixed drink after that. He concocted himself another one as he browsed through her CD collection. Shauni had enough of them to open her own used CD shop. There were thousands of them, thousands, in an enormous wall cabinet.

Rorey was feeling the early buzz of a fresh high when Shauni disappeared into her back room. When she returned, she'd exchanged her party clothes for silk panties and a matching tank top. He dropped a CD jacket on the floor when his eyes found her posing seductively against the wall, in all her splendor. Her toned legs and perfect surgically augmented breasts looked good enough to nibble on. Everything looked good enough to eat.

The mood was set when her primal scent rushed through his nostrils. Victoria's Secret couldn't have created a potion as potent as the vibes she was sending off. It was all-natural and intoxicating. Like the atmosphere, he inhaled deeply and breathed her in. He wanted to look away but he couldn't. She was the most womanly image he had ever seen up close. She was only twenty-one, but her body was far from the nineteen-year-old's he'd etched in his memory. She was put together well and there was no denying it. The hours most students her age spent working on part-time jobs, she used to work out at the gym.

Shauni smirked sensually. "What's the matter, Rorey? You look like you've never seen a grown woman before." He hadn't and it was reflected on his face by a dumb, scared, mouth-open, lost-in-the-woods gaze. "Are you gonna just stand there gawking or are you gonna give me a kiss?" A kiss wasn't quite what she had in mind, but at least it would warm up the pot that she wanted him to stir up later.

"Oh shhht," he mouthed. "I was just going to change the disc."

He found himself at a crossroads. Knowing his terminal condition, he wanted to leave but couldn't. The attraction was too strong and the alcohol he drank ruined his defenses. "I need another drink, that's what I need. Why don't you put on something we can dance to." He fixed another cocktail while she watched him from the hundred and one disc-changing machine.

"Rorey Garland, if I didn't know better I'd think you was afraid of me." He wasn't the least bit afraid of her. Well, maybe a little. But he was very afraid of intimacy. He didn't want anyone to have to go through life like he had to, with utter fear, shame, and knowing people would be afraid to touch him if they knew.

Shauni sauntered nearer to him and began to unbutton his shirt. With each button she unfastened, she eased closer, until all the buttons were undone and she was pressed against him. She smelled so good, too good. It was more debilitating than the double shot of bourbon he'd just finished off. He rationalized to himself that he could kiss and fondle her tight body but stop when it got too heated. He shouldn't have underestimated the amount of heat that an attractive warm body, too close to deny, could generate. Somehow, he allowed the euphoric passion from her wet tongue kisses to draw him in. In what seemed like seconds, he found himself on his back, butt naked, caught up in her web of lewd intentions as they kissed furiously underneath her satin sheets. Shauni had already tried at least twice to maneuver his throbbing penis inside her. She had become frustrated. "Is there something wrong? Why don't you take me, baby," she pouted. "Go for it, I'm on the pill. We don't need a condom."

Rorey was shocked at her irresponsibility. He knew that if she didn't require him to wear a condom, she probably hadn't asked anyone else to, either. Suddenly, he didn't feel as apprehensive as before, but he still insisted on strapping on protection. "Shauni, I think we should use one anyway. You never know. Where do you keep them?"

She rolled her eyes and crawled out of the bed in a huff. "I think I might be able to find one somewhere in the . . . " she mumbled, while looking in an old shoebox in the closet. "Here's one, but I can't stand these things. I like to feeeel it."

Rorey hesitated. He rolled it around with his fingertips, then meticulously strapped it on before pulling her close to him.

Shauni moistened her lips with her tongue and closed her eyes as she became swept up with her own ravenous anticipation. She noticed that his hard muscular body seemed even harder now and his penis was much larger than she expected it to be.

They spent over forty-five minutes with their legs entangled in fiery, passionate, animalistic sexual acrobatics. He didn't want to stop, but they both needed a chance to catch their breath. Shauni pushed him off her playfully, with an attitude suggesting she wanted to continue later on.

After climbing out of bed, she gathered herself before going for dry bath towels and something to drink. Rorey's chest heaved up and down as he lay on his back. He caught his breath while coming down from the high of their exhausting interlude. His alcohol-sustained buzz was gone now, and reality stormed back into his life with a vengeance.

His conscience began to bother him, although he attempted to ignore it. He wondered what he was doing there when he knew perfectly well he had AIDS. It was as much a precautionary method as it was using good sense to put that condom on, which reminded him he needed to relieve himself of the beers he drank earlier.

He stumbled into the bathroom and searched along the wall for the light switch. When the light came on, fear raced down his back along with streams of sweat. The condom was gone. All that remained was the remnant around the base of his penis, a yellow synthetic latex ring. It must have torn during their window-rattling escapades. A knot developed in the pit of his stomach. He knew better than anyone that a broken condom was a useless condom.

Rorey forgot what he went into the bathroom to do when his knees buckled. Everything else was insignificant by comparison. He sulked back into the bedroom. Shauni was stretched out on her king-size bed, wrapped in a large beach towel, resting up for round two.

Standing only a few feet away from her, he didn't see her lying there through the haunting haze that eclipsed his vision. He figured out what must have happened, but he didn't know how to tell her, what to tell her.

Shauni, still caught up in the rapture of ecstasy, rolled over in bed only to find that he had begun to gather his clothes off the floor to get dressed. She was determined to entice him to stick around for another torrid episode. "Oh, I see. You've had enough. Well, I haven't and I want some more, Mr. Quarterback." He continued to put on his clothes in a slow, methodical manner, neglecting to speak or acknowledge her presence. "Hey, Rorey, don't tell me you're leaving." He didn't answer her beckoning him to return. "Don't do this to me," she threatened. "I'm not kidding with you. I've waited a long time for this and I've only gotten half the show."

Somberly, Rorey walked past the bed to get his other things in the den. Shauni became aggressive and demanded more sex while stroking his chest and whispering lewdly to him. He continued to ignore her as he put on his coat. That was the last straw. Shauni wasn't used to rejection. She tore into him. "So what they say about you is true, after all. You don't really like girls, do you?" Rorey stopped and jerked his body around like a demented mass murderer, but she continued to shout insults at him. "Prove you're not a queer. Come back and finish the job!" Her voice got louder until it became unbearable.

"You don't understand, Shauni!" he shouted back.

"Oh, I get the picture, all right. You're a sorry excuse for a man, you—"

"You don't understand," he repeated, only much softer. "It busted. The damned condom busted."

Sadness filled his eyes as silence filled the room. He was afraid of what needed to happen next. He had to tell her about his condition, but he wasn't sure if he could do it. Maybe he could have pretended that it didn't happen. Maybe he could have pretended he didn't have AIDS. Other people do it all the time. They knowingly put sexual partners at risk and go home as if nothing ever happened.

"Calm down," she suggested confidently. "It's okay. I told you I was on the pill. Don't worry, I'm not going to get pregnant."

He shook his head before walking out the door. "Of course not. What was I thinking? You're on the pill." His harsh sarcastic tone went unnoticed. Shauni didn't get it. She completely missed the boat. He disappeared into the darkness, leaving her unaware of his true concerns.

She probably never once thought about contracting sexually transmitted diseases such as herpes, syphilis, or AIDS.

Marshall thanked his lucky stars when he discovered that the diner was still open. Better yet, it was empty, just as he needed it to be. Marshall forced down several cups of coffee, although he couldn't stand the taste of it. He had been there over an hour and was more than ready to talk to Rorey.

He headed down the Row again, wondering what he would say when he found his friend who needed his support. He was concerned about saying he was sorry without sounding like a chump. Saying "I'm sorry" was difficult for Marshall. He knew it was going to be tough and he'd made up his mind that he was going to be, also.

Empty beer cans and bottles littered the front lawns of fraternity houses on either side of the Lambda's, where the once-hopping party had slowed down to a crawl. Most of the die-hard partygoers were

borderline toxic-poison statistics, extremely close to consuming le-
thal levels of alcohol, but that wasn't Marshall's concern.

Legacy counted his money and put away his sketch pads and
drawing tools after making over three hundred dollars. He must
have drawn over half the female booties in the party. And some of
the guys, too, who paid extra. He didn't usually do men's butts.
That wasn't his thing. Now, his caricature sketches of the women
profiling from behind, they were something to see. He always found
a flattering way to accentuate even the most unsightly of tooshies.

"Heyyy, Marshall, where ya been?" a member of the marching
band asked from behind a twelve-ounce beer bottle. "The party's
over, man. They're outta beer. This'n here is the last one." He smiled
at the bottle, then hoisted it like a coveted award.

"Yeah . . . that's messed up," Marshall responded, to patronize
the inebriated student. He continued to look over the remaining
partiers who danced on with hopes of coupling up for the night.
"Have you seen, uh . . . Rorey Garland tonight? His truck is out
front."

"No, I haven't seen him, but I'll tell him you're looking for him
if—" Realizing the young man was so drunk that he may have seen
Rorey and forgotten, Marshall walked away while he was still talking.

Marshall checked, but he didn't find Rorey passed out in any of
the upstairs bedrooms or bathrooms and concluded he simply wasn't
there. Big Love saw Marshall on his way out of the frat house and
stopped him. "Man, where have you been all this time? That's cold-
blooded of you not to show up until it's over. This victory party is
mostly because of you and Rorey. At least he came on time."

Marshall wanted to apologize but had no time for that. "Rorey
was here, tonight?" he asked anxiously.

"Yeah, he was. Left over an hour ago. He got so wasted. I tried
to look out for him 'cause I know you superstars can't handle y'all's
liquor. But I'm sure he'll be all right. Some chick was sneaking off
with him."

"Over an hour ago?" Marshall confirmed. "Thanks, Big Love . . .

I really appreciate it." He took off, walking toward the dormitory a few blocks away.

As the candlelight flickered off the plain white walls in Rorey's dorm room, a half-empty bottle of whiskey rested near him on the floor. He sat on his desk staring out into space as sweat mounted on his forehead. He played his music louder than he should have, but it was Friday night, so initially no one complained. He sang the words he knew of a hit record performed by an English rock group called the Nobodys, as it played on his stereo, between taking monster swigs of whiskey. "She's a good woman . . . nothing like her momma. She loves chocolates and good kisses too . . ." Rorey was headed for self-destruction. The self-pity he anguished in wasn't enough to drown his emotions, so he downed alcohol by the mouthful.

The more he drank, the louder he sang; the louder he sang, the higher he had to turn up the volume on the stereo. The louder the music got, the more he drank; the more he drank, the more vicious the cycle became, until his singing became annoyingly shrill, *"I'm the epitome of lonely . . . just leave me be . . . please, just walk away from me . . ."* Someone knocked at the door, but he ignored it as he went on as singing uncontested. *"Just walk away from me . . ."*

Rorey was soaked in his own sweat but continued to wail along with the music. His expression grew blank and disturbed as a single tear rolled down his face after another long hit from the whiskey bottle. He sang along, *"Just walk away from me . . ."*

The knocks at the door became harder and more impatient and were accompanied by shouts to turn the music down. "Hey, Garland! Rorey! Party's over, man, turn that noise down!" Several people congregated around his door and pleaded for him to turn his music down.

When a heavy voice outside the door threatened to break the door in, Rorey sang louder than ever, to the point of screaming out the words. *"Promise you'll tell my momma that I'm sorry . . . and promise that you'll never cry Billie . . . promise that you'll walk away from me . . ."*

Marshall approached the dorm at the exact same time the campus police drove up. They were answering a disturbance call on the sixth floor. The two white officers who arrived were good-old-boy wanna-be cops whom Marshall had had a run-in with before. They had spotted him urinating behind a tree late one night while he was coming from Jasmine's apartment. They had tried to make a federal case of it. That was hardly a misdemeanor, but this was a case of life or death.

Instinctively, Marshall had an idea something was wrong and that Rorey was involved. He had to beat the rent-a-cops up to the sixth floor. They stopped by the residential assistant's desk for information. Marshall couldn't make it on the elevator without them seeing him, which was always followed by harassment, so he hit the stairwell at top speed. As soon as he did, the rent-a-cops stepped into the next available elevator.

The oversized student who'd grown tired of making threats from outside the door was outdone when the elevator doors opened. Two officers stepped off. At the same time, Marshall burst through the metal doors leading from the stairwell and sprinted from the other end of the long corridor toward the crowd of people gathering around. The music played on from inside the room, but Rorey had stopped singing. The group of students swelled outside with no one able to speculate why he refused to open up.

When Marshall reached the scene outside Rorey's door, the police recognized him immediately and were not glad to see him, either. Marshall pleaded with the rent-a-cops to let him try to get the door open, but they refused to listen to him. Despite their objections, he maneuvered his way through the students and grabbed the doorknob.

Hysteria filled the hallway. Marshall sensed his friend was in trouble, but the cops wanted to exercise their egos and students wanted to get back to sleep. One cop wanted to break the door down and the other was busy making a case to arrest Marshall for meddling in official police business.

Meanwhile, Rorey slowly opened his bottom underwear drawer and pulled out an old handgun with the paint worn off its handle. He held it up to inspect the chamber. There was a large slug, set to be fired. He sat solemnly on his bed with a blank stare tattooed on his face. The loaded .45-caliber pistol rested on his thigh. It seemed lighter and easier to handle than all the times he and his father used it to shoot at rattlesnakes while fishing.

Marshall yelled out, "Rorey! Open up the door . . ."

Rorey heard his closest friend's voice but couldn't turn back. The hand he used to steady the gun began to tremble. More sweat beaded up on his forehead. He took one last gulp from the bottle, carefully sat it at his feet, then tentatively waggled the gun upward from his lap and opened his mouth wide.

The heated atmosphere outside the door escalated into chaotic proportions when one of the campus police grabbed Marshall from behind and tried to put him in handcuffs. "Hey, man, get your damned hands off me!" he demanded. "Man, let me go!"

They wrestled him down to the floor. He fought feverishly to get away from their grasp. Students began screaming and yelling at the officers to release Marshall. Pandemonium filled the hallway.

"Hold him down, Earl!" one of them ordered. "Hold him now, and I'll cuff him."

Amid the student's frantic shouts for freedom on the star athlete's behalf, the scuffle became more ferocious. Sweat poured down Marshall's forehead as he grimaced while working to liberate himself.

Officer Earl panicked when he sensed Marshall gaining the upper hand. With reckless abandonment, he reached for his gun. His company-issued roach-brown clip-on tie fell to the floor.

Bannnnnnnnnnnnng!!!

A thunderous gunshot rang throughout the dormitory. All movement and sound ceased to exist at once. A short, dark-haired coed's scream, at the top of her lungs, was the exclamation point to a desperate conclusion.

Everyone looked at Marshall, who was lying on his stomach. Officer Earl's hand shook, clutching his service revolver, but it hadn't fired. The shot that stopped time in that bewildered hallway had come from inside Rorey's dorm room.

Marshall reluctantly climbed to his feet, stared both the officers down, and threw his shoulder against the wooden door. It flew open. Rorey was lying on his bed with the back of his head plastered to the wall behind him. The bottle of liquor had been kicked over on its side. The remaining contents poured out onto the floor, much like Rorey's blood poured from his body.

A few of the students looked on, horrified at the disturbing sight. Marshall had seen this tragic scene before. He was accustomed to a fresh pool of blood and the smell of gunpowder, but he was a stranger to that which was self-inflicted. The rent-a-cops pushed past him and made their way into the bloody suicide den. Obviously, they weren't properly trained to handle it. Both of them threw up vomit all over themselves, soaking their two-tone polyester uniforms to the skin.

Marshall simply turned and walked away. It was over. His facial expression bore no witness to the pain circulating through his veins. It was over.

Rigamarole

Legacy entered the small tollbooth and let the door slam, then tossed his brown leather backpack on the change counting table near the back of the booth. In spite of the random scheduling, he pleaded with another employee to let him work booth number seven, lucky seven. It was his favorite booth regardless of the ratty black rotary telephone stored inside the Northwest Highway tollbooth.

His thick, dark brown hair fell into his eyes before he could quickly brush it away. Considering it was a winter month, the weather that day was unseasonably warmer. His light denim jacket would be more than adequate for the evening, even when the temperature dropped. No matter how cold it got, he wouldn't normally wear much more than that, and he preferred baggy blue jeans to just about anything else. He had worn the same size pants, thirty-two waist and thirty-four inseam, and large T-shirts for over seven years. That's what he liked. That's who he was, loose jeans, oversized shirts, and boots. Never cowboy boots, but just about any other kind would do. Mostly combat boots or Timberlands. He liked feeling taller than five feet ten inches.

Legacy's skin tone resembled that of the mulatto and Creole soldiers he had met while in the military. Not white, not brown, creamy maybe, or beige. Kind of hard to peg, but it was smooth and even. It didn't appear he had to shave often. He did look his age, though. A fair description of his looks would classify him as being more cute than handsome and easy to look at, but he didn't date anyone on a regular basis. He hadn't found the time to enjoy life. He was too busy making a living. Working hard for promises of a good life was worth the sacrifice. "Been poor" was destined to be a declaration for the past. He was too focused on his future and getting paid to allow anything to deter him from reaching that dream. He just didn't know how he was going to get there.

It was five o'clock in the evening on Tuesday. He worked at the Dallas North tollbooth exchange every Tuesday through Friday from five until nine. The booth was made up of a brown brick and panel construction, virtually a five- by eight-foot box. The other tollway employees jokingly referred to them as prison cells because workers were confined to them for the duration of the work shifts. There were twelve other such booths along the fifteen miles of freeway stretching from downtown Dallas north to Plano, a wealthy neighboring suburban community.

The coin sorter rattled loudly like a busted chain saw when he turned it on. "Ahhh, damn! It's broken again. When are they gonna fix this crap . . ." He turned the old machine off and proceeded to repair it like he had to do at least once a month. It was a relic but it still worked sometimes, and that was enough for the tollway authority to keep it in service.

Moments later, he had replaced the machine's rusted cover and screws that held the cover on, all just before the evening rush hour began. He really didn't mind the busted coin sorter much; the ancient heater worked less than the sorter did. The monotonous duty he performed, handing out quarters in exchange for one-dollar bills, was tedious, but tollbooth number seven allowed him the opportunity to see her entering the tollway after work. *Her*. The one reason he put up with substandard equipment and rude customers. *Her*, in the blue Mustang. Thin, fair-skinned, dark-brown shoulder-length hair, and gorgeous. *Her*.

She would whiz through the toll drive after waiting behind someone who didn't have a prepaid window tag and had to dig in their purses and ashtrays for coins, which happened often. Drivers who had window tags couldn't stand being detained behind the tag "have-nots." If there were too many tag have-nots in a row, the line to enter the toll drive grew ridiculously long, jamming up the busy street behind it. Then people would lean on their horns to speed up those who searched for change, but not her. She always waited patiently for her time to pass through. Legacy noticed that about her.

Fifteen minutes after five. He pushed the shirttail deep down into his blue jeans and tried to maintain some form of neatness just in case she noticed him today, but she probably wouldn't—she hadn't before. *Her*. Regardless, he always kept an eye on the next four cars. That would give him time to reel off enough quarters to make change for all of them if he needed to. Just in case she noticed him. Maybe he could get in a few words or something. Although he didn't know what he'd say, given the chance.

Each time he saw her, he managed to work on the pencil sketch he had started months ago. But sometimes she whizzed through too fast and he'd be forced to draw from memory. His refined quick-draw skills had even impressed the art director at the university. Six months of practice paid off. He had trained himself to memorize an image, then draw it from his memory. The detail was uncanny. Everyone knew he was talented. He knew the drawing proved that his desire to meet her, Ms. Blue Mustang, had evolved into a need. He was drawn to her but had no idea how to get close enough to be noticed. She had him in a bad way and didn't even know he existed.

Several cars passed through, then the Mustang approached. There she was, two cars back and moving forward, but her window was rolled up. Now she was almost even with the booth, not ten feet away. The glare from the sun on her window ruined his range of vision and obscured his view. Just like that, she was gone. Damn. Sometimes it went that way and he couldn't get a clear look at her, but it didn't stop him from wanting to.

Kennedy endured a hectic drive home and parked her sports car in the garage after picking up a few things from the Eatzi's market on Oak Lawn, the best take-out market in town. Lady Eleanor met her at the door as usual and brushed against her leg to say hello. "Hello, yourself, Eleanor. How was your day today? Catch any mice?" She didn't have mice but thought it would be cute to suggest that if she did, Eleanor could handle them.

After changing into her workout gear, she picked up the remote control and channel-surfed until she found *Wheel of Fortune*. "Good, it's just coming on," she said, while opening the blinds in the den. The light from the setting sun shined through her window. The burnt-orange rays rushed between the cracks in the blinds with a welcoming attitude, as if they had waited all day to be invited in.

She set the timer, then straddled the treadmill rails with a watchful eye until the belt went fast enough for her to step on and begin her workout. Attempting to guess the first puzzle, she continued standing instead of walking. Finally, she guessed it correctly and wondered how some contestants made it on the show only to perform so horribly. She quickly realized it was probably much different when the gigantic cameras were there, the tape was rolling, and it counted. All things considered, some of the guests were still pretty lame.

The treadmill churned and Kennedy was twenty-two minutes into her forty-five-minute workout when the phone rang. She tried to listen in as the answering machine recorded a message, but the television was up too loud and drowned out the machine. If she climbed off, she would have to locate the remote control, turn down the volume on the TV, turn off the treadmill, and run to the phone before the caller hung up. That would take much too much effort, and besides, who would be important enough to go through all that rigamarole for?

When the phone rang again, curiosity got the best of her. "Hello," she said, short of breath. "Who? No, you have the wrong number. There's no one here by that name." Climbing back on the treadmill, she knew it was a bad idea and a bad practice to stop exercising to get the phone, but it might have been Simpson trying to return one of her many calls to his office. A girl can dream, can't she? Or disillusion herself, same thing. Perspiration formed in her lime-green elastic headband. Her heart rate was up and she only missed one of the puzzles during the entire show. She was moving right along until the phone rang again. She continued to walk at a steady pace but stared at the phone as it rang for the fourth time. On the fifth ring, the machine picked up. "Let it ring. Simpson's not calling today. Probably someone selling something or another wrong number." It stopped ringing. She went back to looking at the tube, not really watching it. Just looking at it. *Jeopardy!* had just come on, and although she did enjoy challenging her wits against that show's contestants, too, her mind was still tied up, trying to guess when Simpson would return her calls.

Fifteen minutes later and a fountain of perspiration for her troubles, the power-walk workout was over. It was rougher than normal because she had smoked more cigarettes than usual. The smokes kept her company. They gave her something else to do while pining away for her man, but more than anything they fed her nicotine addiction. And that felt good. At least she could count on her buzz when she needed it.

The cigarette lighter would not cooperate at first, but it did after a little coaxing. Not five minutes had lapsed after finishing her workout and she was furiously puffing away. She'd just spent forty-five minutes working the last pack of them out of her system.

Her face was still moist as she blotted it with a washcloth. She collapsed on the sofa with her legs crossed at the ankles, then cursed out loud when she noticed that the message light on her phone was blinking. When she could no longer resist it beckoning for her attention, she pulled her tired thin frame from the comfort of the sofa. Hitting the playback button produced Simpson's voice on the other end. The excitement overcame her. In the middle of celebrating, she accidentally brushed the hot cigarette against the twenty-four-ounce Blue Mountain water bottle in her other hand. Fire flickers jumped on her crop top and workout shorts and fell between her legs on the couch. "Ouch! Oh! Oh, oh, oh!"

She hopped up and tried to kill the sparks by whipping at them with the end of the towel before they burned holes in the sofa. Too late. They were already there. Back to the phone. Kennedy didn't hear a word of the message. Rubbing the new holes with her fingers as if to soothe the couch and apologize, she pushed the red button on her answering machine to replay the message. "Hi, uh, Kennedy. This is Simpson. Remember, Simpson? Well, I've missed you and would like to see you, but no more drinking. If you can agree to that condition, call me and I'll arrange a meeting time. Bye."

She sat there smiling like a small child with a fresh two-scoop ice cream cone and listening to the message over and over again while puffing away merrily on another cigarette. Obviously, she had quickly forgotten how miserable she had been when in his company lately. She figured, in a twisted sort of way, that staying involved with a somewhat controlling significant other was better than letting go of the years she'd invested in the relationship. Besides, he could change, after all. She chose to hold on to that tiny ray of hope, no matter how his love for her continued to diminish.

"Hello, Simpson . . . ?" she said anxiously into the phone.

"Hello. I'm not available to take this call," his recorded voice announced. "I'm either out making money or spending it. Leave a message."

She was disappointed and wanted to hang up, but the phone beeped, urging her to leave a message. She blurted out the first thing that came to her mind. "Uhh . . . this is Kennedy. I'll call you back." How uneventful.

"Where could he be" crossed her mind more than once. Sure, she could have paged him, but she didn't want to seem desperate, even though she continued calling his apartment until midnight. He never answered.

Kennedy arrived at work early the next day, as she had in the last couple of weeks, but she was on edge that morning. Morris noticed but decided to stay out of it, which was difficult for him to do. He knew it had everything to do with her man, but Morris was never good at man-woman relationships.

There was no smoking allowed in the art gallery, so Kennedy lit up her fourth cancer stick of the morning and froze outside the building's main entrance. If Mr. Johansen had known she was out there, he would have had a cow. Professionalism was everything to him, even outside the gallery's doors.

While shivering as the cold wind seemed to wrap around her head and squeeze, her ears rung and her nose turned bright red as her teeth chattered. She began to feel awful, but she had to hit another one. Her usual opportunity to light up and relish a smoke or two was lunchtime, since Mr. Johansen didn't allow for smoke breaks during working hours, but she was in a bad way, a very bad way.

Kennedy emerged through the double glass doors with her long gray winter coat wrapped around her body tighter than it was designed to fit. She continued to shiver after she had returned to the warmth of the gallery. The strong Texas winds had blown her silky brown hair into a jungle of warring strands. Reeking of cigarette smoke, which seemed to cling to the wool fabric for dear life, she smelled like a rank, overfilled ashtray, as did her car and apartment. Whenever she experienced major stresses in her life, she increased her habit. Before long, her current stress was sure to be a barn burner.

"Oh, girlllll! You're a mess!" Morris shrieked. "Look at you."

He was appalled when he saw how damaged she looked after battling the outside elements. "And you stink! You need to come on in and warm up before you catch your death of cold. The temperature is still dropping. I heard it on the news."

Kennedy nodded, acknowledging he was right as she shed the thick coat. Her teeth chattered less by the time she journeyed back to her office, although she had not completely thawed out yet. Chill bumps multiplied on her arms when she thought of how cold it was just on the other side of the thick glass office windows.

Morris quickly returned with another cup of his hot herbal tea remedy; that was his prescribed medicine for most of nature's intolerance of us humans. Got a cold, hot tea. Been rained on, hot tea. Got a stomachache, hot tea. Stomach cramps, Midol. Morris wasn't stupid. There were some things warm tea couldn't quite manipulate.

She could easily see the steam rising up from the cup leading Morris into her office. Her hands anxiously reached toward it when she anticipated how good it would make her feel. She handled the cup gingerly, like a woman dying of thirst, ever so delicately watching it leave his hands and receiving it into hers. She puckered up and pressed her thin, soft lips against the rim of the coffee cup and ingested as much of the tea as she could before her tongue felt the scalding wrath. "Oooouch! Morris, it's too hot!" she complained.

In response, he pressed the fingertips of his right hand over his heart. "I'm so sorry. Let me fix it. It's a new blend. You'll enjoy it when I cool it for you." When he took one step toward her, she leaned over it like a small child shielding his last cookie from an older brother's clutches.

"No!" she replied sharply. "I'll hold it until it cools off. Thank you. It smells good." She watched him carefully and began to blow the edge off the blistering-hot liquid.

Morris threw his head back and proceeded to exit her office. "I guess my work here is done, again. Smooches." He scurried away.

Kennedy enjoyed the spearmint-flavored tea from one of Morris's coffee cups that read "My heart isn't the only thing I left in San

Francisco." He owned several. They were sure to spark conversation, just as he planned. He was not a private man. There wasn't a discreet bone in his body.

Her morning was almost over and she was no closer to solving her dilemma regarding Simpson than she was the night before. She ran it through her head over and over again. "He finally called and I missed it. But when I did call back he didn't answer, not all night. Maybe he turned in early and slept right through the ringing telephone. Maybe he had an early day at the office and turned his ringer off. Maybe he's playing some wicked little game that's turning me into a disgruntled deranged loser lunatic," she heard herself saying. "Maybe I am deranged. Hell, I don't know anymore, but I'd better find out."

Excuses came a dime a dozen, and she could have rationalized the situation until it sounded plausible, but it would not have been any different. She called her man after days of noncommunication and he wasn't to be found. It didn't matter where he was or what he was doing. He wasn't doing it with her. She knew that for sure and all the herbal tea in China wouldn't change that.

She'd been staring at Simpson's photograph displayed on her mahogany credenza in an eight-by-ten picture frame for the past hour and she hadn't accomplished any of the items on her things-to-do list. Her time had been spent going over in her head all the nasty arguments they'd had, despite the good times. Their relationship wasn't all bad, just all bad lately. She wondered if she'd changed during the course of the relationship because of how he'd treated her or if he'd treated her the way he did because she'd changed during the course of the relationship. Confused, scared, and lonely. She was all three at the same time and despised each of them. Control had always been her saving grace. Whenever she began to slip up or falter with boyfriends gone by, her control prevailed every time. No broken hearts, no regrets until now and she couldn't stand it.

Suddenly, she sprang up from her desk and snatched the phone receiver off its base, then immediately returned it to its place. She repeated this futile exercise a few times and continually mumbled a rehearsed speech to herself while pacing back and forth. "You can do this. You're a big girl and you've always handled things like this. You're good at it. Just pick up the phone and call him. Get it over with. What's the worst he can do?" She paused for a brief second to reflect on her situation. "Dump me and not see me again, ever. That's what he can do." With that, she plopped down in her chair and stared at the phone as if she were waiting on *it* to do something. Tell her what to say, do, something, anything. But it didn't. It simply sat there until she mustered up enough courage to dial the private phone line in his office.

With each button she pushed, she said the digit aloud. "Five . . . five . . . five, zero . . . one . . . zero . . . zero." The phone rang long and slow. "Maybe he won't be there and I could leave another message." No such luck, he answered his line on the first ring.

"Hell-o, this is Simpson."

She froze up.

"Hello?" he repeated.

"Oh, hi. You're there," she said nervously. Butterflies performed aerial assaults in her stomach. "I thought I had your voice mail."

"Kennedy? That you?"

She began fidgeting with the ink pen on her desktop. She bounced it on its point at first, then spun it around with her thumb and index finger. "Yeah, but you're probably busy and I just—"

"I am on my way to a very important meeting," he interjected, "but I do have a second or two. What's on your mind?"

Her fidgeting grew increasingly worse. The pen even flipped off the desk onto the carpet underneath it. She bumped her head harshly when she instinctively went after it, but she refused to let on to Simpson that she'd hurt herself. She had made up her mind to be stoic and tough. Determined. "I . . . uhm. I called you back last night. You know, after I got your message. But you weren't in." Kennedy wanted so badly to question him on his whereabouts, but she didn't have enough gumption to pull it off. So much for stoic, tough, and determined.

"Yeah, I had to work late. Something, uh . . . came up and I had to leave town overnight." He started to thumb through his daily planner as they spoke. "Oh, listen, while I have you on the phone. I have two courtside Mavericks versus Bulls tickets if you want to go tonight."

Her face lit up. He still wants to see me, she thought to herself, as she began to sway in the chair from side to side. "Yeah. Sure, what time?"

"Let's say around seven. That'll give us time to get there and get settled in. It should be fun. Jordan is averaging over thirty-five points."

"Okay, I'll be ready. See you then." Kennedy didn't know much about basketball and didn't care. She was going to be with her man again and that's all that mattered.

Morris stopped by to look in on her and reclaim his coffee cup. "Heyyy, Morris," she said merrily. He smiled back and folded his arms across his thin torso.

"Let me guess. The miraculous healing is a direct result of (a) a phone call from Simpson Stone, (b) an invite to jump in the sack with Simpson Stone, or (c) the grand prize . . . a proposal of marriage from whom, I wonder. Let me see . . ." Morris pretended he had to actually consider from a vast list of all one of Kennedy's love interests. "Would I be correct in guessing . . . Simpson Stonnne?"

He made Kennedy laugh. She spun completely around in the chair with her legs sticking out before answering him. "You're partly right. It's only A but it could lead to C. I'm so happy, Morris. He's taking me to the Chicago Bears game tonight. Everyone has been talking about it."

"You mean Bulls, dear," he said, correcting her. She looked puzzled. "The Chicago Bulls. Bears are football," Morris explained further when her almond-shaped face still wore the same befuddled expression. "Never mind. But they're gonna clobber the poor Mavs, bless their hearts. Maybe that kinky Dennis Rodman will rip off his sweaty jersey and . . ." He stopped and placed the back of his hand against his forehead, acting as if he were going to faint. "Oh, I can't go on. Just thinking about him makes me swoon. He's so big, so strong, and so open to trying new things. He's got more hair colors in his bag than I do. Wonder what else he's got in there? But that's another story for another time. Umm . . . umm . . . umm. What a man!"

Morris sauntered off, fanning himself briskly with his other hand. "Enjoy the game," he shouted over his right shoulder.

"I will."

Eight

Yesterdays Are Forever

*B*lack suits and dark eyeglasses filled the private viewing room in the west chapel of the Mount Zion Baptist Church. Rorey's religious faith was First Baptist, but his family concluded that a Southern Baptist church was just as good. A haunting aura surrounded the body in a closed casket. Hundreds of flowers covered the metal tomb. They were sent by adoring fans and other college teams in their conference, all sad to hear about the tragedy and wishing the UTC students strength to get through it. Incense had been burned earlier to freshen up the room. The fragrance lingered. It did assist in smothering the essence of the occasion, but somehow, like any chamber in an old church, it still smelled much like an old library.

Flea virtually disappeared behind Big Love's eclipsing stature, sitting on the end of the second row. He purposely sat there to hide his emotions from the others attending the wake. Most of the team members sat near the front, anchored down by grieving faces and heavy hearts or continually wiping the tears that ran from beneath their sunglasses. Not many of them had slept much since the suicide, and neither did several thousands of the other members of the student body. Rorey's death rocked the university. So many questions were left unanswered. He was a hero, their hero. His future seemed certain. A professional football contract, worth millions, was at his fingertips. "Why" was the prominent question plaguing the campus. Why would a young man who seemingly had everything to live for take his life and check out early? Marshall knew and the coaching staff had a good idea. Various rumors spread but no one could really piece it all together.

Heartache overcame the jam-packed room when they opened the casket for viewing, and Loretta Howard, the homecoming queen, sang "Precious Lord Take My Hand" accompanied by piano. Her voice was beautiful. The gifted soprano belted out tearful heavenly notes that choked up every living soul in the sanctuary, except for one, Marshall's. He didn't shed a tear when Rorey died or at the wake. He didn't have anything to say about the matter. Denial is what they call it when people refuse to deal with an issue; Marshall's was severe. He just sat there and stared at the flowers surrounding the casket while Jasmine along with countless others cried their eyes out.

Coach Dean staggered his way up to the front and said a few words before he became too weak to finish what he had written down to say and had to be helped back to his seat by two of his own players. Others made valiant attempts to put what they felt about Rorey into words, but each one's comments faded into tears and uncontrollable muttering. Sorrow overwhelmed the room. Loud shrieks calling "Roreyyyy!" poured out occasionally. The service had to be cut short when three female students passed out, undoubtedly due to a deadly combination of grief and heat from a vastly overcrowded room. The constant fanning and tear-wiping dissipated as the crowd slowly spilled out into the cool parking lot just outside.

Initially, Jasmine was surprised that Marshall could hold his composure, but she began to understand. The other students and faculty in attendance dealt with their pain in their own way. Marshall's straight face and cold expression was his way of dealing with the death of his best friend. He wasn't ready to say good-bye, so he didn't.

Instead, he stood at the head of the casket and leaned in to pick a carnation from the montage of flowers present. When a renegade tear seemed to escape from his left eye, he turned his face away and took a deep breath. That was it. He placed the carnation in a small black pouch with drawstrings, then tucked it away in his suit coat pocket and slowly walked toward the exit, where Jasmine watched and waited with her head hung low.

The assortment of young men with their suit coats now opened and shirttails hanging out anchored themselves to the benches in the Wrangler locker room. Bottles of cheap wine and whiskey circulated throughout the close-knit circle of friends. Marshall passed on the first few rounds as the others indulged in the libations and talked about tough games they won with Rorey at the helm, and they kicked around a few anecdotes in his remembrance.

"I remember when Rorey showed up on campus from Oklahoma City in that old beat-up Ford truck four years ago," one player said, smiling as he thought back. "It was old and beat up even then. Looked like it barely made it from OKC." The others laughed cordially, but Marshall remained silent and hid a smile behind his lips.

"Y'all remember when that country fool didn't want to practice the first Saturday we came back last year because Channel Twenty-one was running that *Bonanza* marathon on TV?" Flea conferred. "So he turned on the water sprinklers and let 'em run all night long . . ."

"Yeah, yeah," Big Love interjected, "and the practice field was all soaked. Yeah, I remember that. And old Coach MacIntyre made us practice in the mud anyway. That was the best practice we ever had. Rorey had more fun than any of us. I didn't know he was behind it but I should have."

When Marshall thought back, too, it touched him. The previous head coach was an old war veteran and didn't fool easily. Pranks like that one were around long before movies like *Bull Durham*, which is where Rorey got the idea. Big Love was right about one thing, though. Rorey did enjoy that particular practice more than anyone else did. He was simple to please and everyone's friend when they needed one. But he was gone now.

Legacy sat atop a seven-foot ladder just on the side of the lockers opposite where the athletes were thinking back on yesterdays and paying homage to a fallen comrade. His worn blue jeans displayed just about every color he had used on a life-size painting covering the entire sixteen by ten foot wall near the locker room entrance. It was clear he had been at it for some time and it was nearly finished. He listened while they reminisced and he enjoyed the stories along with them, but he wasn't one of them. Legacy was different. He wasn't a jock like them. His scholarship had been earned through service in the military, and he lived in Dallas, nearly an hour's commute away.

He had sneaked his way into the locker room the day before with paint and brushes in hand. The lighting wasn't perfect, but he was used to working aided by flashlights. That's how he had to sketch at night when he was in the orphanage and the military. He was a hard worker and much too tired to be that high up on the ladder. When he dozed off and almost fell from his perch, one of his paintbrushes tumbled down and bounced off a water bucket he used to soak his brushes in. The loud clank alarmed the other men. They jumped up hastily to investigate, only to find him searching the floor for the dropped brush, looking as guilty as sin when they startled him.

Big Love stirred in the bad lighting, grabbed Legacy by his collar, and proceeded to shake him. "What the hell are you doing here? You spying on us?"

Before the weary artist could defend himself, other players noticed the paint and assumed he was there to vandalize their hallowed ground. Most athletes would confess to feeling more at home in the team's locker room than just about anyplace else. It was sacred.

Marshall flipped the light switch on, illuminating the entire large room. "Freelance!" he yelled in Big Love's direction, as the giant held Legacy in a tight clench.

"You know this clown, Marshall?" he asked.

"Yeah. He's cool, he's cool. Just put him down."

What the young men saw brought about bright eyes and respect. They all stood in awe when their eyes found the artistic scene painted on the wall. It was a mural edifying Rorey and his accomplishments at UTC. Legacy had copied a photo he found months ago in the *Dallas Morning News* showing Rorey shedding a tackler to make a throw downfield. It was colorful and angelic.

"Freelance, you didn't have to do this," Marshall uttered with a lump in his throat. "But it is beautiful. Man, it's . . . it's a masterpiece." Everyone agreed it was just that, a masterpiece.

"I had to sneak in without the coach's permission," Legacy informed them in his own stead. "He'll probably have it painted over and have me arrested." Marshall disagreed and shook his head slowly.

"Naw, not this painting. Ain't nobody gonna touch this. Nobody. You just finish it and we'll see to it that it continues to have a long life and a home."

"Freelance . . . it's Freelance, right?" Big Love asked, just to be sure. "We gotcha back, podna! This is really special, man. You did a beautiful thing."

Everyone who saw the mural would know that Rorey's winning spirit was with the team, and it would forever serve as a reminder of his leadership as well as his friendship. It was truly something to behold. The others slowly piled out and moved their congregation to a nearby park, but Marshall couldn't leave. He wanted to but had difficulty moving his legs, so he took a seat and observed the artist apply the finishing touches.

*   *   *

After Legacy wrapped it up and began packing his things to leave, he stared at Marshall, who was in a daze. "Hey, you all right, man?" Legacy asked out of concern. He had watched Marshall study the artwork for almost an hour without saying a word.

Marshall snapped out of it. "Oh, yeah, I'm much better now. Thanks to you."

He was happy in a time when it seemed impossible to find joy. His ace, his teammate, his best friend had been immortalized on that wall. It was the greatest gift anyone could have given him. "Hey, Freelance, I want to thank you for doing this for Rorey and all. I mean . . . I wish I could pay you for this, but I'm busted right now."

"You don't have to pay me anything. You think I put Rorey Garland up on that wall for money? Naw, I put him up there because that's where he belongs. He tutored me for two years in calculus and trigonometry for free and never asked me for nothing."

Legacy saw that Marshall was embarrassed for offering compensation for his work. "That's why I put him up there. He's the kind of guy that gave everything he had and expected nothing in return. He belongs up on that wall."

Nodding his head agreeably, Marshall shuddered as they stared at the finished product a while longer, then took the paint supplies out to Legacy's 1985 Suzuki Samurai. The jeep had a busted radio and a worn-out plastic covering, but a custom paint job of him standing next to a fiery-red Lamborghini sports car graced the side of it. The Lamborghini was the dream car Legacy had saved up for over eleven years to buy. Some men need dreams to push them in the right direction. Some men just need to dream.

Even though Legacy "Freelance" Childs wouldn't have accepted money for the painting if Marshall did have it to offer, he did ask for future business referrals instead. "Marshall, I do want you to remember that I'm a starving artist. And when you get settled next year, I'll probably still need some work." They laughed and shook hands, then parted ways.

*   *   *

Jasmine was cleaning her apartment furiously. She wore yellow rubber gloves, a checkered red and white scarf wrapped around her head, and faded jeans with a gray UTC sweatshirt. She cleaned meticulously when she had something on her mind that she couldn't deal with straight on.

Seeing her man emotionally strung out like he was about Rorey's death was difficult because he wouldn't let her near him. Not emotionally, not intimately, not at all.

Marshall knocked at the door. Jasmine heard the raps on it but hesitated. She didn't want to see anyone who hadn't called ahead first. When she stood against the door on her tiptoes, looking through the peephole, she recognized Marshall immediately but was confused. She opened the door slightly and let him push it open the rest of the way while she washed up for dinner.

The previous week had been strange and painful for her as well as for him. He lost Rorey and it seemed that she was losing him. Marshall's warm side disappeared. That wasn't a good thing to lose during a Texas winter.

"Hey, honey. Come on in. Why didn't you use your key like you always do?" she asked with her hands under the sink.

"I guess I wasn't thinking," he replied with a blank expression. "Hmm, just trippin'. You gotta look over me for a little while. I'm just trying to get my head straight. I'll be fine. I'll be fine."

His expression did not change, but hers did. It was initially stained with sorrow for Rorey, but sadness crept in along with Marshall and beat it out for the starring role. She tried not to show it. He probably wouldn't have noticed either of them, anyway, regardless of which one she wore as he turned on the TV without initiating any decent conversation with her.

Jasmine's eyes were still somewhat puffy from all the crying and wiping she endured earlier. He hadn't noticed that, either. Time was what her man needed. She'd convinced herself that time was all he needed to get over it. Time heals all wounds. That's what she heard someone say once. She hoped that whoever that someone was knew what the hell they were talking about.

"Marshall, I'm going to jump in the shower," she yelled from the other room, as she began to peel off her clothes. "Maybe we can catch a movie or something." When she heard no response, she sat down on the side of her bed and stared into space, just as Marshall did in the living room. They were in the same apartment but not on the same planet.

Nine

Why Do I?

*L**ady Eleanor raised her head,* then sprang up on all fours when someone knocked at the front door for the second time. Kennedy rested a half-smoked cigarette in an ashtray she kept on her makeup counter. After turning off the curling iron, she peeked her head out of the bathroom. "Hold on, I'm coming," she yelled in the general direction of her front door while putting on an earring.

The cat lay next to the door, blocking its entrance. Kennedy made her way to the living room and approached the door. "Move . . . Eleanor," she urged. But the cat didn't comply. "Hold on . . ." She quickly put on the other earring and straightened her clothes, knowing who stood on the other side of that door. It had been weeks since she'd seen him.

When she bent over to harness Lady Eleanor, the feisty feline snapped and hissed angrily. "Lady Eleanor," Kennedy gasped, in a tone filled with surprise. "What's your problem this evening?"

Eleanor fought to get away from Kennedy's clutches, but she managed to corral the cat underneath her arm. She unlocked the door and pulled it open while securing her pet, who still wiggled through a last foiled attempt to get away.

Simpson was standing in the hallway impatiently. He checked his watch and unzipped his black designer jacket. "You finally got it open," he joked. "They can be tricky sometimes, doors, I mean."

"Yeah, I uh . . . finally did it," she said, reciprocating his dry humor. "The years of training paid off."

After they smiled uncomfortably at each other, he strolled into her apartment without a hug, a kiss, nothing. She took note but opted not to make a big deal of it.

Eleanor stared at Simpson and arched her back. It was obvious the cat did not care for his presence. If only humans were equipped with like instincts. Simpson stared back but the cat won out. "Damned cat," he grunted under his breath.

"I'll be ready in a moment," Kennedy yelled, standing over the bathroom sink, brushing her hair. "You can help yourself to anything in the fridge." That was not a great offering, since her refrigerator rarely stored any items from the four basic food groups, a fact that Simpson was all too well aware of. However, Diet Coke was a staple, by the liter.

He studied her living room as if he expected some things to have changed. The couch still had a small rip on the arm, the scratches on the leg of the oak coffee table were still as apparent, and strands of white cat hair already affixed themselves to Simpson's navy corduroy pants, all compliments of Lady Eleanor. That damned cat. And he couldn't stand any of it. Not the cigarette burns in the couch, the scratched coffee table leg, and especially not the collection of stray cat hairs. None of it.

Kennedy reappeared from her bedroom wearing a thick red wool jacket, black ankle-length Lycra leggings, and a brand-new, out-of-the-box pair of fly Kenneth Cole leather ankle boots. She threw a black leather purse strap over her shoulder. "I'm ready. Let's go." She grabbed his hands and pulled heartily as if she could lift him off the couch herself. His phony smile revealed he was not amused. It was another pleasant gesture gone unappreciated.

"Hurry up, Simpson," she whined. "We'll be late. Downtown traffic is getting worse every day." Kennedy was not that interested in the game or getting there on time. She just couldn't wait another minute to begin their date, thinking this one would be different from the others somehow. She still loved him, still hoped for better days. Although lately, her reasoning for doing so was as clear as Louisiana gumbo. Not even the smallest ray of hope stood much of a fighting chance in the same ring as Simpson's increasing rudeness and arrogance. Loving the wrong man can be a dangerous thing. Loving a man who refuses to return that love can be disastrous.

She smiled, staring face forward, when she reached her door. "I'm glad you got the tickets. It'll be so much fun."

"It should be quite a game," he replied plainly on the way out, as he slowed to sneak a glance at the wine rack in her kitchenette. Two bottles of '87 Moët champagne he hoped would still be there rested on the bottom rung, just where he'd left them.

Traffic was not as convoluted as they had anticipated. Their drive over to the Reunion Arena Convention Center was painless. Simpson flashed his VIP parking pass and the garage attendant waved him ahead of other cars battling to merely inch forward in the long line. Porsches and VIP passes, that's the lifestyle he led and cherished above the picket fences and PTA meetings that Kennedy had in mind for them both.

Filing into Reunion Arena, she walked closely behind him as they made their way through the maze of ticket holders. Kennedy felt awkward dodging people rushing to find their seats or hurriedly pushing toward the Chicago Bulls souvenir tables, which was an invariable vendor's paradise. Bulls paraphernalia didn't sell cheap but it always sold out. Dallas Maverick team garb usually sold at half price by halftime. The struggling home team was usually well behind in points by then. And nobody wanted to represent a loser.

"Popcorn . . . peanuts . . . hot dogs . . . ice-cold beer . . . " one hefty concessions worker bellowed continually, with the authority of a town crier.

"I haven't eaten, honey, hot dogs sound good right about now," Kennedy suggested to no avail.

Simpson was at home in the prime courtside seats and too busy watching the players warming up and executing their pregame passing drills to hear her. "I'm sorry. What did you say?" He refused to divert his attention from the display on the basketball court.

"Yes, I said I wanted something to eat," she answered to the back of his head, as he gazed at the players at the far end of the court.

He reluctantly shoved his hand inside his jacket pocket and pulled out a roll of twenties. "Here." He reeled off one, then quickly handed it to her. "Get what you want from the vendor. That'll give you something to do." In that short span of time, he had already become annoyed with her.

Kennedy reluctantly accepted the twenty. She contemplated handing it back to him with the same foul attitude that he offered it with. Thinking better of it, she decided to be the bigger person. "Can I get you anything, darling?" came across clearly, despite her saying it with her teeth clenched together.

"No, no, nothing for me, thanks."

The squat-built concessionaire wiped sweat from his fully flushed cheeks with a soiled white handkerchief he rolled out of his lint-filled pocket. While Kennedy viewed this unsightly spectacle, her appetite fled but her stomach continued to growl. She was repulsed but starving. Hunger prevailed. She bought two hot dogs and a bag of roasted peanuts for later.

After devouring one hot dog in a matter of what seemed like milliseconds to the two college-age men seated behind her, one of them remarked, "She'd better slow down before she gets a speeding ticket." Even though the comment was meant to be between friends, she overheard it and was immediately embarrassed. The other dog was savored in hopes of eluding additional ridicule.

Between roars from the crowd, Kennedy asked various questions regarding what had just happened on the court and why the fans were angry with the officials. Each time she demanded his attention, Simpson became less willing to interact with her and more pissed off that she wanted to converse with him. He had other ideas. "Listen, Kennedy, these courtside tickets were very expensive and I plan to enjoy watching the game, not giving you a play by play. I'll answer all of your questions later. Just try to sit there and do what you do best, look pretty. Okay?"

Although insulted, she nodded her confirmation and vowed to just shut up until the game came to a complete stop.

Simpson studied the court like a professional basketball scout for a rival franchise, making mental notes and mouthing defensive assignments to the Bulls each time the Mavs displayed decent ball movement. "Do your thing, Jordan. Yeah!" he shouted, as Jordan stole another ball and glided downcourt to move the crowd with a rim-rattling slam-dunk. "Wow! Did you see that?" he asked rhetorically.

Yep, she saw it, but it didn't matter, the outcome on the court was of no consequence to her. She didn't understand the game of basketball, nor did she have a handle on her man. The night was young and she was zero for two and drowning in a sea of indifference.

By the end of the second quarter, Kennedy had sunk far below the unhappy camper strata on the Upset Girlfriend's Pissed-Off Chart. But a successful man like Simpson is what she wanted, or at least thought she did. Besides, her mother always told her that a woman could fall in love with a rich man as easily as she could a man with modest means. In either case, making a difficult relationship work took sweat and tears. Unfortunately, hers had begun to require a lot more tears than sweat.

Simpson's pager went off while Dennis Rodman dribbled at the foul line, struggling to make his second free throw shot. He had missed the first one and exhibited his frustration toward the home crowd. The page wasn't acknowledged because the loud screams, from Maverick supporters trying to distract the shooter, drowned it out.

Kennedy squirmed about restlessly in the stadium chair, wishing she had brought something interesting with her to read. Seventeen thousand screaming fans and she never felt more alone. And she dared not strike up a conversation with Simpson for fear of getting her head bitten off. Those two college students sitting behind them would've loved to have seen that.

With one minute left in the first half, his pager went off again during a called time-out. Simpson heard it but decided not to respond until halftime. He didn't want to miss out on any of the NBA action. It was fantastic.

Kennedy also heard the pager beckoning him to answer it. She glanced down at it long enough to see a 911 code entered in behind a return phone number. She wondered who needed to reach him badly enough to submit an emergency page. When the action on the floor resumed, she searched her purse for an ink pen. Found one. She quickly scribbled the callback number on a used napkin. Afterward, she eased the napkin into her purse, then placed it beneath her seat. It was not so much that she distrusted him, but it did pique her curiosity; he had not been spending many of his free nights with her.

A herd of fans emptied into the aisles when the halftime buzzer sounded. For the first time in as much as fifteen minutes, Simpson thought enough of Kennedy to share some of his bright conversation with her.

"So what do you think so far, some game, huh?"

She nodded slowly with her jaws still clenched closely together. "Yep, some game, all right." She was referring to the game he was running on her.

Simpson didn't notice she was bored stiff as he enjoyed the atmospheric intensity in the arena. "I see why Jordan and Pippin get paid the big bucks," he marveled. "They put on one hell of a show. Don't you think?"

Again she allowed her head to rock back and forth. "Uh-huh. This is quite a showing," she replied quietly. "Yes indeedy, a real treat."

Kennedy was in the midst of fading into oblivion when the thought of why he brought her there, only to ignore her, crossed her mind. Then she quickly realized she was not an active part of his evening and it did not appear likely she was going to be. Like a ton of bricks, carrying that weight on her shoulders further diminished her self-esteem and began to break her spirit.

Where was that sweaty vendor with that disgusting soiled handkerchief when she needed him? An ice-cold beer would have hit the spot and helped her deal with the boredom accompanying the frustration. Much to her dismay, the vendor was nowhere to be seen amid the busy concrete walkways. Besides, she had promised Simpson she would abide by his no-drinking policy while they were together. Actually, two long-necks and a hot slice of cheese pizza would have been more accommodating than what she got from him.

The athletes jogged on the court to shoot around before the start of the second half. Most of the people attending the game had returned to their seats, preparing for the action to start up again. Simpson's pager sounded for a third time. It seemed to beep louder and with grave urgency. When he unclipped it from the waistband of his pants and held it up to read it, the message field read in triplicate. That meant three pages from the same caller. Someone was extremely serious about getting in touch with him. He barked at the pager and threw up his hands in protest. Kennedy tried hard to appear uninterested and unfazed as he excused himself and stormed off, heading up the ramp with cellular phone in hand.

Kennedy glanced up the ramp to see if Simpson had gotten far enough up the steps to work out her little devious plan. Good, he disappeared into the tunnel leading to the rest rooms. Before she could clear her thoughts as to what course of action she wanted to take first, she had entered the number from his pager into her cellular phone and pressed "send."

The hair on the back of her neck stood up as she held her breath while the phone rang. She was not prepared to do or say anything in particular if a woman answered. Her heart pounded faster with each ring. Just as she was having second thoughts of invading his privacy and decided to hang up, a man answered on the other line with a harsh voice.

"Yeah, this is Richey. Is this you, Stone? You prick!"

Richey's Brooklyn accent spilled out with each word he uttered. Kennedy's brain malfunctioned, which was just as well, because anything she could have said would have sounded ridiculous. Her hand began to shake when the man's voice became more insistent and disturbed.

"Who in the hell is this!" he shouted. "Hello . . . !"

She peered over her shoulder again as she fumbled to get the phone turned off and as deep into the bottom of her Coach bag as possible. Who could that man have been, she thought. Kennedy didn't know of anyone who talked to Simpson that way. He was frightening. The thought of someone more powerfully obtrusive and more demanding than her man horrified her. And, she could tell by the way he said those explosive words, getting what he wanted was just one of the many things he was known for.

Richey slammed the receiver down hard on his desk. The club's doors were not opened yet, but bartenders stocked the shelves with whiskeys, bourbons, and scotch, anticipating a busy night. Club Matrix was a successful watering hole where the right kinds of people lounged when they felt a need to be among others like themselves, other important people, those who had deep pockets, long money, and the predilection for the wild side of life.

Before Richey got deep into a mad tirade, the phone rang again. "Hello?" he said violently into the receiver.

"Hey, Richey . . ." Simpson's voice was pleasant but coated with impatience. He was as unaware of the impending circumstances before him, like a blind man who was headed for a cliff. "I got your page a second ago. What'd you need?"

"This Stone?" the gangster asked angrily, in a way that made Simpson wish he could have been someone else. "Oh, you just got my page? Then tell me why I wasted the last twenty minutes trying to reacha, huh?" Richey's dark, gel-soaked hair was in disarray. He had been running his fingers through it. A nervous habit he despised about himself; he never liked having a thing out of place, not even one single hair.

"I called as soon as I could," Simpson replied routinely. "I'm at the Bulls game, for Christ's sake."

"I don't care if you was shooting hoops wit' Christ himself. When I page your ass, you'd better break your neck getting back to me before my phone gets cold. You hear what I'm saying?"

Simpson heard him loud and clear and had no other choice but to bite his lip and stay in that man's good graces. People who fell out of those good graces were sometimes found in the Trinity River. Sometimes they were never found at all.

"I'm sorry, it won't happen again. What can I do for you this evening, Mr. Glass?" Simpson used the mobster's family name to assure Richey that he was all ears and all business.

"I need some blow; at least five grams. Got high rollers in town from Vegas. They're gonna wanna party and I don't plan on disappointing them. Know what I mean?"

Of course, he knew what Richey meant. He knew what the tough guy wanted before he returned the page. The one reason Richey ever called him was to mule illegal party favors to the club that couldn't be tracked back to his organization. Drugs were still out of bounds to some of the old-school mobsters. Drug dealers were as unpredictable as abusers because drugs and all of its trappings promoted irrational thinking.

Richey had gone out on a limb by bringing in someone from outside the family and setting up Simpson's side gig a few years ago. He taught Simpson how to stay small enough to go unnoticed by the law and other cocaine hustlers. That provided Richey the luxury of having it at his disposal when he needed to get his hands on some. And to top that, he could get it at wholesale prices without having to be concerned with storing or moving it. The risk and profit fell equally on Simpson, with two provisions. The deals that he made would only be small ones and done on a part-time basis. That's what they agreed on.

Richey was no dumb schmuck when it came to minimizing his illegal business risk. The mobster knew that being caught with large amounts of cocaine wasn't smart. He also knew which kind of men would spill their guts to the Feds if it meant getting their own necks off the chopping block and which kind wouldn't. He had Simpson Stone pegged right. The wealthy pretty boy would sing like Patti LaBelle if his neck were on the line and he had hard jail time stacked up against him.

Simpson's loyalties became questionable. He stuttered when answering Richey's question of coming up with enough drugs for the party that night. "Uh . . . uh . . . that depends, Richey."

"Depends!" he shouted. "Don't you screw around with me, Stone!"

"Don't sweat it. Uh . . ." Simpson stalled, choosing his words carefully. ". . . I'll handle it. Don't worry."

"If you disappoint me, you should be worried," he threatened. "People I do business with expect me to deliver what I promise 'em." Fear was a well-utilized tool when Richey Glass Wiseguy needed it to be. He counted on it.

Simpson paced in the men's room and explained what his limitations were. "I won't be able to get the package there until after ten o'clock. I have a woman with me and I'm at the game. Jordan's putting on a jump-shot clinic as we speak."

Richey looked at his diamond-studded wristwatch. "Don't show up here later than eleven. It doesn't take that long to get your rocks off."

The pretty boy weakened. His knees were like weary pillars of an ancient plantation house, barely strong enough to serve their purpose and ready to get wave at any time. If the mobster were to discover that Simpson had been making big deals with anyone who could afford the premium drugs, the penalty for breaking the contract would have been painful and thoroughly administered. Before Simpson could get up the nerve to offer a rebuttal, Richey had slammed the phone down.

When he returned to his seat inside the area, Kennedy wasn't sure of what to say, so she decided to play it cool. "Hey, did you get lost up there?" she asked jokingly, trying to shield how uncomfortable she had become with the whole incident. She regretted making the call but liked the idea of having one up on Simpson for a change.

Simpson leaned back with his eyes glassed over. He looked as if he'd seen a ghost. "No, I uh . . . it just took a bit longer than I thought." Tension took control and would not relinquish its hold on him for the rest of the game.

After the ball game concluded, not one word was uttered during the drive back to her apartment. Simpson didn't offer to take her to a late dinner or stop by Café Brazil for coffee. He was focused on getting her home, then getting to his gravely pressing business. Preoccupied does not begin to describe Simpson's state of mind. What had he gotten himself into, dealing with mobsters and drugs, two things that could definitely get a person killed.

Kennedy glanced his way occasionally, looking for any changes in his demeanor, but no changes were detectable. He was still visibly shaken by the phone call at the game. She hadn't seen that expression before. Seeing him scared the way he was almost made her feel sorry for him. Almost, but she had a strong intuition that whatever fix Simpson found himself in, it was his own doing that landed him there. She was right. He was in way over his head.

Ten

Lost My Way

*J*asmine *pulled out of the theater* parking lot in her Honda Accord after she and Marshall caught the eight o'clock show. The reviews were good, but neither of them enjoyed it too much. Personal issues weighed too heavily for them to detach themselves from their own painful realities. Jasmine was concerned about her relationship and the man who came along with it, but he was still dealing with Rorey's tragic death. Marshall was devastated and his outlook on life was becoming adversely affected. Some of the valued issues that once sustained his focus began to drift away into minutiae. His bond with Jasmine ultimately mattered less, as did his commitment to keeping her at the center of his life. She was the bright spot in his world, but suddenly and without warning the wonderful illumination grew dim.

When they rolled up to her modest apartment complex, Marshall began thinking of all the excuses he could use to get out of staying the night. He hadn't prepared himself to get close again, not to anyone, including Jasmine. The more she reached out for him, the further he withdrew. The deep wound had not yet begun to heal.

As her key chain jingled when she unlocked her dead bolt, he realized the best thing for him to do was just to tell her how he felt. "Jazz, I'm kinda tired. I'm gonna go on back to the dorm and call it a night." He could not look her in the eyes when he said it.

"What? What do you mean you're tired!" instinctively rolled off her tongue, before she could stop it. The stress of Rorey's death was getting to the both of them. "You know you can stay here anytime you want. Anyway, I haven't seen much of you lately and I was hoping we'd spend some quality time together."

"Hey, I just need some rest and could use some time alone is all." He continued to look at the ground. "I'll call you in the morning."

Jasmine exhaled slowly. "At least you could look at me when you tell me you don't want to be with me."

Throwing his hands up, Marshall slowly backed away. "I just need some time is all."

The disturbing thought, that he did not want to be with her, tugged at her heartstrings. She couldn't remember a time when he rejected her company. Times were changing. Jasmine could see it happening but felt helpless to stop it.

Marshall buttoned his letterman's jacket and pushed both hands inside the warm pockets. He wished the months would rush by so that his thoughts of Rorey wouldn't bear such an intense sting. Unfortunately, they were still in front of him, as were the means of getting past a best friend blowing his head off when he had some life left to enjoy.

Flea, some of the members of the get-drunk Tow Down (TD) Crew, a roughneck non-Greek fraternity of partying misfits, and other ballplayers lounged in the athletic dorm lobby playing dominoes and making cracks at each other, which is what they looked forward to doing each time they had a spare minute.

Marshall strolled into the busy lobby but was unaware of all the activity going on around him. He walked past the couple in a lover's quarrel near the big-screen TV, female students playing spades and giggling as he glided by, and the loud hurrah taking place at the domino table. He was in his own world, until Flea got his attention.

"Watch this . . . watch this," Flea said to the others observing the game. Then he yelled across the lobby, "Hey, Marshall, the missus let you off for the night? You must have put your work in early."

Friday night on campus was the best opportunity for students to get their late-night freak on, since there was neither class nor church to get up early for the next morning. Optimistic students prepared their overnight creep sacks on Thursdays.

The group of young men around the table erupted in laughter when they heard Flea's crack. Marshall smirked as he began marching toward them. Flea looked surprised when it seemed there would be a response to his street-corner antics. Normally, Marshall didn't indulge in the ghetto stylings of "wise-crackin'," so with each step he took toward them, anticipation of what his comeback might be manifested in elbow bumping and loud "ooooh"s from the gallery of players, wanna-be Macs, and male Ho-Dogs present.

"Come again, lil' man" was Marshall's initial shot of retaliation. He'd broken one of the fundamental rules of cracking, that it was solely for entertainment purposes; Marshall got personal.

"Awe, see, you're wrong for that," one member of the TD Crew contended.

Flea leaned back in his chair and scratched his head. "Naw, naw . . . it's gone be all right," he said, nodding his head vigorously. Flea stared his opponent down. "Oh, I know what the problem is. Yeah, Queen Jasmine rode him hard and put him up wet. Or couldn't you get it up?"

As the onlookers scoffed and snickered, another of them, wide-eyed, looked at his watch, then quipped his two cents worth, "Well, it is early," suggesting that Flea's presumption may have held merit.

Marshall sidestepped that comment and stayed locked in on his target. He looked Flea in the eyes and asked, "Is that the best you can do? I heard you're supposed to be the face crack snap master."

"I don't know about all that, but I do get off a good'n erry now and then," Flea proclaimed, with his chest stuck out. "Gotta admit, though, I am mighty surprised that yo' shorty let you outta her sight on a Friday night. For as long as I can remember, you've been on weekend lockdown. I'm talking house arrest," he boasted. "What up? What up? Time off for good behavior? Shawshank . . ."

Others standing in the lobby heard the fallout from that barrage of insults and drew near while Flea backers and TD Crew members high-fived one another.

Marshall raised his brow, then flashed a smile that grew into a chuckle. "Ahh, you . . ." he said, now laughing, "you got me. You got me." True enough, he had been with Jasmine every Friday evening since he could remember. That didn't necessarily mean he would let it slide, though. Marshall had a thing or two up his sleeve. "That's a good one, but tell me something," he remarked, in a sly manner like that of a cunning fox. Now he had not only Flea's undivided attention but also that of everyone else who had gathered around. "It's Friday night, right?" he continued, laying the trap.

"Riiiight," Flea answered naively.

"And you're hangin' wit the crew, right?"

Flea looked around, surveying his good friends in the crowd, acknowledging his boys. "Riiiight." The poor fellow had been set up and didn't even see it coming.

Marshall held up his right hand as if he were taking an oath of some kind. "Well, I've got an idea why you're free this evening, since you're all up in mine."

Flea shined a bigger smile than before. "So gimme yo' best shot. Why am I free tonight?"

Marshall leaned in slowly to capture his audience's undivided attention. "Palm-Ella musta gave you the night off," he said calmly.

Then he closed his fist and proceeded to shake it back and forth. "I know she's your favorite."

The uproarious laughter Marshall received was much louder than Flea's ovation. One of the fellas was so beside himself, he lost control and fell out of his folding chair at the domino table. That feat received the biggest laugh of all.

"Aw-ight, aw-ight, my bust. You got me." Flea conceded defeat, then threw up his hands as he began to sing, "Why can't we be friends . . . why can't we be friends . . ." he repeated in jest, as they slapped hands and agreed to call a cease-fire. It was all in good fun, all in good fun.

Jiving with the boys was the first time in a long time for Marshall that he realized he actually had something to laugh about. That brief interlude of male bonding felt good, damned good. It reminded him of the way he and Rorey used to trip on each other's inadequacies or rub it in when the other one made a trivial mistake, like mispronouncing a word. All in good fun.

While the others standing around attempted to catch their breath from all the merriment that had taken place, Marshall quietly backed away and headed for the Snapple vending machine. Big Love motored through the lobby with his face buried in a large pizza pie box. He would cut pizza slices on the way home the way most people nibble on a French fry or two. Half the pie was usually gone before he made it to his room.

Marshall counted the coins in his hand as he approached the machine. "Two Snapple lemonades, coming up," he muttered to himself as he looked straight ahead.

Big Love smacked on a slice of pepperoni, black olives, and triple cheese, studying it as he bit into it. Wham! He walked over the top of Marshall. Change for the vending machine went flying in the air as the big man held his pizza box firmly. Not one crumb had escaped from it.

"My bad, Marshall," he apologized, with pizza crust hanging from his mouth, "but I ain't had no Fat Man's pizza since Rorey passed. He had a hookup over there. Now they act like they don't know a brotha, tried to charge me full price."

Marshall collected all the coins he could find on the floor. "Yeah, I know, Biggie. Full price ain't no joke."

After Big Love mentioned Rorey, he felt compelled to ask Marshall how he had been getting along. "Too bad about your boy. How you been holding up? Ain't seen you around much since . . ." He paused to shove another slice in his mouth. "Well, you know."

"I'm cool, but I never would have thought I'd be buggin' like this. I can't explain it, but it's like someone ripped off my right arm or something. I miss that crazy white boy." Marshall's eyes started to water. "Sometimes I still expect to see that rusty beat-up-ass Ford pickup rolling through the yard. Man, I get twisted about it if I think on it too hard, but I'll get through."

"Keep it light," Big Love offered as his only words of advice, before he pushed his way into an already crowded elevator.

Once Marshall selected the Snapple he wanted, there was nothing left to do but wait on the next elevator going up. Flea exited the men's room nearby with the kind of look on his face that suggested he was up to something.

"Marshallll, we still cool, right?" he asked, extending his hand for some dap.

"Yeah, you know it. Sorry about that lil' man thing, but you caught me off guard."

"No problem, don't even sweat it. I know you got nothing but love for the brothas; besides, I'm still trying to get used to seeing you without yo' lady."

"Is it like that? You act like I can't be without my squeeze for a minute," Marshall argued. "Like . . . like we're joined at the hip or something?"

Flea didn't respond. He simply cocked his head to the side and stared back at Marshall as if to confirm that's exactly what he meant.

"Oh, now you're really trippin'," he protested, knowing all the while that Flea was right, because he'd spent all of his spare time with Jasmine.

"I'm just sayin', maybe you should hang with the Crew sometime and take a breather. It ain't that bad. You could probably use some time with the boys." Flea smiled when he saw that Marshall was coming around. "Check it out," he continued, "we about to head on over to the Kappa party at the roller rink. Why don't you come and hang? You're about to go to the damned NFL and ain't never hung with your boys."

Nodding his consent, Marshall smiled. "You're right. You know that? I'll be gone this spring and haven't spent any time with my dogs." He was slipping fast and it wouldn't take much longer for him to fall directly and completely on his face.

Flea rubbed his palms together slowly. "That's what I'm talking about. The real college experience."

They were five deep in a dropped-down Chrysler station wagon. There was Flea, Tut, Pig, Busta, and Marshall, with forty ounces in hand and bumping a vintage Tupac rap CD all the way to the roller rink, a legendary party spot off campus.

Booties swayed, players played, and the music seemed to hypnotize the coeds who felt intoxicated by another Friday night throwdown jiz-am. The brothers of Kappa Alpha Psi stepped in precision with striped canes in hand as other Greek organizations fell in line behind them. Marshall found it electric. The atmosphere was thick and festive. Frat brothas, sorority sistahs, and Me Phi Me non-Greeks all partied in perfect harmony. It was the first time Marshall conceived of so many black folk of different backgrounds and interests being in one hot place at the same time with no fights breaking out. The mood was unity and amusement, both contagious.

Watching the sororities step around the outer edge of the party, he noticed something else he hadn't before. There were scores of beautiful African-American women attending the same school he did. Up till then, he could only see as far as Jasmine. Unfortunately, a man's perspective has been known to change sometimes. Without warning, it can flip on him, rear back, and slap the taste right out of his mouth.

The DJ kicked the latest tunes, keeping the dance floor full until he decided to slow it down. The first slow record he played nearly cleared the dance floor, but he urged the men in attendance to stand up and be counted. That challenge was well received. It didn't take long before twosomes found their way to a slow groove with the lights turned down. Even Flea convinced a young lady to share some time with him on the floor, and that was no small task. It was common knowledge that he was sexually deprived but tried real hard to rectify it, real hard. But most women saw him as a pest and generally blew him off.

Marshall gazed out into the herd of dancers and felt good about what he saw. He was also glad he came. Enjoying college festivities without Jasmine was a new deal, but he convinced himself he needed it, deserved it.

After a few more slow songs, the music picked up again. Most of the students who had been on the floor vacated it for a necessary visit to the rest rooms. Flea collapsed on the table Marshall used as his observation station.

"Woo, this party is off the hinges. Them Kappas always throw a live jam," Flea contended. "See what you've been missing?"

"Yeah, I see your point," Marshall affirmed, as he stared at a high yellow sistah in tight blue jeans.

Watching his newest running buddy get an eyeful of some forbidden fruit, Flea threw in a bit of advice, for the sake of keeping the record straight. "Slow your roll, man. I know this is your first time off the leash, but you can't expect to go after big game right away. Now, you might want to start at the bottom and work your way up, wit' maybe a freshman female or something of that nature.

See that? That there is the honey of all honies. Your woman excluded, of course."

"That goes without saying. But who is she?"

"That there is Heretta Malveaux from New Orleans," Flea explained, rubbing his hands together again. "A ragin' Cajun. Good hair, French blood, I'm talking gumbo. Everythang in the pot, she got. Booty, tiddies, class. And don't let that mustache fool ya. She's all woman."

"Oh yeah, niggah, I believe it. Damn, she's fine. Who's gettin' wit' that?" Initially, Marshall had merely swayed off course. Now he was on his way to being lost. If Jasmine were to find out, he was likely to come up missing. He began innocently enough, just looking, then he had to go and inquire all about the woman.

Flea began stroking his chin as if it aided in his recollection of the latest 411. "Let's see. She's dating some Dallas Cowboy or somebody. He bought her a Mo-say-tees, C class, to get her to stay after she told him it was over."

"So . . . what did she do?" Marshall asked impatiently.

"What? Awe, she ain't to be taken lightly. Them's USDA prime-cut grade A breast and thighs. We ain't talking bal-on-ey."

"So she kept the car, huh?"

"Naw, she didn't keep it. She demanded an E class instead."

Marshall's eyes widened. "E class?"

"It's right outside. Chrome rims, leather, gold package. Oh, it's sho' 'nuf laid."

Pig and Tut appeared wiping their faces with paper towels. Marshall couldn't take his eyes off this woman nor her statuesque frame, although the fellas he came with made mention of several others they had interests in.

Pig's real name was Eric Polk, but Big Love's Southern pronunciation was Poke, as it also was for pork, or "poke" chop. Anyway, it stuck and the nickname Pig was an indirect result of a ghetto colloquialism.

When Pig noticed a young coed who seemed much too young to

be checking out Marshall, he got the star athlete's attention. "Check it out over there. Ol' girl is clocking you pretty hard."

"She is a cutie but kinda young. Probably a fresh fish," Marshall reasoned. "I'll let you have her. She'll be fine, though, when she grows up."

He'd kept his hands to himself but kept an eye on Ms. Malveaux, as she was often called, even though she was an undergraduate student. It was out of respect for her mature ways. She was the kind of woman who always looked older than the other girls her age.

Looking at her more intently now after learning of her appraised value, Marshall thought about what Flea said earlier. "It's laid, huh? I bet it is just that."

Flea began to realize what had taken place. Even though he lived by questionable morals himself, he couldn't sit idly by and say nothing. "Hey, wait a minute. I see where this is going and I don't think it's cool. Jazz would kill you if she saw you jonzin' for that sistah. Hell, I might come up missin' for bringin' you here, and I ain't tryin' to get my picture on the back of no milk carton. You feel me?"

"Ain't nobody talking about getting with her," Marshall replied halfheartedly, mostly to convince himself. "I just want to get close enough to see if it's all as tight as it seems to be."

"Aw-ight, then. I'll introduce you, but if Jazz finds out, it's your funeral. When she comes looking for yo' ass, my name is Pruitt. I don't know nothing about it, and sure as hell didn't do it."

Eleven

He Left the Toilet Seat Up . . . Again

O uch!" *Kennedy yelled, squeezing her eyes* shut when he tried it for the second time. "Simpson, I told you before that I didn't like it that way. It really hurts."

He slapped her hard on the butt, not to add to the pleasure of sexual intimacy but rather as a disciplinary tactic, as he overtly ignored her objections to engaging in anal sex, because that was what *he* wanted.

"And, I told you before that my woman has to please me in all the ways I need to be pleased, if she wants to keep on being my woman. There's a lot of women who'd love to give it to me, any way I like."

Although Kennedy didn't agree with his idea of pleasure, she knew that he was right about other potential women agreeing to be his sex slave for the sake of having a chance at real love. She'd done some things she wasn't quite proud of, either, for that reason.

Kennedy had been pondering that very reason lately, while Simpson's predisposition for anal penetration became more prevalent and more of a chore for her. She loved him and feared losing him, plain and simple, at least enough to feel compelled to please him, even if it were at her own expense. Compromising sexually was her cross to bear. Reluctantly, she gave in each time and with each dreadful occurrence, she hated it exponentially more. This time was no different. Before she could inhale deeply and prepare herself for it, he mounted her from behind and began to forcefully work himself into her anus. "Awwwwe!" she wailed loudly.

Again Simpson ignored Kennedy's cry of pain as she bore her face deep down into the pillow to get through it, like a virgin on her first sexual escapade. She experienced a fountain of emotions all at once. Although she felt abused, she was more ashamed than anything else because she didn't make him stop. Wincing throughout the entire episode, Kennedy wondered why so many other women raved about doing it that way when she detested it so. Some things can't be explained, she reasoned, while praying that he would just hurry up and finish. It lacked the passion, excitement, and stimulation that used to keep her up all night wanting more.

When Simpson was finished with her, Kennedy hid herself beneath the thin cotton sheets, wishing she had a hole to crawl into. Just like the other times, she felt misused and utterly violated, much like she had for the better part of the past year.

Long bouts of silence commonly followed their coming together intimately. Both of them seemed to reflect on totally different avenues of life. Kennedy was thinking of ways to move closer to loving the kind of man she'd read about in romance novels, the kind who loves his woman so wholeheartedly that there is no room left for another. Simpson, however, usually reflected on thoughts of making more money and living life to its fullest, unencumbered by traditional commitments of the heart.

*   *   *

Faint streams of moonlight sifted through the drapes covering the large windows in Kennedy's bedroom. The smell of expensive cologne and contempt lingered in the air. The repulsive aroma that sexual trauma emits has a way of doing that, lingering. Sort of as a reminder that though the act has been completed, that doesn't mean there won't be consequences to bear.

Simpson sat quietly, in abutting darkness on the edge of Kennedy's bed, buttoning his long-sleeve shirt. She wasn't at all surprised that he was on his way out the door, but she felt she had the right to inquire about it.

"Where are you going?" she asked, although she had an idea the phone call he received earlier had something to do with it.

"I've got to stop by the office tonight. Something came up."

"Something . . . ," she repeated, in such a way that would force him to elaborate. "Something like what?"

He turned his head toward her and frowned in disbelief. It had not been her nature to question him or his business exploits before. "Hey," he responded, massaging his temples, "it doesn't concern you, all right?" She heard what he said but she also knew what he meant. That it was none of her business where he was going.

"So that's it? You're just gonna hump me like a dog in heat and disappear into the night?"

"I said I had business!" he barked. "It's not up for discussion."

By the time he was fully dressed, she found herself wondering exactly when it was he stopped loving her, or if he ever had. Consciously or subconsciously, his demeanor had changed. He used to take her out on the town religiously and show her off. He used to kiss her softly in parting. There was even a time when he had to tear himself away from her presence. That was then.

Simpson disappeared into her bathroom. After the toilet flushed, he left her lying there, without as much as a smack on the cheek or a good-bye. He shrugged on his jacket and made his way to the kitchenette. He checked his watch, then peeked around the corner to see if she was stirring. After making sure the coast was clear, he pulled one of the bottles of Moët off the wine rack, then held it up in front of his face to inspect it. "Yes. This is a very good year," he whispered to himself. Then he twisted the bottom of the bottle until it was completely removed. Two zip-lock bags filled with a fine white powder fell from the bottle. Stashing it at Kennedy's apartment allowed him access to it if an emergency occurred. Richey's hostile insistence constituted just that, an emergency.

Moments after Kennedy heard the door close, she climbed out of bed. Purposely leaving the lights off, she felt her way to the bathroom through the calm blackness that surrounded her. The blind silence of the dark was comforting. She didn't want to see herself and be reminded of who she had become. An unloved, unappreciated relationship-caretaker who didn't possess the fortitude to demand something better for herself. The sort of woman she'd seen while growing up in Oregon. The sort of woman she despised for being weak, the same sort of woman who allowed her man to come and go as he pleased without so much as a hint of tangible commitment. And wouldn't you know it, he left the toilet seat up. Again!

A group of Japanese businessmen sitting at a nearby table applauded when Legacy finished another booty sketch on the first floor of Club Matrix. The young lady he immortalized on canvas thanked him with a soft smack on the lips, then happily strutted off to the dance floor with abundant attitude. Her boyfriend rudely smirked at the talented artist but passed him a fifty-dollar bill for his time nonetheless. Legacy smiled thank-you and wondered how much the boyfriend would have paid if she hadn't kissed him.

Between sketches, he drank a few sips of bottled water and checked out the club scene. Some of Hollywood's notables dropped by to socialize with the Dallas "A" crowd and soaked up some of the atmosphere the city had to offer. Eight-time Grammy winner Sonja Fairchild arrived fashionably late, danced a solid hour, and paid a hundred bucks to have her personal booty sketch created only to autograph it for Richey, the club's owner. Richey was so proud to have it; in fact, he gladly handed Legacy another crisp hundred and thanked him for making his night.

Richey was rough around the edges and didn't like too many people. You could number the ones he did like on one hand; Legacy was one of them. Having a young, aggressive, opportunistic college student around who utilized his talents to make a legit living while earning an education appealed to Richey. It was the club owner's way of giving back to the community. Carte blanche was offered to Legacy to work the club anytime there was a big function or if an exclusive party took place. All of Richey's women had portraits of their dorsal views made. Some of them even bothered to clothe themselves for it. Legacy didn't mind it when they didn't bother, and he was smart enough not to ask questions.

He also knew his part-time boss was a corrupt cutthroat with several unmentionable businesses, as well as business partners, but the mobster maintained a fondness for him. Richey had given him a break when he caught Legacy peddling sketches on the club's sidewalk a year or so earlier. It was a matter of respect. No one did business on Richey's property without getting his permission first, then cutting him in on a piece of the take. It was how things were done.

At a few minutes till eleven, Simpson pulled up in front of the valet booth at Club Matrix, as ordered. His frightened glassy-eyed daze from before made another appearance, but he fought diligently to shrug it off. Barging in the club's entrance with his pride scarcely in check, Simpson neglected to speak to Franky, who always stood at the door, before giving the place a once-over.

Simpson noticed the guy sketching a woman's well-put-together backside. The Japanese businessmen were drunk and riotous by then, and the attractive guest he summoned had arrived by taxi, just as he instructed. But no Richey. Simpson had made up his mind on the way to the club to dissolve their partnership. He was tired of being involved with the likes of uncultured, brutish career criminals. He preferred to deal locally on the low end with fashion models, producer types, and other club owners. His high-end clientele had flourished to include European commodity dealers, beautiful peo-ple—all of which constituted a better class of felons than the thugs he was initially directed to do business with. Simpson figured that if he played his cards right, he could score some major deals with South Americans, go solo, and cut out the middleman while dou-bling his profit.

When Simpson stopped by the woman's table, where she sat and waited alone, Richey grabbed him by the arm. The mobster wrapped his thick, strong fingers around Simpson's triceps and squeezed hard. Simpson grimaced and instinctively backed away from the table. Without any salutations to speak of, they both headed toward the opposite side of the club.

The short walk to the back staircase seemed like an eternal jour-ney for the disgruntled part-time drug dealer. It presented enough anguish for him to rethink the new business proposal he planned to spring on Richey, the one that was mobster-free. The pain that ran through his arm up to his shoulder wouldn't come close to the hor-rible fate he would be subjected to if he crossed Richey Glass, busi-nessman.

The two men reached the top step and entered the upstairs man-ager's office. The huge bodyguard took his usual place outside the door. Richey extended his hand, motioning for the cocaine. "Where's my package, Stone?" he demanded, without raising his voice. The no-nonsense expression he sported said more than he could have with threats or inflammatory words. "You got some nerve. You know that?" The mobster's demeanor hardened as he stared at Simpson. His voice began to rise. "You've got some nerve, you little shit. Stopping by a table to yap wit' some whore when you got business with me."

Simpson stared back with eyes displaying fear and uncertainty. His hands trembled as he laid the bags on the desk. Getting too close to Richey when he was that upset wasn't advisable. It was rumored that he cut a man's ear off for a lesser offense, so Simpson tried to slide into it.

"Uh . . . Richey. I've been thinking and umm . . ."

"You been thinkin'?" the mobster interrupted. "You take your time getting here and when you do, you stop by to chat with something in a skirt. You think I give a damn about what you've been thinkin'?"

Simpson became more cautious than ever. Everyone knew that Richey had a short fuse and it had already been lit. He turned his back and exhaled deeply. "I'll tell you what," he reasoned, while stroking his hair back with an open palm, "I'm a fair man. Tell me what you've been thinkin'. Tell me?"

The post–Ivy Leaguer stood with both arms by his side. He peered down at the floor and poised himself to make a statement. It was obvious he had something profound to say, but did he lack the courage? He knew that Richey was not a peon at some fancy upscale restaurant or some skinny-kid valet. He was the real deal. Murder and mayhem were his usual bedmates and they always came through when he needed them. The things Richey willed to happen with a single phone call made the headlines.

There was no room for Simpson to ego-trip this time. In the big league of joy and pain, he was a flyweight. He contemplated his fate and swallowed hard. "I, uh. Just wanted to say I'm sorry, Richey." The yellow streak that flashed down his back had just lengthened his life. Being smart enough to be afraid was a much better choice than being brave enough to be dead. "I need to be more businesslike. I admit that."

"Damned right you do," Richey agreed fully.

When Simpson managed to muster a smile, albeit scrawny, Richey knew he was being patronized. "Listen, Stone. You have pissed me off and I am seriously discontented. Don't let this happen again. From now on until I tell you different, I want you to send the packages instead of coming here. I don't want to see your face for a while."

Simpson didn't feel inclined to ask for the money to be exchanged for the cocaine. He did well to write it off and chalk it up as a learning experience.

"Oh, and Stone. I know what you've been doing with your so-called lady friends." Simpson froze and listened with bated breath. "I should have you whacked for that alone. You sick bastard. Now get out of my sight!"

He gladly left the office and Richey's company, thinking about all the things the tough guy could have found out about him: maybe taking his money, buying drugs wholesale overseas, skimming additional profits off the top before distributing the goods, or supplying it to models. No, he couldn't know about that, Simpson thought, or he'd already be dead. Whatever it was, he needed to fix it before he caught Richey on a bad day and ended up getting whacked on general principle. But for the time being, he decided to play it by the book, do just as he was told, make the deals and run the wine-distributing warehouse. That should keep him breathing.

He walked down the front staircase used by regular guests of the club. The Japanese businessmen were gone, probably run off by Franky for being drunk and disorderly. The artist was packing up his supplies. Simpson's long-legged date waited, though impatiently, as he drank the remains of her white wine in one fast gulp, then rushed her out of there and double-timed it back to his ritzy home in Plano.

The time slipped by with the grace of a cunning thief. It was getting late, later than Legacy expected to be peddling drawings at the club. Richey Glass came down and slapped him on the back, thanking him again for the Fairchild sketch. When Legacy attempted to share his earnings with the owner, Richey refused it but swelled with pride when the hardworking college kid did the honorable thing, offering him a piece of the take. He would never have accepted it, but it felt nice each time Legacy offered. It made Richey feel like a big boss back in Brooklyn, getting a piece of the action from everyone else who was under his wing.

Heavy fog rolled in after midnight. It wasn't thick enough to cause serious driving hazards, but the streets were less occupied than usual. Legacy was tired after a long day but not sleepy enough to go back to his empty apartment on a Friday night. He was lonely but managed to keep busy and occupy his mind with other things. He found himself reading the late-night menu at a small table near the back in Planet Hollywood. Three African-American women were seated at the table next to the one where he enjoyed coffee and a spicy shrimp appetizer. They were all attractive and decked out in interesting multicolored Kemetic garb. Two of them sat facing each other, at either side of the table, and one sat directly facing him. He tried not to listen in on their conversation but he couldn't help it. They discussed exotic excursions to Belfast and France and talked about men and what minefields black women should prepare themselves for in the new millennium.

He noticed that their ways of expressing themselves were as dynamic as their printed foreign gowns. They used their hands and facial expressions to display exactly what they explained with their words. Before he knew it, he had sketched a portrait of the lady who sat facing his direction. Her facial features were so defined. She was a beautiful brown, he thought, the color of his coffee with two splashes of cream. A golden cloth wrap rested atop her head like a crown. He noticed that, along with the complicated smile she wore beneath it. During the few instances when she did allow herself to enjoy the conversation, inklings of a sentimental mood loitered near. It was painfully obvious, even to a stranger, that she was preoccupied with something else.

Legacy studied the sketch he'd drawn of her. He was pleased he could capture the essence of her but was disturbed that the picture actually mirrored her distress. Offering it to her might have cheered her up, but it also could have offended her if she didn't find it flattering, only making matters worse.

After he'd stared in her direction for what the other two ladies felt was too long, they inconspicuously consulted each other while taking turns staring him down. Eventually, they decided to let the local muscle handle it and the restaurant security was summoned. Legacy snapped out of his daze when the over-sized bouncer wearing a tight black Planet Hollywood T-shirt nudged him to get his attention. A few of the other tables noticed there seemed to be friction. "Hey, buddy, whadda you think you're doing?" the cocky bouncer demanded, awaiting a response. "You're scaring these ladies. Staring at 'em."

"Uh . . . I didn't mean to offend anyone," Legacy answered in his own defense. "I was just admiring them." When that answer wasn't what the security officer wanted to hear, he proceeded to gather up all the pencils lying on the table and forcefully remove Legacy from the premises.

"That's it, partner, you've got to go. Git your stuff!"

"I'm going but I didn't do anything." Legacy collected his things and attempted to down his third cup of coffee. "I just sketched her, that's all. Is that a crime?"

The woman, whom he had sketched with amazing detail in only minutes, looked on while her two companions seemed to lean in and stand guard. She studied him now as he was being escorted out of the restaurant. He didn't own the eyes of an evil man, she thought, contemplating.

Legacy apologized as more people began to look on. "I'm very sorry, ma'am. I didn't mean to cause a scene."

The security guard had heard enough and had enough of Legacy taking his sweet time. When it appeared imminent he would finally be removed, the woman asked what it was he put into his pocket. "I'll check it out, Ms. Badu," answered the man, who grew more frustrated with each passing moment.

Legacy threw his hands up to prove he had nothing harmful to conceal. The man pulled his large hands from Legacy's coat pockets. The napkin he had sketched on fell to the floor. "There!" she exclaimed. "That's what I want to see."

Now she was going to see the drawing, he thought, and get scared or offended, then he would be on his way to jail under the new Texas stalker laws. She looked curiously at the sketch. "Wait . . . ," she demanded, then examined every warm line and complimentary contour on the paper. "We've made a mistake, he's the friend I came here to meet, but he didn't look like I thought he would." Honestly, she had never laid eyes on Legacy before that night, but his spirit told her that he had something she needed.

"Are you sure, Ms. Badu? If he's bothering you ladies, I can toss him out on his butt."

"No, it's all a mistake. We're very sorry for all the commotion. Thank you very much, but you can go now." She shooed the bouncer away with one hand while pulling Legacy toward her table with the other one.

"Yeah! You can go now," repeated Legacy, and began waving him away, too. The other two women stood nearby, gazing at them. They were confused when their friend suddenly came alive and handled the investigation personally.

"Friend," the attractive woman said. "Please accept my humble apology, but you must understand. . . ."

"Erykah," one of the ladies interrupted, "are you sure you know what you're doing? You don't know this man."

"I know, but by looking at this magnificent drawing, he already knows me." She turned toward him as if to behold his face in its entirety. "Please be my guest at this table. We seemed to have ruined yours."

Legacy stared more intently at the woman the bouncer called Ms. Badu and felt uneasy. All the time he'd spent caught up in how bewildered she seemed, he'd missed the most important part. She was the singing and recording artist Erykah Badu. Ms. "On and On" herself.

"Now I'm really embarrassed," he confessed. "I sat there gawking at you, studying your face. You should probably have me arrested for not recognizing you." He went fishing for something interesting to say, but it kept coming out babble. "You look so . . . ," he went blank, "so pure. So you. I should have recognized you. I've been a fan since you came on the scene with *Baduism*."

She made direct eye contact with both her girlfriends, who turned out to be her personal bodyguards, to put them at ease. "Could y'all please excuse us for a moment," she insisted, instead of asking. "Thanks, ladies. Take a powder."

The more she spoke, the more idiotic he felt. Her sweet sultry voice was extremely distinctive. He owned all of her music but it just hadn't registered.

"Ms. Badu . . . ," he said, smiling.

"Please call me Apples," she suggested politely, "all of my friends do."

"I'll try, but I can't promise. It's not every day you meet someone who offers so much to the music world, to the art world. I mean, the vibe I get from your work is so urgent. I mean, urgent enough to break a man or make him come back home. You know what I mean? Urgent as in right now."

"That's funny you should say that. Do you believe in destiny?"

"I don't know," he answered. "I always thought that life is what you get caught doing while you're busy planning it all out." Legacy laughed but she didn't.

She was too serious to notice his comment was meant to be a witty response. "Well, I do believe in destiny and positive energy and intuition. The whole spiritual realm always revolving in its own spherical domain, I mean. You know, three hundred and sixty degrees."

Legacy made an effort to keep up, but she was a great distance ahead of him. When she realized they weren't on the same page any longer, or the same spiritual plane for that matter, she digressed enough to let him catch up. "I didn't mean to get so heavy, friend, but I have strong beliefs. And one of them is that everything happens for a reason. Take tonight, for instance. I'm caught up in this situation with my man right now. But you knew that. I can look at your work and tell that you knew it, Mr . . ." She paused when she realized she didn't know his name.

"I wish I could start over. How rude of me. I'm Legacy Childs, pleased to meet you."

"Likewise, Legacy. That's an interesting name. I like that," she said, while looking at the drawing occasionally.

After a couple of cups of coffee and hot tea, they had become acquainted. She even laughed out loud once but placed her hand over her mouth to muffle the sound as she drew attention to herself. Legacy offered what he thought would be a surefire way to straighten out things with her significant other. He suggested that she call her man and leave a singing voice message of his favorite song on the answering machine. She agreed it sounded like it might be worth a try and decided to do so as soon as she returned home. "My Man" by Billie Holiday would do rather nicely.

Before they said their good-byes, he learned that she still owned a place in town but lived mostly in New York, and that she was giving a charity benefit in town during the following month at the Phenomenon nightclub. She didn't have all the details but thanked him for the sketch and invited him and a guest to attend. Then she handed him a business card listing private phone numbers at which to reach her. Legacy nodded his head in the midst of silence and wondered if it were sure fate for him to be in that particular place at that particular time. He was in awe.

Her warm smile and heartfelt thanks convinced him it was just that. Fate.

Twelve

Baby, Don't . . .

A vastly overweight student balanced his overstacked food tray
and book bag while pushing his dining card back into his
pants pocket. The ending was inevitable. His hand got stuck
and the tragedy he feared became a reality. As the book bag slid off
his shoulder and knocked his hand from the tray, Jell-O, burgers,
French fries, and soda went flying. There was a loud crash. It startled
the table of female students sitting nearby. Everyone in the large
dining hall looked on, then applauded and cheered his unfortunate
mishap, which was customary at UTC.

"Fat boy didn't need all that food, anyway," Busta reasoned. "By
dropping that tray, he probably just lost ten pounds." Flea nodded
his head in agreement. Marshall bit into a BLT and laughed with
his mouth open.

"He ain't got no business being that damned big nohow. He

ought to spring for some Jenny Craig," Flea added. "And who was he trying to fool with that Jell-O?"

Busta took a sip of iced tea from his cup. When his eyes rose up, they found Jasmine wandering through the corridor outside the lunchroom. He tried to conceal a mischievous smile, but it was a futile effort. "Hey, man," he said to Marshall, "the word on the yard is you got with Ms. Malveaux."

Marshall stopped chewing, then swallowed hard. He looked at Flea, who was purposely looking away to avoid eye contact. "The yard, huh?" he replied. "Would the yard be sitting his little butt at this table? Is that the yard you heard it from?"

Pig smiled and bit into a second hamburger. He was not much on words, especially while he was eating.

"I ain't sayin', but that's not important," answered Busta. He leaned in closer to Marshall, sitting across the table. "So, uh, did you sink or swim? They say easy does it, but I want to hear it from you. How was it?"

"It wasn't even like that," said Marshall, as he squirmed uncomfortably. "We met and hooked up but she ain't all that. I'm lettin' it marinate until I can figure out a way around Jazz."

"I told him she was trouble. I told him. I told him," Flea professed, then got nervous when he thought about it. "But nawwww, he had to get to know ha better." Pig nodded in agreement. He was there when Flea attempted to discourage Marshall from approaching the shapely sister.

"Get to know her, huh? How much better, my brotha?" Busta asked, watching Jasmine walk toward them as he purposely kept the conversation going.

"Well, you know, a gentleman never tells," Marshall contended, with a satisfying hell-yeah-it-was-good smirk on his face.

"Hell no, he ain't gonna tell. I wouldn't either, Marshall," Flea argued. "If you were smart, Marshall, you'd take it to your grave. 'Cause if your shorty finds out, Jazz is gonna be on that . . ."

"Jazz is gonna be on what?" Jasmine asked curtly. She seemed to appear out of nowhere. Flea, Pig, and Marshall sat motionless.

Busta smiled, as his ulterior motive was accomplished. "Don't clam up now, Marshall," she added. "Looks like you had plenty to say a minute ago and more to say at the party the other night." She felt like she owed it to him to keep him in check like that. Jasmine fooled herself into thinking it was good for him, like an enema. A brief cleansing every now and then could prove quite effective. It added credence to the old "An ounce of prevention is worth a pound of cure" cliché.

"Baby, don't . . . ," Marshall pleaded from embarrassment.

"Don't what? Baby don't read you in front of your tired little friends?"

"You must have us confused. I ain't little," Busta disputed, with his chest stuck out.

"And I ain't tired," Flea chimed in.

"Opinions vary," Jasmine said calmly. "Marshall, get your things. I want you to walk me to class."

Busta and Flea leaned back in their chairs with their arms crossed. Pig watched from the other side of a half-eaten stalk of corn on the cob. Each of them waited to see if the football star was going to do what his woman instructed him to do. Marshall was caught in a bad place, between the sistah he loved and the brothas he wanted respect from. The tension was as thick as the cut of steak Pig shoveled in his mouth.

"Well, are you coming?" she asked again, growing more annoyed by the second.

Marshall looked at his comrades in harm, then looked up sadly at Jasmine. "Yeah, I'll be right there," he conceded reluctantly.

She began walking toward the exit doors. Marshall got up slowly, knowing the onslaught would be severe when he did. He was right.

"Oh, you're gonna leave your little tired friends, huh?" Busta barked sarcastically to Marshall.

"That's tired and little," Jasmine corrected loudly, without looking back.

"Who's wearing the pants?" Flea asked adamantly. "I told you Jazz is the man. She runnin' thangs."

Pig stopped eating for a split second and washed his food down with a huge gulp of water. "Y'all both know that y'all would do the same thang. Flea, I've seen you do worse for a sistah who wasn't even yours. And Busta," Pig added, with his head cocked to the side to help illustrate his point, "don't let me get started on you. We ain't even gonna get into what I've seen you do to keep some drawz. Hmm, and some of it was illegal."

"What? What?" Busta uttered in his own defense, knowing all too well that Pig was dead on. Each of them had succumbed to the wishes of other women they shared lesser ties with. During school days, a brother had to do what he could to maintain. Sometimes, to get a shot at some new action, he'd have to beg, borrow, and steal just to see the panties. And some sisters would put a man through all three.

"Hold up, Jazz!" Marshall yelled, catching up to her as she exited the dining hall. "Baby, how are you gonna play me in front of my boys like that?"

"Your boys?" Jasmine repeated loudly. "How are you gonna play me? A month ago, you wouldn't have claimed knowing those scrubs. Now they're your boys?"

"Yeah. Well, you know what I mean. They're cool people. Busta, Flea, Pig."

"Oh, they must be. Real cool people. So cool you'd rather hang with them than your own woman. The woman you're gonna marry." He stood speechless without mustering up a single comment. All he could do was listen. "I never thought I'd see the day, Marshall. Come on now, a Busta, a Flea, and a Pig." She wrinkled her top lip. "That sounds like a circus if I ever heard of one. Is that what you want? A circus life?"

"No, baby. No . . ."

"Don't you baby me. As far as you know, my name is Ms. Jasmine Reynolds."

"Okay, be that way, Jazz. But I just had to get out for a while."

"Get out? Let's see, if I remember correctly, and I'm sure I do. You told me you needed to go home. Be alone. Alone with who? The Flea, Pig, Busta, and the bearded lady." Marshall's eyes widened. Surprise engulfed him. "That's right! I heard about you and that tired tramp Hairy He-retta Malveaux. And it had better be just school-yard hearsay, because if I find out it's not, I will become a mem-o-ry so fast your head will spin. I'd rather be a cherished part of your past than to be your present fool, Marshall. You got that, baby?"

He stood silently with his lips pressed together. He understood, all right, but he didn't like it. "Yeah, I got it," he replied finally. "I also get the fact that you've turned into something I never thought I'd see from you. The fellas told me that you'd be trippin' sooner or later. You've finally turned into that jealous sistah that every man hates knowing. Ain't no cause for it 'cause ain't nothing going on. Who're you gonna believe, anyway, your man who loves you or some trifling haters around here who don't want to see two people in love stay that way?"

Jasmine twisted her lips while staring back at him with uncertainty. "Whatever, Marshall, whatever. Just letting you know that I've never been a fool and I don't plan on trying it out now to see what it feels like, so don't play me stupid because I don't play. Remember that."

Legacy sidled up behind Marshall, who was standing alone on the sidewalk, as Jasmine walked away. Marshall's demeanor displayed the thoughts going through his mind. Doing the same thing and doing the same woman for four years had him in a quandary. He was young and had the world to explore, along with other women.

"Hey, Marshall, was that Jasmine Reynolds? We have Cultural Appreciation together." Legacy's question fell on deaf ears as they both watched her strut down the long sidewalk.

Marshall blinked repeatedly, then glared at Legacy as if he were coming out of a daze. "What?" He was still trying to get over the discussion he just had. "Oh, Freelance." He acknowledged Legacy's presence but didn't take his eyes off Jasmine until she disappeared into the Cultural Sciences building.

"That Jasmine's a good student. She helped me with African and East India Studies and now I'm showing her some of the different European art masters. You know, Monet, Gauguin, Rembrandt."

Marshall grinned devilishly. "That's all good, but I have a little somethin' you might be able to help me with." Legacy stared back intently while Marshall laid his plan. "You know Jazz is my girl and we've been together for a while now, but I've got some other things to do, on the down low." Legacy knew exactly what he meant. "I just need you to stay close and tell me if some other brothas try to step to her. You down wit' it?"

"Yeah, that's cool," Legacy agreed. "I'll see you around." They slapped hands and parted ways.

Thirteen

Don't Confuse the Two

Kennedy tugged at her torn panty hose. A long run spanning from ankle to calf appeared from what seemed out of nowhere, as they all do. Morris passed by her office and witnessed her appraising the damage. He could not refuse an opportunity to chit chat.

"Yyyes. You do need new ones. They're absolutely mangled," he said, adding his unsolicited two cents.

"Yeah, I know," she agreed, without looking up. "But I just paid a lot of money for these and they're supposed to be guaranteed against runs."

"Well, looks like you're gonna have to run your little self back to that store and demand they be replaced. Look at them! They're clinging to your leg for dear life. You know Mr. Johansen is not going to be pleasant if he sees your hose falling apart."

"You're telling me. Maybe I'll take off early for lunch and pick up another pair then."

Morris looked at his watch, then scurried off in haste. It was almost nine o'clock on the nose. He turned up the volume on a small clock radio sitting on his desk. Tom Joyner, the fly jock himself, came back over the airwaves to notify listeners of another clue to the radio station's latest promotion. "All right. Here is the ninth and final clue for the all-expense-paid 'Ladies Night Out on the Town' contest. The grand-prize winner will receive a ladies night package for her and six of her friends. The limousine is provided by Lasting Impression Limousine, whose motto is 'It's how the stars ride but they gotta pay too.' So please listen carefully because I can only play it once. Who said it and in what movie."

Morris poised an ink pen on the notepad he had written all the other clues on and listened intently. The announcer's voice faded out and a portion of an audio clip began. "Besides, I don't believe in financial portfolios when it comes to what makes the heart go pitter-patter," a man's voice contended.

"What do you believe in, then?" a woman's voice asked.

"The softness of a woman's skin," a man's voice answered. "That Tiger Woods's consecutive slam is golf's first and only grand slam. I believe that Malcolm X's assassination was a coup to silence one of American's finest leaders. I believe in bubble baths after hot steamy sex. Great wine and good novels go hand and hand. I believe there ought to be one man for every woman. I believe in the G-spot and that every man who cares about his woman ought to spend as much time as it takes discovering hers . . ."

Kennedy approached Morris's desk while he leaned in closer than before to the small radio. The clue was tough, much more difficult than the others, which he figured out right off the bat. For two weeks he'd listened and collected clues. "Shhh . . . ," he insisted, shooing her away.

She frowned and continued to annoy him. "Hey, what—"

"Could you please?" he said abruptly. "This is serious business."

She stood there looking at him, trying to figure out what had him all worked up. Kennedy eased closer to his desk. Again he shushed her. "Shhhh, you're making me miss it."

The audio from a popular movie played on. "I also believe in saying thank-you and please because it's the right thing to do and neither'll cost you one thin dime. And I believe in window-rattling escapades that'll last all night, and if it's really good, halfway through the morning, too."

The woman's voice followed by simply replying "Ohhh my" in response to all that her costar had to say.

Tom Joyner's voice faded back in. "That's it, the final clue. I'll take the first caller who has all the clues, in proper order, for the Ladies Night Out grand prize."

Morris sat there looking disappointed, still tapping the pen to the notebook, but slower now. The wheels had fallen off his hope train. He was clueless. The actor's voice sounded familiar, but he had no idea what movie it was from. Kennedy smiled when she figured out what he was up to. Morris had talked about winning that contest for the past two weeks.

"What about that excerpt would you like to know?" she asked with a knowing grin.

"It's no use. I don't have the slightest. It was too hard!" He let his head fall forward until it was flush against the desktop. "Oh, why'd they have to make it so complicated?" he whined.

Kennedy stood over him. "I knew right away who said it and in which movie."

His head sprang up from the wooden surface like a jack-in-the-box. "What do you mean? You know it?"

"I sure do. It's Isaiah Washington and Nia Long in the hit movie *If You Knew,*" she answered matter-of-factly. "It's one of my favorite successful-man-who-has-everything-but-the-right-girl movies. This guy falls in love with an audience member while watching *The Oprah Winfrey Show* and . . ."

Before she finished her statement, he was on the phone dialing the number to the radio station. The line was busy. He continued pressing redial and listening to the radio as women from all over the Dallas–Ft. Worth Metroplex area called in to take their shot at the prize. Kennedy shook her head and backed away. "Good luck." Other than the radio and the telephone, he was oblivious to anything in the open foyer. Constant redial had become his sole thought for the day.

Westwood Mall was less than four miles from her office, so a quick dash and grab should have taken only a few minutes. The well-furnished shopping center had just opened its doors for business. Although Kennedy practically had all the stores to herself, minus four or five sets of "get fit after fifty" seniorly power walkers burning up the walkways during their health laps, she had a task at hand and needed to stay focused. Straying off course could have been disastrous. Not enough time, never enough money.

Kennedy was proud of herself for passing up several remarkably dressed window displays, making a straight beeline to her favorite department store. She randomly selected several styles of hose and headed to the checkout register. When she asked the sales attendant what he advised about the size differences of each brand, he turned his nose up and looked and away as he returned to his personal phone call and cleaned underneath his fingernails with an outstretched paper clip. "I'll be with you in a moment," he spat at Kennedy in a dry tone, then continued with his conversation. "I'm back, it was nothing. Just some sistah with an issue. Like I care."

Kennedy was livid. *Some sistah!* He caught her at the wrong time. Her own man was not on his job and nothing else mattered.

"Hey!" she yelled. "If I were you, I'd get my butt off that phone and tell whoever that is that you're talking to that you're about to feel the full extent of this *sistah's,* as you put it, issue. You don't know me like that."

Mr. Rude checkout man sighed deeply, as if she were wasting his time. "I know she is not trippin'," he whispered into the phone. "Let me go before I—"

"Before you what?" she interrupted. "Yeah, you'd better get off of that phone."

He slowly put down the receiver as if he were collecting himself.

Most apathetically, he offered, "Now look, even a retard can see that the sizes are all marked accordingly on the packages," without really moving his lips.

"Excuse me! Unless you own this place, I suggest that you check yourself and address me better than that. I spend a lot of my hard-earned money here and even if I didn't, I'd still expect a higher level of respect than you're giving me."

The cashier placed his hands on his hips and spat back. "That's the problem with you *Cosby girls*. You get a little money and expect people to bow down to you. Well, you've got the wrong number, honey. This ain't information, so figure it out for yourself."

Before she knew it, she'd had a nasty altercation with a snooty cashier who most vehemently refused to replace the hose; his supervisor finally had to be summoned. The floor manager had overheard the last bit of their tiff. He appeared, apologized, and instructed Mr. Rude to exchange the hose and give another fifty percent discount on a second pair for her trouble.

In her triumphant moment, Kennedy snatched the panty hose off the countertop. She got what she came for, but suddenly that wasn't enough. She squinted her brown eyes at Mr. Rude and held her head up high. "Let that be a lesson to you. And don't act like you're better than me. I'm the customer. Remember that, *Ronald*," she said pointedly, looking at his gold name tag. "*I* shop here. *You* work here. Don't confuse the two."

The tall, thin cashier rolled his eyes behind her back. It felt good to blow him off as he'd done to her when she initially arrived. Now she enjoyed a leisurely victory march, at his expense, all the way back to her car.

Driving back to the office, she noticed that street construction workers had closed off another lane on Northwest Highway, an extremely busy thoroughfare. The light was changing, and the lane she traveled in began to peter out. She had to make a decision fast, either speed up and fly through the tail end of a yielding amber traffic light or slam the brakes and hope that some driver would be courteous enough to let her in. But she had grown accustomed to Dallas drivers and she didn't count on anyone giving her a break in line.

"Come on, light . . . don't change on me. Don't change," she pleaded, mashing down on the accelerator to make it through the light.

A man saw her approaching the intersection and riding the shoulder to get by. Out of pure meanness, he pulled out in front of her, blocking her passage. That ridiculous maneuver forced her to slam on her brakes, but the car was traveling too fast to stop. The driver, who had pulled his car in front of hers, panicked when he realized it. His eyes grew wide. He ducked inside that shiny Lexus of his, bracing himself for the impact sure to total his car and probably break a few of his bones. Her blue Mustang hydroplaned as it skidded closer to an impending collision. She closed her eyes and screamed. The car was out of control atop loose dirt and gravel from the construction in progress. Somehow, she miraculously guided it around the Lexus.

The sports car came to a jolting stop when it bounced off several bright-yellow hundred-gallon construction drums, each filled with water and bound together with bungee cord. Those drums stopped her car before she killed anyone and probably saved her from serious bodily injury, although the impact did severely wreck her front fender and annihilated her radiator. She was lucky to be in one piece.

Construction workers who saw the accident dashed over to assist the damsel in distress while the man who caused it simply adjusted his rearview mirror and scoffed, "Lady drivers, boy, I'll tell ya," as he drove away without a hint of concern or remorse.

Kennedy climbed out of her car as the workers attentively sought to help her. She was fine. Just shaken up. As the construction workers moved the automobile off the street, she assessed the damage, then called AAA to have her car towed.

Later, while Kennedy gathered her nerves, she called Simpson to come pick her up. His receptionist answered after several rings.

"Stone Imports," she said, giggling into the telephone.

Kennedy looked curiously at her cell phone. "Hello. Is Simpson Stone in? This is Kennedy James."

"I'll see if I can get him for you," she said sharply, with an altered tone. The young blond stopped giggling and shoved the phone underneath her dress. That's where Simpson's head was. They were fooling around in the wine cellar at his office.

"Yeah, Simpson Stone here." He was panting to catch his breath.

"Simpson? This is Kennedy. I've had an accident and I need you to come and get me."

"An accident?" he repeated, still fondling between his employee's legs. "How serious was it?"

Kennedy became more agitated. "Serious enough!"

"Yeah, how serious? I mean, are you hurt?"

Kennedy looked down at herself to note any obvious injuries but didn't see any. "No, I don't seem to be, but I am stranded."

"I'll have to send a taxi for you. I'm all tied up." Simpson smiled at the young lady who was pulling on his necktie and motioning for him to get off the phone.

"A taxi. You're really not coming to see about me, are you? I don't know why I bothered to call you. What if I were standing here bleeding . . ."

"But you're not so why are we discussing it? Tell me where you are and I'll send someone to—"

"Never mind, I wouldn't want to inconvenience you." She was so embarrassed and emotionally wounded that there was nothing else to do but hang up the phone. That's just what she did.

"I wouldn't want you to inconvenience me, either," Simpson agreed joyfully, before finding his way back underneath his young receptionist's dress.

Kennedy had already suspected he might be having an affair with the ambitious and hot-in-the-panties, I'm-anxious-to-get-ahead-with-my-legs-wide-open younger woman. Deep down inside her soul, she knew very well that it was going on, but she wasn't ready to do anything about it. Not yet, anyway. Come to think of it,

Kennedy came to know him the same way the receptionist had, by getting her kicks at the same place she got her paycheck, when she worked at Stone Imports. It was a nice arrangement before their relationship got in the way of her work. It was the same kind of *working* arrangement he was involved in when she called him. Kennedy knew Simpson's philosophy regarding working hard and playing hard: as often as he could, both at the same time.

The tow truck came and the driver hooked up the crippled automobile. He pulled it into the nearest service station to adjust the belts attaching it to his truck. Morris arrived on the scene and parked his 1968 hot-pink Volkswagen Beetle, which proudly sported a 69 BUG vanity plate, next to the wrecker.

"Are you all right?" Morris shouted through the car window before he stepped out.

She nodded, affirming that she was, but tears of mascara had long since stained her cheeks. Nonetheless, she was glad to see him coming to her rescue. "Thank you so much for coming, Morris. It was awful. I tried to make the light and then this Lexus pulled out in front of me. Then Simpson . . ." She started to cry again.

"It's okay. Slow down. Slow down. It's okay. Don't go to pieces on me. Momma's got happy plans today." He put his thin arms around her like a mother does to comfort her child. "Why don't you go in the rest room and fix your face. I'm sure you'll feel better if you look better. It works for me." He was glad that she took his advice and stepped into the women's room at the back of the service station.

Morris sauntered around to the front of the dented car and looked it over, curious to see how much damage was done. He peered over the tow truck driver's shoulder. "Oh, that's ugly. Simply tragic. She can't drive it all beat up like that."

The tow truck driver, who wore tight blue jeans, a short, thick navy flannel jacket, and a tan cowboy hat, looked over his shoulder when he heard something in Morris's voice that didn't sound quite right to him. When he saw Morris's meek feminine attributes, he flinched hard and fell out of the way, as if a strange animal had wandered up behind him.

"It's okay, slim," Morris offered, attempting to appease the man who stared back at him so apprehensively. "I'm not in the mood either, honey."

Kennedy emerged from the women's room with her face made up as best she could, considering what she had to work with—trembling hands, bad nerves, and worse lighting. Her new panty hose were a full size too big and sagging at the knees and ankles.

Morris took one look at her and placed his hand over his heart. "Oh my!" he said, with his mouth hung open. "Who jacked you up in the powder room? Never mind. That's why I told Mr. J. you would need the rest of the day off. I figured you'd be a total wreck. Boy, was I wrong," he added sarcastically.

"You're such a good friend, Morris. You're right. I do need the rest of the day to get my head together. My life is falling apart in front of my eyes and I can't seem to do anything about it."

The wrecker guy watched them closely. That annoyed Morris enough that he voiced his objection. "Hey, can we have some privacy here? This is a distraught woman at the brink of hysteria. She needs a moment!"

He continued to stare but now only at Morris, who had thrown his hands on his hips in opposition to being gawked at.

"I'll bet that pink 1969 bug over yonder is your'n, ain't it?" the wrecker guy asked suspiciously.

"See, that's where you're sadly mistaken," Morris remarked boldly. "I can't stand it when people try holding others up to blazingly unfair preconceived stereotypes. But if you must know, that's a *1968* Volkswagen," he declared, pointing at his pink car with a dramatic limp wrist. "*I'm* the sixty-nine bug!" Snap! Snap!

Kennedy was slightly embarrassed at Morris's antics. The driver hurriedly backed his way to his truck, jumped in, and quickly whipped out into traffic, weaving in and out with Kennedy's car in tow.

Auto insurance cards, AAA membership receipts, and other various paperwork cluttered Kennedy's purse. She dug through it to the bottom and looked relieved when she found it: a half pack of Marlboro 100's cigarettes. The first long drag hit her like a narcotic sedative. She savored it while looking at the smoke as if it mesmerized her. "Wow, that's good. I can always count on you," she heard herself saying, before she took another drag.

As she approached the pink bug, Morris threw his hand up to stop her. "Oh, no. Don't even think about smoking that stinky thing in my car. You know the rules. No smoking in the love bug unless it's under the stars and in the backseat, with me. And for that, you don't qualify. So lose it."

She jumped inside the car with it still lit and much to Morris's dismay. "I need this cigarette. You don't understand. My life is crap. Nothing is going right."

"Oh, darn it . . . if you must." Taking into consideration her recent trials, Morris was nice enough to roll his window down. But in protest, he stuck his head out and dramatically gasped for breath. "Forgive me, Loretta. Momma's so sorry," he said to the car. Then he shouted orders to Kennedy. "You're going to have to roll your window down, too, before you suffocate us to death!"

"But it's thirty-five degrees today," she protested in return.

"I don't care. My cleaning bills are atrocious as it is and smoke ruins the fabric. You decide whether you'd rather puff on that thing or freeze!"

"Okay, okay. I'll throw it out." She took another long drag before she tossed it out onto the street. "Umm, that was so good. I can't believe you. That was such a waste."

"What are you complaining about? I don't understand why you do that to yourself. At least you could have chosen a brand that's less butchy, like Virginia Slims or something. You look like someone about to rope a bronco with those things hanging out of your mouth. Yeee-hah!" They both laughed at his ridiculous perspective on cigarette brands and their target-marketing strategies.

The waiter strolled over to take their drink orders as soon as they were seated in the small diner. Kennedy looked at her watch. The crystal face was smashed. "You believe this? Now my watch is busted, like my relationship. What else could go wrong? I'm almost afraid to set foot outside my front door."

Morris had been surveying the restaurant for something eye-catching. He saw a few men he used to know and his old acquaintances saw him, too. "I'm sorry, honey. What did you say?" It wasn't so much that Morris had a one-track mind that hinged on the men in his life. He couldn't concentrate because his mind could only stay on one track at a time, his or hers.

Kennedy was upset that he wasn't listening to her complaints. "Oh, it doesn't matter," she whimpered. Her tone of voice bordered on pitiful. "I was just trying to decide whether I should slit my wrist or get my nails done, that's all. But you were too busy flirting to hear my desperate plea for help."

Morris frowned, not taking her seriously. "Anyway. I've got great news. Are you ready for this? Guess who won the radio contest? Me, me, me . . ."

She was amazed. "You're kidding. You really won it? That's great!"

"I owe it all to your clue from that movie, *If You Knew*. That clinched it for me. I mean you."

"What do you mean me?" she asked, almost terrified at what the answer might be.

"Well . . . and don't get mad, but I had to say I was you, Kennedy. It's a girl's night out and I would have been disqualified if I showed up to claim the prize. So please pretend to be me. I mean you. You know what I mean. Please, please, please," he begged. "You could go with us. It'll be a blast."

"Us?" she repeated with a raised brow. "Oh, no. I'm not going to be a party to fraud and escapade around the city with a bunch of . . ." She stopped because of what she was about to say.

Morris's eyes saddened. "Go ahead and say it, Kennedy. A bunch of what? Faggots?"

"No, that's not what I was going to say, Morris. You know I

don't think of you and your friends that way. I tell you what. I'll do it and I apologize for being selfish. You've turned out to be the closest thing I have to a best friend. It's the least I can do."

"Good, then it's settled." His eyes were happy again. "We'll ride over to the station after lunch and pick up the details."

"Aren't you stretching your lunch hour a bit as it is?" Kennedy looked across the table to get a look at his watch for the correct time.

"I've got that covered," he answered with a mischievous leer. "After I won, uh, after you won the contest, I took off for the rest of the day. Mr. J. thinks I have water damage at my house, so he's not expecting me back until tomorrow."

They pulled off the identity switch at the radio station and collected certificates for limousine service, passes to several area nightclubs, and five hundred dollars of fun money.

After several hours of shopping with Morris's newfound cash, Kennedy picked up a rental car and started for home. She fidgeted with the instruments on the dashboard to become familiar with them. The white Ford Escort was a far cry from the Mustang she was used to, but it would have to do. She'd grown tired and the evening traffic had already filled the freeways.

Legacy stacked and sorted coins to make it faster to give change. He set up rows of quarters each time he worked. He figured if he stayed on top of the change situation, he would have a better chance to see Ms. Blue Mustang each time she came through the tollbooth. Six o'clock had come and gone. Legacy kept close watch throughout the past hour, but no dream lady appeared. He knew she normally drove up between five o'clock and five-thirty but never after six o'clock.

The flow of cars started to slow, as most of the people who regularly accessed the tollway at gate number seven were well on their way home by now. He was making an hourly transaction report when a buzzer went off inside the small booth. It alerted him someone was going through without paying the fifty-cent toll fee first. A white car had driven past his window and waited for the gate to rise, but it wouldn't. As he stepped out of the tiny building to investigate, the car began to back up toward him. It was Kennedy. She rolled the window down and began to explain that she had had an accident that wrecked her car and that she was so scatterbrained that she didn't remember, amid all the drama, to get the prepaid toll tag from her own car before AAA took it away. "I'm sorry, but I usually come through here every day. Well, Monday through Friday, anyway. But this isn't my car. It's a long story but I—"

"It's okay, go on through." Legacy stood near the driver's side door, looking in. He was blown away from the moment he recognized her. She was more beautiful, up close, than he thought. "I know your car," he informed her. "You're Blue Mustang. I mean . . . you drive a blue Mustang. License plate number SBGSSL. I see you coming through here all the time." Other cars began to pile up behind her. "Go on through. This one's on me." He tossed two quarters in the basket to raise the toll access arm.

Kennedy thanked him. She also noticed he was handsome but didn't think much of it until she pulled away and caught a glimpse of his tight behind in her rearview mirror. "Oh, the toll guy is fine. I should have been going through the change line years ago," she said loud enough to hear herself, noting that he seemed to know who she was and wasn't too proud to admit he'd noticed her many times before. His dark-blue company-issued Dickey brand utility pants, which he was forced to wear after another employee reported, that on several occasions he was out of uniform, showed her more than she expected to see. He was physically fit and easy on the eyes.

When she finally entered the tollway, Legacy smiled calmly before returning to his office space to celebrate. "I met Ms. Blue Mustang," he chanted, as he danced inside the small building. "Ms. Blue Mustang. Ms. Blue Mustang. Yeah!"

Fourteen

Burdened

*S*hauni Woodbridge giggled through the playful girl talk with a sorority sister when they saw Marshall and Busta approaching them on the sidewalk near the administration building. She was extremely interested in getting to know Marshall in the biblical sense. It was no secret, but he had never reciprocated the kind of welcoming responses she had hoped to receive after her many seductive innuendos. His mind and heart had belonged to Jasmine for years, but things were changing. And Shauni, along with most of the other students traveling in the same A-crowd circles, knew a bomb was destined to fall and eventually find its target, inevitably blowing up the neat little package Marshall had always considered to be his prized possession, his relationship with Jasmine.

"Heyyy, Marshall, you're looking fine today," Shauni said. "As usual," she added, while batting her blue eyes at him. "Hi, Busta," she said flatly, accompanied by a sour, twisted smile. "How're your babies' mommas?"

Busta grabbed his crotch and tugged at it. "Oh, they all aw-ight, but you know they can't get enough of these N-U-Ts."

Shauni knew about all four of Busta's illegitimate children, each of them with a different mother. He had more kids than a day care but would not concede to strapping on a condom, so he only slept with women who were stupid enough to agree to be involved in such a careless act. What he didn't realize was that the women who'd allowed him to put their lives in jeopardy had allowed countless other unprotected men to do the same. But gonorrhea and the other venereal diseases he had contracted during his butt-naked exploits weren't enough of a deterrent for him. Skin on skin was the trap he kept falling in. A man like Busta doesn't get it until he gets it. A-I-D-S. As In Dumb Sex.

Marshall still had his head buried in the latest edition of *College Football* magazine. He managed to tear himself from it long enough to speak. "What's up, Woodbridge?" He always treated her like she was just an ordinary student, not like the spoiled sex vixen she really was. It turned her on more that he didn't seem to notice her tight, painted-on blue jeans and bulging cream-colored sweater showcasing a pair of ultra-firm brand-new out of-the-box D-cup breasts. But Busta certainly noticed. He licked his lips while staring at her every curve. And when she noticed Busta undressing her with a nasty glare in his eyes and rolling his tongue over his lips, as if he were about to get a taste, she focused her full attention toward Marshall. She turned her back on the ravenous wolf.

The vicious manner in which both Busta and Shauni shamelessly went after who they wanted to get in bed suggested that they were well suited for each other, although she would have no part in sharing her satin sheets with her raunchy classmate. He was much too common for her taste, and too crass to tolerate. Even for her.

"I don't care about you turning your back on me," Busta said frankly, but without malice. "I think I like this view better, anyway. You sure yo' momma wasn't gettin' it on with the butler?" He eyed her shapely behind. "From back here it looks like she's got some splainin' to do," he joked in his best Ricky Ricardo impersonation. Oddly enough, he thought it was a pretty good compliment. The sick humor in it was lost.

Shauni grew tired of his crude comments. As much as she wanted to stick around and visit with Marshall, she refused to put up with Busta's menacing discourse. "Let's go, Susan, the air just got a little foul," she said evenly. "Marshall, I'll catch you later when you're not so, uh . . ." She smiled enticingly as she reached out and pressed her manicured fingers against his muscular chest. "Burdened with company."

"Burdened. What the hell are you talking about, burdened?" Busta thought about what she'd said and although he wasn't sure, it sounded like she sneaked in an insult of her own at his expense. But the insult she fired didn't nearly dent his ego as much as her obvious and harsh rejection did.

As the women walked away, Busta turned and yelled in their direction. "Didn't nobody want your old . . ." He paused and looked around to see who was in earshot of his mutterings. "Naked in the backseat debutante ass anyway."

Busta watched Marshall shake his head in disagreement while flipping through the magazine again. "What?" Busta asked, looking at him curiously. "What are you shaking your head for? That rich skank ain't too good to be clowned, now. I don't care how much money her daddy's got. Straight up rich or project po', if I get dissed I'm clownin' the ho'. You know that's how I do it."

"You need help, Bus. I mean serious help, a professional with a degree and everything. Brothas at the barbershop can't do nothing for ya, man."

"You can't just treat broke people worse than you treat people with money."

"It don't have nothing to do with who's got money and who don't," Marshall reasoned. "Busta, you insulted the girl. You basically said her butt was finer than her face, then you called her momma a tramp."

Busta countered quickly. "I ain't never said nothing about her momma."

"Oh, she should've overlooked that comment about her momma and the butler, then, huh?"

"You know her mom's probably been getting freaky with the help. I heard how them rich white women get a lil' loose when their husbands leave town on business and they ain't got nobody to turn to during them cold lonely nights, excepting for old black Elmo downstairs in the slave quart . . . ," he stammered and had to catch himself, "uh, I mean in the servant's quarters."

"You need help, Busta," Marshall reiterated. "You need help."

Glen Allen Lancer leaned against his brand-new champagne-colored Cadillac with chrome rims in the parking lot adjacent to the athletic dorms where Marshall lived. He was as polished as his car. His kind always was. His kind wore charm like a freshly starched shirt. The bronze complexion he sported, it was authentic. Expensive trips to tropical locales secured his golden year-round tan, expensive trips paid for by his clients.

"Hey, Marshall Coates." Glen smiled and extended his hand. "I watched you play all last season. You're really something to see. Caught every game." He stood next to his car with the sparkling paint job. His arm was still poised, sporting a diamond-studded Movado watch, waiting on a handshake as Marshall stood in front of him with a straight face. "I'm sorry, I didn't introduce myself. I'm Glen Lancer. But you can call me Skip."

Marshall continued to look him in the face, then took a once-over of the fancy man's clothes and car. "You a pimp, pusher, politician, or promoter?" he asked in a routine manner.

"Well, I'd guess you'd say I'm kind of a promoter." He reached into his jacket pocket and flashed a business card. "I'm an NFL agent."

"Like I thought," Marshall scoffed. "A pimp."

Skip was caught by surprise. He had waited for the past hour only to be subjected to Marshall's wrath. Usually, his appearances impressed young, naive, and unaware college ballplayers. Unfortunately for him, Marshall was neither naive, unaware, nor young. On the contrary, he was tenacious and wise beyond his years in the avenues of survival. He had been ghetto aged, which meant he was forced to become a man before his contemporaries on the proper side of the tracks knew there was such a thing called making the rent.

Marshall began to turn and walk away. "No thanks. Mr. Lancer? I don't feel like being ho'd out today. Why don't you get back into that fancy whip of yours and *skip* your tired butt on back to Dallas or wherever you came from. I've got an education to complete, podna."

Other students passed by without noticing the two of them in an irregular conversation. Skip looked perplexed for a moment, then conceded defeat. "Okay, okay, Marshall. You win. But it looks like I must have mistaken you for a man who cared about his future." The agent began to look down at the business card he had taken out. "It's here if you want it."

"What's that?" Marshall asked condescendingly, holding him in an ice-cold stare. "A chance to get screwed by a has-been or, what's worse, a never-was? I don't think I need your services. My talent speaks for itself."

"Maybe so, but without proper representation . . ." Skip leaned in closer to Marshall, then shoved a business card into the pocket of Marshall's letterman's jacket. "You could lose big. It's not such a long way back to the projects."

Marshall was insulted but felt like he owed it to his community, as well as himself, to put the overconfident know-it-all in place, still remembering what he learned as a child: Be intelligent when you put people in check, especially white ones with more money and more clout than you. "I have a distinct feeling that either way I'm gonna get screwed, but I can guarantee it won't be at the expense of a professional money minder like yourself, Mr. NFL Agent. And I'm glad you reminded me that home would never be too far away.

Tell you what, why don't you roll up off this campus before I call the NCAA and NFL to let them know what you've been up to." Marshall never would have reported him nor the other agents who had come calling already. He wasn't the type to snitch on anyone. However, the agent had underestimated Marshall's intelligence. They all had.

As soon as Marshall reached his dorm room, he dialed the phone number of a pro player who was part of the Denver Broncos organization. Ray Crocket was from the Dallas area and Marshall happened to meet him while visiting Jasmine's church one Sunday. Ray had instructed him to call anytime he needed to have questions answered or if he just wanted to vent from all the upcoming pressures before and after he entered the league. Marshall looked outside his window from the seventh floor. The agent was still there, running the same lines down to Big Love, who happily climbed into the car and rolled into the purple-skied afternoon.

Marshall sat at his desk and unconsciously drew pass routes on notebook paper. "Hello, Mr. Crocket? This is Marshall Coates from UTC. You might not remember me but—"

"Yeah, I remember you," Ray answered. "You're Jasmine Reynolds's friend. You have a lot of cornerbacks already talking about ways to stop you and you haven't been drafted yet. That's a good sign."

"Thanks." Marshall seemed uneasy because he still didn't know who he could trust. Ray did seem like a nice enough guy and he was kind enough to offer his counsel for free.

There was a brief moment of silence while Marshall got his thoughts together.

"Marshall, man, you okay?"

"Yeah, I was just thinking about running something by you."

"Shoot. If I can help you with it, I will."

"Well, these agents have been coming by here pretty regularly lately and one real smooth one showed up on the yard today. Shiny car, jewelry, the works."

"That sounds like an old friend of mine," Ray thought aloud. "Skip Lancer."

"Yeah, that's what this guy said his name was. Skip Lancer. What's he all about?"

"Marshall, unfortunately they're pretty much all alike. Agents are bloodsuckers, but they are necessary, and some of them even do a great job of representing players. It just depends on who you end up with. Skip is not as bad as most but worse than some. In the grand scheme of things, every new contract negotiated puts another agent's kid through school or buys a house for another mistress. If I could have, I would have gone solo years ago, but most owners won't deal with a player because it gets too personal. Sometimes, players grade themselves too high and can't get the money or package they think they deserve, so they hold ill feelings for the organization and the coaches, even after the deal is signed. But it's never personal and always business."

They discussed how the games behind the game worked and other changes as well as challenges to expect. After they hung up, Marshall felt much better about following his instincts about professional agents, but it was all happening too fast. In a few months, he would graduate and be pulled into a millionaire's lifestyle from making zero money and be expected to handle it.

The more Marshall thought about his tomorrows, the quicker it became apparent his yesterdays were fleeting. Flea wasn't all wrong at the Kappa party weeks ago. Marshall did owe it to himself to enjoy the remainder of his college days amid all the seriousness he had to deal with his whole life. That's how he justified it to himself, each time he sneaked off to see Ms. Malveaux or when other women showed up at his dorm room late in the night and tapped softly at his door.

Fifteen

Pretenders

*K*ennedy *had gotten dressed* in a long black evening gown and dark pearls. She had the toughest time finding something to wear, not really wanting to go after all. She would've rather stayed home and sulked because her relationship with Simpson was in ruin. But it was part of the grand scheme, since she pretended to be the caller with the right answers to win the contest. It was supposed to be a festive event, a ladies night out on the town; however, she couldn't seem to pull herself together.

After several loud knocks on the door, Kennedy rushed to open it, fearing the knocks would get more impatient. When she opened it, there stood Morris decked out in a Vera Wang beaded gown draped with a full-length mink coat, a short blond wig, and wicked high-heel come-and-get-me pumps. He was something to see. Pretty and ridiculous, both at the same time. Actually, pretty ridiculous would describe exactly how Morris looked, although in his own mind he was something else.

Kennedy stood there with her mouth as open as her front door. She stared at him in his expensive gown and didn't know what to say first, that she was surprised at how he looked or that his party attire looked better than hers.

"Close your mouth before something flies in it," Morris said evenly, with his top lip turned up.

When she backed out of the way slowly to let him pass, Lady Eleanor looked on as if she were in awe as well. Morris excused the cat, but he couldn't overlook Kennedy's outfit. "I know you're not going to be caught dead in that drab thing. We're going to a party, not a funeral. Off with it. I refuse to be seen with you dressed like that. I have an image to uphold."

Kennedy's loss for words continued. She was baffled. Not only did her male friend show up dressed like a rich man's woman, he also insulted her selection of clothing. Looking down at her dress, then at his, she acknowledged that he did have excellent taste in women's apparel and conceded to let him select something from her closet.

"Just sit here and let Momma hook you up," Morris quipped. Instant excitement came over him as he laid his mink on her bed. He'd loved playing dress-up since he was a kid, spending several hours a day in his own mother's closet.

After laying out several dresses to choose from, he decided that a sleeveless tangerine-colored Gucci sequined gown would best serve her. She threw her hands up as if to say "What the hell," then she put it on. Morris also convinced her to put on much more makeup than she was accustomed to before they glided down the hall and into the elevator.

The long white stretch limousine idled at the curb. Bradshaw, the doorman, opened the door for them to exit the apartment building. Kennedy said, "Thank you, Bradshaw," but he didn't recognize her at first. As the limousine driver helped them into the car, it occurred to the seasoned doorman who it was hiding behind that painted-on face. When he leaned forward to get a better look inside, he opened his mouth to acknowledge Kennedy, but he found it difficult to speak when his eyes found what they did, six flamboyantly gay men wrapped in some of the finest evening gowns he had ever seen. Morris made seven. Seven penises in lipstick, he thought to himself, while being so startled by their appearance; he jumped back like he had come face-to-face with a rattlesnake.

Bradshaw closed the car door, then rubbed his eyes in disbelief and mumbled, "That had to be seven of the prettiest men I've ever seen in my life," as he returned inside the building.

"Ooh, may-on-naise . . . Gucci looks good tonight. But, uh, who's the fish stick?" one of Morris's guests asked in a condescending tone.

"Don't mind her, honey. She's always jealous of a real woman with original equipment," another of them added.

Among the loud chatter buzzing in the back of the limo, Morris's voice emerged. "Ladies, ladies. Quiet on the set! Time for introductions. This is my good friend Kennedy. She's straight but she's cool and the one responsible for our outing tonight, so be nice."

Hellos, hi's, and charmed to meet you's rang throughout. "Kennedy, this is Chas and Drew. The three dressed alike in the spearmint ensembles are, starting from left to right, Robbie, Tonie, and Joie. They're known as the downtown trio. Uh, don't ask why."

Tonie raised his head, softly stroked his neck with his long, bright-red press-on fingernails and looked away while answering. "She's a big girl and I'm sure she knows why." Numerous oohs, laughs, and finger snapping ensued. "Awwwwe riiiight!"

Morris continued. "And the rude one you already met is Sahara. She's confused but she's family."

"Confused. Who's confused?" Sahara quipped. "Hmm! I bet I could show you a thing or two, Ms. Thang!"

"Well, we'll never know," Morris replied. "You're much too much woman for me."

"Any woman is too much woman for you." Sahara knew that Morris only liked gay men who looked straight, as opposed to those who openly exhibited their feminine side.

"I guess someone is on the rag again," Morris fired back loudly, toward Sahara.

Kennedy didn't quite know how to take the spat, but all the others laughed and began to pour cheap champagne provided by the radio station. What's a little catfight between friends.

Morris noticed Kennedy's uneasiness and sought to offer comfort. "Sweetheart, don't you let these queens frighten you. They're harmless, unless you're a tall, good-looking, strapping man."

"Willing and able," shouted Drew, while finger combing through his wig.

"Oh yesss . . . ," Morris remarked seductively. "Willing and able. Then that's something totally different."

"Totally different," Sahara added, with his index fingers extended about twelve inches apart from each other, as if to suggest how totally different men and women are from one another. "Sometimes there's a foot-long difference."

The downtown trio chimed simultaneously, "If you're lucky," followed by more oohs and overhead finger snaps.

The limo pulled next to the curb of Winfrey's, a classy gay establishment on Cedar Springs, in the heart of the predominately gay district of Dallas. When the doors opened, the party began immediately. With purses in hand, they sashayed into the busy nightclub as if they owned it. Everyone was in gay apparel. Lavish gowns and expensive leather pumps filled the room, though there were a few men who were straight looking, dressed in casual eveningwear.

Kennedy looked over the room. She saw men in drag coupled with other men standing dangerously close to one another. Some of them even smacked on the lips, and she blushed at the thought of seeing them tongue-kiss. She thought she was as liberal as the next person, but this was too much. There was no way she could have been prepared for anything as extravagantly gay as this.

Music began to play loudly above the conversational minglings of the noisy room. As the stage show started, the girls took their seats. Kennedy tugged on Morris's arm to stall him at the bar. She seemed reluctant to touch anything. She simply didn't belong, but she pretended to be unaffected by the entire grandiose affair.

Morris played big brother or big sister, whichever the case may have been. Again, he noticed her tension. "Kennedy, are you all right?"

"Yeah, but I . . . ," she began to say, before pausing when she saw one man playfully grope another one. "I don't know if I can handle this."

"This is your first time at a drag show, huh?"

"I'm sorry, Morris. Is it that obvious?

"I'm afraid so. Your constant teeth grinding gave you away and I wanted you to have a nice time. You could really use it."

Kennedy continued to work on relaxing her way through the evening as she looked over the crowd of people curiously. There were men dressed as women, women dressed as men, and some she couldn't tell which. "I would feel a lot better if I could tell who was who in here," she admitted finally.

"I think I can help you with that one. Look over there at the bar. See that guy with the soft pastel gown that doesn't fit quite right and the pumps that are altogether wrong with the outfit?"

"Yeah, what about him?"

"He is one of the nicest, most perfectly normal gynecologists I've ever met. Though not professionally, of course."

Kennedy fought it, but a brief chuckle came roaring out of her mouth. "Of course not," she agreed.

Morris pointed to another man at the bar. "That man cozying up to that woman is an established businessman. He's bi—"

"Bisexual? That's gross."

"No. Biodegradable. Of course, bisexual. He's what you might call a pretender."

"A pretender? What's that?"

"A pretender is a man who likes men in drag but pretends not to be interested in men at all. They usually bring a woman here or pick one up as a beard, a cover, all the while scouting for a drag queen to take home. They're twisted, if you ask me, and I'm just as liberal as the next queen, but I think it's dangerous because they sometimes regret what the night watched them do by the time the morning comes."

Kennedy winced, then saw an attractive brown-haired waiter making rounds and delivering drinks to various tables. She pointed at him. "Morris, what about him? Is he gay or pretending?"

"Oh, honey, I wish. That's Mars. He's dreamy but not gay. I think the owner's his brother or something like that. He's working his way through college. Hi, Mars," Morris yelled from a few tables over. The young man looked up and smiled back. "A girl can dream, can't she?" Morris shrugged his shoulders and squeezed out a nervous giggle. "Some of us just prefer the flip side of life. You know, the B-side. Not everyone enjoys the same old worn-out A-track after it's been played too often."

"That's what I mean, Morris. Drew, Robbie, the others, all made up like women. Why? And Sahara, I can't even begin to go there."

"Let me begin at the beginning," he suggested, noting her obvious anxiety. "I invited you here because you didn't seem to be the judgmental type. You never once frowned on the way I chose to live or my sometimes wicked ways. So please don't ruin my faith in you by disapproving or trying to understand why I am the way I am. And please don't condemn me for it. Let's get something understood. I don't want to be straight or hurt. I just want to be me and be okay with being just that. Me. Right, wrong, or indifferent. Me."

Kennedy's eyes fell to the floor momentarily, like a child caught doing something in which she had no business, then she looked into Morris's eyes. "Please forgive me. I'm really sorry, but this will take some getting used to, I guess. And as for your lifestyle, I've never judged you because I see the love and compassion you show toward everyone else whether they approve of you or not. But you're right. I do owe you more than that. I should be ashamed of myself."

She held out her hand and offered it to Morris. He refused it but hugged her tightly instead. "Yes, you should be ashaaaamed. But I forgive you. I'm over it already." He flashed her an overexaggerated, eyebrow-raising smile.

"Friends?" she submitted.

"Friends," he accepted.

The first act on stage, a YMCA Village People parable, was over and the second act began. A Tina Turner look-alike in a spiked wig, short leather skirt, and five-inch pumps appeared in a cloud of smoke, lip-synching Tina's hit song "Private Dancer," while a tall muscular man in tight black patent-leather pants with a matching vest and hat accompanied the headliner in a sensuous private dance of his own. That made Kennedy blush beet-red. Among all the applause and accolades from the audience, she still found it difficult to watch attentively.

Later in the evening, Kennedy stopped in the rest room to use the facilities, but there were both men and women loitering near the stalls. She quickly changed her mind and stepped out into the lounge area feeding into both rest rooms. When it came to her that the rest rooms displayed "His & Hers" and "Everybody" signs, it reaffirmed she was at the wrong party altogether.

She nearly broke her neck marching back down the long, dimly lit corridor leading from the ballroom. She bumped into two people heading her way, but she didn't think to stop and apologize. When she returned to the brightly lit gala setting of Winfrey's lounge, it was like swimming upward toward the water's surface and breaking through to get that life-sustaining breath of fresh air she needed. Kennedy was drowning, suffocating in something she knew nothing about. It was time for her to kick-paddle toward shore.

With Morris prodding, the party girls poured outside to reengage the limousine, as the girls made a move to their next destination. Simpson's car was parked neatly near the valet stand, right up front like he liked it. Kennedy's heart stopped beating when she saw it.

She couldn't blink as she pulled Morris aside. "Maybe it would be a good idea for you all to go on ahead. I suddenly don't feel so good. I'll see you at the office next week."

Morris didn't understand. "Are you sure? Is something wrong?"

"It's not your problem. It's mine. It's just that I see Simpson's car over there and I wonder what the hell he's doing around here." She pointed to the extravagant foreign sports car with a straight forefinger.

"Kennedy, how could you be so sure that's his car?"

"His vanity plates. 'NV THIS.' Besides, I'd know that car anywhere. I helped him pick it out last year."

"I'm sure there's an explanation, but this is not the time or the place. It's probably harmless, but if it's not, I don't want you to lose your dignity in there. Come on. Let us take you home." Morris had a good point. There was no sense in embarrassing herself if she didn't have to. If Simpson had been in that queen-for-a-day hideaway without a damned good reason, all hell would have broken loose and Kennedy would have been in the eye of that tornado.

The limousine returned Kennedy to her building, then darted off to resume the rolling party brigade elsewhere. Bradshaw came out to meet her. Her sulky demeanor and pouty lips said that she wasn't in the mood for conversation, so he didn't press. She couldn't help wondering if the right decision was to question Simpson concerning his whereabouts later or beat it back there to storm into Winfrey's, demanding to know why he was there and who he was there to see. Ultimately, she had too much pride to go back and look for him. She was forced to wait and worry about what he had to say on the matter. Maybe she was just making a big deal out of nothing. A deficiency in self-esteem can play tricks on a person's mind. But since worrying was free, she'd take as much of it as she could carry.

Sixteen

Ain't Nobody's Business

The sun peeked out among the thick blanket of overcast clouds and shined its rays on the small sandwich shop. Kennedy became frustrated when Morris studied the menu but couldn't seem to make a selection. They sent the waiter away twice because of Morris's indecisiveness. "Morris!" Kennedy shrieked, louder than was necessary, to get his attention. "Could you please pick a damned sandwich before the sun shining through that window bakes me to a crisp. Good grief. It's a sandwich, not rocket science." She was still fuming over her boyfriend's possible indiscretion.

Morris cocked his head to the side. "I know you didn't go there on me." He leaned back in his chair, pressed his hand against his narrow chest, and sighed deeply. "Oh, my. Aren't we testy today?"

His feelings were slightly bruised. "And who pissed in your corn-flakes this morning?"

"I'm sorry. I didn't get much sleep last night, so excuse me if I snap. I feel like old tires. A lot of miles on my back and no appreciation."

"Some night, huh?" he asked, in his usual nosy tone. "Who needs sleep when you can stay up all night and get balanced and rotated. I know I could use another twenty thousand miles on my back."

She overlooked his comment. "Morris, please. I'm trying to be serious here. Simpson didn't show up, again, last night and I couldn't sleep a wink wondering where he might be. I just don't know anymore."

"Well, what did he have to say about the other night at Winfrey's?"

"He was very angry that I asked. Said something about the club owner being his client, then he blew me off." She stared out the window and squinted into the sun's brightness for a moment while Morris looked on with sympathetic eyes. "He does that a lot these days," she added. "Blows me off, I mean. I wish he were more like he used to be. More honest, more thoughtful . . ." She looked across the table at Morris as she became more upset. "He used to give a damn about what I thought and about me. Before he started caring so much about how successful he was. Even though he assures me that he's doing it for us, I'm not so sure I want it."

She was lost so deeply in the backwoods of denial, she had convinced herself that Simpson's lack of attention for her had something to do with his dedication to his job. She knew better than that. She knew as well as Morris did that he wasn't spending quality time with her anymore because someone else had taken her place.

Simply by chance, Morris had already found out who that someone else was. And as much as he enjoyed being in other people's business, he warred with the idea of telling her. But he'd made up his mind to stay out of it as long as he could; and that was no small feat. He also considered the fact that she probably wouldn't have believed him, anyway. As difficult as it was, Morris's better judgment prevailed. Besides, no one can save a woman in love from her own self. Especially after she decides to trade in her soul for her man's busted promises. If she's lucky, she'll get way past tired of being a fool for him and nerve up enough to demand her soul back. Sometimes . . . way past tired comes too late.

Morris looked out the window, too, searching for something appropriate to say to a friend whose man had all but collected his personal items, which were folded next to the delicates in her panty drawer. He had to say something. Knowing the truth and keeping silent about it would have surely killed him. So he decided to do what came naturally to him. He opened his mouth and expected the right words to come pouring out.

"Kennedy, we've been working associates for a while now, but I want to know if you think of me as a true friend?"

"Sure, Morris," she answered casually. She could tell he had something he was leading up to. "You're probably my only friend. Why . . . are you asking me that?" While she waited on an answer, it came to her that she'd allowed all of her other friendships to fall by the wayside when she centered her life around Simpson Stone. There was not one single close girlfriend to confide in and share her pain with, one to lean on. Not one to shoulder her woes. Not one. It was then she realized just how much of a true friend Morris had become.

"No reason in particular," he innocently responded. "I'd just like to know where we stand, that's all."

"Does this have anything to do with the other night at the club? Because if it does . . ."

"Don't be silly," he answered nervously. "We've gotten past that. I just can't stand seeing it eating you up inside like this. I always hoped for the best for you and Simpson, but sometimes you've got to know when to cut bait and get off the pot."

Kennedy narrowed her eyes and tilted her head slightly to the side. "I believe that's fish or cut bait, and crap or get off the pot."

Morris looked confused. "What?"

"You didn't say it right. I can't stand it when people try to turn a phrase and say it wrong."

"Whatever . . ." He rolled his eyes back in his head to show his displeasure. "I might not have said the analogy right, but you know what I mean."

"Actually, it's more of a metaphoric cliché than an analogy, and no, I don't know what you mean, Morris. What is it you're trying to say?" She knew exactly what he meant and she also knew that he was right. But she still felt insulted that he suggested she make a decision to stay in the relationship or not. She wasn't ready to face the inevitable that stared her in the face.

Morris sighed deeply and leaned in toward her. "What I meant to say is, maybe it's time to stop letting Simpson Stone the Third lead you around by the nose and dump on you when he damn well pleases." Morris wasn't fazed when she gazed back at him with astonished wide eyes. "Did I say that right?" he added coarsely.

They sat there looking somberly at each other for a moment. Suddenly, Kennedy burst out laughing. Morris peered back at her peculiarly before laughing aloud, too. "I guess we are friends," she surmised. "Because only a friend has the right to say something like that and expect to live."

"That's why I prefaced this conversation by checking to see where we stood. It did come across harsher than I expected, but enough is enough. If it were me, and my man was making me very unhappy, diminishing my quality of life, I would want to lean on you to help me pull out of it. But it's not me, it's you. And it's your turn to lean."

"Thanks, Morris, but no thanks. You've helped me, in five minutes, clearly see something that has been a blur for a very long time. You've done enough already, more than enough, but I refuse to drag you further into this mess. It's my mess and I'll find a way out of it, on my own."

He agreed to let her walk the last mile alone. "All right. You win. I promise to stay out of it, but I have just one more piece of advice."

"And that is . . . ?"

"That when you realize you have something very precious, you'll cherish it no matter what. And if it breaks down, promise to get it repaired by someone who knows what he's doing." Kennedy was confused. Her perplexed facial expression suggested that she needed clarification. "Your heart, honey," Morris answered. "I'm talking about your heart. You can't replace it, so it's important you get it repaired."

He extended his arm, then reached his hand across the table. Kennedy grabbed it and squeezed tightly. She wanted to agree wholeheartedly, but she knew they would only be empty words. Simpson was the only man she ever considered marrying. He had the right career, right connections, and great looks. A real Prince Charming on paper. As far as she knew, he did have it all. And she wanted the suburban lifestyle that came with having the right stuff, including 2.3 kids. The problem was, her Prince Charming hadn't treated her like royalty since she could remember.

Seventeen

Come What May

The bell sounded when the elevator doors opened on the basement floor of the library at UTC. Legacy stepped off and immediately made his way over to the Info-Net computers, which were used as quick reference guides. It accessed a brief summary on most of the articles found in the library's periodical section after they had been bound into hefty volumes. Unfortunately, his computer skills weren't as prolific as his artistic ones. He tried several times to query for an article written about African-American contributions to the art world from the 1920s to the present. He was mostly interested in the Harlem Renaissance, the rebirth of the artistic movement among blacks that began in Harlem, New York, then spread like wildfire throughout the country.

After several attempts and coming up empty, he began gathering his things to adjourn upstairs. Jasmine watched from an adjacent table, covered with books, along the far wall. "Freelance Childs," she said, just loud enough to get his attention, "remember, you have to back-slash shift."

Legacy turned to acknowledge her, then quickly attempted one last time to get the computer system to work. Since he didn't back-slash shift, it didn't work. He grabbed his book bag and headed over to the cluttered table where Jasmine had parked herself for hours of monotonous research.

"Hey, Jasmine . . ."

"Freelance," she answered back, with a tired smile.

"I can't get that stupid computer to do what I tell it to. It might be user-friendly but it sure ain't Freelance-friendly."

"That's cause you didn't push the right keys. Back-slash shift gets it to work. Didn't you read the instructions? Of course you didn't, you're a man," she answered, not allowing him a chance to quote the obvious.

He stood there trying to think of a clever reply, but he came up empty. "Well, I would have read the . . ." Legacy stopped himself when he realized that he sounded like a sorry excuse for the entire male population, but he couldn't risk being seen as a complete idiot. It was too late for that. "But I was in a hurry."

"In a hurry, huh? Men are always in a hurry these days. If y'all took time to pay attention and read instructions, y'all would know what was going on and get it right the first time."

Legacy decided to make an attempt at redeeming himself and score one for his brothers in arms, male-bashing victims, who'd been ripped to shreds all too often at the hands of some unrelenting female. He sat down at the table across from her, looking on intently while pretending to outline her would-be psychiatric evaluation. "That's good. Uh-huh, that's very good. Misplaced aggression, yes. I'm sensing hints of female dominance. Pent-up hostility. Give me some more, I could use the extra credit. It'll make a good psych case."

"Very funny. Ha ha ha. You're a riot."

"I had to say something. You stopped me in my tracks. I had to strike a blow for my brothas."

"Yo' brothas?" she repeated, in a manufactured ghetto vernacular.

"Yeah, my brothas. Men. We're all in this together. Me, Marshall, all the way up to the president."

"Be careful. You sure don't seem to mind placing yourself in suspect company."

"Who, you mean the president?"

"No, I'm talking about Marshall. He's the one you have to watch." They laughed a while and seemed to forget all about their brief war of the sexes.

Legacy began looking at the titles of the books on the tables. *The Arts: An Introduction, Painting and Sculpting*, and others in the same realm. "Hey, what did you pull down all these books for?"

"Unlike some people," she replied sarcastically, "I have to study art in order to understand as well as appreciate it."

"You're trippin', but I know what you're getting at. I know art, but it's only because I've made it a part of my life. It's the same with you and black literature, jazz, and theater. You know so much about that stuff that Professor Cuington has to check with you before he can grade the exams."

She returned the smile he'd flashed her. "Now you're trippin'. I know my stuff from growing up in a house filled with books about great music pioneers: Cab Calloway, Bessie Smith, John Coltrane, Billie Holiday, and a lot of black folk from the Harlem Renaissance. But you don't know nothing 'bout that," she boasted.

"You're right, you're right. I don't, but I do know about art, and by the looks of all these books, you know less than nothing 'bout that," he scoffed jokingly.

"Freelance, you make me sick. A man with a quick wit. In some states that would be considered a dangerous weapon. Yeah, I could use a podna like you."

"Coo'," he responded, in a street vernacular of his own.

While they shared ideas on term-paper themes and how important accessing the right information was to completing the assignment, Legacy felt guilty for admiring Jasmine so much after he'd
promised Marshall to spy on her.

"Well, I need to take a trip to the city," he informed her. "Maybe
you'd like to come with. I'm going to the Dallas art mu-se-um. You
just might learn something if you're not too careful." He quoted Bill
Cosby from his animated cartoon show, *Fat Albert*. He knew it
would pique her interest.

"Hmmm, let me think. Stay here and grow old with these text-
books or take a joy ride to Big D. That's a hard one."

"Oh, no, you must have me confused with some other man. I'm
gonna educate you on the finest things this life has to offer: the arts.
Ain't gonna be no joy ride. I hope you got your parental permission
slip, because this is a field trip."

"Okay, you sold me. I would love to go, just promise me one
thing."

Legacy studied her face momentarily, then asked what that one
thing was. "Yeah . . . what's so important?"

She could barely contain herself while thinking about it. "That
we'll have to stop in Deep Ellum and pick up some of Uncle Otto's
fried pies."

Legacy laughed at how the pies must have held extreme significance for her. "Sure, I live near there. We can get as many as you
want."

During their excursion to Dallas, they shared stories about their
first year in college and found they had a lot in common. He respected her and thought to himself that she just might've been the
smartest African-American female college student he'd ever met, and
he wondered if she looked at him as a white boy because he wasn't
black. He would learn in time that she did often wonder what racial
category he belonged in, but she also respected him, regardless of
how his ancestors arrived in America. Whether it was above deck
or cradled in the belly of a slave ship, she was much too sensitive
to delve into something as deep as ethnicity. Besides, some people

are touchy about race, especially if their ethnic background involved more than one. She could tell that his did.

When they stopped along the way at Deloache's convenience store to purchase the fried pies she'd raved about, Jasmine asked him why she never saw him with anyone. Male or female. "I've seen you on the yard before this term, but I can't ever recall seeing you with anyone in particular. You a loner or something?"

His expression saddened. "I never had much use for a lot of friends. Plus, when I was growing up, I would get caught up in my work sometimes and stay indoors for weeks. Kids my age thought I was strange. They were probably right."

"I'm sorry to hear that. Kids can be so cruel." She took a bite out of a pineapple-flavored fried pie. "Hey, I was wondering how you know Marshall. You know, since you're not a jock."

"Everyone knows Marshall, he's the biggest thing to hit UTC since integration. His name and yours comes up a lot in general conversation, mostly in the same sentence. And when I met you in class, I knew you had to be the one special enough to hook a talented brotha like him."

She smiled. "Taught him everything he knows. Now he's dangerous, too. But what about you?" She thought better about asking him his personal business, but she couldn't take the words back. There was something about him that made her want to get to know him better. Not sexually, just better.

"What about me?" he snapped, with playful street attitude.

"Whose name comes up in sentences with yours?" she responded, just as playfully.

Legacy looked at the ground, then smiled at Jasmine like a second-grade boy with a crush on the little freckled-face girl at the head of the class. "I have this particular woman in mind, but I can't seem to get next to her. I'm not even sure what I'd say if I ever got the chance to."

Jasmine nodded. "Good for you, Freelance. What? Is she a junior? Senior?"

"No, she lives here in Dallas." He assumed. "I guess she does."

She looked curiously at him. "You don't know? Let me guess. She has no idea you exist?"

"Yeah, I paid a fifty-cent toll fee for her once."

"Well, that almost makes you engaged," she joked.

"Hey, how'd you know? How'd you know she doesn't know me?"

Jasmine bit off another piece of pie. " 'Cause if she did, she'd already be yours," she replied, with a knowing wink.

He explained his part-time job and that he was too shy to ask his dream lady out on a date when he saw her. Besides, it would have been next to impossible to ask a woman out for dinner all those times she whizzed through the toll lane with her window rolled up.

Legacy's trip with Jasmine was one of enlightenment, as their new friendship broke ground; however, there was a glitch in the program. The art museum was closed for the remainder of the week due to renovations. The sign posted on the front door listed several area galleries temporarily housing pieces from their art exhibit until the construction was completed. Legacy knew where all the galleries were. He remembered there was one he hadn't had a chance to visit before, even though it was near the tollway on Northwest Highway.

On the way back to the office, Kennedy apprehensively confided in Morris that she didn't feel real comfortable about having anal intercourse with Simpson, although she had allowed it to happen more than a few times. Morris was embarrassed to share intimate sexual details with a heterosexual female, but they were becoming closer each day. In his infinite wisdom, though blushing and trying to seem unaffected by the whole conversation, he offered her words to live by. "If you really have a problem with back-door action, then don't give up the booty. And I mean that literally."

Kennedy giggled at his comment but understood how serious Morris was as well as what he said. They'd spent the last three hours in a team meeting with Mr. Johansen, a dry coming together to share projected earnings. Both Morris and Kennedy were subjected to fighting tooth and nail to stay awake. Mr. Johansen did finally show a bit of compassion when he allowed them to take a one-function break, just enough time to take care of one issue. Whether it was a rest room visit, to make a short phone call, or to refuel with fresh caffeine. Both of them decided on the latter.

They bolted out of the meeting and raced to the break room. Morris entered the small room first. He estimated the coffee's shelf life had long since expired, it was as thick and murky as muddy water. Kennedy pulled out two one-dollar bills from the pocket of her suit coat. "Almond Joy or Mounds bar?" she asked, as she headed for the vending machine.

Morris continued to methodically set up the coffee machine for its brewing sequence. Without stopping to give her question much notice, he answered very matter-of-factly. "Girl, please, Almond Joy's got nuts, Mounds don't."

"And sometimes you feel like a nut, sometimes you don't," Kennedy chimed in playfully.

Morris looked up after placing his coffee cup underneath the drip spout. He suggestively replied, "I always do," as he snapped his fingers twice over his head.

"Why do I encourage this?" Kennedy said rhetorically. "I've got to sneak in another function before we get back." She fed fifty cents to the soda machine, took her Diet Coke, and started toward the door. "I'll see you back there? I'm about to burst."

Kennedy exited the break area, making a beeline toward the rest room. Her arms were swinging as fast as they could to keep up with her fast-paced stride when she bumped the can of soda against her thigh and accidentally flung it in the air. She scrambled to catch it before it fell to the floor but inadvertently popped it up and over the upstairs railing. The soda can flipped and twirled downward toward the gallery level as Kennedy leaned over the rail with outstretched arms. Panic struck an alarming chord deep down in the base of her spine. It was headed for two people studying some of the works in the David Park exhibit from Berkeley, California.

She yelled out to warn them. "Nnnnnno!"

They looked up from below in time to dodge it. Splat! The soda can exploded on impact, then hissed like an angry snake. She dashed down the staircase as quickly as she could to apologize to the couple. "I'm sorry, please forgive me. It was an accident."

She looked at the large puddle seeping from the busted soda can onto the floor. The man standing there graciously accepted her apology. He looked familiar, but Kennedy couldn't place him. The woman with him didn't seem quite as accepting, nor had Kennedy ever laid eyes on her before. The two of them standing there, dodging the killer beverage, were Jasmine and Legacy. In a strange twist of fate, he had come face-to-face with the one woman he dreamed about, completed several sketches of, and adored.

Morris, Mr. Johansen, and others crowded around to assess the damage, which mostly consisted of frazzled nerves. Fortunately, they were minimal. A maintenance worker appeared and quickly attended to the mess. Kennedy continued to sneak brief glances at Legacy. She was sure she knew him.

Jasmine sensed an obvious but ignored chemistry between the two of them and thought it was odd that neither seemed willing to delve into the obvious. They were both interested, that was the obvious part, but neither Legacy nor Kennedy pursued the opportunity to move forward with something that immediately took on a life of its own, and that was peculiar.

Jasmine decided to break the ice. "Oh, it's really not a problem. We come to art galleries all the time when we're running low on excitement. By the way, I'm Jasmine. And my shy colleague here is Freelance."

Instantly, Legacy was caught in the midst of a bad case of cottonmouth. It surprised him that Jasmine initiated the conversation. "Uh, actually, it's Legacy," he said, with an excitable grin.

Placing her hands on her hips, Jasmine lowered her head. "Legacy . . . ," she repeated, now almost laughing. "Your name is—"

"I think Legacy is a wonderful name," said Kennedy. "I'm

pleased to meet you, Legacy and Jasmine. I'm Kennedy." She continued making subtle eye contact with him. "And again, I'm sorry. Now if you'll excuse me." She took one long last look at him before she headed up the staircase.

Morris had been sent out to find her in order to resume the meeting. He saw the whole sordid mopping-up incident. He was glad not to have missed it. "You should be ashamed of yourself. You hussy, you," Morris teased, as soon as she climbed the stairs. "First, you almost maim the poor couple, then you shamelessly flirt with girlfriend's man."

"I wasn't flirting. You can't really call that flirting. Anyway, that wasn't her man, although she is a smart one. She introduced herself as his colleague only to allow me the freedom to browse without causing static."

"Well, how was it? The once-over," Morris asked.

"So nice, I did it twice," she answered with an air of confidence.

"I know you did. Boyfriend was fine. That exotic Mediterranean look is hot this year."

"Don't fool yourself, Morris. Looks like his are never out of season."

They laughed and pretended to fan themselves as they returned to the boring meeting on the second floor. Kennedy's homeless smile subsided before the moment had expired on its own. Thoughts about Simpson looming in the background brought her back to her dim reality. She loved a man, deeply, but for all the wrong reasons, and she still didn't clearly know why.

Legacy pulled Jasmine outside the art gallery without saying a word. She found herself on the sidewalk of St. Paul Avenue wondering what happened or what she'd missed. Legacy stared at her with a glare of contempt. His dark-brown eyes were cold and still. She looked back at him curiously.

"What?" She shrugged her shoulders.

"What?" he repeated. "You know what you just did? You . . . you just introduced me to the woman I'm gonna marry." As his serious glare transformed into a joyous, beaming smile, he reached out to give her a big hug. "That's what you did. Jasmine, I owe you big time. Whoo-hooo!"

"Wait a minute . . ." she uttered. "Calm down. Wait a min-ute. Before you met Miss uh . . . I'm-so-sorry-I-almost-killed-y'all, you were telling me how some other woman had you all twisted. Some tollway mystery lady. Remember her?"

Legacy pulled up on his belt and tucked in his shirt with the other hand as if he had just closed a profitable business deal. "Yep, yep, yep, little lady. That's the beauty of it. She's the one. The One. The same one I've been telling you about. Now, thanks to you, I know her name. Kennedy, and it's a beautiful name, might I add. I know where she works and I know that she is *foy'n*! Jasmine, you've got to help me get that woman." All the way back to the parking lot, he asked for her assistance. Then he continued begging her help after they were in his jeep and on their way back to the campus.

"I don't know, Leeeegacy," Jasmine taunted playfully. "Looks like you might be too far gone for me. You got it bad."

He looked at her anxiously, then asked, "I've got what bad?"

"A bad case of 'I've fallen and I don't want to get up.' One of the worst cases I've ever seen. And I've seen plenty. I don't know, Freelance, you seem desperate and I don't deal with desperation, on any level."

She was adamant about not getting mixed up in something that serious, something that she didn't have control of. She had seen her older sister stalked to within an inch of her life, thanks to an over-zealous admiring coworker who couldn't seem to comprehend the words "Hell no!" She had also seen too many just-add-water instant relationships fail before the lovers could spell each other's last name right.

"You don't understand," he explained. "I need that woman in my life. I don't know why. And I'm not mental, either, but I knew that our paths would cross the first time I saw her go through the toll lane. Thousands of women pass through every day, but I knew she had to be the one."

Jasmine studied him up and down, then flashed him an approving crooked smirk. "I hope I'm not wrong about getting involved in this." She may have regretted it somewhere down the line, but she wished the best for Legacy and wanted to give him a few pointers on what women really like.

"Thank you, thank you. You won't regret it, Jasmine. I promise you won't," he reassured her, as they headed down the forty-mile stretch of Interstate 35.

Eighteen

Day-Old Cookies

The heavy steel bar came down slowly. Marshall exhaled and pressed the two hundred and fifty pounds off his chest for the tenth repetition. His workout was completed. After a routine training session, he had worked out his powerful thighs, muscular biceps, and his tremendously shapely chest that looked strong enough to protect the world's finest cargo.

After a few moments of noting the progress from his heavy weight lifting in the full wall mirror, he pulled a thick sweatshirt over his head, then collected his things before stuffing them into his gym bag. Like always, he had the full attention of several female students also working out in the Physical Education building. One young lady wearing spandex tights and a matching leotard stopped him at the water fountain. She wanted an autograph and his phone number. She got them both, slipped him hers, and promised to call soon.

As soon as Marshall stepped out the exit door, Shauni appeared in shorts too tight to be legal and a thin windbreaker over a crop top. It had to be less than forty-five degrees out, but it wasn't obvious by what she had on. Marshall cordially spoke and engaged in a little small talk as she flirted hopelessly, but he didn't have the time to entertain the same thoughts that danced around in her head. The kind of dancing that happens underneath silk sheets. He had become a busy man, too busy for her, anyway. He had bigger fish to fry. Marshall wrapped a large towel around his head, then climbed into the passenger side of a red Mercedes-Benz parked at the curb. He kissed the driver on the lips just before the car pulled away.

The Quadrangle Mall was busy, just as it always was due to twenty-seven thousand college students in the midst of a typical college town. Jasmine stacked the last of the fleece warm-ups on the sale table. She had worked part-time as the assistant manager at the Lady Footlocker for the past two years, but her tour of duty was up. She punched her time clock for the last time. Preparing for upcoming career interviews and university recruitment workshops was imminent and more important. She told the manager she was grateful for the opportunity, collected her things, and headed toward the exit door of the mall.

Marshall found himself thirsty after the lengthy exercise and wanted more than water to drink. The nearby 7-Eleven was just the place he needed to get what he wanted to quench his thirst, a twenty-four-ounce strawberry-lemonade-flavored Snapple, his favorite. While he was in the store trying to select the coldest bottle possible, Heretta Malveaux stepped out of the Mercedes to see what was taking him so long.

Coincidentally, Jasmine decided she'd stop by the same convenience store to get coins for the copier at the library. When the light changed, she drove into the store's parking lot and parked next to the red Benz. She noted how nice and shiny the car was before she realized who it belonged to. Just as she did, she looked inside the large glass window and saw Marshall with his arms wrapped tightly around Ms. Malveaux as he kissed her playfully on the neck, much like he'd kissed her softly for the past three years. She was in shock and her lips became incredibly dry. The large lump that started in her throat quickly sank deeply into the pit of her stomach. Jasmine was devastated and confused about what to do. The rage within her suggested she storm into that store, give Ms. Malveaux a piece of her mind and a fat lip, and take her man back. But the pain weighed heavier on her heart than the two hundred and fifty pounds Marshall bench-pressed earlier.

Something from deep within Jasmine compelled her to stay in the car and fight back the tears. She knew she would have lost every shred of her dignity had she burst in the store and caused a major scene. It might have been worth all the drama to rip some of the hair off that tramp's lip. On the other hand, she figured Marshall was a big boy and had made his choice. Although it wasn't supposed to happen like that. They were to be married and live happily ever after with a picket fence and all the other grandiose imagery that went along with a fairy-tale marriage. How could it all have gone wrong, she thought. When did it all go wrong?

Before she knew it, she had peeled out of the lot and sped down College Street toward the library with tears streaming down her face. It was awful, simply awful, for her to find out that way. Marshall was giving his time to another woman, other women. But she knew now and had some choices of her own to make.

Legacy was at the computer when Jasmine made her way into the library's entrance on the first floor. He was gathering additional information for his term paper when she whizzed by him. Even though she almost bumped into him, she didn't have the slightest idea he was there.

Eventually, he pulled all the data off the printer and started out in the direction she'd headed in. After searching the rows of books and periodicals in the basement and coming up empty, he thought she might be in the women's rest room. He stood outside the door for a couple of seconds, uncertain about whether he should risk it and go in or not. He had finally worked up enough courage to barge right in to find her. As he took a deep breath and placed his hand over his eyes, he heard sobbing coming from the other side of a huge shelved wall of books. He approached with caution and wasn't quite sure of what he might find. A few more steps revealed Jasmine with her head in her hands sitting against the shelf with her books sprawled out on the floor. She was distraught and looked as if she had just witnessed someone's violent death. In an indirect, twisted sort of way, she did: the end of her relationship with Marshall.

Legacy quietly looked on. He was apprehensive about going over to comfort her. What if she didn't want him to? The concern he felt crossed the line of classmates and forced him to react and do what was right in his heart.

Slowly, he walked over to her and dropped to his knees. "Hey, you all right?" he asked softly.

She looked up at him with a river of effortless tears pouring from her sad brown eyes. "Uhhh, Freelance." She was startled and tried to wipe away the tears, but it was a futile effort. She just further smeared her mascara. "Where'd you come from? I'm sorry. I thought I was alone."

"I saw you zoom past me and thought maybe I should see if I could help. I don't mean to get in your business, but you looked like you could use someone to talk to."

The tears subsided eventually, but she was still a nervous wreck pretending to be over whatever had her in such bad shape. It wasn't too believable. After she cleaned up her face, she filled him in on the torrid details and reflected a lot on how it used to be.

Once she began to cry again, he tried to convince her to be strong. That's what he had always been told as an orphan and in the military. Be tough, don't show your emotions or it will be seen as a weakness and a character flaw. He couldn't remember the last time he cried or for what reason, but it had to have been when he was a young boy. He wasn't sure that it was even possible for him to cry, but it didn't matter. It wasn't his tears he was concerned about.

"I've got something that should cheer you up." He had a suggestion that was so far off the wall that it just might work. "I know of this little bakery not far from here that sells day-old cookies half price. My treat."

"Day-old cookies?" she said, with a look of contempt. "You think you can bribe me and distract my feelings with some day-old cookies?"

He smirked and felt stupid after realizing how ridiculous it must have sounded, considering all she had been through, but he had offered it and he meant it. "Well, yeah."

Jasmine contemplated a while. "They have oatmeal raisin?"

"Sure they do. They've got all the oatmeal raisin cookies you can eat." He sounded so sure, you'd have thought he took inventory. In actuality, he had no idea what cookies they had left over.

"You buying?" Her interest was piquing.

"Of course, I'm buying. I said I was treating, didn't I?"

Jasmine perked up. "I just love day-old cookies."

"Come on, then. Let's pick up these books before someone sees you and thinks you were crying your eyes out."

"Who, me? I always cry my eyes out and make a fool of myself like this. You should see the fool I make of myself when I don't like the lunch menu at the cafeteria."

The cookies were delicious, even at a day old. After five or six oatmeal raisins, Jasmine opened up and elaborated on her wounded love for a man who was losing himself in his sorrow for Rorey and a newfound determination to catch up for lost time in the woman-hopping department. Any way she looked at it, Marshall was surely lost.

Legacy knew he would eventually be caught in the middle between Jasmine and Marshall. He wanted to be fair and impartial but didn't know if he could be. Marshall had asked him to keep an eye on his woman while he tended to other so-called business and had also spoken up for him and saved his neck in the locker room after Rorey's funeral. On the other hand, Jasmine did help him to understand other cultures, women, and himself better. She'd explained how real women wanted to be treated and respected. And when he divulged he'd felt like he had been pushed around his whole life, she made him promise that when adversity struck, he'd start pushing back. His loyalty drifted to Jasmine, hands down.

Nineteen

You Again

*L*egacy *marched up the stairs* to the administrative offices of Johansen's Art Gallery with one dozen long-stemmed yellow roses. He didn't know what he'd say when he reached the top of the stairs and would have to ask for the beautiful lady he dreamed about getting to know, although he had rehearsed it many times during his shifts at the tollbooth. With each step he took, the tension mounted exponentially. He was nervous, but he was tired of not having enough nerve to step out and get the things he wanted. Jasmine was enduring the ending of the kind of love affair most people only dreamed about, and he hadn't once experienced it for himself. This was it; his time to grasp the brass ring had come.

When Legacy climbed the last step and found himself walking toward the business reception desk, a man had his head buried in the leading national tabloid magazine. It was Morris engrossed in some story about cloning two-headed potbellied pigs in Arkansas, so he didn't look up immediately to acknowledge Legacy approaching his workstation.

"Pork, it's the other white meat," Morris said aloud, before he realized he wasn't alone. "That's cute."

Legacy hid the flowers behind his back, but Morris saw a couple of them sticking out from behind his jacket. "Hello," Morris greeted, with a big smile. "You can leave those beautiful roses here. I'll sign for them." He obviously assumed Legacy was a delivery person.

"Nnnno," Legacy muttered, "I think they need to be delivered personally."

"Well, I guess that'll be okay. Who are they for?"

Legacy's nervousness multiplied even more. "They're for, uh . . . Kennedy." He felt stupid when Morris looked at him, expecting him to say her full name.

"Kennedy, huh?" Morris grew suspicious. "Kennedy James?"

Legacy exhaled and nodded emphatically. "Yes. That's right. Kennedy James." Knowing her last name made him feel better somehow. Almost connected. "Is she in?"

Morris answered as emphatically as Legacy asked him. "Yes. She is. And I'll get her for you, Mr . . . ?"

"Oh, uh . . . Mr. Childs."

Morris was sure he had seen him somewhere before. He gave Legacy a long, hard once-over, the kind of once-over that would have made any straight man uneasy. It was the type of head-to-toe-and-back-down-again that considered what Legacy might be like in bed. "Are you sure I don't know you?" he asked, after he stood from his chair.

"No," Legacy answered most assuredly, in a homophobic tone. "I'm real sure we've never met."

As Morris forwarded his telephone lines to a prerecorded voice message detailing the gallery's business hours and current exhibits, he continued to stare at Legacy but now suspiciously, then stepped into a nearby office. Legacy let out a deep sigh of relief and began pacing in small circles.

Kennedy was on the telephone when Morris ducked into her office and closed the door behind him. She was in the middle of getting information about an artist who wanted to tour the Southwest, especially Dallas. Morris pressed his back against the door and wrapped his arms around himself as he proceeded to caress his own shoulders in a comically provocative manner to get Kennedy's attention. She eventually looked up from her notes with a perplexed, what-in-the-hell-is-going-on-with-you look on her face. After he had her attention, he began to entertain her with a sultry rendition of a calypso lover's two-step, implying it was about to be on.

She attempted to shoo him away by pointing at the phone, but he was relentless. The more she shooed, the harder he sambaed until her expression revealed she had become quite a bit more curious than perplexed. "I'm sorry . . . ," she apologized into the speaking end of the telephone. "Can you hold on a moment, please?"

As she pressed the hold button and moved the receiver away from her mouth, she shouted at him for carrying on while she tried to conduct business. "Morris! Have you lost your mind? I'm on the phone and you—"

"I am the bearer of good news," he announced heartily, "that's who I am. And you'd better change your tone or I just might forget to inform you that there is a gorgeous flower delivery man outside with one dozen long-stemmed roses for guess who."

Kennedy pressed the hold button to reconnect with the party waiting on the line. "Thanks for holding. Something just came up. Can I get back with you later on for the details? Thanks. I'll call you back this afternoon."

Morris placed his hands on his hips with an air of an arrogant know-it-all. "Should I send him away?"

"Why is he still out there? You usually sign for them and send the delivery guys packing."

"First of all, this one is too fine to send anywhere, unless it's to my place with the house key, okaaaay. Secondly, he doesn't seem like the type who could be sent away. And thirdly . . . ," he said before pausing, "when I did offer to sign for them, he said they had to be delivered, and I quote, per-son-ally. End quote. At any rate, he is out there waiting to deliver them, himself."

Kennedy stood up from her desk and walked around it to see what all the fuss was about. "Did he say who sent them?"

"Not a word. But he did say that Mr. Childs was his name. After you come on out, you'll understand why that's all you'll need to know," he said with assurance. "And oh, don't come running out like you know what's going on."

"That'll be easy. I don't know what's going on."

Morris straightened his clothes and primped his short hair with his fingers as if Legacy were waiting in the foyer to see him. His smile overshadowed his ploy to act natural when he returned. "She'll be right with you, Mr. Childs. You can have a seat if you like."

Legacy took Morris up on the offer. As soon as his butt landed in the chair, he felt like a small boy waiting for the principal to come in and execute his punishment. Waiting was murder. Knots formed in his stomach.

Morris looked up occasionally, giggling quietly to himself when he did. The whole scene put him in the mind of a young couple's first-date jitters.

Kennedy strutted out of her office with a plain expression, which was hard to keep after she saw him, immediately realizing he was the same man she almost injured days before with the runaway soda can. Morris could see that she liked what she saw, as she did when she made his acquaintance the last time he was there, although she pretended not to remember him.

"Hi. Mr. Childs," she said effortlessly, while extending her arms to receive the roses. "I understand someone sent me flowers."

Legacy handed them to her as if they were an Academy Award. One she had worked tirelessly for. "You don't remember me, do you?" he asked, with a tone that affirmed his embarrassment.

She remembered him, all right, she just didn't let on at the risk of seeming too anxious.

"They're beautiful." She drew the bright-yellow floral arrangement close to her nose and breathed in. "I'm sorry, what was that?"

Morris snickered louder than he meant to when he witnessed Kennedy's sappy but successful Oscar-caliber performance of coy. It was so loud, in fact, he placed his hands over his mouth and turned his face away. Legacy was already uncomfortable as it was. Morris's obtrusions made it almost unbearable.

"I was saying that uh . . . I just thought you would have remembered me, but I guess I was mistaken." Legacy took a couple of slow backward steps when he felt he had made a foolish mistake showing up at her office with flowers in hand. What a schmuck, he thought of himself. "Maybe I should just go." With a lump in his throat, he muttered just above a whisper, "I'm sorry to have wasted your time."

When he turned around to walk toward the staircase, Morris sprang up from his chair and flashed a disappointing, frightful, clenched-teeth grimace at Kennedy. He'd seen her initial reaction when she laid eyes on him, and he knew her well enough to know that she was interested, very interested. What he couldn't understand was why she was letting him slip through her fingers, as fine as he was.

Legacy never felt so dejected before. When he bought the roses, it seemed like the right thing to do. Jasmine had pumped him up and convinced him to be assertive, but it seemed to have blown up in his face.

Kennedy smiled back at him and silently mouthed "Chill out" in Morris's direction. As she carefully watched him approaching the top stair, Morris panicked and placed his hands over his eyes. He couldn't stand to watch this man vanish as easily as he appeared. "Legacy!" Kennedy called out, loud enough to get his attention.

Legacy stopped and turned toward her, confused. It sounded like she called his name, but he had to be mistaken. Just moments before, she didn't seem to have a clue who he was. He was reluctant to say anything. What if it was only his imagination? What if he merely thought she called his name, and he would only further embarrass himself? But it wasn't his imagination. She called out again.

"Legacy. That is your name, right? Or should I call you Freelance?"

Morris and Legacy both shared the same dumbfounded expression. Neither knew what was going on, but Legacy was the first to speak.

"Legacy will do just fine," he answered, still puzzled but smiling.

Kennedy started out toward him, with Morris following closely behind. "Are you going to leave before I get a chance to thank you for the roses? They're yellow, for friendship. How sweet." She was standing a close two feet away.

"You're very welcome," he replied, without hesitation.

Kennedy changed her approach after being drawn to his seemingly shy ways. "Did you come all the way up here just to deliver flowers, or was there something else you wanted?"

Morris flashed a confused frown when Kennedy dropped the coy act and went for the gold. He didn't know what to make of it. Initially, she acted as if she didn't know her visitor, then she called him by name, and when it seemed certain she wasn't interested, she came out with this Mrs. Robinson routine. It was like a bad episode of *Friends,* nothing made sense. Morris was in the dark as long as he could take it, then he snapped. "Wait . . . wait . . . wait a minute." He insisted that he be debriefed. "Not another word until somebody explains to me what's going on here."

"Haven't you been keeping up, Morris? Mr. Childs was here last week. He and his girlfriend . . ." Kennedy explained.

"Colleague," Legacy corrected.

"That's right, he and his *colleague,*" Kennedy repeated, for sake of emphasis. "They were viewing the David Park collection downstairs and I almost took them out with my soda can. You remember, Morris."

Morris's eyes widened. "That's right! I knew I had seen you before. I never forget a . . . well, never mind what, but I never forget one." Kennedy smirked at Morris, who noted her objection of his comment as he quickly dismissed himself from their company. "I think I'd better leave you two alone," he suggested. "I think I may have already overstayed my welcome. Toodles . . ."

"So, Mr. Childs," Kennedy continued, "why did you come back here today?"

Remarkably, all the nervousness he'd felt earlier and the remnants of dejection had mysteriously faded away. She laid it all out on the table for him. He had rehearsed it a thousand times in order to prepare himself if he ever got the chance to get this far. Well, this was it. He took a deep breath, then took his best shot.

"As a matter of fact, I did come with more in mind than just delivering flowers. I think you're a beautiful woman and I would be honored if you'd allow me to get to know you better. Are you available for dinner?" It came out just as he'd practiced it, without a hitch.

She was impressed. He was direct and to the point without a hint of apprehension. He knew what he wanted, and with a decent opportunity, he asked for it. Kennedy sized him up and liked what her brief evaluation rendered. "I'm not available. I am seeing someone at the moment, but . . . I am free tomorrow night. If . . . you promise this will be a simple friendship date, I would love to accompany you."

Legacy was overwhelmed with excitement, but he couldn't afford to show it. He'd finally met his dream woman and secured a date. A friendship date or not, it was still quality time with her, Ms. Blue Mustang. He would get an opportunity to get to know her, how she thought, and what things she thought about. They exchanged phone numbers and found it was mutually agreeable to share a meal together.

Twenty

Can You Blame Her?

The wind seemed to blow a little calmer, a little sweeter the following day as Legacy sat on the bench outside the General Business building. His mind was on Kennedy and making the best of perhaps his only shot at what he considered heaven on earth. Her. The anticipation was resounding within him but comforting at the same time. And he couldn't wait until Jasmine returned from her job interview in Houston. He wanted to fill her in and thank her for helping him work through his situation. That's what friends are for. Sometimes we're not strong enough to maneuver through our own road hazards but can exude more than enough direction for our friends in need.

It was eleven o'clock when Marshall exited the business building with a few students and saw Legacy. He brushed the students off and plopped down on the bench. "Freelance, where you been, man?

I thought you were supposed to be keeping an eye on my honey for me. Something's up, 'cause she's been tripping lately and igging me."

"Oh, yeah, Jasmine," Legacy remembered. "I've been thinking about that, Marshall, and I ain't really down with it."

"Don't shortchange me, Freelance. I thought we were tight like that."

"Yeah, we're still tight, but not like that. Jasmine is a great girl and I owe her a lot. She got my back and—"

"She got your back!" Marshall shouted. "What you mean, she got your back? Is that why she's tripping on me, 'cause she got your back?"

"Nahhh, that's not what I'm saying at all. She's putting in work to hook me up with a potentially serious female situation. But even if she wasn't, she deserves better than me playing Columbo."

Marshall looked away in disgust. Although he knew Legacy was right, it didn't help his situation any. His jaws were still tight. "So you and Jazz are tight like that now?"

"Just like that," Legacy answered, with certainty and fearlessness. The attitude with which the smaller Legacy answered assured Marshall something had happened with Legacy, Jasmine, and their relationship. His pride wouldn't let him conceive the thought of his woman sharing her time with another man, but she hadn't bothered to return his calls, nor did she have much to say when he did catch her at home.

Marshall leaned forward, rested his elbows on his thighs, and briefly massaged his temples. "My bad, man. I didn't mean to accuse you of getting with my girl, but I can't figure it out. It ain't like it used to be. She ain't trying to give a brotha no time."

"Can you blame her? How do you think a woman is supposed to take seeing you wrapped up with another one?" he asked rhetorically. "You broke her heart, man."

"What are you talking about? Who got busted?" He had no idea why Jasmine had been avoiding him. What's more appalling, he was too caught up in his other business in the streets to pay attention to what was going on at home.

Legacy leaned away from him to get a good look at his face. "You really don't know, do you? Jasmine busted you at the store slobbing down Ms. Malveaux."

Marshall raised his head and looked at Legacy in disbelief. "She saw it? You're sure?"

"She told me herself. Crying, cussing, the whole bit. You may as well change your name 'cause Marshall Coates ain't never getting back in there."

Marshall popped off the bench and began pacing back and forth, ranting while Legacy watched silently and shaking his head. "I've gotta fix this. I've gotta . . . she's coming back from Houston on Saturday, right?"

Legacy smirked. "As far as I know."

"Well, that gives me a couple of more days to worry about that. In the meanwhile, I gots other business to tend to. Know what I'm saying? 'Preciate the heads up on that, though."

Making a mental note, Marshall concluded that he didn't intend to make any wholesale changes in the way he'd been handling business; at least, not in the next couple of days. Things had changed between him and Jasmine because of the decisions he had made for himself. He couldn't even recognize himself anymore, nor could he remember who he used to be.

Remo's on Oak Lawn was a popular see-and-be-seen eatery. The food was good but the atmosphere was better. All the yuppie Dallasites frequented it. Kennedy, a buppie in her own right, was no exception. She had grown quite familiar with the upscale restaurant while spending many evenings there with Simpson when they were seeing each other regularly.

Legacy wandered in behind a crowd of people sipping cocktails from the busy bar while they waited to get a table. Lines were good for business and the employees were well trained to take their sweet time seating empty tables. It was expected. Legacy looked around the restaurant, but it was too active for him to see if Kennedy had already arrived. She had. A cute, petite redheaded hostess dressed all in black approached him and asked if he was there to dine with Kennedy James. When he nodded that he was, she escorted him past several tables decorated with appetizing menu items and attractive customers. Cigarette smoke charged him when he turned the corner and entered into the section nearest to the back door, the smoking section.

Kennedy stood up and smiled when he arrived at the table she'd commandeered just before he got there. "Hi, Legacy, I'm glad you made it. The food here is great."

"Hello, you been here long?" He was quite happy to see her again.

"No, just got here a little while ago, but I know Cinnamon, the hostess. We use the same hairstylist."

"I guess it does pay to know the right people," he said assuredly. "I heard them say it was a forty-five-minute wait up front."

Kennedy quickly took her seat, then reached for the burning cigarette resting on the ledge of the glass ashtray sitting on the table. Legacy hadn't noticed it until then. Cigarette smoking repulsed him, but he'd just met her and if he wanted to see her again, he thought maybe he'd better play safe and endure it.

After she took a drag on the cigarette and blew the smoke out, she offered him one. That presented him with an opportunity to ask her to put it out, but instead, he simply declined. He wanted to say, "Hell no, I wouldn't like to kill myself slowly, but thank you anyway."

The waiter stopped by the table. He introduced himself and wrote his name upside down, Tom, on the white paper tablecloth so that they could read it right side up, then he took their drink orders. She asked for a glass of chardonnay; her date opted for light beer. Tom the waiter nodded and immediately excused himself.

Before they fell any deeper into small talk, Kennedy looked as if she were surveying the items on their table. Legacy noticed her doing it and began looking over the table, too. "What, do you need something?" he asked.

"Well, I was just looking for more flowers," she joked. "That is what you do, right, bring flowers?"

He chuckled, appreciating her wit. He began checking his pockets as if he were expecting to find some flowers in them. After he looked under the table and underneath his seat, he responded, "I can't seem to find them anywhere, but I'm sure I brought in a couple of dozen or so with me. Maybe they're in my wallet. I could check."

They shared a good laugh. It started as a great beginning, one that he'd longed for. She told him where she was from and the funny story about missing her train to Chicago and getting stuck over the weekend in Dallas, her assimilation into the Texas culture, and a difficult adaptation to the extreme hot and cold weather. Legacy was more evasive, but he did divulge the first time he ever saw her at the tollway. She was embarrassed that she didn't recognize him from the time she'd wrecked her car and he'd graciously tossed fifty cents in the basket on her behalf. Then he talked all around his past, which was nothing like hers, so he focused mostly on his love for art, something they both had in common.

Over an hour had passed before she realized Simpson had not crossed her mind. Not once. When the thought of him did occur to her, she felt guilty and wondered what she would do if he walked up and caught her having dinner with another man. Then she remembered seeing his expensive Porsche parked at Winfrey's. As soon as she did, his car and the thought of him vanished from her mind as suddenly as they entered it.

By the end of dinner, Legacy had sketched a flattering portrait of her on the white paper tablecloth. Actually, it was pretty good, considering he had to do it with the crayon the waiter used to write his name with. She was surprised he was so talented and more than impressed that he took the time to create her image. What she didn't know was that he had done it in his mind hundreds of times before. Her image was etched in his memory.

The check came and Kennedy offered to pay for her own meal and one glass of wine, which she didn't even finish, but he wouldn't hear of it. It wasn't that she wanted to prove she was a modern woman, it was more of a gesture to remind him it was strictly a friendship date. He picked up on it and let her know that he did.

"If you like, you can treat me next time. That's what friends do, right?"

"Right." She agreed with a naughty leer as she lit up another cigarette. "But who said there would be a next time?"

He was pretty sure of himself, and the evening had gone better than she had expected, too. She knew as well as he did that there would surely be a next time. All was well until Legacy began fanning the smoke away from his face. She was offended that her smoke offended him. Without displaying any hint of emotion, she asked, "Is there a problem?"

Legacy was confronted again with his severe distaste for smokers and an opportunity to say what had been on his mind all evening. He had a decision to make, shut up and pretend not to have a problem with something he despised, or risk a chance at furthering the relationship by speaking up and telling her what he really thought about her habit. Before he could decide, he blurted out what was on his mind.

"Yeah, as a matter of fact, I do have a problem. I think you're much too beautiful to be sitting there with that cigarette sticking out of your head."

Kennedy was taken aback and didn't know quite what to say. "Oh, you do, do you?" was her best effort.

"As a matter of fact, I do. And I also think that people who smoke cigarettes are killing themselves. Or maybe they won't kill you right away, maybe they'll just shrivel up your lungs like little dried prunes and make your life and the lives of those who care about you a living hell."

His short dissertation was poignant. It contained merit as well as truth, but she wasn't stirred up enough to put it out. Instead, she took another long drag and blew a dense stream of smoke across the table, directly in his face. The stale air around them thickened along with the tension, which attempted to wedge itself between them. "Oh, that's . . . that's really cute," he said sarcastically, before laughing out. "And you're so talented."

She felt the strain but laughed as well. It seemed like the thing to do at the time. They'd just met, had one dinner, and were fighting like old lovers. An instant bond was forged from it. Kennedy didn't know what to think about this brash young aspiring artist who worked part-time at the tollbooth near her office. She thought his comments about smoking were out of line, but she kind of liked it. It reminded her of the way Morris fussed, more out of compassion for her than for contempt of what she did. So she gave him that victory but didn't concede the war.

"Listen up, Freelance . . ." Freelance, ooh, that left a mark. "We've had a nice time tonight and I would like to see you again, as friends. But I don't want to if you're going to preach at me for lighting up. I'm a big girl and I know what I'm doing. I like to smoke, it makes me feel good."

Legacy saw the road ahead and it was dusty and unpaved. He had more to sort out than he anticipated. Perhaps this was too early in the game to go for the win.

Jasmine talked to her mother on the telephone as she lay across her bed looking over business letters she retrieved from her mailbox when she returned to town. "Momma, I know it sounds like a good opportunity, but I'm still not sure," she reasoned, as she sighed into the telephone receiver. "No, I shouldn't talk to Marshall about it. It has nothing to do with Marshall. Besides, he's got other things on his mind. I already told you he wasn't ready for what I need. Somehow, he's not the same man I used to know. I've gotten over it, now you and Daddy need to. Yes, Mother, but I won't promise you anything. I'll tell him if I see him. Gotta run. Love you, bye."

Jasmine received a job offer to organize the Urban Flava line of Victory Sports apparel, based in Houston, Texas. Even though it was less than three hundred miles from her folks, she still had reservations about it. She neglected to tell her mother why she was hesitant to accept the best offer she'd gotten after months of interviewing, but Mom still figured it out in the first two minutes of the phone call. Somehow, mothers always know when we're still in love with the one who did us wrong. Her mother was no exception. As soon as Jasmine hung up the phone, she realized it, too. She and Marshall may not have been together for a while, but he still had her heart locked up tightly in a glass jar. The problem was, he had placed it on a shelf along with other forgotten collectibles.

She looked at the clock sitting on her nightstand. It was eight o'clock on a Friday night and she didn't have anyone to share her good news with. After flipping through the latest issue of *Essence* magazine, she got the idea to call someone else. Maybe he'd like to get dressed up, hit the town, and celebrate. She pulled out her art history notebook from inside her book bag. It had a phone number written on the back of it. The phone rang three times before the answering machine picked up.

"Hi, this is Legacy. You're talking to the machine because I'm not in to take your call. If you're a burglar, this would be a great time to rob me. If you're not a burglar, leave me a message. Bye."

Jasmine smiled to herself. She thought the message was cute and accurately exemplified his personality.

"Freelance, this is Jazz. You're probably on a date or working one of those jobs of yours, and I know you didn't expect to hear from me until tomorrow, but I wrapped it up early and caught the next flight out of Hobby airport. I'd like to tell you all about it. Call me."

It was extremely difficult for her to sit there when she wanted to get out and tell someone. All the years of making good grades and the right connections finally paid off, but being forced to look for someone to party with reminded her that in four years of college she hadn't made many friends. Rorey, Marshall, and Legacy were it. Rorey was gone and Marshall was black history.

*   *   *

Jasmine strutted through the double doors in the lobby of the athletic dorm decked in high-heel pumps, gracing a tight black mini dress under a stylish black sheer raincoat. She was striking. Her legs were purposely bare because she knew Marshall thought women's legs looked sexier when not confined to panty hose. Her hips swayed casually like someone rocking in a hammock from side to side.

There were Spade and Tonk card games going on, along with smashing dominos, but when Jasmine added a little extra wiggle to her walk, all the activities stopped. The young ladies at the Spade table looked on and nodded their approval. "Go on, girl," was saluted from the other group of females.

Each of the bad boys, at the men-only table, put their dominos down and gave her their full attention with their mouths hung wide open. Most of them wished they knew her well enough to have a shot at getting with her, but they knew better. Marshall or no Marshall, they knew better. And she knew that she looked as good as they thought she did.

Halfway through the lobby, Jasmine stopped suddenly and gave it a full viewing. She didn't see Marshall or any of his new immediate so-called friends, so she proceeded to the Resident Assistant's (RA) desk to call up to his room. After she dialed his number, she turned away from the chunkily built white male student on duty, who stared with the same amazement as the black domino players.

With her behind pressing against the face of the long desk, she peered out over the lobby and noticed something that didn't look right. No one had resumed their games. No one was concentrating on their cards to steal the next book. No one was slamming bones for a big score to get a leg up on points, either. No one moved. Some of them looked in her direction while others glanced over toward the big-screen TV, near the east elevators on the men's wing of the coed dormitory. She didn't catch on at first, but a second look revealed what the others already saw: Marshall and his boys sitting on the sofa playing an NFL Live computer game on the oversized TV set.

She slowly laid the receiver down on the desktop. The phone continued to ring. Jasmine and the RA had to be the only ones in the entire place who didn't have a clue as to what was destined to happen next. With each step she took toward the TV, Jasmine's smile grew increasingly larger, until she was almost directly behind them. With Busta and Flea studying the screen, Pig maneuvered the video game's hand controls and successfully marched down the field with the Atlanta Falcons team. There were two seconds left on the clock before the game would be over.

When Marshall stopped Pig's team from scoring, he and Flea cheered as the time ran out. "I told you 'bout running with them sorry Falcons. You can't hold me," Marshall taunted. "I done told you and showed you. You can't hold me. Ain't that right, baby?" he said softly to someone sitting between his legs.

Jasmine overheard that last comment. Her brilliant smile was gobbled up by uncertainty. She couldn't see anyone past Marshall's broad shoulders.

"I'm next," Flea shouted, as he pulled the controls from Pig's sweaty hands. "And I ain't going out like that. Gimme Denver so I can put a lil' blitz on that ass . . ." He panicked when his eyes found Jasmine standing over Marshall. "Hey Jazz," he said pleasantly, but with a nervous tenor. It was undoubtedly more for Marshall's benefit than hers.

Marshall whipped his head around quickly. His eyes bucked like someone who saw a tall building falling on him but it was much too late to get out of the way. He pounced up so fast, the young lady on his lap stumbled to keep from falling to the floor. Jasmine smacked her lips and shook her head slowly from side to side in disbelief. That was the defining moment in their relationship. She felt stupid that it took seeing him with another woman twice before she finally got the message.

"No! Don't get up on my account," Jasmine said to him. "I should have expected as much. Pig, Busta, Flea, and the bearded lady. How's life under the big top, Marshall? And how long have I been wrong about you? Never mind, it doesn't matter."

Marshall took a step toward her, but she checked him to a standstill with her flat palm extended outward like a veteran crossing guard stopping oncoming cars at an elementary school crosswalk. "Don't! You've already made a big enough fool out of both you and me."

Ms. Malveaux punched Marshall in the chest as hard as she could. "What's she talking about, Marshall? I thought you said y'all were finished a long time ago."

He just stood there with a stupid look on his face, numb to the straight right hand she landed on him.

"Well, he was half right," Jasmine answered for him. "We're finished now."

He looked over the crowd watching the spectacle he was responsible for but had no power to control, although that didn't stop Marshall from trying. "Jazz. Don't do this," he begged with sorrowful eyes.

"You already did . . . this," she replied, and then turned to walk away. "Oh, yeah, my momma says hello," she added with her back turned toward him.

Normally, there would have been a lot of hoopla and loud cracks made about Marshall getting busted the way he did, but there wasn't one sound in that lobby to be heard. As Jasmine casually strolled past the game tables with her head held high, the men stared again. Only this time it was different than before, with respect instead of lust in their eyes. The congregation of women parted to let her through. Admiration best describes the nodding heads that she received from them. One large-size sister dressed in pajamas, Greeked out in her sorority's colors, signifying her bond for life, stood near the exit doors smirking. As Jasmine passed her by, she held up her hand like someone taking an oath. Jasmine slapped her a mellow high five on her way out. "Hm!" was the only salutation offered. It said what words couldn't have possibly communicated. Simply put, it conveyed, "You did what you had to do, girlfriend! 'Nuf said."

Everyone watched Jasmine until they could no longer see her travel down the concrete walkway. Marshall watched her, too, but for him it was different. He watched her walk out the door and out of his life, just as she promised him she would if it came to this. Simultaneously, all the attention reverted back to him, looking pitiful and alone. After Ms. Malveaux shoved him in the chest in passing, there was only one thing left for him to do: Call Tyrone to help him come pick up his shhhit. . . . For the first time in his life, he was alone.

Jasmine climbed into her Honda and slammed the car door. She started up the motor but she wasn't ready to leave, probably because she was all dressed up with no place to go. Handling herself in front of all those people was easy, but she couldn't hide from herself behind that facade she'd just played out back there. When she felt her eyes misting up, she pulled down on the face of the rearview mirror until it was angled enough to see her own saddened eyes glaring back at her. "Uh-uh, Jazz," she said aloud to her reflection in the mirror. "No more tears. No more . . ."

Inside a little coffee shop just north of downtown, Morris continued to stir his cup of Colombian blend long after the sugar had sufficiently dissolved in it. Each time the spoon made a complete revolution, it made an annoying clink against the rim of the cup. That usually irked Kennedy, but this time she didn't think it was enough of an issue to mention. She was more concerned with the predicament she found herself in. A bad relationship that barely hung on by the thinnest of hopeful threads and a new admirer who didn't quite fit the résumé of the man she wanted to get serious about. She couldn't see herself with an aspiring anything, artist included.

The torment and embarrassment she experienced as a young girl having to accept hand-me-down clothes and other accessories from the county club crowd, after her father died of a heart attack, was still with her. Deep beneath the expensive apparel she now treated herself to whenever she got the chance, and deep beneath her well-rehearsed facade, festered the memory of the secondhand wardrobe of her youth and one miserable welfare Christmas after another that she and her mother endured.

She'd watched her father work himself to an early grave while doing the best he could with a limited education. For fourteen hours a day, six days a week, Kennedy watched her mother grow more lonesome while he worked seemingly endless hours just to make ends meet. After his death, her mother took on odd jobs as a cleaning woman but never really got over losing her husband at age forty-eight or her longing for him to come home at a decent hour without being too worn out to do anything but fall asleep as soon as he did. Kennedy witnessed the disheartening and continual episodes day in and day out. Feeling helpless and burdensome, at age sixteen she promised that she would never allow herself to get involved with any man who didn't have himself together financially. She refused to take a chance on putting other children through what she knew all too well and feared ending up like her mother, who died of a broken heart, owning only one pair of shoes worth being buried in.

All those years later, Kennedy still harbored the resentment of dreadful days gone by. Muddling through the past, scarred by circumstances she couldn't control back then, proved conclusively that she didn't have the wherewithal to work herself out of it now.

She snapped out of her stupor when the waiter stopped by the table to check on the odd couple after they'd been sipping coffee and espressos for over an hour. They briefly looked over the dinner menu and decided that their warm potions were sufficient for the evening. As soon as they were alone again, Morris lapsed into a lengthy dissertation about the latest Ellen Tracy outfit he'd just purchased. He went on and on about the deep-purple, two-piece velvet ensemble, then began to describe the black riding boots he planned to wear with it, when Kennedy awoke from her previous catatonic state.

"Morris, what do you think about the guy who delivered those roses the other day?" She spoke without realizing what was happening.

"Who, that Legacy guy?"

"Yeah, I mean what impression did you get?"

That was right up his alley. Talking about men he'd just met was one of his favorite pastimes, whether the man was his or not. "Well, I thought he was just gorgeous. Those jeans and that pretty-boy inner-city street appeal of his, I thought he was hot. Sizzling."

Kennedy stared down into her espresso as if she were expecting to see her future in it somehow. "That's what I thought you'd say. He is handsome, I agree, and he does have this sexy way about him, but he seems too nice, too normal."

"Would you listen to yourself, honey. Handsome, nice, and normal is what every sane girl wants in a man. I'd say those are the things that bubble baths and dreams are made of."

"Maybe I'm not sane, then. Maybe I like the fast, furious, and dangerous type that—"

"Oh I see," Morris interjected. "A bad boy. Is that the type of dangerous you're talking about?"

"Yeah, someone who's mysteriously dangerous but good for me at the same time."

Morris squinted his eyes in objection to what she'd just said. "Mysteriously dangerous but good for you. Are you kidding? There is no such thing. These days, mysterious is scary as hell and dangerous sounds like a broken heart, a penicillin shot, and a prison term. You already have one bad boy and what has that gotten you? More dates with a single gay male, that's what."

Kennedy took her ribbing quietly. She knew he was right but had her heart set on a man who could provide drama and challenge to her life. But after enduring a reality check and a close look at her present empty and painful love affair with mysteriously dangerous, she had second thoughts about handsome, nice, and normal.

Morris added more cream to his coffee, then began to stir it slowly, much like he planned on doing to Kennedy's personal business. "Why all the talk about this Legacy, anyway? Is there something you haven't told me?" His eyes were wide now and his ears were wide-open as well.

The corners of her mouth raised slightly as a pleasant smile fought its way through her thin lips. "I did, um, go out with him the other night, but just as friends. I didn't want to give him the wrong idea."

"What idea would that be, Ms. James?" he said, like a prosecutor who laid the trap, knew the butler did it, and was about to forge a confession, Perry Mason style.

"The idea that I was maybe interested or something. I have some-one already and I made that very clear. Besides, he's not what I'm looking for."

Morris in his infinite wisdom laughed and leaned in for the kill. "Sweetheart, if you are so clear about the man you already have, then why are you thinking so hard about another one?" Nothing said guilty like the blank helpless stare that hung on Kennedy's face like a thick veil. Morris had her looking into the depths of her very own soul, perhaps for the first time in her life. By her own admis-sion, she was looking for something else in a man, something other than what she'd already tolerated for much too long. Considering that, there was no way she could have told him that Legacy shared his sentiment for her cigarette habit and that he cared enough about her to ask her to quit. That surely would have been used against her in a case she was already losing. It was hopeless. She was forced to take the chance to see what Legacy was really like, what he had to offer, and if she would want it when she found out.

Twenty-one

Enough about Me

*T*he crowded bowling alley was filled with young adults coupled up and numerous invigorated families. Loud crashes were abundant as the heavy black balls thundered down the long glistening lanes. Cigarette smoke and the smell of stale beer occupied the air along with excited yells of triumphant "way to go" and disappointed "ahh" and "almost" commingled therein. Kennedy instinctively turned up her nose when Legacy suggested their next outing include time at Don Carter's Bowl-a-Rama lanes. It was one of the places he was sure friends spent time in. Kennedy was adamant that this date, just like their last one, be a friendship outing exclusively. Legacy figured she might not like it at first, but with some careful maneuvering and a little luck, she just might find herself having a wonderful time. He also figured on some of the places she would probably feel most comfortable. All of those places were crossed out because he wouldn't be comfortable in them. He reasoned that helping Kennedy reach a higher level of consciousness and self-awareness was more plausible than him pretending to be someone he wasn't willing to imitate. Wanting to please her was one thing, but he wasn't willing to lose himself in the process.

"Red vinyl," she said, complaining to no one in particular, openly unimpressed by the cheesy upholstery. "Why am I not surprised?"

Legacy ignored her comment while continuing to lace up his personal bowling shoes, then set the scoring screen with their initials.

Kennedy surveyed their immediate area. "Uhh, where are my shoes?"

"Your shoes? Oh, that's right, you've never been bowling before. You probably don't have your own shoes. No problem." He grabbed her by the hand and pulled her up from the small plastic table in the bowler's gallery.

"Where are we going? To buy me a pair of shoes, I hope?"

"Nope. The pro shop is closed already. We'll just get you fitted with a pair of rental ones. What size do you wear?" he asked casually. She smirked her disbelief that he would even suggest she wear shoes that were worn by hundreds of other people she didn't know. Again, he ignored her. "You look like about an eight narrow to me."

Kennedy quickly corrected him. "Excuse me. I'm a seven'n a half, thank you." It was bad enough that she had to wear those ridiculous red and blue clown shoes; at least he could guess the right size, she thought.

"Spray them again," she demanded when the attendant whisked the shoes through a sanitizing spray machine. "I mean, can't be too safe." She handled them with the very tips of her index fingers and thumbs as if they were two dead, smelly fish.

Legacy smiled about it. This would definitely be unlike any date she'd ever been on, he thought. Which was the point Legacy wanted to make.

He helped Kennedy search along the racks to find a lightweight ball that felt comfortable to her fingers, then headed back to the lane they'd rented. Just when she began having second thoughts about agreeing to see him again, she noticed how Legacy looked out for the small children who darted between them, in that carefree way kids love to do it, just behind the gallery tables. His face lit up as they laughed aloud, enjoying their simple childhood game of "tag, you're it." She couldn't remember seeing Simpson affected in that way at the sight of children playing together, nor any other man in her past, for that matter. There was something refreshing about it, but she thought she'd keep it to herself, since she was determined to have an awful time.

While firing up a cigarette, Kennedy watched other bowlers hurl balls toward the pins positioned at the end of the alley. In the next lane was a great bowling duet. The tall, slender-built blond young man couldn't have been more than twenty-two years old, and his girlfriend was a short, petite brunette who looked a year or so younger than him. It was obvious that they were both utterly in love, almost too in love to watch. She would knock down all the pins or clean up the spare with her second attempt, and he would reward her with a sweet smack on the lips when she did. Kennedy observed the ritual, thinking, what an incentive to do well. Each time the thin blond male lovebird made a strike, he would strut back to the gallery with a cocky swagger to claim his reward. Another kiss. It was almost repulsive, especially since Kennedy didn't have the same kind of thing going on for herself.

"Do you see how that couple is carrying on? Young hormones are sickening to me," she complained. "They need to get a room and spare us the details."

"They're in love," Legacy argued. "You can't blame 'em for that. I think it's great that they're not afraid to show their feelings in public. They want the whole world to know they love each other."

Without giving it another thought, Legacy approached the lane carefully, stepped up to the line, and released the ball with a smooth touch. It flew straight down the lane and swept all ten of the pins away. "Ooh, yeah!" he shouted, and strutted back to receive some form of exaltation, but Kennedy wasn't impressed. Actually, she was embarrassed because Legacy's masculine prance was almost as shameless as the other guy's.

"Not you, too?" Kennedy said in a disapproving tone.

"What? Not me, too."

"That ridiculous parading. That macho strutting is way over-rated. You men act like it's so difficult to knock all those poor little pins down with that big old ball."

Smiling politely, Legacy stepped aside, yielding her complete usage of the lane. She awkwardly placed her thumb, index finger, and ring finger in the round holes of the ball. It was a sign of the comical times to come.

Kennedy marched up to the line but stopped way short of where she needed to be. When she pulled the ball back to gather herself, it slipped out of her hand and took off toward the gallery behind her. The young lovers ran for cover when the ball catapulted in their direction. Legacy made a desperate leap and caught the menacing ten-pound bomb before it could do any real damage.

"Whew . . . sorry about that." He apologized to the alarmed couple as they apprehensively took their seats. "First time out and she's a little aggressive."

Kennedy stood motionless near the ball return machine. "Oops, I'm so sorry," she apologized. "Are you all okay?"

No one answered. They just glared back at her like deer on the highway, frozen by the headlights of an oncoming eighteen-wheeler. After everyone calmed down, she fell into her seat with her hands pressed between her thighs. She was more afraid than they were. She didn't want to move an inch.

"It's still your turn," Legacy whispered, as the young couple cautiously looked on.

"You're not expecting me to get back up there after I nearly took out two innocent people?"

"I stepped back up to the plate after you almost took me out with that soda can. You could at least give it one more try. I'll help you, come on."

Kennedy let out a huff. "I really need a cigarette."

Legacy picked up the ball and held it out. She still wasn't sure about making another attempt at what she previously thought to be a cinch, but she reluctantly accepted the ball, anyway. Then he pulled her close to him.

"Okay. Now place your fingers in the holes. Use your left hand to support the ball from the bottom."

He stepped behind her and wrapped his arms around hers, then walked her through the motions slowly. "Left foot, right, left, then release. See those arrows painted on the lane? That's your guide. Aim for the middle one."

She listened carefully, but the soft way he whispered in her ear made it difficult to pay attention. His warm breath made her think of other things, things that friends didn't usually engage in together. "Take it slow and relax. You'll be fine," he assured her. "Just remember, left-right-left-release."

As Kennedy poised herself, the male lovebird stood at the end of his lane watching her. "You can go ahead," Kennedy offered. He declined, apparently still leery of her skills.

"No, I'll just stand right here and . . ." He swallowed hard, preparing for the worst. "And keep an eye on you."

Kennedy knew he had a right to be afraid, very afraid. She lined up with the arrows, marched up to the line, pulled the ball back, and blindly flung it down the lane. The ball immediately rolled into the gutter, then miraculously bounced out of it to knock down three pins. No one knew what to make of it. They marveled because the gutter didn't normally relinquish anything that it caught. Maybe it was sympathetic or maybe it was a sign from the gods that every attempt deserved some gratification. Either way, it wasn't a lost cause. Kennedy turned around bright-eyed, hoping to gain approval from the gallery. Legacy applauded nobly. The male lovebird said, "Cool," and nodded his endorsement, but the female lovebird continued with the deer in the headlights gaze.

From that point on, Kennedy knocked down more pins with each opportunity. Legacy encouraged her with high-fives, and both lovebirds nodded and smiled. They were just happy they no longer had to fear for their lives.

In the last frame, Legacy needed to sink nine pins to break a score of two hundred. He winked at Kennedy, who had really gotten into it by then. With his patented approach, he glided up to the line and let it fly. Before the ball crashed into the pins, he turned around and confidently strutted back toward the gallery. Crash! All of the pins flew into the mat behind them, a perfect strike. Kennedy stood up and sensually strolled over to Legacy, who was still reveling in his grand finish. She threw her arms around him, like the female lovebird had done when her man scored well, and planted a big wet one on the lips. Then she sneered seductively at the young lovers before winking at them. The lovebirds looked at one another for joint signs of approval, then simultaneously flashed smiles back at her. "Cool."

When Kennedy's hands were too sore from holding the bowling ball to continue, Legacy sat on a stool, enjoying a long gaze at her blue jeans, which seemed to contract and tighten around her butt when she leaned over the edge of the long pool table to get a better angle on the shot she wanted to take. Kennedy wasn't very good at shooting pool, either, but she was good at other things. Getting a man's attention was one of them. Each time she had a tough shot, she chose the most difficult angle. It really didn't matter whether she made the shot. Pool wasn't the game she was playing; enticement was.

After midnight, the Bowl-a-Rama lanes began clearing out. The night-cleaning crew waited for customers to finish their pizzas and beers so that they could start preparing the bowling alley and game room for the next business day. Legacy dealt with more secondhand cigarette smoke than he was accustomed to, including Kennedy's. She enjoyed their nondate immensely and wasn't ready for it to end. She couldn't remember the last time she'd laughed so loud at herself, and she had him to thank for it. She also noted how well-rounded he was. He could speak with the enunciation of a foreign dignitary or the flat diction of an urban homeboy, and not one of the kids in the arcade could equal his score on the Galaga video game. Kennedy was intrigued by it because Legacy was somewhat mysterious but not dangerous, and he was anything but normal. And the youthful arcade dwellers knighted him king. He was altogether different from any man she'd ever known. That much she was sure of.

When he pulled his Samurai jeep up to the front of her apartment building, where their evening started, Bradshaw stepped out to get the door for her. "So this is it?" Legacy asked, looking down at nothing in particular.

"Yeah, I guess this is it," she repeated.

"Okay, then, umm, I guess you'll call me when you have time again?"

Before she could stop it, "I have time now" rolled off her tongue. "I mean . . . I know that we decided, well, I decided, that it would probably be better if we didn't get too friendly, but I'd really like it if you came up for coffee." She was afraid that if the night ended, she would never be able to recapture its charm again.

The nervous desperation in her voice was comforting to him. He'd felt the same way since she allowed him to help her improve her previously ridiculous bowling technique. But he was glad it was her idea. He wanted to prolong saying good night, too, but didn't have the nerve to risk it.

They exited the elevator on her floor. "Excuse the mess, but I didn't think I'd be inviting you up tonight." When Kennedy opened the door, the cat purred. She was glad that her roommate was home. "Look out, Lady Eleanor doesn't like . . ." Suddenly, the cat rubbed her long white hair against Legacy's pant leg, then purred even louder than before. ". . . men. I guess I stand corrected. She seems to have taken a fancy to you." She looked curiously at the cat that always hissed at Simpson.

"They say that animals and small children are great judges of character," Legacy added in his favor.

"Uh, yeah. I have heard that somewhere before." She smiled

briefly, then pulled off her jacket and made her way into the kitchen. "Can I get you some coffee or a Diet Coke?"

"I'll take some coffee, thanks."

"Cream? I have amaretto."

"Please, if you don't mind. That'll be nice."

She scurried around in the kitchen, trying to make the best of what few edible items she had available but didn't have much luck. "Hey, Legacy, got my car back today," she yelled, with her head in the refrigerator, grasping for avenues to utilize that nervous energy. "Isn't that great news? Yeah, they've had it longer than necessary as far as I'm concerned." There wasn't one decent thing to eat in the entire place, unless you could count Lady Eleanor's Perfect Pet food.

While she was busy in the kitchen, Legacy looked around the room. He saw the treadmill, the expensive foldaway kind advertised on TV. He noticed the rip in the couch and the several cigarette burns it was forced to wear. An educated woman in her position wouldn't normally let her sofa go like that, he thought. It just didn't fit. Other than that, it looked like he figured it would. The place was actually very nice. She had a few quality reproduction prints of Van Gogh and Monet.

"Do you mind if I check out some of your artwork?" he shouted back in her direction.

"No, be my guest," she said, still studying the contents of her refrigerator.

He ran his fingers along the contours of a decent oil painting hanging over her fireplace. It was a picture of a small girl dancing in torn ballet shoes. It was detectable, to his trained eye, that a novice had painted it, but the colors were very dramatic and it definitely had soul. It reminded him of someone he knew growing up. Then an eight-by-ten photograph caught his attention. The picture looked more like the kind they sell with the frame than that of a real person. The man in the picture was a pretty boy with perfect hair and teeth. It had been airbrushed or at least touched up to give it a more polished appeal. Legacy leaned in to get a better look. The man in the photo looked familiar, but he thought it was his imagination.

"Here is your coffee, I hope you like it. It's a flavor I get from Starbucks." She sat the serving tray on top of the assorted magazines spread over her coffee table. "I really had fun tonight. I never would have thought something as simple as bowling and pool could be so much fun."

"I'm glad you liked it, but that was nothing. Give me some time and I could show you some really simple stuff." They both laughed as she sidled up next to him, examining a piece of artwork. "I was looking at the painting of the young girl dancing. The coloring is different from anything I've seen. Who did it?"

"I painted that when I was sixteen. I used all natural coloring. Mud, sand, octopus ink, egg yolk, and clay."

"Octopus ink? Egg yolk? You're serious?"

"Yes, I am. My father was a butcher and I was going through this young tragic blue funk phase. Good thing it lasted only four months."

"Who's the model? She seems happy to be dancing, even with torn shoes."

"Torn shoes . . . funny you should notice that. It was a self-portrait. I titled it *Borrowed Shoes*."

"That's original. Why . . . ?"

"When I was growing up, my father worked all the time and my mother helped out, too, but they had no money for things as frivolous as a girl's dancing shoes, so I was given the old shoes after the little rich girls were finished with them and on to a new pair. They always had a new pair."

Kennedy wasn't afraid to admit she'd grown up poor, at least not to Legacy, although she constantly regretted divulging her humble upbringing to Simpson Stone, of the Austin Stones, who continually threw it in her face when it benefited him.

Legacy smiled to himself. "I would have never guessed that you had two parents who worked; much less, worked hard for a living." The Kennedy he thought he wanted to know and help achieve a semblance of consciousness and self-awareness was exposed as a fraud and he was glad.

The cat stretched out by their visitor's feet. Kennedy took further notice. "Enough about me," she said, eyeing her pet. "I want to know all about this Legacy Freelance Childs whom Lady Eleanor can't seem to get enough of." The cat had been on her heels for the past ten minutes.

"I knew a girl like you once." He continued to study the painting. "She loved to dance, too. Sabrina was her name. She would dance all day if they let her."

"They?" Kennedy asked.

"They, at the orphanage. That's where I spent the first thirteen years of my life. I had forty-seven brothers and twenty-six sisters when I was graduated. That means I was too old to stay there any longer. The Child's Orphanage in Greensboro, North Carolina, didn't want to add to their problems by keeping children there who were old enough to make more babies. So, on my thirteenth birthday, I was graduated to the state's foster parent program. Graduated, that's funny." He never thought about how ridiculous that sounded before then.

"Child's Orphanage. Is that where you got your last name?"

"Yeah, all the children who were left there are referred to as baby John or Jane Doe for thirty days. If no one claimed them, they assumed the last name of Childs. The Greensboro phone book is full of Childses." Legacy smiled when he thought of how confusing it must be to look up the right name in the phone directory.

Kennedy became very interested in his past. "That's really something. Why'd they name you Legacy?"

"It's been so long since I've thought about that." He drifted off into his past for a moment before responding. "Well, the Greensboro school had a surefire way to name each child left there without a birth certificate. On the kid's thirty-first day at the school, they figured the parent wouldn't be coming back, so they'd get out the daily paper, the *Greensboro Gazette,* and choose a name from the headlines or from the leading story."

Kennedy's eyes widened. "You're kidding?"

"No. No, I'm not." He laughed, too, when he realized how ridiculous it was to choose a child's name from the newspaper. "On my thirty-first day, the headline read 'King Muhammad Farad Dies and Leaves Legacy: As Well as Millions to Homeless Children of Quatar.'" He could barely finish before he erupted into unbridled laughter.

Kennedy tried to be sympathetic, but she lost control, too, when she felt the need to probe further. "Wait . . . wait. You mean you could just as easily have been named Quatar?" She was rolling on her sofa with her arms wrapped around her stomach as if trying to hold herself together.

Legacy thought about it and began to laugh even more hysterically. "That's not the worst of it," he confessed. "There's more. Another kid was abandoned the same day I was."

She braced herself. "What'd they name him? Farad?" she asked, straining to hold it together, thoroughly enjoying his preposterous story.

He shook his head, catching his breath before he could answer her. "No, they named him King Muhammad!"

Kennedy laughed so hard that she fell off the couch, landing butt-first on the hardwood floor. Lady Eleanor stared through their amusement, wondering what was going on. When they continued falling all over themselves, the cat cowered away from them and hissed her discontent, then made tracks into the bedroom. She'd had enough. They were much too animated for her taste.

A delightful evening rolled along smoothly as they shared other humorous stories, and some not so humorous, from their childhoods, while drinking coffee and listening to Kennedy's Beatles LPs for the rest of the night. Her apartment hadn't witnessed that kind of revelry since she'd moved in. By the time the sun peeked through the blinds, Legacy knew he'd found the woman he could call his own. But the airbrushed eight-by-ten photograph was lodged in his mind, blocking a clear view to what he hoped would turn out to be love.

Twenty-two

God Musta' Blinked

Two long months melted away. Marshall spent most of his time working out for professional football scouts from the New England Patriots, Kansas City Chiefs, Green Bay Packers, and Minnesota Vikings. Each of them showed up in rented luxury cars, timed his forty-yard dash, and tested his agility and strength.

After viewing film footage of his past collegiate performance, they all rated him as an excellent draft selection. The scouting deadline was only a few days away, which was just as well. The excitement of jumping through hoops for the NFL faded away for Marshall after the Chiefs' representative made his notes, thanked him for his time, and climbed into his rented Lincoln Continental and drove away. Marshall thought it should have been a blast.

Maybe if he still had Jasmine in his life to share it with, the experience would have been a lot more exciting.

"Marshall, I'd like to introduce you to Don Shanklin," Coach Dean said. "Don is with the Atlanta Falcon organization. He wants to spend some time with you today, work you out, and see what you can do." Marshall smiled courteously and nodded while he shook the man's hand.

"We've heard great things about you, Marshall, on and off the field. I know that other scouts have been here to see you, but we really need good receivers next year, and if what they say about you is true, we'll do everything we can to make sure you become a part of our organization."

Marshall liked the idea of living in Atlanta, just as he had New England, Kansas City, Green Bay, and Minnesota, but just long enough to realize that no matter where he ended up, it would be without his friend Rorey and the love he threw away trying to grab something that was never meant for him.

At three-thirty in the afternoon, the sun was still high in the sky. The smattering of clouds couldn't add relief from the unrelenting heat beaming off the hot AstroTurf. The UTC track team practiced their baton exchanges on the track surrounding the football field. Some of the Wrangler underclassmen, along with other senior athletes, kneeled around the forty-yard line where the Falcons' Don Shanklin stood ready with his stopwatch poised.

"Whenever you're ready, Marshall!" he shouted, forty yards away.

The head coach grinned assuredly when Marshall pulled off his sweatpants and T-shirt. He knew how fast his star athlete was, as did Ken Arlan, the head track coach who never forgave Marshall for refusing to anchor his sprint relay team. While Marshall went through his ritual of stretching his arms over his head, Don Shanklin looked at the younger college athletes and asked, "Is he really as fast as they say?"

Each of the young men agreed simultaneously. "Faster."

Hearing their overwhelming endorsements, the scout rubbed his potbelly as he laughed. He didn't understand then that Marshall Coates wasn't just another flash-in-the-pan college superstar. He epitomized the hopes of those less fortunate players who figured their only way to get to college was on an athletic scholarship and their best shot to get their families out of the government housing projects was to get to the NFL. To them, Marshall was a hero on his way to lassoing that dream.

"Come on, baby, come on, baby, come on, baby," Marshall whispered, looking at the ground beneath his feet. Don steadied his thumb to move the start button on his stopwatch when Marshall took his first step. "Nowwwwwwwww!" he yelled as he blew out of his sprinter's stance.

His powerful thighs contracted and extended with the fury of a thoroughbred racehorse, pumping as his knees drove up to his chest. Before he reached the ten-yard mark, he was flying like the wind. The players, looking on intensely, noted every long stride he took. Their mouths watered as he glided past them.

"Ahhh! That's good . . . ," Marshall murmured when he blazed through the finish line.

The underclassmen stood up, slapped high-fives, and cheered. Don looked down at his stopwatch. It read 4.4 seconds. He wiped over the watch's face feverishly with his thumb, figuring he had to be seeing it incorrectly. After shielding the watch from the sunlight with his other hand, he shook his head.

One of the players asked, "What'd you get?"

The pro scout looked at the clock again. "It must be wrong. I clocked him at four point four. Not many athletes his size, in the world, can run that fast."

The young player nodded his head and agreed. "Maybe there is something wrong with your clock. He usually runs a four point three." He continued nodding as he turned and walked away.

Don took off his hat with the Falcon insignia on it and scratched his head in disbelief. When Marshall was asked to run the forty again, he did, only faster.

After the star athlete jumped through the other hoops, Don made a note of Marshall's physique, positive attitude, and athletic talents. The word he put by Marshall's name in his completed scouting report was "awesome." They said their good-byes and Don thanked him, then climbed into his rented Lincoln Continental and disappeared.

"Another Lincoln," Marshall said to himself. "They must get some kind of discount."

He sat on the green AstroTurf of the football field and began stretching his long muscular legs. That was his last scheduled workout and he was glad it was all over. Now he could get back to concentrating on wrapping up his last college semester and putting his mistakes behind him. He finished his cooldown routine and stood up to put on his T-shirt.

When he stuck his arms through and popped it over his head, he could sense that someone had walked up behind him, but he acted as if unaware. Maybe it's Jazz, he thought.

"Guess who?" came from whoever it was now holding her small hands over his eyes from behind him. He knew it had to be a woman, but he didn't recognize the high-pitched voice. "Take a guess," she repeated.

"Okay, I give. And I'm tired."

With that, she removed her hands and leapt in front of him. "It's meeee!" she squealed.

Marshall's anxious smile drooped when he saw who that high-pitched squeal belonged to. "Oh, what' up, Woodbridge?"

Shauni continued to smile at him despite his obvious disappointment. "You don't have to be that glum about it. I just thought I would surprise you and stop by to say hi."

With suspicions, he looked her up and down. The loose-fitting white nylon shorts she wore adequately covered her bikini bottoms underneath, but the bright colors shone through, screaming out, "Please notice me!"

"Well, I'm surprised," Marshall admitted, "but how'd you know I'd be here?"

"I come out on Tuesdays and Thursdays to catch some rays,

usually up there as high as I can on the fifty-yard line." She pointed toward the top bleachers. "You'd be surprised what can be seen from way up there."

"Oh, yeah? Like what?" He began collecting his other things.

"Take that guy who you met with today. He was excited and desperate. I could tell that by the way he had a big old smile each time you finished one of those drills. He was much more impressed than that other man from the Minnesota Vikings."

"Oh, he was, was he?" Marshall seemed more interested in what other observations she'd made. "How do you know so much about football?"

"I don't know that much about football, but I do know a lot about people. I like to watch 'em. Sometimes I can tell what they're thinking." Shauni was cunning. She set him up to ask the question she wanted him to, and he did.

"All right, Woodbridge, tell me. What am I thinking right now?" Marshall was sure she had no idea what was on his mind.

"What do I get when I get it right?" she whined seductively.

"You mean, if you get it right?"

"No, when I get it right. I told you I know a lot about people and I'm good," she replied, more suggestive than before.

"Okay. If you get it right . . ." He looked down at the ground to think of something she might want as a prize but couldn't come up with anything. "Why don't you tell me what you think is fair, if you get it right."

"I'll get it right, then I'll tell you," she answered. Then she tilted her head forward and looked up at him to read his facial expression.

Thinking she could never guess it correct, he agreed. "Let's have it, Woodbridge. Tell me. What's on my mind?"

Shauni was enjoying this contest she initiated. Playing by her rules, the game began. "You are thinking, I'm tired. Too tired, after putting on a dog and pony show for the National Football League, to be standing here with this spoiled rich white girl trying to read my mind. Oh, now you're wondering how I knew. Now you're nervous because you know that I have guessed it correctly and you have no idea what I'll want as my prize. Tell me, Marshall Coates, aren't I right?" Marshall's eyes blinked nervously. He thought about lying. "And Marshall, don't try to lie to me. I can spot a liar at one hundred yards. My father's a liar, one of the best, and I can bust him with my eyes closed."

Marshall reluctantly nodded his defeat. "You got me, Woodbridge," he conceded, with an I-don't-believe-this smile on his face. "So, what will it be, since I don't read minds?"

She licked her lips. "I'll think of something while we celebrate your achievement, but until I do, you'll have to stop calling me Woodbridge."

He just loomed there in his own broad shadow, impressed as hell and utterly defeated.

Shauni opened the door to her Corvette and motioned for Marshall to get in. Although apprehensive at first, he eventually obliged and later found comfort in being wooed by another attractive woman.

Outside her apartment, Shauni climbed out of the car and quickly made her way around to the passenger side. After opening the car door and escorting him upstairs to the privacy of her luxurious abode, the royal treatment continued as she popped the cork on one of the chilled bottles of Dom Perignon she stored in her refrigerator. "This would be a good start. Don't you think?" she asked sensually.

Marshall drank more than he should have on an empty stomach. Before he realized it, he'd finished the bottle by himself. Shauni sipped on her first glass while he muttered on about how frustrating the whole NFL scouting and selection process was. "And if I wanted to play for a particular team, it doesn't matter because they draft who they want and that's only if the player is still available, I mean if no other team has picked him by then."

Shauni patiently listened until Marshall had drunk himself into a faulty state of mind. As he rattled on, nearly in an inebriated stupor, she crawled on top of him and began to undress him slowly.

"Marrrshalll, I just decided what I want my prize to be."

Of course, she knew what she wanted long before then. She took the empty crystal champagne glass from his hand, then led him to the bathroom shower. Marshall had been rendered helpless, just as she'd planned.

After a long hot steamy shower together, Marshall stumbled to the bed for support. He could hardly stand on his own. Shauni was close behind with an oversized bath towel wrapped around her. He was aroused but still exhausted. Shauni climbed on top of him with her legs straddling his waist. The moist heat between her thighs was a pure indication of how badly she wanted him inside her. He was the only man on campus she wanted but couldn't get her hands on or legs around, until then.

He tried pulling away when he felt his long, thick penis penetrating her wet vagina. He was unconscious for most of it, but more than nine stiff inches of him stayed awake to participate. However, Marshall did have the presence of mind to ask for protection. "Where's the rubber," he mumbled, "hey, where's the . . ."

She ignored him; instead, she continued sliding back and forth vigorously, grinding on his hard penis with her knees locked until her head jerked uncontrollably. Then her entire body trembled like a wooden shack during a fierce tornado. Her skin ran cold as she collapsed on top of him.

After the storm, their bodies were limp until five in the morning. Marshall awakened to a room he was unfamiliar with. Clothes were thrown about the floor and he was totally nude on her bed. His mouth was dry and his stomach was empty. It had been more than seventeen hours since he had eaten. When it came to him what drinking the bottles of expensive champagne led to, he was disappointed in himself for letting his guard down long enough to be put in that compromising position.

Shauni heard him washing up in the bathroom. She appeared behind him while he took a whore's bath in the sink. Her makeup had worn off and her hair was severely tangled. "Good morning," she said on the front end of a long yawn. "You're not leaving, are you? I thought we'd start the second half during the sunrise. You, uhhh . . . fell asleep last night."

"Well, too bad," he replied, wiping himself off. "That's all you get. By the way, I didn't see any condom packages in the trash can or on the floor. What'd you do with them?"

She smiled devilishly. "Now, why would I want to waste a perfectly good condom on a fine man like you? I didn't want nothing to come between us."

He threw the damp washcloth in the sink and pushed past her on his way out of the bathroom. "That was stupid. Don't you know there's stuff out there you can't get rid of?" He immediately thought about Rorey. "Sex ain't to be played with. It can kill you, ya know."

She became defensive, crossing her arms as she tore into him. "Just what are you trying to say? That I'm one of these nasty sluts on campus who'll just sleep with any man that comes along? I'm selective and I do know when I should wear a condom or not!"

He put on his shirt and began lacing his leather high-tops. "That's the kinda thinking that kills, right there. No one knows who might have AIDS. You can't tell by looking at somebody. That's why you should never have unprotected casual sex. That's why they make rubbers."

"I know why they make rubbers, too," she repeated, deliberately using the term he had. "And I know which kinds of men to use them with. You and Rorey are just alike."

Marshall started toward the door. "You don't know jack about Rorey," he countered.

"Oh, I don't? I know that you two prima donnas should have been best friends. You're just alike. He thought he knew who I should be using condoms with, too."

Marshall turned and charged her, grabbing her by her bare shoulders.

"What do you mean, Rorey thought so, too?"

She jerked away from his grasp and backed up a few steps. "He got all worked up and insisted that I use a condom when we were together! Didn't matter, anyway, damned thing broke on him before we were five minutes into it. He liked it rough."

Marshall was sick to his stomach. He was as sick as Rorey was when he learned his condom had broken. Marshall moved his lips, but the words didn't come out right away. "Rrr . . . you were with Rorey? When?"

Shauni hunched her shoulders like a small child caught doing something she had no business doing. She didn't understand the possible ramifications of her actions. With her head lowered, the words seemed to barely squeak out. "That night . . ."

"What night!" he demanded loudly. His booming voice frightened her.

She backed up even further. "That night!" she shouted back, before breaking down. "That night . . . the night he died."

Marshall felt faint. His worst fears had come true. He'd slept with a woman who had been with a man diagnosed with full-blown AIDS. His strength failed him as he sank to his knees with his head in his hands.

Shauni saw him devastated but still couldn't understand why. She approached him cautiously. "Marshall . . . you're really scaring me. What's going on?" He didn't answer her at first. Maybe he hadn't finished processing it for himself. "Please tell me, Marshall. What is it?"

His head slowly raised until his eyes met hers. His eyes were red, dim, and glassed over with fear. "AIDS . . . ," he answered, in an undertaker's tone. "The bad news is what they call it in the hood, though. *The* bad news . . . but it don't matter what they call it, Woodbridge. It ain't no joke." Shauni didn't move. She couldn't move as Marshall explained further. "And I'm guessin' that's why he killed himself, Rorey, I mean. 'Cause the damned rubber broke. Crazy white boy. He didn't have to kill himself."

Marshall went on to tell her how Rorey got infected with the virus, but she couldn't comprehend it. The only thing she could decipher was that she'd had unprotected sex with an AIDS victim.

Marshall stayed awake the entire following day and night. The phone rang the same repetitious double ring, which distinguished it as an off-campus call, but he didn't answer. He couldn't think of anyone he wanted to talk to; he refused to talk to Shauni about it because she was a bundle of nerves herself, and he just kept thinking he had no business there in the first place. He soon realized he had made several bad decisions since he started hanging with his boys.

Finally, the strain of bearing the bad news got the best of him. He faded into a deep sleep, followed by a hypnotic dreamscape. His subconscious was dominated by the thought of what his ultimate fate would be. That thought manifested itself and surfaced in a grisly and morbid nightmare. It began down a long dark corridor with the only light at the end of it. He couldn't even see his hands out in front of him, but he felt compelled to move ahead despite what felt like spiderwebs clinging to his face. Suddenly, the corridor lit up somehow, although he couldn't detect where the bright light came from.

He rubbed his eyes briskly, hoping they would focus eventually. He heard sounds that seemed to come from all sides to surround him. When the picture became clearer, he began to run as fast as he could toward the light at the end of the tunnel, but he couldn't outrun the corridor's doom. Embedded on both sides were large continuous steel cages, resembling prison cells, along the walls. Pale, bald, ghost-white prisoners, wearing old dirty tattered shrouds, moaned and gnashed their teeth as he passed each dark cell. Some prisoners were even worse off. Their sickly thin frames pleading for help were more terrifying than the others, who screamed as they reached through the bars to grab at him. His feet got tangled in a thick glue like slime rising up from the floor. He struggled and stumbled to the ground. Someone, or something, threw a bag over his head. He struggled frantically but couldn't breathe. His heart pounded as he continued his struggle to get away. He screamed out, "I can't breathe!" as loud as he could and tore away at the bag over his head.

Someone called out to him. "Marshalllllll . . . waaaake upppp!"

He popped straight up in his bed. "Rorey," he answered feebly. "Rorey, is that you?"

Several of his teammates stood around him in his dorm room along with the RA. They heard screaming from his room and came running to help. Marshall sat on his bed with the covers in disarray and a pillowcase over his head. The top of it had been ripped to shreds. Pieces of it were still dangling from his clutched fists.

"You okay, man?" one of them asked. "We heard screaming and figured you were in trouble. Man, you really freaked out." They had no idea what troubles he'd seen.

"You were calling out for Rorey," another one added.

"You think you might wanna go and talk to Coach about it?"

Marshall sat dazed on the edge of his bed. "Uh-uh" was his sole response.

As they piled out of his room, he heard one of his teammates mutter, "Poor guy's having a nervous breakdown and this close to the NFL draft."

Twenty-three

Forgetaboutit

harlie, the head bartender at Club Matrix, counted the cases of beer that had been left by the back door earlier in the day. "Stu-pid idiots. They never get anything right." He crossed out the number sixteen on his inventory check sheet and wrote a six in its place. "How many times do I hafta call down 'ere an' threaten 'em schmucks before they get da orda right," he cursed, as Legacy passed by the bar to set up his drawing stand.

"Hey, Charlie. How's business?" Legacy said back to him.

"Hey, kid. Oh, business? Business is always da same. Nothin' a couple a broken legs won't fix. Ain't that right?"

"Yeah, that's right, Charlie." Legacy liked to ask him how business was because it gave Charlie a chance to rattle off some tough thuggish answer. Since Charlie came to Texas with Richey, he was like a fish out of water. The rules were different down south. When tough guys broke arms or legs of southern customers who didn't pay up, they called the police to report it. In New York it was a different game. Customers in the Big Apple who didn't repay on Richey's terms expected to get something broken. It was an unwritten law of the streets. And, thinking about reporting it to the cops, "Forgetaboutit." Even though Charlie was over fifty, he had a lot of leg-breaking left in him. He was probably more suited for heavy lifting than bartending, but he was honest, something Richey expected from all of his employees.

Just before the club opened, Simpson came in dressed to the teeth in an olive-green three-button Armani suit. He appeared anxious and reluctant when he stopped by the bar to drop off a package with Charlie. Simpson intended to drop off the package and get out of there before Richey saw him. He was still on punishment and didn't want to run into the quick-tempered gangster if he didn't have to.

"Where you going, Stone?" Charlie asked in a threatening tone. "Da boss wants ta see ya. Go on up."

"What does he want?" Simpson asked, not really expecting an answer. It just caught him off guard.

"How da hell am I 'posed ta know? He wants you, not me."

As soon as Simpson hit the back staircase, Charlie picked up the black phone behind the bar and notified Richey he had a visitor. "Hey, boss, Stone's on his way up."

Simpson tapped twice, lightly, on the door. He waited until he was invited, then opened the door and went in. When Simpson came out minutes later wearing a pissed-off expression, he motored down the stairs like he had been in a discussion that didn't prove too favorable for him.

Legacy was on his way to get more Wet-Naps and assorted supplies out of his jeep. He hoped it would be busy, because he planned on making up some of the money he'd spent on those new supplies and gifts for Kennedy.

Suddenly, Simpson walked directly into him with a hard jolt as he returned through the club entrance, knocking several items from

Legacy's hands. "Hey, kid, watch where you're walking before you get yourself hurt," he snarled, checking his suit for damages.

Legacy stood firm. He might not have been as tough as Charlie or Richey, but he was no chump, either. An expensive Armani suit wasn't going to back him down, at least not that suit. Simpson curled his top lip in opposition as he ran his fingers through his hair. Then he backed off.

After Simpson left, Legacy picked up the items that the suit had knocked out of his hands. He remembered seeing Simpson somewhere before, but he knew it wasn't at the club.

Charlie stood behind the bar, smiling with the pride of a brand-new father. He had witnessed the brief cockfight and nodded with his lips puckered. "Uh-huh. See, dat's whut chuss gotta do. Stand up fer you'self and jerks like dat will back down every time. Guar-un-teed."

No one had to tell Legacy that; he'd learned it in the orphanage, fending for his own health in the foster homes, and fighting for his country and himself in the military. He also learned when to pick his fights.

"Thanks, Charlie, who was that dude, anyway?" Legacy asked. "He looks familiar but I can't place him. I'm sure I've seen him before, somewhere."

"Who, Stone? Don't concern yourself with scum like dat. Da prick! You don't wanna know his kind. He's bad news."

Legacy knew that was all he would get from Charlie, but it was eating him up inside. Who was that?

Half the night had gone by when it came to him. "Eight-by-ten glossy," he said to himself. "I knew I remembered his face from somewhere. So, Kennedy's uptown fella works for Richey. Well, I'll be . . ."

The following day, Kennedy sat in her office arranging the latest set of flowers Legacy had sent over. Morris tried to help, but four busy hands around one flower arrangement were two too many. The office looked more like a floral shop than an avenue for business, but no one complained, especially not Kennedy.

"Aren't they beautiful, Morris?"

He began to rearrange them again. "Yes, they are. But they would be more beautiful if . . . you . . . set it up like . . . this. Ahh, now, that's simply charming." They both leaned back in their chairs and sighed in unison, "Ahhhhhhh . . ."

The flowers were gifts of friendship and a hint of something much stronger that Legacy felt inside but that was still much too premature to talk about. Kennedy shared what her past four weeks were like. She laughed the loudest when she described how she beat Legacy at table air hockey and ping-pong at the city youth recreation center where he'd done some pro bono artwork. What she didn't know was that a lot of energy went into letting her win and making it look like she did it on her own. Legacy was an air-hockey-playing, ping-pong-tournament-winning fool as a kid and in the military. Those were low-budget games the Child's Orphanage could afford.

He and Kennedy had other dates, as well, but the ones she truly enjoyed included games or walks in the park where children were playing. There was something therapeutic, energizing about it. Legacy told her that he wanted to have a whole house full of children when he got married. Before he met her, he'd never given children or being part of a family a thought because his past experiences wouldn't allow him to take it for granted. Kennedy was always too busy trying to handle right now to think about something that far down the line. And Morris, he was very excited about the whole thing.

"I told you that handsome, nice, and normal were the things dreams were made of," he said, basking in the flowers' beauty.

Kennedy corrected him. "You said that's what bubble baths and dreams were made of, if I remember correctly."

Morris leaned in with grand surprise written all over him. He braced himself for some juicy details. "Whaaat, bubble baths? You don't waste any time, girlfriend. Give it to me straight and don't leave out a single tickle." He was on the edge of his seat.

"Slow down, Morris, I don't have any details. Not yet, anyway. But I can definitely see the possibilities brewing in the sometime near future. On the other hand, I just don't know." She turned to look at Simpson's picture on her desk.

Morris sneered at it. "So, I take it you haven't told Mr. Stone about your newfound love?"

Kennedy became uncomfortable. She couldn't refuse the urge to squirm in her chair. "Well, I do plan on discussing our future. It's just that he's been real busy lately."

"You mean, he's still not returning your calls?" Morris was obviously disappointed. Kennedy found in Legacy what she said she'd always wanted, someone who was attractive, attentive, and attached to her. "I see," he moaned, when nothing else seemed appropriate to say.

"Don't do this to me, Morris!"

"All I said was, I see."

"You know damned well what I'm talking about. Don't push! I recognize that condescending tone and I already have enough to think about without being hurried to make a decision." She turned beet-red. The frustration she apparently felt inside seemed to cry out when Morris struck a nerve. Truth be told, she'd realized before then that she had a tough decision to make: Legacy or Simpson, a promising future or a hopeful promise.

Morris calmed himself and took a deep breath. "Kennedy, you know I love you like a play cousin and I usually try to stay out of your affairs." When Kennedy flashed him a you've-got-to-be-kidding wide eye, he tried to save face. "Well, I do try. I'm just not good at it. But I can't sit idly by and watch you throw away all this happiness." He thought he would never tell what he knew about Simpson's so-called other women, but Kennedy needed help seeing things for what they really were. He also realized he would put their friendship on the line when he told her. Regardless, he felt compelled to do just that. "There's something you should know and . . ." He couldn't look her in the eyes. "I probably shouldn't be telling you this but . . ."

Suddenly, the phone rang. They both looked at it but neither of them moved. She was prepared, or at least thought she was, for whatever Morris had to say, only Mr. Johansen was passing by her office when it rang again.

"Is someone going to get the phone or are we closed for today?" His insistent tone forced Kennedy to react without thinking.

"Hello, Johansen Arts. Yes, Mr. Childs, she is in. How are you?" The tension that engulfed the small room a short moment ago was broken immediately. Morris smiled while getting up to leave. Maybe it was for the best. Either way, he took it as a sign to shut up and let things play out.

The pleasant blush returned to Kennedy's cheeks as she swayed in her seat. She happily confirmed their date for Saturday evening. Each time Legacy called, all was restored in paradise.

When Saturday arrived, Legacy picked her up at seven o'clock sharp. She loved being on time when they had plans. A minute past would have been overbearing. Lady Eleanor loved seeing him, too. She would follow his every step around the apartment. That cat acted as if Legacy were as much her company as he was Kennedy's.

Legacy previously requested that his date wear something swanky. Her short royal-blue beaded gown with matching sling-back pumps did nicely. The new tuxedo he bought for this special occasion draped his body like a second skin. Legacy was ready for a GQ magazine spread. No one could tailor fine clothing at a discounted price like Ms. Othella Harper. She'd been performing her magic at the Greenville Avenue COX Cleaners for over twenty-five years.

Kennedy had several questions that might lead to finding out where their mystery date would take place. Legacy just continued on with his congenial but evasive silence as they drove nearer to Club Phenomenon, a happening upscale club on the north side of town. The valet line was extraordinarily long. Anxious drivers awaited their chance to park and enter the busy nightspot. Kennedy wasn't familiar with the club, but that wasn't her thing, anyway, so she sat quietly until she realized most of the people getting out of the cars ahead of her were African-Americans. She casually turned toward Legacy, wondering for the first time if he preferred this kind of party atmosphere to what she was used to, when she did go out on the town. "Uhh, what type of club is this?" she asked finally. "It sure is packed tonight. There must be over a hundred people standing in line."

Legacy shrugged. "I'm not sure. One of my clients sent me a couple a passes. That's all I know." Of course, he did know what type of club it was, as well as the special event taking place that night. He wanted to see how Kennedy would react to being in the midst of her own people. So far, Legacy had room for concern. As far as he could tell, nothing about her was black except her parents. And he'd seen his share of black folk who were so far removed from themselves ethnically to the point of searching job applications and checking the "other" box before they even began to fill the darn thing out. He had to know where she stood.

After waiting fifteen minutes and making no noticeable progress to reaching the valet stand, Kennedy became restless. Her twisted lips confirmed it. She wiggled in her seat and glanced at her watch more than twice. Legacy noticed it but pretended not to. Just when he began to feel the pressure from her anxiety, he noticed one of the club's owners getting something from the trunk of a Lexus sedan. He rolled down the window and called out the man's name.

"Priceless . . . Priceless!" Priceless Michaels and his brother Jamie owned several nightclubs in Dallas, all very successful, each one legit. Priceless was average height and well built. His skin was dark, smooth, and flawless, accented by a tailored, short fade haircut. He wore the finest suits he could find and owned several pairs of horn-rimmed designer eyeglasses. He looked more like a cross between an NFL tailback-slash-stockbroker than a nightclub owner as he strolled over to the jeep that was at least ten minutes away from reaching the valet stand. Kennedy was about to implode. Anticipation had gotten the best of her. Priceless recognized her date immediately. Legacy's skills came highly recommended by Marshall, who had grown up in the same community with the Michaels brothers.

"Freelance . . . what's going on, man?" Priceless hailed. He smiled at Kennedy. "Hey, sistah, how you doin'?"

It had been a long time since anyone called her that. She quickly made note of the reference and fought back a smile when he said it. She realized how much she'd missed the inclusion in her own race and that feeling of belonging when people who look like you accept you for just being you.

Legacy tapped the face of his watch with his fingertip. Priceless understood right away what he was getting at. He laughed and reached in his jacket pocket and came out with a VIP pass. It was a hot-pink, five-by-seven handbill.

"Here, take this and park in the VIP section. You should have had one of these, anyway. Just tell Jackson you're on the menu. He'll take care of the rest."

Legacy thanked him for the hookup and broke out of line. His jeep was parked in no time and they were ushered past the multitude of people standing in line to get in and escorted up the side elevator that opened into the exclusive club's third floor.

Once they were seated at a table inside the area roped off from the common partygoers, Kennedy had a chance to soak up all the extravagance and electricity that permeated the large ballroom. Their table was extremely close to a three-foot-high platform decorated as a makeshift stage. She smiled when she looked over the instruments. "Hey, there's going to be live music," she said, with the innocence of a homegirl on her first date out of the hood. "I love a good band." She still had no idea what to expect. The mood was more festive and fortified with celebration than anything she'd come to know before. It reminded her of the Grammy and Academy Award bashes she'd seen on television year after year.

Couples paraded around. Women were adorned in fancy gowns and men in tuxedos and other dark evening wear. The whole place was polished. "Spectacular" was the word for the occasion and Kennedy still wondered what Legacy had done to be awarded a place in such an auspicious setting.

As soon as they were comfortably seated, a nicely built waitress, wearing a twisted hairdo quite fashionably, stopped by and poured two glasses of expensive champagne. She didn't ask whether they wanted it. Her job was to pour everyone in that section champagne. After their glasses were full, the waitress asked if they needed anything else before she sauntered off to the next table.

Kennedy continued to gaze about the room. She noticed many professional athletes she recognized from television sitting at tables nearby. They all seemed to know one another. It brought a calmness to the excitement she found herself starstruck by. "Legacy, what exactly did you do for Priceless to grant us all this attention?"

He made his best attempt at looking confused. "Huh, oh, it wasn't anything to speak of. I just did a little favor for a mutual friend."

Before she could get another word in, the house lights were turned down. The packed club erupted with screams and cheers. After the vibrant noise subsided enough to start the show, a single spotlight flashed on stage where Priceless stood holding a microphone. He beamed the biggest and most brilliant smile he could muster, then greeted the crowd with the grandeur of a circus ringmaster.

"How y'all feel out there!" Everyone responded with more cheers. "Are you readyyyy!" Again they responded, "Yeaaaaah!" The drummer led in softly with a hypnotic beat. "Live at the Phenomenon, our very own earth-toned south Dallas brown bonnnne. Errrrrrykah Baaaduuuu!"

The club went wild amid the music, which held its same soft pitch echoed by melodic mixtures of female vocalists crooning, "Baaduuuu . . . Baaduuuu . . . Baaduuuu . . . Baaduu . . ." Then the lights came up. The band was dressed in black slacks and tight stretch Lycra long-sleeve tops. The three female vocalists looked enough alike to be sisters. The main attraction was none other than

Erykah Badu herself, wrapped in a multicolored, Afrocentric gown with a matching headdress. Her back was facing the audience. She was frozen in a pose with one hand on her hip and the other extended up like a tea spout. She resembled a poster advertising *Dreamgirls* on Broadway. Next to her on stage was a life-size painting of her striking the exact same pose and wearing the exact same outfit she had on, except the painting displayed her frontal view.

The lights went out again. When they came back up, the audience roars swelled into a frenzy. She stood next to the painting, which was so well done that it appeared to be a life-size snapshot. The resemblance was uncanny.

Ms. Badu flashed her beautiful smile and winked. "It's good to be home, Dallas!"

Again they cheered even louder. Kennedy wondered who this obvious celebrity was. Everyone else knew. She was the one they stood in line and paid thirty dollars each to see.

Ms. Badu lowered her head as if she were in deep thought, but you could tell she was just feeling the sultry music behind her. She began to speak softly, in that mellow Billie Holiday voice of hers, without raising her head. "I'm home and it's hard to believe, but I finally made it back to where it all began. Oakland Avenue, now known as Malcolm X Boulevard, M.L.K, Hatcher, and little old Peabody Street. Some things have changed, too much has stayed the same, but there's always tomorrow. Before I go any further, I have to say a how've you been to my kinfolk . . . old friends and hello to my not so new ones. I love and cherish each . . . and every one."

The music stopped abruptly but only momentarily. When it started again, the spotlight was shining on the oil painting. Ms. Badu said in her warm and loving voice, "Y'all like this?" More applause. "It looks like me? Does it capture me?" The applause grew even louder. "Yeah, I guess it does. Doesn't it?"

She took the spotlight and walked across the long platform and down the stairs leading to the floor where the VIP tables were. She waved to some of the athletes she knew and named them as she recognized their faces. When she reached Legacy's table, she stopped on a dime and stared at him.

"This . . . this is the one whom we have to thank for that beautiful painting, my good friend Legacy Chiiilds." She accented the "I" in Childs with a sexy growl because she knew it would move the crowd. And it did.

She reached out and grabbed his hand as she called his name and asked him to take a bow. Legacy was embarrassed. Everyone in the place was looking right into his mouth. He wanted to hide his face, but the spotlight found him, making that an impossibility. So he stood up briefly, grinned and bore it, then nobly nodded his affection to her.

As she turned and walked back toward the stage, she looked back at Kennedy and winked. "He's a good one, honey, helped me with my situation." Then she broke into a hit song of hers, "Next Lifetime."

Legacy was beside himself. He figured that's what Priceless meant when he said, "Tell Jackson you're on the menu."

Kennedy was in awe. All of her dates with Simpson combined couldn't have come close to equaling this. She felt tremors deep down in her soul because Legacy was admired for his talents and his work, not for the money he had. He was adored as well as appreciated for just being himself. She never knew something so simple could feel so good. Not to mention that the concert was urgent and off the hook. It made couples laugh, reflect, and fall in love all over again. By the end of the show, the audience was more than ready to try some of the things Erykah Badu sang about in her heartfelt lyrics.

After the show, Kennedy gazed at her date with happy eyes all the way back to his jeep. "That was the best time of my life. Legacy, thank you so much. I could never ask for more than that." He smiled and winked just as the singer had. She laughed and leaned over to kiss him, but he playfully dodged it.

"Don't be trying to kiss all on me 'cause I know Ms. Er-y-kah Ba-du. The lyricist herself." She tried to kiss him again, but he dodged another one.

They were both still laughing when Kennedy asked to go to his place instead of taking her back to her apartment. Since she nor any other woman had been to his place, he was apprehensive. She sensed it but pressed anyway, "Don't give me that look. We go to my place all the time and I've never been to yours. I won't take no for an answer." She pouted and stuck out her bottom lip like a small child who'd dropped a lollipop in the mud.

Legacy pulled over on the shoulder to give her his complete and undivided attention. "And why would we be going to my place, Kennedy?" he asked suspiciously.

"Because a person's home says a lot about them and I want to know as much about you as possible." That sounded like a plausible reason, and it was enough to convince him to give in.

Legacy steered the jeep down several dark back alleys until he was deep into the industrial district. Three-and four-story warehouses muddled up the concrete terrain. Cement trucks rested, from long hard workdays in the city, in a locked parking lot across the street. Huge bundles of steel beams bound by thick wire lay alongside a warehouse door with CHEMICAL WASTE painted on it. The door was dirty. The door was also the entrance into Legacy's warehouse apartment. Kennedy's face fell when she realized that ratty old warehouse was their destination.

"You're kidding, right? This is some kind of a joke?"

Legacy opened the large iron door as anyone else would have opened a normal one. "Nope, this is what you've been waiting to see." He was more concerned by her distaste than she was for his mental health. "You change your mind? This is hardly what you expected, isn't it?"

She surveyed the entranceway. "No, no, it's not quite what I pictured, but you artist types are a strange breed."

He didn't understand that comment, but it didn't sound like a compliment to him. Nonetheless, he invited her in. She entered like someone apprehensively walking into a home where a murder had taken place, thinking the body might still be inside.

Legacy allowed her to voyage ahead. She didn't get two steps inside before the thunderous snarl of a large barking dog slammed her into Legacy as she tried to escape through the front door.

"Ahhhhhhhhhhhh!" she screamed.

He grabbed her around the waist before she hurt herself. "Wait, wait . . . Kennedy, wait a minute. It's okay. There's no dog, no dog."

He began to laugh as she moved behind him with the agility of a WWF wrestler, still expecting to see a giant starving animal charging her way. "There's no dog. It's part of this alarm system I put together. Dog Pound Surround Sound." She wanted to believe him, but her pounding heart wouldn't allow it. He had to prove it, so he programmed the alarm system to bark again. When it did on command, she straightened up and moved out from behind him. Peeping around corners.

"You . . . could have killed me!" she said, catching her breath. "Why didn't you warn me?"

"Well, I thought I'd let you find out on your own how secure I am living down here. If anyone gets past Big Bruno the barking alarm system, I have the whole place wired to go up in flames, trapping the would-be thief inside to die a gruesome, hellish death."

"They'd be trapped inside?" she repeated in disbelief. "Uh-uh, no way. This is way too serious for me. I'm getting out of here." She started for the door.

"Kennedy! I'm joking. A joke, remember? It's a thing that's supposed to make you laugh. Don't be so mental."

"Mental?" She stood in her how-dare-you pose with both hands on her hips.

"Yeah, mental. It's not that serious. If someone wants to break in and get what's mine, they can have it. I'm not willing to kill anyone over it. Besides, since I painted CHEMICAL WASTE on the front door, bums nor the druggies come around here anymore."

Legacy raised both arms like a king admiring all that he owned. "All this is mine." Then he hit the light switch. Four sets of lights came on individually. The shocking luminescence made both of them squint until their eyes could focus. "I hate when that happens," he said, walking toward several objects covered by canvas tarps.

When Kennedy's eyes focused, Legacy's enormous warehouse apartment wasn't rundown or dirty at all. On the contrary, it was quite spectacular. She uncovered his furniture, all art deco pieces. There were a pair of bright-red comfort chairs large enough to be love seats and an oversized deep, royal-blue sofa shaped like a wave. He began to cover them again, but she argued the point. "Don't," she insisted. "These are some of the most exclusive pieces sold at the New Age. You can't even get their catalog unless your income is six figures." She looked at him from the corner of her eyes. "You don't make," she motioned with her hands because she was embarrassed to ask after she'd started, "six . . . ?"

"Figures? No, not hardly. Remember, I'm just a lowly college student." He returned the same corner-of-the-eye glare she'd flashed him. "Honestly, I know Hymrick down at New Age. Designed his showroom, painted a few walls, and threw in a sketch or two. He let me take anything I wanted. A couch and chairs were all I needed at the time. No need in being greedy. I'm just saving 'em for my art studio, when I get enough money to afford a real one."

He pointed to the far corner of the room where he stored a drawing table and paintings covered with smaller tarps than the others. Kennedy strolled off in that direction. Legacy followed close behind.

"Hey, they're not finished," he yelled, and picked up his pace, but it was too late.

She saw him coming and ran over to them. She pulled off the first one. It was a replica of her teenage painting, *Borrowed Shoes,* only much better than the original. The next one was a collage of the furniture in her apartment. Only she could have recognized the pieces, because they were intentionally distorted. It was a masterpiece of Expressionism, but she'd never seen it done with ordinary house furniture.

He grabbed her hand before she could unveil the third one. "I'm not sure you want to see that one. I don't know what you might think of me if you do," Legacy explained.

She stared at his desperate, panicked expression. His nervousness scared her. She became afraid of what might be under that cover, so afraid that she needed to see what it was.

After Kennedy contemplated a moment longer, he felt that she wouldn't do it, but she did. In one fell swoop, the tarp hit the floor. Legacy wanted to reach out and stop it from happening, but he couldn't. When her eyes met the canvas, she was astonished. She couldn't believe what she saw. Among the striking pastel colors plastered to the cloth background was a portrait of Kennedy in a long white flowing gown similar to a Roman toga. She was in a flower garden of some kind. She was angelic. Her hair was shiny like dark copper, and the contours of her face were smooth and subtle.

"I call it *The Lover's Muse*," he announced, standing behind her.

She whipped around as if his voice startled her. She had forgotten in that short time that she wasn't alone. "I'm so sorry," she said nervously. "You were right, I had no business looking at your work when you told me no."

They stood there looking at each other. He didn't know what she made of him immortalizing her like he did without her permission. She hoped he would forgive her insensitivity.

The room was quiet until Legacy stepped out on what he thought to be a limb. "Well, now that I'm exposed. What's your verdict?" He stood firm and expected the worst.

"I think they're just . . ." She seemed to have a momentary loss for words. "Uh, marvelous. They're simply breathtaking. All of them. Each and every one." She placed her hand over her heart. "You've got to have a showing. How many of these do you have? Seven?"

"More like seventeen."

"Legacy, you've to got to show the world what you can do. It's amazing."

"I don't know. They're not finished. I'm not sure I'm ready yet."

"I say you're ready. And what do you mean they're not finished?"

He stood there looking at the paintings before he answered. "I
haven't signed them yet."

Kennedy found it difficult to buy in to his excuse. "You haven't
signed them? That's weak. That's really weak. You could have come
up with a much better one than that." She simply didn't understand
him. He left the signatures off purposely. That way he could hide
behind nameless masterpieces. Even after all he experienced in life,
the shy little orphan boy was still deep inside him.

"It's hard to explain, but I don't sign them because I don't know
who I am. I don't know who my parents are, what they looked like,
or where they came from. Actually, I've been thinking a lot lately
about changing my name."

"To what, King Muhammad?" she teased, trying to break the
tension. It worked.

He tried to discourage the troublesome smile peeking between
his lips, but he couldn't. "No, that name is already taken." They
both laughed thinking back on the fun they'd had getting to know
each other the first time he went to her place.

She looked back to admire the paintings again. "People need to
see your work and know who produced it. It doesn't matter how
your name came to be. You can make it famous, anyway. This is
your purpose, Legacy, and it was heaven-sent. You could enlighten
the world for generations with your talents." She still sensed apprehension but was determined to rid him of it. "You listen to me, Mr.
Legacy Freelance Childs. God blessed you with something special,
you owe him that much to share it!"

"Is that your expert opinion?"

"No, my expert opinion wouldn't be enough to do your work
justice. You need a real expert to see what you've done with the
colors, the shading, and composition. It's beyond me, way beyond
me. But, I will say this: Through your work, you could live forever.
That's a gift from God. Please don't waste it."

He walked over to where she stood and looked at the last one she'd uncovered, then looked at her. "What about that?" He pointed to the portrait of her. "You mad?"

"Mad?" She laughed oddly. "Mad? What would I have to be mad about? *The Lover's Muse*? I still can't believe you see me that way. If I looked like that, I'd be . . ." She couldn't think of anything grand enough. "Uh, the most beautiful woman in the—"

"You are to me," he interjected. "You are to me."

For a moment, she was frozen in time. "That's why I'm so crazy about you, Legacy. You do *it* for me," she whispered. Her lips were only inches away from his.

He thought about every word she'd just said but he didn't get "*it.*" "*It?*" he repeated.

"Yeah, *it*. That very elusive *it*. You know, that *it* little girls dream about as children making mud pies. The *it* that drives them insane when the cute new boy in school likes them back and all their friends get jealous. The same *it* that grown-up girls dream about, too. All our lives are spent preparing ourselves, looking for, and expecting *it* to come along one day. Well, here *it* is. Finally . . ." She began to cry. "That mystical, magical *it*."

Legacy knew at that exact instance what love felt like. It was so powerful that it moved him closer to understanding himself and forgiving his parents for abandoning him. Without allowing another second to pass, he placed his hands on Kennedy's trembling shoulders and pulled her against him. His tongue pushed between her lips gently. She moaned helplessly and wrapped her arms around him tightly as if to never let him go. The heat between them was more than enough to take it a step further. What they shared with each other drifted well beyond mere tongue dancing.

Legacy slid his hands down her shoulders, along her waist, until they found her soft behind. He caressed it again and again until he realized he couldn't stand it any longer. Suddenly, Kennedy withdrew and pushed away from his embrace. "Did I do something wrong?" he asked, alarmed.

"No . . . this. This isn't right," she answered, backing away and wiping her lips with her thumb and index finger. I'm sorry, Legacy, but this isn't right. I have to go. Please forgive me."

He couldn't understand it at all. The passion was real. They both felt it. Things were hot and then, out of nowhere, she wanted to go home.

The ride back to her apartment was completely quiet the entire way. The only words spoken came from Kennedy when she stepped out of his jeep. She didn't turn to face him when she said, "Please forgive me, I'm sorry."

He watched her storm through the glass doors until she caught the elevator going up. All that business about finding *it*, that very elusive *it*. What happened to all that? Legacy couldn't begin to figure *it* out. He was hopelessly lost, but he couldn't let go.

Sometimes, love is like a bad perm, you can spread it on thick and it still won't take. Sometimes.

Twenty-four

No Means Not Tonight

*K*ennedy dragged herself out of the elevator. A frosty layer of speculation engulfed her. She had just left the man she'd fallen in love with when the reality of what confronted her grew to be too much to handle. She found herself slouched on the sofa with her head in her hands, staring at Simpson's photo. It seemed to come alive for a moment, grinning back at her in that demeaning manner Simpson was known for.

She turned her head away; the mere sight of him made her sick to her stomach. Before another waking minute passed, she became determined to resolve the issue that had her caught up in a web of despair. Kennedy's life had been put on hold and nearly all the dignity entrusted by her ancestors was gone. At that very moment, she was stripped to the bare essentials of her soul. Her saving grace, however, was realized in the one thing she could always count on but never knew she possessed, the inner strength that black women pay for with tears but carry as proudly as their own name.

She rumbled through her purse, eventually finding her cigarettes. Before the match went out, the first long drag filled her lungs, providing an anticipated rush of nicotine to help her handle it all while she dialed his home number.

Simpson answered the phone on the first ring. "Stone," he said quickly, as if bothered by the interruption.

"Simpson, we need to talk. I'm tired of getting the runaround from you."

There was no immediate response, then he asked rudely, "Who is this?"

Kennedy was appalled. "What in the hell do you mean, who is this? It's Kennedy, damn you. After three years you still don't know my voice?" Trying to refrain from yelling, she felt herself losing it, but the drama was overwhelming. "Just how many other women call and bitch about getting the runaround from you?"

Again there was a long stream of silence before he answered. "Look, Kennedy, I can't deal with this right now. I'm all tied up."

Suddenly she lost it. Snapped. "I can't believe I'm hearing this from you!" she screamed. "Don't you know our relationship is hanging by a very thin thread? Does that even matter to you anymore? You've got to come up with some answers, homeboy. And I mean right now. Yeah, you're on my time. And I'm sick of this shit. Sick of it!"

While she ranted, he held the phone in disgust. It was difficult for him to carry on with his business at hand, a late-night houseguest.

"Look!" he whipped sharply, "I said, now isn't the time."

Shock waves traveled through the telephone at the speed of light and subsequently knocked some sense into her head. Her entire constitution underwent a thorough and immediate self-assessment, and she didn't like what she found. There was one thing left to do: Rectify that I'll-stand-by-and-wait-until-my-man-is-finished-making-a-complete-fool-outta-me-before-I-get-ready-to-stand-up-for-myself character flaw.

"Let me tell you something, Stoney . . . you no longer have the option to tell me when I can and can't see you, nor when to lie down and roll over. Tonight things will change . . ."

Simpson's patience had exceeded his capacity. He felt assured, like all the times before, that he still had the upper hand and there was no way she would risk jeopardizing their relationship; that had always been his trump card, held closely to the vest.

"Are you finished?" he asked, as calmly as he could. "We'll discuss it tomorrow. I already told you, I'm tied up and I don't have time for this tonight."

More irritated than angry, he slammed the phone down, composed himself, and then poured two stout glasses of champagne. Back to the business at hand.

The windshield wipers worked overtime as the blue Mustang glided along the empty wet streets of Dallas. Kennedy couldn't stand being treated as if she were anything less than a lady any longer. After being with Legacy, she knew what it felt like not only to be loved but also to be cared for, and there was no going back now.

Rain poured down in buckets as she exited the tollway at Parker Road. She drew nearer to Simpson's home in Plano. Possessed and driven to see his face after telling him that he no longer held her mind and body in check, Kennedy needed to see his reaction. She deserved at least that much. But even more, she had to know if she could actually pull it off.

No one can keep a hold on you like a lover who robs you of self-esteem. Kennedy was hell-bent on getting hers back tonight.

The rain continued to fall as she motored down those pretentious suburban streets. Large homes aligned the dark and somewhat dreary landscape. If any other cars traveled along those roads with her, she hadn't noticed. She couldn't see anything clearly past the angry incantation that swelled inside of her, contaminating her every thought.

When she reached his ridiculously overpriced two-story abode, sitting at the end of a vast cul-de-sac perpendicular to the road she was on, all the lights were off in the front of the house. But she knew he was still there. Simpson didn't like driving his precious car in the rain, afraid that other drivers didn't possess the skills necessary to avoid an accident. He was all about himself, which was another thing she came to despise about him, remembering he'd purchased that particular home because of its grand drive-up appeal. Everyone who entered the subdivision admired it. That's why he had to have it. It was his showpiece, the setting for many extravagant social gatherings.

Kennedy ran her front tires over the curb, leaving a thick black stripe over his cement walkway. The car door swung open with such fury that she didn't bother to close it. Storming toward the massive front door on a mission, she was prepared for whatever awaited on the other side.

After several failed attempts to summon him by ringing the bell, she began pounding on the door until her hands were red and severely bruised. It hurt like hell, but she was too mad to acknowledge the pain or the fact that her clothes were soaking wet. It was war, a war of the hearts, and she refused to surrender.

Suddenly, Simpson snatched the door open, catching her by surprise, but she remained focused on what she went there to do. He was bare-chested in his silk sleeping pants and leather house shoes.

"What in the hell are you doing here? You know I don't allow you to stop by without my permission!"

Those words put a crazed scowl on her face. "Permission! Who do you think you're talking to, somebody's child? I don't need permission. I'm an adult, a grown woman. And I come and go where I want, when I want. You got that? Stoney!" Since she'd only called him that when she was drunk, he assumed that she was then.

"Look," he said, trying to get her to lower her voice by controlling his. "I don't need this kinda shit happening at my front door.

This ain't the ghetto. And I've told you . . . I just don't have time to see you right now."

He attempted to slam the door, but Kennedy instinctively threw her petite frame against it. Although he managed to outmuscle her enough to get it closed, she managed to catch a glimpse of a woman's purse resting on the sofa table in his family room.

The short skirmish was over and it seemed that Kennedy had lost. She had been literally thrown out into the street, in the rain, no less, by the man she thought she'd spend her life with.

Despite being worn out and wringing wet, the crazed scowl still masked her face, and it gleamed more than ever now.

Kennedy marched back to the curb and climbed into the car. "I'll show you. You asshole!" she declared loudly, as she drove her fast car to the end of his street. The stop sign seemed to beckon her. She slammed on the brakes. "That's it!" she shouted, maneuvering a 180-degree U-turn to spin the car around. Peering down the pretentious street with overpriced houses, she unleashed a grin so sinister, the devil himself would have envied it.

She revved the motor twice as if to signal a warning like bulls do before they charge. "Mr. Stone," she called out, as if he were in front of her car. "I think we have a jacked-up understanding of one another's feelings. But I'm about to straighten all that out right now. Zero to sixty in under five seconds, huh? Let's see if that salesman was bullshitting me."

She floored the gas pedal. The Mustang spun its wheels, then took off like a jet down a runway, rapidly approaching Stone's house. Doom and destruction rode with her. There was enough room for all three of them. When Kennedy knew it was too late to turn back, she closed her eyes and gripped the steering wheel for dear life.

"Ahhhhhhh!" she screamed as her front tires hit the curb, sending her airborne over his finely manicured lawn. It was the thrill of her life to go crashing through Simpson's prized imported plate-glass window with the force of a pissed-off hurricane. *"Boommmm!"* Destroying everything in her path. Hurricane Kennedy.

Glass shattered, walls caved in, and thick clouds of confusion filled the abruptly redecorated room, with a new Ford Motors motif.

Lights in the house came on as she fought to dig herself from underneath the rubble she'd caused. The car door was smashed up and refused to open, so she climbed out through the window on the driver's side. Her head bled profusely and her body was wracked with pain, but she managed to greet Simpson when he made his way into what used to be his prized dining hall.

He couldn't believe his eyes. His mouth flew open like the gaping hole in the front of his house. He was speechless but Kennedy wasn't. She had a few things to get off her chest. "Uh-huh, bet you can see me now, huh, Simpson." What appeared to be a tall, thin attractive woman emerged behind him, wearing lacy panties, thigh-high hose, red high heels, and an open-to-the-waist nightshirt, which was the mate to Simpson's sleeping pants.

"My, my. . . . Mr. Stone," Kennedy offered, her brow raised, "and what have you here?" A closer look revealed that it wasn't a woman at all. The tall, thin person standing behind him was the companion he had been seeing, the same one Morris began telling her about when Legacy called. The same companion Simpson went to Winfrey's to see on the evening they had the Ladies Night Out. Marlana, he called himself, Ms. Drag Queen International 1997. Simpson always did like the best of everything. As it turned out, he was one of those pretenders Morris had warned her about. The charade was over.

Kennedy, Simpson, and Marlana stood there looking at one another until years of frustration began to boil over from within Kennedy's troubled soul. She shouted at the top of her lungs in a fit of embittered rage. "It's been three years! I've been putting up with your tired ass for three long years . . . treating me like my feelings didn't matter! All the time thinking you were working late for our future! You had me thinking I was inadequate when all along, you'd rather do this"—she paused to get another look at his half-naked lover—"than do me!"

Staring at Simpson's date, Kennedy began inching closer to the two of them while taking the opportunity to catch her breath. "Oh, how inappropriate of me," she continued, now standing directly in front of Marlana. "I'm not minding my manners. Hi, I'm Kennedy. Maybe you've heard of me. I'm Simpleton's ex-girlfriend. And who might you be?"

Marlana didn't budge or make any attempt to enter into a war of words that were sure to follow, so Kennedy started in again by herself. "What's wrong? *Cat* gotcha tongue? No, that couldn't be right, because you're supposed to be the *caaaat*."

Simpson knew that an argument would further aggravate the situation and was just what his intruder wanted. He wasn't willing to provide the neighbors with any more of a spectacle than they were already getting while gathering around, beneath their umbrellas, outside the house to investigate the car hanging out of it. Some of the onlookers were more interested in what was going on inside the house as they peeked in from the outside.

Kennedy presented her hand to Marlana as if she were honestly seeking an introduction. "Where was I? Oh, yes. I was asking your name, wasn't I? Was it Michael, Mike, Harry, Hank, Frank, maybe . . . ? Nnno, I've got it." Kennedy smiled as brightly as she could manage. "You definitely look like a *Dick* to me."

Before Marlana knew what hit him, Kennedy snatched the wig off his head and held it high over hers, waving it joyfully at all the nosy bystanders looking on as if she'd just been awarded a coveted first-place trophy. Simpson's date attempted to cover his head while ducking out of the room.

After the cat was out of the bag, or closet, Simpson made one last attempt at damage control. "Kennedy. I know you must be upset, but don't you think you've done enough? I mean, my neighbors are watching." It was obvious that he was more concerned about dealing with the fallout after his neighbors began snubbing him.

"Like I care what your neighbors see and hear! I'm sure they already know that you're an insensitive, egotistical, poor excuse for a man! I thought you could change." Her voice was calmer now. "But I was wrong about you. You can't help it. You're a sick bastard."

Feeling faint, she raised her arm and brushed her forehead with the back of her hand. When it fell down to her side, it was covered with blood. Simpson exhibited a disturbing expression that suggested Kennedy may have been badly hurt. Instinctively, she followed his eyes to her hand. Her eyes widened when she saw deep-red blood dripping from it. The next thing she remembered was being hoisted into an ambulance with police officers and flashing lights surrounding her.

Twenty-five

Stay Clear of My Misery

arshall hadn't run into Jasmine on campus. Maybe it was due to his conscious avoidance of all the places he knew she would be. The fear and shame he carted around wore on him like a steady stream eroding a great mountain, reducing it to a small rock and voiding it of significance. His one-night escapade with Shauni Woodbridge changed his life, but he was yet to fully comprehend its magnitude and the road his mistake would lead him down.

The spring was in full bloom and the buzz of graduation resounded among the UTC seniors. Marshall sat on a bench outside the Zoology and Life Sciences building on the far east side of campus. Normally, premed, botany, geology, and other science majors were the only students who traveled the walkways where he collected his thoughts or fell deep into another paperback novel. That's how he dealt with his anguish.

He learned quickly to busy his mind with other people's thoughts, those of authors who had something to say through the characters they wrote about. It was a defense mechanism he adopted while refusing to get tested for AIDS, choosing not to address it. It wasn't so much to combat his denial as it was for him to continue life as he knew it, with a promising future. Without hope, he would have felt compelled to consider other alternatives, just as Rorey had.

The eleven o'clock hour was approaching. He had a nonverbal communication class to get to and more than enough time to get there. While casually standing, he brushed the back of his walking shorts with one hand as he continued reading with the other. The direct course to the Liberal Arts building was through the union courtyard, but that meant being near Jasmine's next class. He didn't want to risk it, so he took another route through the back parking lot. Many students scurried to find parking spaces while others casually made their way to various destinations. Marshall thought about the chapter he'd just read in Walter Mosley's mystery thriller *White Butterfly*. An incompetent physician diagnosed one of the main characters with syphilis years ago, and then the poor man later found that it was just a pimple on his penis. If only he could be so lucky, Marshall thought.

While he waded between rows of idle cars in the full parking lot, he continued to ponder how syphilis was the worst sexually transmitted disease a person could get back then. His mind was on everything but where he was going. When he stepped off the curb, a car slammed on the brakes, creating a loud and urgent screech of the tires. He instinctively jumped back onto the curb and held up his hand to apologize to the driver for being careless. As he and the driver made eye contact, Marshall froze. Jasmine sat behind the wheel of that car with a blank expression staring back at him. Marshall wanted to acknowledge her and wave hello, but by the time that thought came to him, she was gone. It was perhaps better that way, since there was nothing left to say between them. She had given him walking papers a couple months ago, but he'd already walked off the job long before then. There was nothing to say between them.

Twenty-six

Wounded

Kennedy woke up in the hospital three days later with a concussion, a gash in her head, four bruised ribs, and a fractured bone in her forearm. Considering all that pain and soreness, it would have been nearly impossible to drive a car. It worked out just as well because her car was totaled. It took all of four hours and two tow trucks to put that car out of his house.

Legacy had been in the room she shared with a hernia patient every minute since Morris called him two days ago. Washing up in the tiny bathroom and sleeping in an uncomfortable chair were small prices to pay for Legacy, if he could be there when she regained consciousness.

Morris had just arrived with several more magazines for the both of them to share. Legacy was standing near Kennedy's bed. "Hey, sleepyhead," he whispered, holding her hand.

"Sleeping Beauty, arise," Morris added.

Kennedy licked her dry lips to moisten them. She moved slowly and looked around the room. Her face was dark and bruised. Bandages were wrapped around her head. She tried to raise her injured arm and grunted in pain as she failed. When she looked at her arm in a cast, she winced and sighed.

"Easy, Kennedy," Legacy instructed. "You have to take it slow. The doctor said it would be a couple of days before you can even think about getting up. If your tests come back all right, then we'll see about another game of air hockey." That promise transformed her wounded frown into a crooked smile.

She looked at Legacy, then Morris, then over to the next bed, where the female hernia patient was resting. There was a sixty-something redheaded heavy-set white woman, Mrs. O'Dougal, smiling and waving. She was nosy but kind. Legacy had learned more than he ever wanted to know about a hernia operation as she explained every excruciating detail to Morris the day before, when he helped to fix her hair before her family came to visit. She'd say, "Now, Morris, don't do anything too risqué. I'm not a loose woman and I'd hate to give that young doctor the wrong idea. Just make me look respectable for my folks, who'll be coming by to see about me. Just make me respectable."

Morris took great pride in his work. They decided that Suzanne Somers had more tucks and lifts than she admitted publicly, but both agreed that her latest hairstyle was to die for and suited Mrs. O'Dougal to a T. Morris cut and styled as the old woman read the tabloid articles aloud. Now they were the best of buddies. They'd spent the entire day sharing gossip and perusing the Hollywood rags for celebrity breakup stories.

"Awwwe, how long have I been here?" Kennedy groaned. "I feel like death warmed over. I must look a mess."

"You'll be fine," Mrs. O'Dougal answered. "Morris can do your hair when . . ." She stopped herself when she realized Kennedy's head was bandaged.

Morris cocked his head and shunned her for that unwarranted comment. "I think Mrs. O'Dougal and I will work a crossword puzzle while we let you two talk." Morris grabbed the dividing partition and whipped it around until he and the older lady were on the other side of it.

"But I don't like crossword puzzles," Mrs. O'Dougal complained from the other side of the curtain.

Legacy's face displayed worry behind a bright but manufactured smile. "Good afternoon. I was beginning to think you didn't want to come back to visit us."

"What day is it?"

"Tuesday."

"Tuesday? Do I still have a job?"

"Yeah, your boss was here yesterday. He said not to worry and to take as long as you need to recover."

She squirmed a bit to get more comfortable. "Did I really drive my car through Simpson's house?"

"Yeah, that's what the police report said, anyway."

Kennedy's eyes roamed the room again, expecting to see some armed police guard, but she discovered Simpson coming through the door instead. "The police won't be bothering you," he affirmed cheerfully. She had not heard so much excitement coming from him except when money was involved.

Simpson sat a crystal vase, crammed full with pink carnations, on the small table next to her bed. Legacy hadn't said a word, but he did study Kennedy's face. He still wasn't sure if the incident wasn't an accident. No one knew what possessed her to park her car in Simpson's front room.

Simpson held up a bouquet for Kennedy to see. "I figured you would be awake sometime today, so I brought you these."

Morris cautiously stepped out from behind the huge divider. He saw it coming before the others did. "Is . . . everything okay over there, Kennedy?" he asked, as if he could have prevented it if it weren't going to be.

Before Kennedy could answer, Simpson stepped toward her and grabbed her weak hand. "Everything will be fine," he answered to Morris in general. "As a matter of fact, you can all go now that her husband-to-be is here. But don't get me wrong, I do thank you for looking after her."

Kennedy was stunned and confused. Husband to be? Wasn't he the man whose chandelier she'd turned into a hood ornament? Why all the newfound honor and respect? These were the questions of all the others in the room, too. Even Mrs. O'Dougal knew what had taken place. She was nosy, after all.

Kennedy mustered up enough might to pull her hand away from his grasp. Legacy became alarmed but held his ground to see where Simpson Stone was going with his Mr. Good Guy routine.

"Don't worry, darling," Simpson said in his most pleasant voice. "I didn't press charges. All is forgotten, but we do need to talk about our future." He glanced at Legacy, then sneered at Morris before continuing. "So you can tell your little friend there and the paintbrush kid they can both run along." The tension was too much for Morris, so he left the room in a huff.

Simpson scoffed, staring Legacy down. "That's one down, one to go. Maybe you should run off behind him with your tail between your legs, too. Yeah, I remember you from the club and I didn't think much of you then, either."

"I'd like to see your best effort at running me off," Legacy snapped loudly. "Please . . . try and make me leave? I'm begging you."

He stationed himself like a fearless jungle cat protecting his lioness, ready to pounce at Simpson's slightest move. The gauntlet had been cast down at the feet of his adversary. Legacy hoped that the man standing in front of him would do something stupid. He wouldn't be disappointed.

Simpson motioned toward him with both arms half coiled in a position used to push heavy objects. Ultimately, he wouldn't get the chance. Legacy quickly sidestepped him and clocked him on the chin with a straight right-hand jab, wobbling him, and prepared to hit him hard again when Morris appeared with the doctor. He was a Marcus Welby look-alike accompanied by a stout male orderly.

"Hey . . . that's enough of that. Break it up!" the doctor demanded, throwing his arms around Legacy's.

The beefy orderly smiled at Simpson, who staggered to keep his balance while holding his face. Beefy didn't know Simpson, but that didn't stop him from disliking his pretentious first impression. "You two should be ashamed of yourselves," the doctor reprimanded. "This patient needs rest and you're in here duking it out like thugs. I have the mind to throw you both out, but she does need mental stimulation. Obviously, one of you has to go."

Legacy and Simpson flashed matching contemptuous jeers at one another. Neither one seemed willing to relinquish their territory.

Simpson exhaled his frustration, then sought to forecast a decision. "So who's it going to be, darling, me or paint boy?"

No one moved but Kennedy, who tried to sit up again. Morris went over to prop pillows up behind her back, then stood by her side. Legacy studied her face again. She seemed uncomfortable while everyone looked to her to solve the dispute.

"Well, Kennedy, I guess he does have a point?" Legacy submitted apprehensively. "Who will it be?"

Kennedy lowered her eyes as if to contemplate the situation before looking up to address it head-on. Her eyes locked on to her longtime boyfriend. "Simpson," she said sadly.

Simpson grinned, sensing victory, but it was short-lived.

"Simpson," she said again. "Please leave. These are the people who love me and I'm convinced that doesn't include you."

Utterly shocked, Simpson began to plead. "Kennedy, you're making a big mistake. Don't turn your back on me, you'll regret it."

He moved toward her, but the orderly interceded with a warning. "You heard the lady. She asked you to leave, and I'm sure you don't want no more of that feller over there." He nodded his head toward Legacy, who was ready for plenty more, if it came to that.

Simpson didn't persist. He was outnumbered. The orderly made sure he found the way to the exit. As soon as the doctor followed them out, Morris sighed relief.

Mrs. O'Dougal pulled the partition back, raised her fist, and cheered. "Good for you, honey! You really told him where to get off."

The woman's bluntness in business that had nothing to do with her made Kennedy smile. And, although Kennedy was relieved, confusion plagued her. She'd never seen Simpson act that way, so pleasant, so nice. Maybe he finally saw the light, the error of his ways. Perhaps finding himself in perilous danger in the middle of the night had led to a life-changing reformation.

Legacy slept on Kennedy's sofa for the first full week she was home. He filled her refrigerator with fruit and vegetables and other healthy snacks, one trip to the supermarket that was long overdue. He filled her nights with laughter and promises of great expectations. She couldn't pretend if she wanted to that love like this was commonplace. Her troubled face bore a radiant glow that confessed openly to never knowing a love like his, one that was so giving and innocent. It was the kind that love songs were written about.

Agony came in the way of a long wait for her body to heal. Anticipation lingered daily, Kennedy wanting to show him exactly how appreciative she was and give back what she felt she'd been receiving in abundance from him. All Legacy wanted was for her to get well and belong to him. If things turned out like he hoped, there would be a lifetime of blissful reciprocity.

After Kennedy regained a good portion of her strength and mobility, Legacy relinquished his personal night-care program and began sleeping at his own apartment again. Two days later, phone calls from Simpson started pouring in. He'd call and plead with the woman he'd lost to see him, although he couldn't explain why it was so important. It was a bad idea, she thought, but he was relentless. Calls at one in the afternoon, midnight, two in the morning, sunrise, something was definitely up with him. He wouldn't let go.

When she finally agreed to meet with him, against her better judgment, she suggested that they arrange a public meeting place. Simpson, however, had other ideas. He demanded to visit her at the apartment, gesturing that it would be easier for her and that she wouldn't have the trouble of catching a taxi. Of course, she didn't buy it, but that wouldn't stop him from trying. Soon after being turned down for the last time, he resorted to showing up at her place unannounced. Kennedy refused to let him in but offered some advice through a locked door. "Stalking is against the law, Simpson. I hope you know that. I *will* press charges." Now his persistence frightened her. Something was very different about this Simpson. She felt bad enough just talking to him when he called, fearing Legacy would find out. She couldn't stand the thought of losing the best thing that ever happened to her, but she had no clue how to handle a desperate ex-boyfriend. The other men in her past were all but forgotten.

Morris stopped by and brought groceries when Legacy was tied up with graduation rehearsals and intern interviews for studies abroad. He had always dreamed of studying art in Europe.

May 26 was a beautiful Saturday. The smell of freshly cut grass supplied just another ingredient to a day meant to last in the memories of the 2,759 graduates of UTC and the loved ones who attended the ceremony. A calm breeze brushed gently against the bountiful flower arrangements at both ends of the stage. University President Karen Morris called the names one by one as the anxious students awaited their turns to receive their diplomas and a farewell from school days.

When President Morris briefly hesitated the commencement ceremony to gain the audience's attention, a lump sprang up in Marshall's throat. She looked at him nearing the stage and smiled at him, then she continued. "Marshalllll Coates!" she announced, with the exuberance of a television game show host.

An outburst of applause, standing ovations, and cheers resounded on the deep-green front lawn. Marshall was shocked that everyone knew who he was. The shell he had crawled into may have forged his new reality of desired solitude, but those who watched him explode on the football field hailed his triumphs tumultuously.

He stepped up on the stage, received his diploma with his left hand, and shook the president's hand with his right one. Flashbulbs illuminated from all directions. During his short jaunt across stage, with thousands looking and cheering, his eyes found Jasmine's far back in the eighteenth row. She was standing along with everyone else, but her sad eyes and a forced smile accompanied her applause. There was joy inside of her, but Marshall couldn't be sure from that distance. It was muddled beneath the pain he'd caused her.

After the ceremony, parents congratulated, friends rejoiced, and everyone celebrated. Legacy reintroduced Jasmine to Kennedy, who was healing nicely but still had her arm in a sling. The stitches were removed from her head and she was glad to be outside. Several weeks of home confinement presented the worst kind of cabin fever.

Marshall walked away from a group of well-wishers and supportive fans when he saw Jasmine. Maybe he hoped that they could recapture what was lost or that just being close to her would be enough to better his good-byes. When he approached the group, Legacy's face lit up. "Marshall, we're finally finished. No more classes."

Marshall manufactured a solemn grin. "Yeah, Freelance, we did it." It was as empty as his heart was.

Jasmine looked away the entire time he was among them. Kennedy noticed her sudden change in disposition but didn't know what warranted it.

"Well, I guess I'd better be getting back. The family's probably looking for me," Marshall said, his voice heavily laden with reluctance. "Freelance, I'll call you when I get settled. Kennedy, it was nice to finally meetcha."

He had the world at his feet, but the woman meant to be his barely looked his way. Marshall's eyes told the story that words couldn't. They were sad, apologetic, humbled, begging-for-forgiveness eyes. And yes, she missed him, too, but her pain still stood in her way. Jasmine's bottom lip was trembling before she trapped it with her teeth. She knew he was trying to find the appropriate words to convey just how sorry he was. He wanted to reach out to touch her hair, her face, offer a hug, something. Anything. But she refused to let herself get caught up again.

Rejected, Marshall understood that it would never be the same between them, as he painfully turned and walked away from what once made him whole. A single tear ran from Jasmine's eye when she heard his footstep dissolve into her memory.

The gathering dissipated. Legacy and Kennedy climbed into the jeep and headed up Interstate 35 back to Dallas. The tassel on his Wrangler-green graduation cap swayed in the wind as he drove on.

When they arrived at her apartment building, Bradshaw met them at the door, made note of the ceremonial headdress, and congratulated Legacy, who wanted everyone he saw to notice his achievement. Even when they were inside her apartment, he was reluctant to take the cap off. He was energized and filled with euphoria.

Kennedy played back the messages on her answering machine. Simpson had finally stopped calling, so it was safe to play them aloud. Morris had called to see how she was recuperating, and there was another message from the county's disease control department. She was confused as to why they'd be calling her. She dismissed the first message they'd left as a mistake. Why would the disease control center be calling her? Maybe she sustained some sort of infection caused by the crash?

Legacy's antics took her mind off it when he began singing Kool and the Gang's song "Celebration" and dancing around the room. "Come on, Kennedy," he yelled, taking her by the hand and carefully swinging her around. She laughed and danced, too, while the sling securely held her other arm.

"Legacy, stoppp! I'm out of breath," she screamed, pulling out of a spin to catch her balance. "You go on ahead, I've got something to slow you down."

Shaking her head briskly to regain her focus, she headed for the kitchen while Legacy continued to dance in circles by himself. "Good," she said when the bottle of Moët was where she thought it was, on the bottom rung of her wine rack. She reached for two champagne glasses high on the top shelf.

Legacy noticed she was having difficulty and decided to give her a hand. "Here, let me get those for you."

His natural high was more ebullient than he thought. The glasses almost slipped from his dancing fingertips, and when he pulled the bottle of champagne from the wine rack, a firm grasp eluded him like a drunk who'd already had too much to drink. The bottle rolled from his clutch. He tried to catch it before it hit the floor, but it was out of his reach. He and Kennedy both expected to hear a splash when it landed, but there was no splash. The bottle hit the floor hard and spun around as if it were instrumental in a young lover's game of spin the bottle. Before it stopped spinning, the base fell off it. They looked at each other and then back down at the bottle. Legacy kneeled down to inspect this strange bottle of champagne.

The bottom had come off but didn't leak one drop of liquid. He cautiously picked it up by the neck. When three transparent bags fell out onto the floor, he sprang to his feet as if they were poisonous snakes. They were sandwich bags filled with white powder. The two of them stood there peering at each other again, but nervously this time. By looking at the way the bags were fastened and taped at the ends with the weight of the contents written on them, Legacy knew what had to be inside. He'd seen enough bags like that while he did tours in the Air Force to recognize them. It was pure, uncut cocaine.

"Who . . . where did you get this bottle?" he asked. His harsh tone of concern alarmed Kennedy.

"I . . . uh, Simpson. It's Simpson's. It's been here for a while. There were two, but I noticed one missing after the last time he was here." She tried to think back, but the fact that enough cocaine was sitting on her floor to cause someone a lot of trouble overruled her thoughts. "I'm . . . almost sure of it. But it was just champagne, so I didn't mention it to him. Simpson has a whole warehouse full of this stuff. I figured he couldn't care less about one bottle."

Legacy shook his head, referring to her comment. "Not bottles like this, he doesn't. That's a lot of money in those bags. A lot of money."

Kennedy squinted and shook her head slowly while Legacy became concerned with her state of mind. "Are you okay?" he asked.

She continued looking on. "Yeah, I'm fine. It's just making more sense to me now."

"What is?"

"I've been racking my brain trying to figure out why Simpson showed up at the hospital as if nothing happened. Why he didn't press charges for all the damage and embarrassment I caused him with his neighbors and why he's been trying to come by here to see me after I sent all of his belongings to his office."

Jealousy consumed him. "What do you mean, he's been calling to come by? Here?"

"Yeah, that always puzzled me. He's been begging to see me, but only if he could come here. And when I refused to, he immediately changed back into his usual contemptible self. I didn't understand it then, but now I know. He'd been storing his drugs here and, casually as you please, picking them up when he needed them. I can't believe this, a hundred and one ways to screw Kennedy James over."

"Well, believe it. And I bet I know who he works for. Richey Glass. The club owner I told you had connections with the mob." He remembered the first run-in he'd had with Simpson at Club Matrix when Simpson was terrified to go up and see Richey. "He's in it deep. Richey doesn't play when it comes to money. But why would he keep it here? It's almost like he's hiding it from someone. I'm surprised Simpson didn't come up here and demand it back."

Just when it came to him that Simpson delivered a parcel package to Richey's office no more than two inches thick, which couldn't have contained a bottle of any kind, someone knocked on the door. Kennedy hesitated. "I'm not expecting anyone."

Legacy pulled a sharp knife from her silverware drawer. "Go ahead. Check it out."

She cautiously approached the door. When she leaned against the door, her heart began to pound. Darkness was all she found when she looked into the peephole. Someone had their hand over it from the other side. "Who is it?" she asked apprehensively.

"Open up and you'll find out," a friendly voice replied.

She turned to check with Legacy, who was holding a sharp knife behind his back.

He nodded and whispered, "Open it."

As she opened it slowly, someone pushed hard against it and knocked her down. She lay on her back with Legacy running over to see if she was hurt. He dropped the knife on the floor by her side. When the door slammed, they both looked up to find Simpson and another shorter man standing over them. Simpson wore a tan suit with a maroon silk shirt opened at the neck down to his chest. A large gold medallion hanging around his neck and a semiautomatic machine gun accessorized the other man's expensive clothing. The short man, with an unkempt dark-brown beard, appeared to be Cuban at first glance. Legacy had spent his whole life studying different ethnic characteristics. After a closer look, he was sure the hired gun was Colombian.

"Isn't this cute?" Simpson snarled, looking at them on the floor. "And what is that knife for, Paint Boy? Protection? Don't you know you should never bring a knife to a gunfight?"

Legacy clenched his jaws tightly but was afraid to make any sudden moves for fear the foreigner might shoot and not stick around to ask questions later. It was obvious he was there to discourage that sort of thing. "Kennedy, I recall hearing these words, 'I bet you'll see me now.' Don't you remember those words? Yes, it does have a nice ring to it."

For the first time she saw the cowardly little boy Simpson really was, one who paid other people to do his dirty work. How could she have wasted all that time thinking he was the one she wanted?

He motioned for the gunman to hold them at bay while he got what he came for. "And shoot them both if they move an inch," he added, kicking Legacy in the stomach before stepping over him.

As he clutched his ribs and tried to catch his breath, the gunman watched attentively. He was paid to be the muscle. Killing two people he'd never seen before would have been bonus money.

The gunman watched them as Simpson discovered they'd found his stash. "I see. That's what the knife is all about. You got me. Here's your chance. What are you gonna do about it?" He was standing over Legacy, who remained still. "That's what I thought. Not a damned thing." Before he exited the apartment, he looked down at them and sneered. "You can have her now. I'm through with her. Oh, yeah, a word of advice. Forget about what you've found and I won't have to send Gustavo here back to pay you a visit." The foreigner laughed as they headed for the elevator.

Legacy's eyes were red and deep with anger. He wished Simpson had shown up alone, without hired insurance. "You okay?" he asked, helping her off the floor.

"I'm fine. I've been through worse spills lately." She smiled a bitter smile and dusted herself off. Legacy went to the window and looked down to the street. He watched Simpson and Gustavo along with two other foreigners get into a long, black Mercedes sedan and pull away.

Kennedy knew Legacy was thinking something that could get both of them killed. "Please don't do anything rash. Legacy, it's over and good riddance. Don't let that jerk be a part of our future like he's been in our past. He doesn't want me and he's got no other reason to ever come back here again."

He hugged her tightly, but the determined look on his face suggested it was not over. Not for him. He knew that a time would come to rectify the situation, but Kennedy's safety weighed heavily in the back of his mind. He didn't know how long it would take, but the time would come, he'd make sure of that.

Twenty-seven

Sorrow, Addressed to Me

*K**ennedy stood outside the building** in a comfortably fitting sleeveless pastel sundress with a floral print. Her arm was out of the sling but still sore and relatively weak. She wasn't sure at first if she exited the DART (Dallas Area Rapid Transit) city bus at the right stop, but the address written on the card she was given matched the one on the building: 1400 Motor Street. She wanted to prove that they had mistaken her for someone with a disease, which they said she had when she reluctantly returned their call, but she couldn't seem to move past the front door as she peered in through the glass. She wanted to storm in and tell them all how wrong their test results were, how very wrong, and where they could stick them. However, the thought of a positive test result wouldn't allow her to throw a mad tirade fit for the ten o'clock news.

As far as she could see from the other side of the glass door, the walls were white, the floors were white, and all the personnel staff's uniforms were white. The place was spotless. That place. That dying place. Everything was ridiculously clean. How ironic for such a place of grief and suffering to be without a single blemish. She went to the Autumn Leaves AIDS Help Center after she'd caught a cross-town bus to the hospital only to learn that her test results could not be explained to her there. The nurse said to take the card and ask for Tonetta Thomas.

She closed her eyes and shamefully went inside. The fear of running into someone she knew or, God forbid, of someone touching her wedged itself in the front of her mind. After all, she didn't have AIDS. Couldn't have. She'd only had one partner for the past three years. That despicable disease wouldn't have had any opportunity to infect her. She was heterosexual and didn't shoot up drugs. Statistics said that she was in the shallow end of seven percent, which was considered low risk. What she hadn't considered was her promiscuous lover who happened to be bisexual and had engaged in risky encounters with many partners, both men and women. She had blocked Simpson so far out of her mind that she didn't once think that it was possible that he had infected her. Sure, she had had unprotected anal intercourse with him, but that didn't necessarily mean she would get AIDS. "Don't gay men and druggies get AIDS?" she thought aloud. That's what she'd always heard.

While she pondered that question, daydreaming near the receptionist's desk, she began to lose her nerve. As she surveyed the waiting area in utter fear, an old man shuffled slowly down the long hallway toward the exit door behind her. He easily could have been death himself, and each step he took was slow and deliberate. "How pitiful and helpless he must feel" were among the thoughts crossing her mind. Each step looked as if it would be his last, but he continued to trod along. Kennedy shook her head in sorrow when he drew nearer, all slumped over and broken, with a ratty belt keeping his pants up around his twenty-seven-inch waist. Maybe he was there by mistake, too, like she was.

When the old man was a few steps from where she stood, she

wanted to turn away. Something about him wouldn't allow her to. Then she couldn't take her eyes off him. His head was enlarged to almost twice the size of a normal man's and his hair seemed to barely hold on to its roots. It looked as if patches of it had been plucked out. He was hideous, broken, tired, and slumped over, but he wasn't old at all. Just a few feet from where Kennedy anchored herself, a heavy black woman in her mid-fifties with vastly graying hair stood up from a comfortable cloth-covered chair in the waiting area. She smiled right past Kennedy. It was meant for the withered man standing behind her.

"You ready to go home, baby?" the woman asked, as if he'd just finished a long day at preschool.

"Yes, Momma, but I'm real tired today," he responded, lacking the strength to raise his head up and speak at the same time. "Could you please pull the car around, Momma? I don't think I can make it to the parking lot today."

A closer look beyond his ashy skin revealed that he couldn't have been more than twenty-five years old. But something, something horrendous had to have jumped him one night. And it had to be at night. Something that could ravage a man's body from the inside out like that had to travel by night; the light of day surely would have exposed it.

Inevitably, when Kennedy made sense of it all and considered the dreadful possibility that she might actually have AIDS and end up like him, she felt vomit pushing its way up from the depths of her stomach toward her esophagus. A young Hispanic nurse, who hastened to assist the young man until his mother could bring the car around, witnessed Kennedy turning green. She pointed to the women's room before Kennedy could ask where it was. She hurried through the door to avoid disaster, but it had already found its place. There went the clean white floors. Vomit spewed from her mouth, although she held both hands over it. The force was too great to be contained.

As she coughed and spat into the sink, a short, attractive black woman with a fair apricot complexion dressed in a flattering cream-colored outfit appeared behind her. The lady quickly turned the cold-water knob to full blast, then doused several paper towels before questioning if Kennedy was all right. When it seemed the situation had become relaxed enough for the lady to ask her state of being, she did just that. Unfortunately, Kennedy was distraught and too emotionally caught up to answer back with clear enunciation. She replied by shaking her head instead, while uttering, "Uh-uh . . . ," before throwing up in the sink again.

It took a lot of cold water and soaked paper towels before Kennedy could calm down enough to hold a conversation with the caring woman who looked important. "Come on in my office," she said, smiling and pulling Kennedy out of the women's rest room. "It's more private in there." The lady's smile was like a beacon, directing her to friendly shores after enduring a rough go at it on an angry sea. Amid all the drama, Kennedy didn't even realize how much her sore arm hurt when it was being pulled on.

Once they were both inside the large office, which looked more like a doctor's examination room with bookshelves than it did an administrator's office, Kennedy wiped her forehead with the towel she held onto, then slowly handed the medical referral card over the desk resting between them. The lady took the card and smiled again.

"Good," she said, looking at the card. "You're my one o'clock appointment. I was beginning to think I'd been stood up. Glad you could make it. I'm Tonetta, Tonetta Thomas."

She was so pleasant, so helpful, Kennedy thought. Too pleasant and too helpful to lash out at her for a mistake the hospital must have made, forcing her to travel downtown and ultimately come face-to-face with some poor man who was obviously disease-riddled and on his last legs. No, this woman was an angel of mercy.

Tonetta read the referral card thoroughly. "Kennedy James, right?"

Kennedy nodded slowly but reserved her comments, as if it would've cost her something to speak aloud, as if it would have validated the tests somehow. The lady pulled out a stack of forms fastened to a clear fiberglass clipboard. Kennedy felt uneasy about the mere thought of her name being entered into some sort of information bin with people who had life-threatening and life-ending ailments.

"Yeah, that is my name, but you don't have to write it down on that form," Kennedy blurted out. "I'm about to leave, anyway. I just came here to tell you that the hospital made a mistake. A big mistake. And you can tell whoever it was to stop calling my house. I don't have AIDS."

Tonetta's eyes lowered. She cautiously laid the clipboard down on the desk, leaned back in her chair, and interlocked her fingers in front of her thin face, like small children do when they have just been taught to pray. "Jesus . . . they didn't talk to you before sending you over here, did they?" Kennedy's face was blank. "Christ, I knew it. I wish they would just once call me and tell me when . . ." Tonetta heaved a thorough sigh to hold back what she really wanted to say. "I'm sorry. It just doesn't help matters when the hospitals don't do their part is all. I'm not blaming you."

Sliding her chair over to the large filing cabinet built inside the wall to hold thousands of files without sacrificing any space, Tonetta read aloud the label attached to the pink color-coded file she'd pulled from the wall. "That's J-A-M-E-S, right? Yeah, that's what I thought."

Kennedy's eyes widened. "What do you mean, that's what you thought?" she asked defensively.

"I looked over your file last week but you didn't show for the first appointment, so I figured you for a denial case."

As she shook her head furiously, Kennedy finally lashed out. "But you don't seem to understand, Ms. Thomas, I don't have AIDS and I wish you'd stop insinuating that I do!"

Tonetta laid the file on her Formica desktop. "Like I said, a denial case."

Kennedy pounced to her feet. Her eyes narrowed as they shot daggers fierce enough to discourage death from approaching. "I came down here to help you fix an obvious problem you've got with your testing equipment or your computer system or whatever the hell it is, but I'm telling you for the last time, lady, I do not have AIDS!"

"I know you're distressed and it's hard to believe that it could happen to you, but . . ."

Kennedy snatched her purse off the floor and turned to walk out of the office. Tonetta was left with no choice, so she opened her file and began to rattle off Kennedy's bio like a military drill sergeant. "Kennedy James! Black female. Age: twenty-eight, height: five feet eight inches, weight: a hundred and twenty-five pounds." Kennedy wrestled with the doorknob but couldn't seem to get the door opened. It was like a scene from a horror movie. While Tonetta continued reading from Kennedy's file, she tried desperately to twist the knob with her hands now sweating profusely. "Blood type AB negative . . . T-cell count 420 . . ." Kennedy's head dropped as Tonetta read on, only calmer now. "Diagnosis: Ms. James, full-blown AIDS . . ."

When Kennedy heard the last note, she stopped struggling with the door. She cried out and fell against the door for support because she couldn't stand above the legs that failed her.

"I'm truly sorry for going there, Ms. James, but sometimes it's the only thing that works to get people to listen." Tonetta did regret using that type of scare tactic, but she couldn't stand to see people out on the streets without the proper information.

Shortly after Kennedy's purse fell to the floor, she did, too. Tonetta crossed her arms and sympathized with her pain, just as she did each time she had to explain to a poor soul that AIDS had infiltrated and taken over their body. It was never easy but always necessary. She'd seen the biggest men fall to their knees like Kennedy did when reality fell on them like a ton of bricks. It was never easy.

She allowed Kennedy to sob, lying cradled on the floor. She was helpless and at her wits' end. After several minutes of crying and moaning, she squealed and sighed deeply. Then, as silence became unbearable, Kennedy asked, in an innocent and childlike voice, "Am I going to die?"

Tonetta peered at the file that lay open on her desk before answering. "Ms. James, we're all going to die someday. But . . . we can talk about your situation when you're ready." Somehow, that was the correct answer. Speaking in general terms about everyone's immortality seemed to lighten Kennedy's burden.

She climbed to her knees and caught her breath. As she began picking up the items that fell from her purse, she looked up at Tonetta's pretty face and stared for the longest time. "How can a woman so beautiful have such a crappy job? It must really suck to get up every morning knowing you'll be faced with people like me." That statement was so profound, it caused Tonetta to smile. Something she hadn't done at the center in a long time, and it felt good despite the circumstances.

Tonetta walked around her desk toward Kennedy to help her get to her feet, but she was met with resistance. Kennedy threw her hands up to deter any assistance. "I'm not that sick, yet, where I need people fussing over me." The counselor understood and graciously backed off.

Kennedy settled back in the chair where many AIDS patients have been notified, confirmed, and counseled. Tonetta opened her bottom desk drawer and collected four pamphlets, *Reality of AIDS, Accepting It, Coping with It,* and *Treatment Options.* As she explained the different classes and support groups Autumn Leaves offered to its patients, Kennedy drifted further into a daydream. She saw three small children in the cutest little bathing suits playing in the front yard of a house with a white picket fence. Between giggles and excited squeals, they called out to her, "Mommmmy . . . ," while Legacy laughed and squirted water from a hose to cool them off on a hot summer's day. It was just a silly daydream.

In the middle of Tonetta's spiel, which fell on deaf ears, Kennedy politely got up and collected her things. She had to make a getaway before the tears started again. "I'm sorry, Ms. Thomas, but I'll just take the information with me. I need . . . I need to go now."

Tonetta's facial expression was subdued. "You sure you'll be all right?" What she really wanted to know, Kennedy answered for her.

"I'm not going to kill myself if that's what you mean." That's exactly what she was driving at.

Kennedy tried to say thank you before she left, but there was nothing to be thankful for. When someone informs you that you've contracted a deadly virus, "thank you" is hardly the sentiment expected in return. She took the information, folded it, and stuck it as far down in her purse as she could, then walked out without being able to utter a single word. Tonetta understood. For her, it was par for the course. The only thing she could offer was a shoulder to lean on and all the answers she could provide, if and when her newest grief-stricken client was ready to hear them.

The bus ride home lasted for two hours. Kennedy rode and rode, peering out the window in silence. Oddly enough, she didn't mind the bus trip home half as much as she did taking it there. Her entire being was numb. She was in too much mental pain for anything else to hurt her. The bus driver figured she was either mentally challenged or on a debilitating drug, because she continued staring out the window as he made stops along his route. He had watched her in his oversized rearview mirror, expecting her to get off each time he stopped.

Finally, he decided to investigate. After pulling the bus over and parking it against the curb, he made his way down the long aisle. He marched past row after row of bench seats. "Ma'am, where do you need to go?" he said loudly. She didn't hear him. Those words were wasted. They went straight through her. "Ma'am . . . ma'am!" he said louder. His strong baritone voice startled her. When she snapped out of her trance, she instinctively jumped and pulled away. "I'm sorry, ma'am, but I'm finished with my runs for today. My shift is over. Next stop's the garage."

She hadn't realized the bus was empty. She had ridden past her stop twice. The large man was perturbed. He scratched his head and walked back to the front of the bus to radio in about one speechless catatonic female. Before he could access someone on the radio, she sprang up and yelled out, "Here! I'll get off here!" She exited the rear door with her head down, wandering the streets of downtown Dallas until the sun made its way home from another long day.

Twenty-eight

Caught Up

uring the following week, Kennedy became a recluse. Her apartment showed few signs of life but at the same time was in utter disarray. She anguished while reading the AIDS literature she'd received from Tonetta over and over until she couldn't stand looking at it anymore. She decided to give her critical care counselor a call.

"Hello, Tonetta. It's me, Kennedy James."

"How are you, Kennedy? Have you had a chance to review the literature I gave you?" Ms. Thomas's voice was mellow and kind. It helped Kennedy calm her nerves a bit.

"Yeah, I've been going over it for days, but some of it is over my head. I get so nervous every time I try to make heads or tails of it."

After Tonetta excused herself a minute to close her office door for what she knew would be a delicate situation, she returned to the telephone with an even more serene style of conversation. "Okay. Now let's see what I can assist you with. And Kennedy, please keep in mind that all of this is new, and yes, frightening, but you can get through it. You're not alone. That's why I'm here."

Making that initial call was one of the most difficult things Kennedy had ever put herself through, but she came away from it with knowledge. She learned that AIDS—Acquired Immune Deficiency Syndrome—was first reported in the United States in 1981 and had become a worldwide epidemic, far worse than the bubonic plague or smallpox. She already knew that AIDS is caused by the human immune deficiency virus HIV, but Tonetta aided in her ability to process the technical aspects of the disease.

"You see, Kennedy, by killing or impairing cells of the immune system, HIV progressively destroys the body's ability to fight infections and certain cancers. Individuals diagnosed with AIDS are susceptible to life-threatening diseases called opportunistic infections, which are caused by microbes that usually do not cause illness in healthy people."

For most of the conversation, Kennedy held the phone and listened. After all, there wasn't much she could add to her counselor's professionally detailed explanation of what she should prepare herself for.

After enduring countless minutes of an agonizing and nearly one-sided phone call, Kennedy sighed deeply. Tonetta observed the cue and agreed that her client had shouldered enough for one day. "Tell you what, Kennedy," she said in her softest business voice possible, "why don't you take some time to let all of this sink in. It is a lot to digest all at once. It's probably a good idea that you try to relax, although it won't be easy, and read over the rest of the information at your leisure, then get back to me for clarification if you need to."

Kennedy agreed to do just that. She'd come away from it with more understanding than she had anticipated. Unfortunately, it was only the beginning.

The pamphlets also noted that more than seven hundred thousand cases of AIDS had been reported in the United States, and it was believed that over one million more people were infected with HIV. The epidemic was growing most rapidly among minority populations and had become the leading killer of African-American males between the ages of twenty-one and forty-five; not drug abuse, not homicide, but AIDS. Furthermore, according to the U.S. Centers for Disease Control and Prevention, the prevalence of AIDS is six times higher in African-American men and three times higher among Hispanics than it is among whites. She also read that a T cell count of less than 500 qualifies as full-blown AIDS. White blood cells, T-lymphocytes, baseline HIV-RNA. All those words were foreign to her before, but now she would have to understand them and what roles they would play in her life. The whole thing was scarier than hell itself, but she felt compelled to become as informed as she could. She had her life to consider, or the remaining part of it, anyway. Cytokines, treatments, therapies, it was all too much to handle at once. So she hid away in the confines of her apartment, listening to the Beatles and watching *Seinfeld* tapes until she could drum up enough nerve to visit one of the AIDS symposiums at Autumn Leaves.

Another week had come and gone and she still hadn't ventured outside her front door. Legacy stopped by every day and pleaded with her to open the door, but she declined to see him each time. Her reasons for turning him away ranged from severe menstrual cramps to a ridiculous quarantine for the measles.

When Legacy explained from the other side of the door that he'd experienced every common childhood disease known to children in the United States, she eventually broke down and asked him to just please go away and forget about her. Some nights he patiently sat outside her door Indian style, hoping she would come out, even if it was to pick up the newspaper. At least then he could have gotten a chance to see her, speak to her. Being separated by the thick wooden door was like being on the other side of the world to him. Everything was going great and then out of nowhere, she estranged herself from him. He figured that Simpson had to be the cause of her strange behavior. He had to be behind the pain and suffering, hers and Legacy's, too.

A few days later, she was sure that Legacy had packed up his sleeping bag and gone home. It was after two o'clock in the morning. When curiosity won out in its battle with boredom, she opened the door. Legacy jerked out of a deep sleep in the hallway. Before he could gather his faculties and ask her what in the hell was going on, she quickly slammed the door and locked the dead bolt.

The following morning, she signed a trespass waiver barring Legacy from the apartment building and demanded his name be removed from the guest list. Later that same evening, Bradshaw saw him entering the building. He advised Legacy of the waiver and apologized for having to carry it out. The sympathetic doorman didn't know what Kennedy was going through, but he recognized that she was gravely afraid of something. And, although Legacy couldn't understand why she went to those lengths to avoid him, he agreed to abide by her wishes, no matter how miserable it made him. What changed her so drastically in such a short time? He had to know.

Kennedy approached the glass doors at the Autumn Leaves Center. That nauseous feeling she dealt with the first time she went there had returned, seemingly waiting for her at the entrance. She feared seeing the young man again, the one who had been sentenced to wear the body of an elderly man. She kept her long arms wrapped around herself as she paced in the waiting area.

Just off to the left of where she found herself milling around in small circles, the Acceptance Symposium, the first of a series, was in session. Twenty or so young adults anchored themselves to plastic multicolored chairs in what was generally referred to by the staff as the Onion Room, because patients who entered it usually cried their eyes out when the reality of their condition hit home. Several races were represented in that particular group session, although no one noticed the apparent cultural diversity as they sat and listened attentively. AIDS is an equal-opportunity killer.

Faces she didn't know seemed to hold the same concerns as hers did. Black faces, white ones, red ones, yellow ones, and brown ones, too. Marshall's college teammate Busta had discovered that his crimes of passion eventually caught up with him. He was seated in the third row, along with two of his babies' mommas and many other careless and unfortunate men and women. Kennedy didn't know any of them personally. She did know that they would all someday meet the same fate.

Tonetta's office door opened suddenly. A rather tall and stately brown-skinned prince of a black man backed out of it slowly, his head bowed. He continued standing there as if he were waiting for something else to happen or be said to him. Kennedy heard Tonetta's voice coming from inside the office. "I'm truly sorry," she'd said to him. It sounded like it was the first time those words had ever come out of her mouth; instead of the two hundred and fifty-fourth time they actually had.

The man's strong frame reminded her of Marshall's, from when she'd met him at the UTC graduation ceremony. Then Tonetta's words hit the man hard enough to topple him over. He looked up with the sad eyes of a puppy being put out on the side of the road by an owner whose children had gotten over the novelty of having a new pet and didn't want it anymore. He felt like a throwaway. Suddenly his knees buckled, causing him to fall to the floor. "Nnnnnno . . . Nnno!" he wailed loudly, without considering who might be looking on. The expensive pants he wore were pressed against the clean white floor tiles. Kennedy couldn't stop watching, even though she was embarrassed to. It was like slowing down to view a terrible automobile accident, only without the blood and guts. But it was just as tragic.

His strong hands trembled against his handsome face while he helplessly continued to sob. Tonetta stepped out of her office and kneeled down beside him. When she couldn't get his attention, two men in starched white uniforms took over. They whispered something to him, then began to help him to his feet. Kennedy didn't hear what they said, but she was willing to bet it had to be something they'd used on other men who weren't used to losing control of their emotions, because it worked. The princely man staggered down the hall like a man headed for the electric chair. An attendant was on either side with his arms around their shoulders for support. He was a defeated man.

Leaving Tonetta's office with tears in his eyes meant he was in trouble. Trapped by his circumstances, choices, and consequences. Kennedy knew all too well what kind of trouble it was. In a short time she'd come to find herself deep in it, too. Troubled and trapped by something that refused to let go once it came calling.

"Ms. James," she heard Tonetta say. "How have you been?" Kennedy thought it was a stupid and insensitive question to ask, considering, but she realized Tonetta meant no harm.

"I've been better than I expected," she replied.

Tonetta ushered her into the office that previously killed her spirit and closed the door behind them. "So, I take it you finished reading the information we discussed?" Tonetta again spoke softly. It seemed that every word was sincere and thoughtfully designed to put her clients at ease, although Kennedy couldn't stop thinking of how she'd probably said those same words to countless others who actually did return after hearing the bad news.

"You must have some questions," Tonetta persisted.

Kennedy took out a sheet of paper folded twice. She painstakingly unfolded it like an archaeologist uncovering a great priceless Egyptian relic. She licked her lips and nodded. "Yeah, there were a couple of things I wanted to discuss a bit more. Um, the pamphlet said that an . . ." She had to compose herself before her emotions got the best of her. "An infected person should expect to experience fatigue, my-opathy, sarcoma, dehydration, chronic diarrhea, and delusions. When does—" Tonetta stepped in to spare her from contemplating each symptom. The mere mention of one more of them surely would have toppled Kennedy. The AIDS counselor had more than enough experience to see it coming from a mile away.

"Let's back up a bit so we can get a clear understanding. Fatigue is a common symptom, as well as chronic diarrhea, which is what causes dehydration and rapid weight loss. Myopathy and sarcoma, which are muscle and tissue disorders, impair the use of limbs and cause soreness in joints. They are both very common, but sarcoma normally becomes a major concern in the later stages." Kennedy looked at her oddly, as if the other symptoms were not serious enough to make a person's life a painful living hell.

Tonetta answered all the other questions she proposed, then set up an appointment for Kennedy to visit with a neurologist.

After Kennedy was mentally and emotionally drained, she exited the office and stopped by the water fountain for a drink before making her way to the bus stop. When she pressed the knob, cool water sprang up from its stainless-steel spout. As she lowered her head to get a thirst-quenching drink from it, a peculiar thought crossed her mind. She stopped herself before the water met her lips, then she pulled her head back and stepped away from the fountain. She didn't want to drink from a fountain that had serviced thousands of AIDS patients, although she knew how the HIV virus was transmitted. Her life and the way she thought about it had changed forever.

When the seriousness of it all began to boil within her, she whipped around to run out of the center. Before she could reach the exit, someone yelled, "Kennedy!" The voice was very familiar. She stopped dead in her tracks, frightened of who might be on the other end of that yell. The truth would be out. No more hiding in her prison of an apartment. No more secrets.

Someone tapped her faintly on the shoulder. She took a deep breath, preparing herself to face the person who could implicate her in the game of tainted love. In the time it took to blink, standing in front of her with a quaint smile, folded arms, and frail body draped in fashionable woman's designer casual wear, was Morris.

"Kennedy, I'm so glad you came back."

She was confused when he didn't seem perplexed about seeing her there. "Hi, Morris," was all she felt safe saying at that point. He extended his arms to offer her a big and much needed hug. She began to mist up around the eyes, realizing that he already knew and was ready to provide the strength she needed to help her get through it.

Morris was on staff as a volunteer two days a week at Autumn Leaves. His lover died from AIDS complications four years ago and many of his close friends had been taken by it since then. He felt it was his duty to assist others battling the disease. Fortunately, he wasn't infected and took precautions to lessen his chances of contracting it. But he knew firsthand, like others whose lives were affected by it, that the only sure prevention is abstinence.

He explained that he had access to all the files that came in and saw hers when it arrived from the county hospital weeks before. After agreeing to secrecy over lunch, he explained other things about the virus he thought she should know. Kennedy was relieved to be able to talk about her condition and share some of her thoughts and concerns while outside of Tonetta's office of despair.

Morris's companionship was magical. It proved that she didn't have to go it alone. He shared stories about others who had died and some who were still fighting for their lives daily. Kennedy learned that a proper diet enriched with vegetables and fruit had helped many patients restore a reasonable amount of health, if the disease wasn't too far into the intermediate stages. At least there was hope. But no matter how much of it there was, there wasn't a way to recapture the future that she almost had, the one that included her and Legacy, healthy adorable little children who looked just like them, water hoses in the summer's heat, and white picket fences. One positive test result changed all that, and there would be no going back.

Twenty-nine

Looking Back

The poignant smell of fresh paint drying filled Marshall's $1.5 million mansion in Georgia. He bought the extravagant seven-room home on a two-acre estate as soon as the Atlanta Falcon football organization drafted him. It was an entertainer's dream home with two oversized living areas, a state-of-the-art sound system built in, a luxury game room with two pool tables, and a six-seat video game play station, each with its own TV screen.

Legacy showed up on his doorstep in the exclusive gated community four days ago with six boxes full of paints, brushes, and other assorted art supplies. Marshall promised he'd give him work when he made it to the big time, and he planned on keeping that promise. Seeing Legacy's friendly face when he opened the door that day was more thrilling for Marshall than for his guest. They spent the first hour touring the large but unfurnished house and discussing about what work Marshall had in mind, then Legacy opened his suitcase and poured out about thirty individually wrapped Uncle Otto's fried pies. There was lemon, cherry, coconut, and chocolate. Each of them was filled with the natural good intention to satisfy and enough saturated fat and preservatives to choke a horse, but they tasted so good.

Sitting down to break bread, or fried pies, they reveled in the opportunity to catch up on the months that passed since graduation and how difficult it had been on both of them. Marshall asked if he had seen Jasmine. Legacy laughed. He wondered how long it would take before Jasmine's name came up. Quite casually, he reached into his shirt pocket and handed over Jasmine's new address in Houston, Texas. Marshall nodded thank you, then shoved it into the pocket of his sweatpants as if it were trivial.

Legacy flipped through Marshall's NFL newspaper scrapbook. Marshall didn't seem all that interested in the press articles. Instead, he diverted the conversation toward Legacy. "Freelance. Since you've been here you've talked about everything from money to music, but you haven't said one thing about that sexy little thang Kennedy you were all cozy with at the graduation."

Legacy's smile immediately dissipated. He rubbed his hands together while he muddled over the thought of her in his mind. Marshall learned, after pressing Rorey to talk about things better left undiscussed, when to back off.

"Hey, man, if it's a problem, don't sweat it. I's just asking."

Legacy sat up straight on one of the few pieces of furniture that had been purchased for the house, which was a black leather E-Z Boy recliner. "Naw . . . naw, it's not any big deal." Sensing that Marshall knew he was lying, he decided to be honest with his friend and with himself. "It's just that her old boyfriend keeps coming into the picture and I bet that's why she's been acting different lately."

"Oh, yeah? Different how?"

"Me and her old man got into a couple of scraps and I thought everything was cool again, and then, out of nowhere, she did a three-sixty. She won't return my phone calls, won't open the door when

I stop by, and get this, she had me barred from coming around her building."

"Whaaaat? You ain't even allowed on the premises? Man, she's really pissed off. Either that or hurt, about something major."

Legacy leaned back in the broad leather chair. "Yeah, it's like I said. I bet it's got something to do with that jerk she used to see." He didn't mention the drugs, the machine gun, or the threats. Probably because he didn't know for sure if they had anything directly to do with the way Kennedy had been acting.

Marshall thought about it for a second, then offered what he thought was good advice. "Freelance, look, the best thing for you to do is get your narrow butt back home and find out what's going on with your woman the best way you know how. When you straighten it out, just catch another flight back here in a week or two. I'll be concentrating on my last two games of the season, anyway."

Marshall ate more pies than he planned to, considering he hadn't seen one since he left Dallas. Those pies reminded him of home, his yesterdays, and of Jasmine. She loved them more than he did. After one fried pie too many, he grabbed a magazine off the kitchen counter and disappeared into one of the home's five bathrooms.

Legacy pondered over what Marshall said. He did want to know what bothered Kennedy so bad that she wanted him out of her life. So he began painting the game room and thinking on it as he did.

By the time the sun came up again, the mural that Legacy came to paint was almost finished. The ceiling was blue and loomed in the backdrop of thick white clouds that looked real enough to hold rain. When standing in the middle of the room, it felt like being on the fifty-yard line of a football field, in a stadium jam-packed with thousands of screaming fans.

Marshall woke up and stumbled into the game room, still dressed in his robe and house shoes. He was rubbing his eyes and yawning while walking a sleepy man's shuffle toward the center of the room.

"Saaaay, man . . . ," he said in the middle of a hearty stretch. "I was dreaming all night that I smelled paint and when I . . ." He stopped when the magic of the room engulfed him. He was in awe and almost heard the roar of the crowd as he stood there. "Freelance, this is perfect. I mean better than perfect. Man, I can smell the grass from right here." He looked down at the rich eggshell-colored carpet beneath his feet. "That's what I need!" he shouted, beginning to jump up and down. "That's just what I need!"

Legacy was happy but too exhausted to join in with the excitement. He had painted nonstop for almost fourteen hours straight. He was bent on getting it finished as quickly as possible so that he could get home and use Marshall's advice, to find a way to get at the reason why Kennedy dumped him without an explanation.

Marshall convinced Legacy to stop painting long enough to eat breakfast and wash it down with Snapple, which was all that he had to offer. Before Legacy had time to get back to work, a man rang the doorbell, saying he was there to lay the new carpet. Marshall dashed to the door wearing a big smile, screaming, "My AstroTurf is here! My AstroTurf is here!"

A truckload of green NFL-grade artificial grass was delivered at his residence to cover the floor of the entire game room. Only a lover of the game could have appreciated it.

Legacy touched up the painting Marshall titled *The Dream Scene*, then washed up and caught the next flight out with a fifteen-thousand dollar check in his pocket. When Marshall arrived home from practice that evening, reporters were waiting on him. Somehow, the terms of his contract were made public and every reporter in town wanted the scoop. The long black limousine stopped and Marshall stepped out of the back of it wearing blue jeans, a Wrangler-green T-shirt from college, and tennis shoes. His limousine driver protested the makeshift media camp set up on his boss's front lawn, but Marshall asked him to ignore them. That's what he did himself, just as he had done all season long. His resistance to granting interviews forced reporters to become brutal in their retaliation of the brass young rookie's shunning them.

After each game, they would line up in the locker room to ask him questions, shout ridiculous comments at him, or make up stories to sell advertising. One rumor was out that he was gay, because he didn't spend time chasing women with other players. Another story suggested that his religious affiliation prohibited him from interviewing with the press. Despite the rumors and speculation, one thing for sure was that his private life remained private. The real story was that there was no story at all. Marshall simply chose not to be caught up in it. He decided not to be a Wheaties box booster, a commercial sellout, or a role model. When one reporter did provoke words from him, it got ugly.

After Marshall compiled a record-breaking 13 catches and 259 yards in one game, a particular reporter decided he was not going to be denied the story of the day. Marshall was undressing in the team locker room with other media blitzes taking place around him. He felt the hot camera lamp shining on his back. Before he could confront the reporter about being in his personal space, the barrage of questions began. "Marshall . . . Marshall . . . you mind telling us what's been your driving force this year? Why all the secrecy? Are you having problems with your success in the NFL?"

Marshall turned and squinted at the bright light shining down on him. "Look, y'all know I don't do interviews," he said, blocking the camera's view with his hands.

"But Marshall . . . the fans want the story, they want to get to know you. You're the leading receiver in the league. No rookie has ever done that. Don't you think your fans deserve to hear from you?"

He smirked at the reporter's nerve to ask questions as if they had a chance of being answered. He looked into the camera and said, "What the fans deserve is a team that can put more W's in the win column." Even though Marshall was having the kind of year that would surely get him in the Hall of Fame, the Falcons always seemed to find ways to blow big leads and ultimately lose big games.

Although he was still perturbed with the man for camping in his personal space, the reporter continued to push the envelope along with his luck. Marshall was sure to make him pay the price.

"So you care about the fans?" the man asked, his fake tone reeking of insincerity. "Then give the people what they want. Don't you think it's time you started acting like a role model?" The mood surrounding the two of them standing in the midst of all the other hype going on became thick and still.

Marshall took one threatening step in the man's direction, then caught himself before speaking. "Role model? Role model . . . let me tell you something about role models. Role models are parents, uncles, and aunts. People who have and keep jobs and provide for their families and show love to their children three hundred and sixty-five days a year. That's a role model, not me. I'm just a guy who catches a football for a living. That's not a role model. I don't even have kids." He was explosive at that point. "Did you get that? Huh? Now get that camera out of my face." He pushed the reporter back into the cameraman standing a couple of feet away. The camera landed hard against the ground and lost its focus. The last shot was of the ceiling.

"There you have it," said handsome talking head in a nice gray suit, with footage of the interview running behind him in a huge ESPN studio set. Charlie Wells, sports anchor, had some comments and questions to share about Marshall's conduct on and off the field. "That was the scene in the Atlanta Falcons locker room after losing a close game to the Redskins, despite rookie sensation Marshall Coates's outstanding performance. Sighting the team's dismal defense for their many losses, Coates is on auto pilot and alone at the top of this year's rookie receiver class. Well, the entire league, for that matter, but get this, he is at the bottom of the list when the question is asked, who gets what?"

Another sports announcer, with a likewise polished persona, took over the story. "Believe it or not, Atlanta Falcons' Marshall Coates is the lowest-paid first-round receiver picked in the NFL draft since the seventies. Why he wanted only one million dollars for a limited one-year contract is the question of the century. Sports agents and everyone else thought he was crazy; well, they thought his elevator didn't go all the way up to the top floor. Present company included. He had no agent, no experience in contract negotiations, and if you'd have asked me six months ago, I would have agreed that he didn't have much common sense, either. But, and that's a very big but, it seems that Mr. Coates had more of an inclination for securing his financial future than he let on. I'll bet that's what the Falcon organization is thinking, anyway."

Film footage of Marshall making spectacular one-handed grabs and one unbelievable catch after another played on the same large screen that showed the reporter getting decked in the background. The second ESPN sports announcer continued, "After his first fourteen Marshall-icious games as an NFL rising star, he has averaged just over a hundred and twenty-five yards per class. And I say class because he takes defensive backs to school each time he steps out onto the field. But, and there's another but, Coates as the individual has another story. No one knows exactly what that story is, and that's a story within itself. We do know that this somewhat reserved young star arrives to practice daily by limo and doesn't seem to have much in common with his teammates. What do they have to say about this strange phenom?"

A taped quote was taken in the locker room after the last game. One of the three-hundred-pound linemen rammed a big clump of dirt-brown chewing tobacco in his mouth and smiled when he was asked about Marshall. He scratched his head and stared into the camera. "I see him every day, but I don't really know him. He's different like that, ya know. I do know that he reads books every chance he gets and that's different. His different is a good thing. We'd rather have his good different that's kinda strange anytime than a bad different that makes sense. You know what I mean?" Then he smiled big and bright as if his explanation made sense to anyone other than himself.

The announcers looked at one another as if the lineman were a blubbering idiot. "Sure . . . we understand. Not. But, there it is again, we do understand clearly that Coates has already shattered the rookie receiving record, earning him an additional, get this, five million dollars. That's right, a special clause in his contract negotiated by him has netted five million for breaking the record and is well on his way to achieving something bigger, yes, more stupendous than that. Here it is . . ." He shuffled some papers on the sports desk as if he weren't reading from the TelePrompTer. "If he can come up with an average of a hundred and twenty-five yards, which is his single game average, add that to his seventeen hundred and fifty yards . . . " He pretended to do some calculations with a pencil on the paper he'd shuffled. "And carry the nine. Holy smoke, it worked. A combined two hundred and fifty yards in the next two games will total two thousand yards in his first season. What is a two-thousand-yard receiving rookie season worth these days, and mind you it's never . . . ever . . . been . . . done before. Well, I'll tell you who gets what. If he does it, it'll be worth ten . . . million . . . dollars." He went into his antics of calculating numbers again. "And that's five plus ten equals . . . that's right, for you all at home with calculators. Fifteen . . . million . . . dollars. That makes for a lot of limousine rides and a lot of sense. Stay with us, we'll be back in a moment." They faded to a commercial advertising one hundred and one ways to serve Spam at tailgate parties.

Thirty

Love Me Enough to Leave Me

The bright sun was blinding as Legacy packed his luggage in the back of the tattered jeep. He had slept all the way home on the plane. But even in his sleep, he could not escape the torch he carried for Kennedy. Thoughts of her captivated his dreams. She owned him mind and soul and he wanted to make it a complete package, including his body. He wanted her to have his babies and become his wife. Not necessarily in that order, but there was a little problem. He couldn't get in to see her. He reasoned that her love for flowers might aid his attempt at resolving whatever issue it was standing defiantly between them.

Bradshaw stood attentive and bold, like a royal palace sentry, at the front door when Legacy parked at the curb. He thought that if he asked politely with persistence, he just might be let in. He ran his fingers through his hair and tucked in his shirttail, trying to make himself look more presentable. He learned that as a child at the orphanage. "Hey, Bradshaw . . . how've you been?" He was all teeth, but the older black man wasn't smiling back. "Hey, I just got back in town and I would love to see Kennedy James. Now, I know my name's been taken off the visitor's list, but I'm willing to forget about all that if you just let me up."

Bradshaw's face was like a stone monument, firm and unyielding. "You know the rules. I wouldn't mind you going up, but I just can't allow it."

Legacy thought about darting past him and catching the next elevator up. Just as the thought entered his mind, an elevator with a young man and woman opened on the lobby floor. He watched Bradshaw watching him as the couple stepped out of it. He looked at Bradshaw and at the elevator again. Bradshaw read his mind. "Son, I know what you're thinking and you could get into a lot of trouble with the law if you make it to that elevator car. And I'd like to keep thinking of you as a nice young man. You've never given me no trouble and I hope you don't start now." Legacy's time was running out. His window of opportunity was slamming shut as the elevator doors began to close. He looked as desperate as he felt.

"Please don't, son," Bradshaw warned. "I'd have to call the law on you."

The thought of making one last-ditch effort crossed his mind, but it was too late. The doors were completely closed and his chance to talk to her was gone. Legacy's expression of utter disappointment was hard for Bradshaw to stomach. A young man who was on the verge of heartbreak was always a tough thing for another man to watch. He put his hand on Legacy's back and guided him toward the exit door. "Look, son. I don't know exactly what's going on, but I can tell you that Ms. James isn't mad with you. In fact, she cried her eyes out when she had that trespass waiver filed against you. She's just taken ill kinda sudden like. Now, I'll say this, it must be pretty serious on account of how so many people keep going up to see her and taking food, and she hasn't been down in a while."

Legacy shook his head. "No, that doesn't sound like Kennedy.

She couldn't be healthier. I just saw her a few weeks ago."

Bradshaw looked back over his shoulder to see if anyone was attending the reception desk. "I shouldn't be doing this, but I will. I guess I believe in giving young people in love a chance." He took out a cell phone and punched in her phone number. Legacy didn't realize what he was doing, but he was smart enough to keep quiet and let it happen. "Hello, this is Bradshaw the doorman. Uh-uh, there's no problem." He eyed the roses Legacy had with him. "I just received some flowers for Ms. James is all. Will she be coming down to sign for them? Oh, okay, that'll be just fine." He turned the phone off and slid it back in his coat pocket.

Legacy's eyes widened with anticipation. "Well, what's going on? Who was that on the phone?"

Bradshaw looked at his watch. "Someone will be down to pick them up, they said."

"They? Who's they?"

Bradshaw put out his hand, palm down, then rocked it from side to side, insinuating a homosexual preference. "You know, the little one who wears women's clothes. I think they call him Marsha."

Legacy stared at the older man as if he were off his rocker, until his gesture hit home. "Oh, Morris. You're talking about Morris."

"Yeah, Marsha . . . Morris. Whatever. The little one." He duplicated the hand gesture from before. Bradshaw referred to him as the little one because the limousine gang had been stopping by lately. All of Morris's friends who attended Ladies Night Out were larger in stature than Morris but just as flamboyant.

Eventually, Morris scurried off the elevator. Legacy ducked behind an eight-foot potted tree. "I'm here to pick up the flowers," the little one said cordially. While Bradshaw pretended to search for a signing pad, Morris began looking for it, too, before he knew what the man had lost. "Bradshaw, what exactly are we looking for?"

"I was trying to find the sign-in board, but I can't seem to . . ." Bradshaw was terrible at deception, but his heart was in the right place. Morris was losing his patience.

"Can I just take these beautiful roses up and sign later?" He began looking for the card that normally accompanied flower deliveries. When he didn't see one, he became suspicious. "And who did you say delivered the—"

"I did!" Legacy shouted from behind him, startling Morris enough to cause an inflection in his voice. "Theeeese!"

Morris instinctively jumped into Bradshaw when he reacted to Legacy. The doorman pushed Morris away before he'd figured out why. "I'm sorry," Morris apologized to Bradshaw, then placed his hands on his hips as he addressed Legacy for startling him. "Legacy, you had no cause to scare me that way. What's gotten into you?"

Legacy grabbed Morris firmly by the shoulders. "I need to know what's gotten into Kennedy. She won't see me, return my calls, or anything. It's that Simpson again, isn't it? Please tell me what the hell is going on before I lose my mind."

Morris grimaced. He was caught in a difficult dilemma. He swore his secrecy to Kennedy, but Legacy was deeply in love with her. Not to mention he was the best thing that ever happened to her.

Pacing back and forth with the roses pressed against his chest, Morris shuddered. "Please don't make me tell you. She'd never forgive me. And at this point, she needs to know that she can trust me." He recognized the suffering and uncertainty Legacy had to be enduring. "Okay, I'll tell you this much. She's just learned that she's very sick and doesn't want to burden you with it."

"Whatever it is," he said frantically, "I know I can help her with it, though it. Listen, I'm crazy about Kennedy and I came here to ask her to be my wife and the mother of our children." He unintentionally squeezed Morris's shoulders harder. "Please tell me what's going on with her."

"Ooouch! That hurts, you brute." Morris pulled away, rubbing the pain from his shoulders. "Babies, marriage . . . now I know I can't tell you." Tears began to stream down his flat cheeks.

"I'm sorry, Morris. I didn't mean to hurt you."

"Don't be silly . . . that's not it. It didn't hurt that bad. You just don't understand, and I can't make you without spilling my guts. Oh . . . she loves you but she . . ." Legacy leaned in. "But she doesn't want to hurt you, and she knows the best way to save you is to let you go. Please believe me. It's better that you just walk away."

Legacy was out of ideas and it looked as though he was out of luck, too. He pulled out a piece of paper and wrote an address on the back of it. "I see that she doesn't want me around anymore. Here, give this to her, and if she changes her mind I'll come back."

He was more confused than when he arrived. He'd just been told that Kennedy was sick and wanted to save him but chose to send him away. He couldn't take it any longer. Not being allowed to help her with whatever it was, was killing him inside.

After he graduated, Legacy had been awarded an all-expense-paid three-month internship to the French University of Art in Paris. He had no intention of accepting it before now, but things had changed. And he had just enough time to accept and get his butt on that plane. Being that close without any hope of seeing her had begun a murderous rampage on his soul. Maybe three months away would be time enough for Kennedy to get well and realize she couldn't do without him, either. That's what he was counting on. He refused to envision his future without her as the biggest part of it.

Thirty-one

If Only You Knew

Sixty-three thousand fanatic spectators booed when the Minnesota Vikings' top receiver, Ronnie Jakes, caught a game-tying touchdown in the back of the end zone. The roof nearly came off the Georgia Dome as the last eighteen seconds of the game rested on the Atlanta Falcons' last time-out. NBC televised the game throughout the United States. Viewers were on the edge of their seats. Jasmine Reynolds was one of them. She sat alone in her Houston town home watching another dazzling Marshall Coates exhibition. The last game of the season was meaningless for the Falcons, who didn't have a prayer of making the playoffs, and the Vikings had clinched their postseason berth by whipping the Jets three games ago. Regardless, the hype concerning Marshall's chance to finish the best rookie season ever recorded and earn an additional ten million dollars was well worth watching.

An NBC sports announcer tied up all the loose ends for the viewers at home. "Well, I'll tell ya. This has been quite a game. It might not mean much to the Atlanta Falcons or the Minnesota Vikings who comes out on top of this thing, but one young man has a lot riding on the last eighteen seconds of this game."

"I'm on the edge of my seat," another one added. "This young man has simply come to the NFL and just taken over. There's a new sheriff in town and his name is Marshall Coates. He has added a ray of hope to the Falcons' organization, which has experienced its share of injuries and problems off the field, but how often does the chance come along to do what he has a chance of doing today?

"Viewers at home watching this game need to understand the magnitude of the last eighteen seconds. That's how long Coates has to make ten million dollars. He has a contractual clause that allows for an additional ten million if he can amass two thousand yards this season. Since it's never been done before, the Falcon organization signed it and agreed to it. All he needs is thirty-five yards to reach two thousand. I gotta be honest here. If I were the team owners, I'd be having mixed emotions right about now. You'd like the win against the heavily favored Vikings, sure. But is it worth ten million dollars?"

The ensuing kickoff was high but short and returned to the Falcons' thirty-nine-yard line, giving them an opportunity to drive thirty yards to set up a forty-one-yard field goal to win the game. The Falcon offense huddled on the sideline. Emotions ran high. The fans screamed louder, almost to the point of deafening thunder. Head coach Billy Blanton kneeled in the middle of the anxious, sweat-drenched offense. When he began to explain how they would set up a field goal attempt, all eyes went to Marshall, whose facial expression was intense. A field goal attempt wouldn't benefit him. And all the extra workouts after practice would have gone to waste. Coach Blanton had an agenda, but the rest of the team had other ideas.

After the coach mapped out his three-play strategy to set up a winning kick, the offense jogged out onto the field. Marshall was spread out wide right. The ball snapped and the athletes collided like Roman gladiators. There was gnashing of teeth as some of the strongest arms and legs on the planet flailed. Thousands of pounds of raw energy mashed, sweat and other bodily fluids flew upon contact. The game was on.

The Falcons' quarterback rolled out to the right side and handed the ball up the field for a fifteen-yard gain to the Viking forty-yard line. The clock ticked on, ten . . . nine . . . eight seconds left. Fans screamed obscenities at their home team's coaching staff. No one understood why a running play was called when they had no time-outs remaining. The quarterback rushed the other players back to the line. He received the ball and quickly slammed it into the turf to stop the clock. The unnerved fans booed. Sports announcers questioned the strategy.

"What's Blanton thinking? Doesn't seem that he planned this thing out too well." Loud boos continued as the other announcer tried to hear himself talk over the loud noise. "You have to question his thought process. Everyone knows you have to run or throw it to the sideline to preserve every precious second when you've used all your time-outs."

"I . . . uh, I just don't get it. And poor Marshall Coates, that just about ruins his chances with only eight seconds left on the clock, and I'm sure Blanton's going to continue with his ultraconservative coaching style and go for the field goal. Well, at this point he's got what, maybe just enough time for one short pass to get in field position, then hope that the kicker's got enough leg strength to pull it off."

"At this point, I don't think they have what it takes to win if it goes into overtime. They've given everything just to have hung in this long. They're spent and it doesn't look good."

The clock started ticking when the ball snapped again. Seven . . . six . . . Marshall was supposed to run a five-yard out toward the sideline. It was a timing pattern. If it worked out right, the coach's strategy to kick a three-point field goal to win would be completed.

Marshall looked at the ground beneath him, then inward to watch the ball being snapped. Sweat ran from beneath his helmet and down his face. "Come on, baby . . . come on, baby . . . come on, baby . . . ," he whispered to the ground beneath his feet. He leaned forward like a sprinter running the hundred-yard dash as he took five quick steps and turned, expecting the ball to be there. When it wasn't, he knew the quarterback was in trouble. The clock continued to tick and the fans were too caught up in the action to count down along with it. Marshall had a flashback to the last college game he played, when Rorey found himself in trouble and scrambled to get a long pass off.

Instinctively, Marshall took off downfield, flying past the cornerback defending him. He looked back over his left shoulder while streaking down the field. As soon as he turned his head to see if the quarterback, who was running for his life, had enough time to throw the ball, it was already spiraling through the air toward him. He had gotten past his defender and seemed to have a clear shot at catching the ball for a winning touchdown, but the Vikings' safety saw it coming, too. His position to catch the ball was better than Marshall's. The defender ran toward it and Marshall's best hope was to meet it as it came down. The final second ticked off the clock, and the stadium was in pandemonium. Some of the fans screamed while others simply held their breath and prayed. The long pass continued to sail as Marshall gathered himself to catch the ball. Suddenly, it began to wobble in midair. It was going to be too short, allowing the defender chasing Marshall to catch up to him.

As the ball descended, the Vikings' safety leapt first to make a play on the ball, then Marshall and the other defender broke stride and jumped into the air, too. All three men looked up toward the heavens as they vaulted themselves upward. It was as if those three athletes were the only ones in the stadium, blanking out all the screaming fans, other teammates, lights, and cameras. They were there strictly for the action. All six arms extended at the same time. The ball continued to fall toward earth as the men's bodies collided with Marshall in the middle. It was impossible to tell without instant replay who did it, but someone tipped the ball up as one of the Vikings fell to the ground. Just when it seemed that all was lost, the ball hit Marshall's knee and bounced up into his hands.

The entire stadium erupted. Marshall fell into the end zone with the free safety holding on around his waist. 30–24, the Falcons won and it was all over. Marshall raised the football high above his head. The fans cheered as they stormed the field and hoisted him on their shoulders. The colossal diamond vision screen flashed "10 Big Ones!" over and over. Jubilation isn't enough of a word to describe the magnitude of celebration that transpired. It was electrifying.

One announcer sat in the media booth shaking his head in disbelief. "If I hadn't seen it for myself, I wouldn't have believed it. Folks, that reception will undoubtedly go down in history as the Ten-Million-Dollar Catch." The diamond vision ran the replay in slow motion; it was Marshall who'd tipped it to himself. "Wow! If you don't believe in destiny, here's a pretty good argument. There should have been no conceivable way for him to make that catch with no seconds on the clock. Wow! I'm all shook up."

Marshall made his way through the player's tunnel beneath the stadium seats and ducked into the equipment room. The excitement of the pomp and circumstance filled his heaving chest. He was elated, but too much had happened for him to enjoy it. The ten-million-dollar catch felt good, but he still had other concerns to deal with. There was the impending doom of AIDS hanging over his head, although he'd been too terrified to go in for testing.

He pulled the football jersey out of his pants. Attached at the bottom, in the front of it, was a small black cloth pouch adjoined with a safety pin. The same pouch he played with each week. It held the carnation Marshall took from Rorey's coffin when he died. That pouch served as a constant reminder that life didn't owe anyone a damned thing, so he played each game for himself, and Rorey was with him each time.

Swarms of reporting news crews collected in the locker room for postgame interviews. Oddly enough, Marshall was nowhere to be seen, so they set up camp and waited, noting two three-by-five photographs taped inside the superstar's locker door. Jasmine's and Rorey's senior-class snapshots served as monuments for yesterday. Both of them were smiling. Both were gone from his life.

When Marshall finally appeared in the locker room, he was half dressed, worn out, and not interested in granting interviews, even though they persisted. "Marshall . . . Marshall . . . !" someone yelled from the back of the herd. "How does it feel to be Rookie of the Year and league MVP?" For the first time since he hit Atlanta, Marshall had time enough to think about how great his accomplishments were. It made him smile, but he didn't lose sight of the fact that those reporters were the same media buzzards who'd hover above his corpse once they knew what he feared they'd eventually find out.

"Y'all know I don't do interviews, and no one has voted for top rookie nor MVP, so I wouldn't know how that feels. No more questions."

They persisted until the team security staff ushered them all out and barred the door. Marshall shook each of the other player's hands and thanked them for being a part of his dream coming true. They didn't know what to make of it, but they had come to understand that Marshall was different. A good different. And that was good enough for them.

Thirty-two

Once Removed

Two weeks later, the balloting was collected and tabulated. Marshall did in fact win both Rookie of the Year and league MVP honors. And, as he promised himself he would do if he achieved both feats, he called a national press conference.

The stage was set up with the Atlanta Falcon emblem in the background. Every major TV and news radio station throughout the country was represented. As Marshall mounted the stage draped in a fine navy double-breasted suit, his legs began to shake. The NFL commissioner shook his hand. A multitude of flashbulbs commenced popping. He was poised but nervous. Long forgotten were the days when he relished controlling a whole slew of media activity with ease. This was a new day. A new Marshall. He pulled a speech from his inside jacket pocket and steadied himself.

Someone yelled, "We love you, Marshall!" from the back of the overcrowded room. That brought a smattering of chuckles from the audience and an unexpected smile from Marshall.

He steadied himself again. "Hey, uh . . . thanks for showing up." The irony of that comment was amusing, considering the press conference was long anticipated. The media had been waiting for nine months to hear what he had to say. He continued, "First, let me say thank you to the Atlanta Falcon organization. They gave me a chance to show the world what I can do on this level. Luckily, the little ashy boy from South Dallas did good." The room responded agreeably once again. "Secondly, allow me to apologize for being somewhat uncooperative with the media, but I have experienced something in the past year that has, uh . . . made me feel alone in this thing." He folded up the speech and stuffed it in his jacket breast pocket. The sentiment he felt couldn't be obtained from a prewritten statement. "And I think I need to explain it in hopes that ya'll will understand why I felt it necessary to do what I did."

He pursed his lips, getting choked up about all that had happened over the past twelve months. "Last winter . . . my best friend and teammate, Rorey Garland, took his own life. He was infected with AIDS and had unprotected sex with a certain young lady. Fearing that he might have infected her also, and not being able to deal with that, he ended it for himself." Marshall stopped to stifle his emotions. Not a sound was heard among the vast conglomerate of media personnel. "That changed my life, of course, but not in a positive way, unfortunately. Instead, I allowed my morals and ethics to become skewed somehow and unwittingly had unprotected sex with the same young lady. And when I learned of the sequence of events, I pretty much shut down and turned off all of my personal relationships with friends and family alike. I didn't want to burden anyone with being associated with me only to be afraid to get too close to me later." He stopped again briefly before continuing. Every woman in the room and many of the men began to wipe the tears from their faces. "Last week I decided to go in and get tested for HIV. The test was negative, thank God, and since then I've tracked down the young lady involved. She was negative also." A loud collective sigh was heard. "But that doesn't excuse what I did and how I've treated people who loved me. I just hope they understand and forgive me. And as for the money, I've made arrangements to set up a five-million-dollar AIDS awareness and prevention foundation in the name of my best friend, Rorey Garland. He'd like that."

There was a long pause of silence, then someone began clapping slowly. Others joined in and soon the entire room let the tears flow as they applauded. The ovation lasted over two minutes, until the same person from before yelled out again, "We still love you, Marshallll!" Laughter broke up the applause.

A heavy stone was lifted off his shoulders. He fought back his own tears and took a deep breath. "I can't believe this," he said jokingly, looking over the vast media campaign. "A room full of reporters and no one wants to ask me any questions."

Immediately, a barrage of questioning ensued. When Marshall was asked why he arrived to practice every day in a chauffeur-driven limousine, he laughed out loud before he could answer. "I knew someone here wanted to know that. Well, it's not because I'm pretentious or think that I'm all that. The simple truth is . . . I never learned how to drive."

They were eating it up and it was the truth, which always makes for a better story than something a public relations person cooks up. The truth was, his family was poor and never owned a car, and he was with Jasmine or Rorey for most of his college days, so it never came up. He was also asked if he would return to Atlanta to play the following year, considering he only signed a one-year contract and now he was the most sought after player in the NFL.

He pondered that one for a moment, then nodded yes in affirmation. Despite the unbelievable offers from other teams, he smiled and answered, "Yeah, I like the great city of Atlanta and I would love to raise a family here someday. If the team will have me back."

The Falcons' owner and general manager, Morgan Heinz, stepped to the microphone and confirmed it. "Marshall, it goes without saying, but let me go on record that we like you all right, too, and want you to stay for as long as you want to be a part of our team. But . . . but we'll have to take another look at last year's contract. We can't afford to make that mistake again."

Everyone in the room chanted, "Sixteen! Sixteen!" referring to the sixteen-million total Marshall earned for his first season.

He agreed to one more question. A beautiful female Asian reporter worked hard to get his attention. She stepped out from among the audience and smiled big and bright. "Marshall, you said that you wanted to raise your family here but you're single. Do you have any prospects?"

Simultaneous "Whoooooas!" rang throughout the large room.

He was embarrassed but was glad someone asked. "Yes, I do, as a matter of fact, but I was a fool and neglected to cherish what we had. And I'm going to catch the next flight to Texas"—he paused to look at his watch—"to see if she'll take me back if it's not too late. Now if y'all will excuse me, I think I have some other business to tend to."

They began to hail him and applaud again as he strolled offstage and out of the media room. The press conference was the national top news story of the day. Highlights of the speech were aired instantaneously. On airport televisions, in hospitals, and in barbershops throughout America, with the volume turned up loud. It was the buzz and topic of discussion everywhere and replayed later by newscasts in other countries.

Marshall was recognized immediately when he entered the airplane. Parents and children alike sought his company during the two-and-a-half-hour flight to Houston Intercontinental Airport. During the trip, Marshall happily signed autographs and talked football with other passengers. The captain announced a hearty congratulations over the intercom, then asked, "Would the Rookie of the Year like to come up and fly the plane?" Of course, they didn't allow him to touch any of the important instruments, but he did get a rush sitting in the navigating pilot's seat.

When the plane touched down, thousands of fans who'd seen the press conference and were proud of their Texan son aligned the corridors in the airport to pat him on the back and wish him good luck. A group of sorority sisters from Texas Southern University had a poster decorated with his picture on it. The sign read AIN'T TOO PROUD TO BEG. That adequately described his strategy. Begging.

Manny, an older tough Greek limousine driver, met him at the gate, holding a sign above his head with the letters "NFL MVP" on it. By the time they journeyed through the airport to the long black car waiting just outside, Marshall had the driver carry a red six-foot stuffed elephant along with several bags of trinkets he'd purchased from stores in the terminal. And they were off.

The spirit in which the general public received him was a mind-blowing experience, but he had to jump back to reality before the limo turned right on Westheimer Boulevard. Two blocks from Jasmine's town home on Chimney Rock Road, he closed his eyes and meditated on what he would say, what he would do. What if she wasn't home? His eyes widened when he forgot to find out if she would be at home, then his mind began to wander like lost kittens in a strange neighborhood. What if she had another man? In all the time they were apart, he hadn't thought of getting over her and didn't consider that she may have gotten over him. Either way, it was too late to change his mind and chicken out.

The limo idled in front of the address Legacy had given him. It had to be the right house. The Wrangler-green Mercedes E-class sedan he sent as a peace offering was parked in the driveway with a bright red bow still wrapped around it.

Marshall hit the power window button. As the window came down, he looked out apprehensively. "Well, Manny, I guess this is it."

The driver looked in the rearview mirror and nodded. "Good luck, Mr. Coates. Just be honest and everything will work out fine."

Marshall agreed that honesty had been a refreshing change lately. He grabbed the flower bouquet off the leather seat and staggered up to the front door with the six-foot elephant in tow. He turned toward Manny for support. The driver saluted him with a stiff thumbs-up. Marshall took a deep breath. The thought of another man opening the door crossed his mind again, but he didn't have any other place to be. This was the only destiny he knew. Besides, he had come too far to turn back now.

He rang the bell and waited. Sounds of footsteps became more prominent until the door opened. Jasmine was standing there in her normal Saturday clean-the-house blue jeans, an oversized tattered flannel shirt, which once belonged to him, and a head scarf old enough to be a longtime friend. She was just the way he remembered her, beautiful in every way imaginable. She looked at him and squinted, then at the limo parked out front. Folding her arms, she leaned against the doorjamb while she pulled off her yellow rubber gloves, one finger at a time. Then she cocked her head to the side and wrinkled her lips like a woman preparing to hear her man tell her for the twentieth time that he'll change if she gives him just one more chance.

Manny observed them while pretending not to pay attention, but Jasmine was certain that he was all ears. Marshall's heart was beating fast. His mouth was dry from anticipation. He was happy to see her but wasn't at all sure of how she viewed his sudden and awkward appearance.

Sizing him up, Jasmine tried to be unaffected by his presence. "Hello, Marshall," she said in a dry, uneventful tone. "Who's your friend?" She was referring to the enormous stuffed elephant blocking her walkway.

He was at a loss for words. None of the things he rehearsed in the car seemed appropriate to say. "What's wrong?" she asked, "you use up all the words you know at the press conference today? Yeah, I saw it but wondered if you would really bring your trifling ass back to Texas for me. Then that Mercedes showed up this afternoon with my name on it. Marshall, do you think you can buy me expensive gifts to get back in my life? No, don't answer that, it might be the wrong one. I can't believe you're here. On my doorstep." Then she looked at him more suspiciously than before. "Wait a minute," Jasmine shouted, "did you stop by Hairy Heretta's house first?" He began to open his mouth but she started up again.

"Ahhp . . . don't answer that either. Marshall, it's been ten months since I've laid eyes on you, except for . . . well, on Sundays, of course. You know . . . on the tube." Jasmine winced when she realized she'd slipped up and showed weakness by admitting she watched him play each week. "Anyway, you didn't have to hide from yourself all that time. I could have helped if you went about it the right way, but you didn't." Her demeanor changed. The tough shell of defense began to wither away as the woman in her began to sift through the cracks. "Hell, Marshall, I just don't know what to think. Until today, I thought you were in Atlanta doing God knows what with God knows who. Then you show up on TV telling all your business like some fool on *Jerry Springer*, and now you pop up at my door expecting everything to be okay and pick up where we left off. Some things have changed." She began to cry but pretended that something flew into her eyes. "And don't just stand there looking at me like that. What do you have to say for yourself?" She threw her hands on her hips in a futile effort to save face and maintain her tough homegirl act.

Marshall hesitated until he was sure she wouldn't cut him off again. Remembering what Manny said about honesty being his best shot, he took it. With a solemn expression, he pleaded his case. "Hi . . . Jasmine. It's great seeing you again, too. I need to say I'm sorry before I say anything else. Whether or not you can ever forgive me for what I did to you and how I carelessly played with the love you gave me in abundance and unconditionally, you need to know a few things." Her expression was hard to decipher, but it leaned more on the side of sadness than heartache.

After he got wound up, the words just flowed from his heart. "Every day that passed was filled with thoughts of you, and the nights went on forever. I see couples taking walks in the park, pushing strollers, and having family picnics and I get so envious. I hope they know what they've got, because I didn't and I'd hate for anyone to lose it, like I lost you. Jasmine . . . I know I have no right to show up here after all this time, and no, I wasn't trying to buy your love or pay my way back into your life, but I just wanted to say thank you for all that you've helped me to become. Lord knows where I'd be if you hadn't . . . hadn't been what you've been to me. For that I could never repay you. If I've insulted you with that car . . ." He pointed to the Mercedes in her driveway. "I'll have someone pick it up this evening. And as far as other women are concerned, the thought of another woman hadn't crossed my mind."

They stood there in her doorway for a moment without so much as a whisper uttered. She tried not to look him in the face. It would have been impossible to hide her true feelings, so she continued to look at the ground. "Jasmine, I blew it. I admit that and there's no other way to say it. But I need you in my life. I always have and I always will. You're the biggest part of me there is. And I want . . . I need you back in it."

She looked up and found his eyes. They were helpless and unsure. She shook her head and threw her hand up to stifle his speech. She took a step back inside her small two-bedroom home. "Don't say another word, Marshall DeShon Coates. You took the best I had to offer and threw it away like garbage and that hurt. It embarrassed the hell out of me. Now that's the past, I know. I also know people can change, but sometimes so do people's lives. Some things have changed in mine, Marshall. It's not like it used to be. What you don't know is that I do have another man in my life."

A lump swelled in Marshall's throat. He feared as much. A woman like Jasmine never had to be alone if she didn't choose to be. At least he'd given it his best shot. Honestly.

She flashed an awkwardly abbreviated smile, then asked him to wait. "If you stay right there, I'll get him so you two can meet."

Sure, that's just what he had in mind. It was bad enough that someone else took center stage in Jasmine's life; Marshall couldn't see himself being friends with the brother. That would be cruel and unusual punishment.

When Jasmine returned, she held a tiny bundle secured in her arms. Something was swaddled up in a soft powder-blue blanket. Marshall leaned in closer to where she stood. It was a newborn baby boy sleeping soundly. The pride of motherhood was exhibited on Jasmine's face.

He smiled at the child, well, as much as he could without falling apart. Marshall never considered another man and a baby. That was too much. But he'd promised himself that no matter what he found when he went there, he'd be understanding. So he tried to be. "That's some baby you've got there," he said, looking at Jasmine. "I'll bet the father is a very happy man."

She looked down at the child again, then hunched her shoulders. "My son is only twenty-one days old. Marshall's never met his father."

"Marshall?" He was confused. "You gave your baby my name?" He was still lost in the surprise of it all. "Why would you give another man's son my name?"

She hunched her shoulders again. "Maybe 'cause Marshall is his father's name."

He thought he knew what she meant, but he wasn't clear his understanding was correct, and that's not something you jump into with your mouth open if you're not sure. She smiled as pretty as she could and gave him the assurance he needed to confirm it. "You went to school, you do the math. Who was still my man ten months ago?"

Marshall was hyperventilating. He was overwhelmed and overjoyed. Everything was happening so fast. "Jasmine, are you saying that I'm . . . I'm a . . . that's my son? Yeah?" He began to lose his mind. "What should I do? How will I . . . tell me, what does he need?"

"He needs a father, Marshall. And his mother thinks it would be a good idea if her baby's daddy and her husband were one and the same."

He felt like a lovesick sixteen-year-old standing on the porch of the first girl he'd kissed. "Thank you, Jasmine. You just don't know how happy you've made me." He began to shout toward the limo. "Manny! You hear that? I'm a daddy! It's a boy!"

While he and his son, Marshall Rorey Coates, became acquainted inside the house, Jasmine had two more issues to address. "Oh, yeah, there are couple of things that need some clarification."

"Name it. Anything." He would have given her the world if she had asked for it.

"When did I stop being Jazz to you? Since you've been here you've called me Jasmine. My mother calls me Jasmine and you do things to me that she can't. And most importantly, you forget about what I said earlier. You know, about all those expensive gifts. Don't you let nobody come by here and take my new car."

Marshall was beside himself. His paradise on earth became a reality. His woman was by his side and his son was in his arms. After all the pain and suffering it took to get to that point in their lives, it was well worth it. Nothing would derail him from enjoying what blessings he'd been given, including his second chance at destiny. It was more than he could have ever dreamed of. Marshall cherished his slice of heaven, ten brand new fingers and ten brand new little toes at a time.

Thirty-three

Damned If I Do

ead flowers rested on the windowsill in Kennedy's apartment. Twelve brittle stems lay flat and still, bound by a single yellow ribbon.

In objection to Morris's housecleaning addiction, Kennedy refused to throw the lifeless roses away. They were the last thing Legacy gave to her and they still meant so much. It was like remembering the faint touch of a lover's hand after the love affair is over. Sometimes the memories are just as good or better than the actual love affair itself.

Life had become a game of desperate measures and trials as well as errors. The neurologist's examination proved what the hospital feared. Clusters of brain lesions were responsible for Kennedy's increasingly massive headaches. Along with morphine tablets to combat the frequent and intense pain, a strict regimen of fresh fruit and vegetables along with bouts of experimental AIDS drugs had taken their toll. Kennedy was not only sickly now; she'd grown tired as well.

In the past three months, she subscribed to using clinical antiretroviral drug combinations known to suppress the amount of HIV present in the blood. A treatment cycle including the drugs AZT, 3TC, and saquinavir constituted the first assault on the virus. When that failed and her T cell count suddenly dropped to 200, quick decisions had to be made. Kennedy was given only six months to live, if that long, so it couldn't be taken lightly.

A more potent drug and aggressive drug, ritonavir, was prescribed as an HIV protease inhibitor to stop the advancement of AIDS. Initially, it had a promising effect on improving her quality of life. But like most experimental drugs, it became ineffective as time wore on, and the virus found innovative ways to break through it. Kennedy quickly learned that new drugs were tested often with hopes of finding a cure or at least offering a more effective treatment, but new strains of HIV continued to evolve daily. Unfortunately, there was no drug available that always achieved success at suppressing the deadly viruses.

The only constants in Kennedy's life had become the seemingly never-ending pain and the nagging beats of the IV drip plugged into her arms to keep her from dehydrating. While numbing her senses, Morris sat by her bedside reading all the latest gossip rags aloud, as if she wanted to hear about other people's problems. He got used to the fact that he'd have to be the one to change the soiled gauze and bedsheets when the chronic diarrhea started up again. Each time her body jerked in spastic convulsions when the pain got too great, Morris turned away and sobbed quietly. He could barely stand to watch the suffering she endured.

When the pain wasn't so bad, Kennedy could perform various small tasks for herself and get around slowly throughout the apartment. One of her favorite things to do was put on a Beatles LP and cater to Lady Eleanor. Morris repeatedly asked her what he should do if, by chance, Legacy should show up. Each time her reply was the same. "There's no need to bring him into my misery. He still has a life to lead. I can't take that from him. It wouldn't be fair."

One Thursday afternoon, Kennedy gave up fighting. She refused to accept any more treatment regimens, despite the immense pain. The morphine was necessary, but the diarrhea had come and gone, so the IV drip wasn't essential. She'd experienced another terrible bout of stabbing pain and nightmares with demonic black crows chasing her. Morris didn't know why he did it, but he decided to contact Legacy. Maybe he sensed the end approaching or maybe he was just plain worn out from going it alone.

Kennedy's skin was sheet-white. With dark circles around her eyes and mouth, not many people who knew her as a lovely woman would have recognized her then. Her T cell count dropped to 25. She should have been dead already. She lay in bed like the dead flowers that rested on her windowsill bound by a single yellow ribbon.

Thirty-four

Just Get Here

French waiters dressed in black slacks, white long-sleeve shirts, and aprons scurried outside Café Bleu. They wiped off tabletops and rolled silverware before the dinner crowd arrived. Legacy decided that the wait wasn't worthwhile, considering he'd eaten there before and wasn't at all impressed with the food. But it was a short jaunt from the apartment the university rented for him.

His French was horrible and he was tired and missing Kennedy more each day, but his plane ticket wouldn't be valid until he finished his course the following week. At least French television was interesting. The daytime soaps and game shows seemed provocative, but he couldn't comprehend much of what was said, so he opted to read American magazines he could purchase at a nearby newsstand.

After searching his small room for the latest issue of *People,* he remembered that his neighbor, who was studying to be an entertainer, liked borrowing his things. Jean was his name. He liked anything American, especially celebrity magazines. His English wasn't nearly good enough to read it, but he enjoyed looking at the photographs of starlit galas and award dinners.

When Legacy tapped on the door opposite his apartment, he heard a Rick Springfield classic, "Jessie's Girl," blaring on an old hi-fi. He knocked harder, asking the young man to please open the door. "Jean . . . *tu ouvis. Ouvis! S'il vous plait. Cest* Monsieur Legacy." Jean opened the door in his favorite "I Love LA" T-shirt and Levi blue jeans. He had several theme shirts with logos printed on them in assorted colors.

"Jean, I . . . I mean je . . ." Legacy stuttered; he couldn't think of the French word for "magazine" but saw it lying on the coffee table and pointed to it.

"Ah, *le revue* . . ." Jean said, reminding Legacy of the word he was looking for.

"Yes. *Le revue*," Legacy repeated, like a schoolboy in French class who had to repeat after the instructor. "Yeah, that's right. *Le revue*. Thanks, man."

Jean sang out in his thick French accent, "I wisszuh that I hud Jezzies gurlll . . ." He didn't care much what Legacy wanted. When he rocked to American music, he was in his own world.

Legacy stepped past him and picked up the magazine. He began thumbing through it. Jean was also known for ripping out pages he liked and keeping them. When Legacy reached the back of the magazine, a thin yellow piece of paper fell out onto the floor. He bent over to pick it up and assumed it belonged to Jean. Something caught his eye. It was Kennedy's name. He almost tore it trying to get it opened. It was a telegram from Morris. It read, "Legacy. Come quick. Kennedy ill. Asking for you. Please hurry." The telegram was dated March 16. That was over a week ago. He freaked, not knowing what to do first.

"Jean!" he yelled above the music. "*Je vais aux Estats Unis.*" Legacy's broken French perturbed Jean. "Awe, forget it. I'm going home! I'm going home!"

He ran across the hall and stuffed all the clothes he could find in a faded-green military-issued duffel bag and headed for the airport. He remembered hearing Jean singing "R-O-C-K in the USA" at the top of his lungs when he reached the terminal.

Legacy convinced the airline representative that the telegram was regarding his sick mother and he needed to make the next flight. They obliged him and arranged a seat in coach, despite his first-class ticket. He didn't mind it at all. He was ecstatic to be on his way home to Kennedy, the only woman he ever loved. No one on the flight knew Legacy's name or asked for autographs. The pilot didn't offer him a private tour of the cockpit, and not one sorority sister showed up to welcome him home and wish him luck. But that didn't matter. He was home.

The taxi slowed to pull over at Kennedy's apartment building. Legacy, who'd been up all night, jumped out before it came to a complete stop. He stumbled, then caught his balance and flew into the lobby. Bradshaw, the doorman, was arguing with a burly delivery person to take his four-ton diesel around to the back. Legacy interrupted the two men. "I know I'm not supposed to be here, Mr. Bradshaw, but I got this telegram in France and I need to get up to Kennedy's."

The doorman seemed to be more concerned about the huge delivery truck blocking his front door. "Yeah, son, go on up. Her friends are up there now." As soon as Legacy started for the elevators, the two men resumed their heated war of words.

The hall was quiet, as usual. He forced himself to calm down, but he couldn't stop the sweat from streaming down his face. Knock . . . knock . . . knock. An unfamiliar man, whose mannerisms were a bit more feminine than masculine, opened the door. He took one look at Legacy's worn travel clothing and sneered. "Yes? Can I help you?" he asked without one hint of sincerity.

Legacy looked past him. He saw other men who were just as soft around the edges, wrapping up plates and glasses with newspaper as they put them into boxes. "My name is Legacy and I came to see . . ."

Morris stepped out of the bedroom. "Ahhh," he sighed with surprise. "Legacy, what are you doing here?" He suddenly appeared frightened. "I didn't think you'd be coming back, since . . ." He halted his speech and gave all the others in the room the eye. They understood and found somewhere else to be.

Legacy began to survey the living room again, then he wandered into Kennedy's room. All the bedding had been removed from it. The mattress and box springs were covered in plastic. He made his way back to where Morris stood, holding the ball gown Kennedy had worn to the Erykah Badu concert.

"Somebody better tell me what's going on here," Legacy demanded. "Where is she, Morris?"

The petite man was afraid to speak. He knew how much Legacy loved her. As the tears formed in the well of his eyes, he began to get flustered. "Legacy, I don't know how to tell you this, so I'll just say it . . ." He swallowed hard. "She's gone."

"Gone? Gone where?"

"Kennedy passed away late Friday night. She was buried yesterday." Morris explained what had taken place and apologized for not divulging what Kennedy was going through. "Please try to understand why I waited until the end to contact you. She loved you so much, it hurt her to be apart from you. Please try to understand. She did want me to give you this." Morris handed Legacy a package, then left the room to give him some time to let it all sink in.

Thirty-five

No Detour Ahead

L *egacy's hands shook as he dialed* a familiar number into the telephone.

"Richey Glass," he heard the gangster announce.

"This is Legacy, I've got a couple a things you'll want to hear." He told Richey about the drugs he discovered at Kennedy's and about Simpson's Colombian connection. Richey thanked him, then made a call of his own.

Simpson casually selected bottles of wine for a special occasion in the wine cellar beneath Stone Imports. His soft, brown-colored suede loafers accented the eggshell-white linen suit and starched white linen shirt. By the time he heard their footsteps, marching with urgent strides, it was too late. Charlie the bartender and big Franky from Club Matrix rounded the last wine rack. Simpson stood there holding a bottle of red wine in each hand. When he realized the thick wooden shafts hanging from their gloved fists were sledgehammers with large steel heads, his eyes bugged out in utter fear. While attempting to make a getaway, he shouted, "Nnnno!" and turned to run for his life.

Big Franky pulled a pistol from his waistband. He pointed and shot, hitting Simpson in the back of the thigh. The wine bottles took flight and crashed against the cold cement floor. Charlie motioned to the shooter that one bullet was enough. The boss wanted it to be slow and painful.

Simpson crawled around on the floor, begging for a chance to get out of it alive. "Please . . . please . . . don't do this. Whatever I did to Richey, I'm sorry. Please let me go. I'm already real sick. Hey, I'll pay you guys off and leave town. Whatever you want. Nobody's got to know."

The two men looked at each other as if they were considering his proposal. Then Charlie shook his head. "Nahhh, I think you've already made a deal with the devil, and he sent us to collect the debt."

Simpson held his leg, grimacing as he continued to plead. "Franky, come on, please. Talk to him. I can make it up to Richey. I promise!"

The two men looked at each other again, then both shook their heads no. "Dis ain't from Richey," Charlie replied. Before Simpson could get another word out of his mouth, the powerful hammers came down hard, smashing bones and ripping the skin from his body. Simpson could hear his own bone and cartilage break under the weight of the powerful blows.

When they were done with Simpson, Charlie and big Franky stepped out of the front door of Stone Imports and rode away in a black Lincoln down the busy Greenville Avenue thoroughfare.

Simpson was found by one of his employees, soaked in a pool of red wine and coughing up his own blood. An ambulance arrived soon after and packed his fractured body onto a gurney wrapped in red soaked sheets. Legacy stood across the street and watched as they rolled him out slowly. Simpson could barely manage to breathe with two collapsed lungs, moaning and rolling his head from side to side. When his eyes found Legacy, casually leaning against a parked car to watch him die, Simpson knew who was responsible for the hit. His eyelids fluttered, then closed for the very last time.

Thirty-six

Subsequently

*B*efore *Legacy knew it, he was* home alone and brokenhearted. In the package, Kennedy had left him some of her personal things to remember her by and a letter. He remembered all the things they'd done together as he heard her voice in the words that she left behind:

> My Dearest Legacy,
> Your reading this letter means I have gone to a much better place, at least I hope. Please forgive me for shutting you out of my life, but once I learned about my condition, I couldn't take seeing your face, knowing that we would never have a chance to grow old together. You'll have to take my word for it. It's better this way. I wanted you

to remember me the way I was, not how I'd become. Hey, remember the first time you took me to play air hockey, it was so sweet the way you let me win. Of course I knew all along, but you made it so much fun for me. I really enjoyed it. You know, it took time getting used to the way you treated me like I was made of glass. You made me feel special every time I saw you. You were never ashamed to hold my hand in public and you let me pout when I didn't get my way. Thank you for that.

By the way, I know you don't care much for cats, but Lady Eleanor misses you a lot. Maybe you can straighten her out. I think she's been taking advantage of me. Oh, yeah, I've left something for you at Johansen's Art Gallery. I hope you like it. Smile when you think of me. I guess I'll see you next lifetime. Hugs and kisses, Kennedy. PS, I finally quit smoking.

After Legacy stayed locked up in his apartment for two days, he realized there was a need to say good-bye to her, too. He found himself at her gravesite peering down at the final resting place of the woman he thought he would spend the rest of his life with. Kennedy's headstone read: AUTUMN LEAVES FALL TOO SOON.

He stared at it for a while, reminiscing about the first time he saw her and the time he showed up at her office unannounced and bearing roses. It occurred to him that their relationship could have stalled right then and there before it even got going, but she had called out to him before he walked out of her life.

Eventually, he rested on his knees near the mound of soft dirt piled over her casket. He didn't know what to say, but he had to say something, if for no other reason than to bring closure to it for himself.

"It's still hard to believe that you're gone and I'll never see you again, but things don't always turn out quite like you plan. I guess life is like that sometimes."

When he heard a faint meow coming from the brown leather tote bag hanging over his shoulder, it reminded him that he'd brought along a gift for her. "I almost forgot. I brought you something." He opened the bag and pulled out a small white kitten. "You were right about Lady Eleanor, she's been a bad girl. Yeah, she's a new mommy . . . quintuplets. I call them the Jackson Five. Morris and the girls took four of them, but I kept this one. He was the whitest of them all. I named him Michael. I knew you'd get a kick outta that." He put the kitten down on her grave to let it stretch out and crawl around for a minute. "I, uh . . . didn't want to get all mental, but I miss you and I wanted to thank you for helping me to realize who I am. You're my best friend and I'll always love you, Kennedy James."

He tried to regain his composure by looking up at the sky before continuing. "Thanks for hooking me up with my first art show at Johansen's. It's next month. I wish you could be there." A single tear rolled passed the bottom of the sunglasses. "Well, I gotta go now, there's some business I need to tend to." He remembered hearing Marshall say that as he left the press conference.

He scooped up the small kitten and kissed it on the forehead, just as he had done to Kennedy many times. Then he slowly backed away.

The Beatles classic hit "Yesterday" played on Legacy's stereo in his dream car, a brand-new fire-engine red Lamborghini. He climbed into it, pulled away from the curb, and drove that new car until darkness devoured the sun.

An extraordinary woman came into his life for a short time. She discovered him, and then helped him rediscover himself. When she left he was changed. Forever.

Like the many budding leaves of springtime look upon long stormy nights and blissful days of sunshine abundant to supply their life-sustaining needs, we, too, require both the pain that accompanies life's trying times and bountiful seasons of joy in order to experience adequate growth. Unfortunately, much like the many budding leaves of springtime, we, too, are often devastated by nature's sometimes suspect sense of fairness when the beauty of autumn leaves vanishes. Inevitably, they do fall too soon.

About the Author

Victor McGlothin is a former bank vice president, who nearly forfeited an athletic scholarship to college due to poor reading skills, before going on to complete his masters degree. His desire to overcome that obstacle has evolved into a talent for sharing the written word through passionate tales of suspense and drama. Victor lives in the Dallas area with his wife and two sons.